'Laura writes fiction like the poet tha
every word perfectly placed. The kind
detail that will have you wondering if she stole your teenage
diaries and rewrote them with clever insights and laugh out loud
humour. I'm not sure I've read a book so perfectly observed.
It's every woman's story of the highs and lows of falling in love,
perseverance and self preservation. I loved it, I loved it, I loved it!'
Dawn O'Porter

'Very funny. *I Love You, I Love You,
I Love You* bursts with energy.'
Matt Haig

'Laura Dockrill is a delicious writer and *I Love You,
I Love You, I Love You* is glorious and tender, evocative
and heart nourishing. I love this beautiful book.'
Salena Godden

'An absolutely gorgeous book. So visceral, nostalgic, mucky,
heartbreaking and bittersweet. Laura captures that weird
pocket of time so perfectly: before smartphones; MySpace
and calling your mates on the house phone and shag bands
and Green Day and all those insecurities and the sharpness
of every new experience and feeling. Just DELICIOUS.'
Kirsty Capes

'A transporting, technicolour plunge into first, and enduring,
love. As ever, Laura Dockrill's voice is entirely her own.
She writes from the inside out and it's beautiful.'
Sophie Dahl

'I laughed, I cringed, I yelled, I clutched my heart and swooned.'
Emily Koch

Laura Dockrill is an award-winning writer from Brixton. Her writing for children and young adults has been shortlisted for the Waterstones Children's Book Prize, the Carnegie Medal and the YA Book Prize, and she has been named a 'Top 10 Literary Talent' by *The Times* and a 'Top 20 Hot Face to Watch' by *Elle* magazine. Laura is one of the judging panel of the Women's Prize for Fiction 2024.

I Love You, I Love You, I Love You is Laura's first novel for adults. Based on her own lived experience, it is the ultimate love letter to her partner Hugo, it draws on first love, true love, from-a-distance-for-pretty-much-her-entire-life love (I know, talk about desperate. . .), but don't worry, she ended up marrying him.

I LOVE YOU

I LOVE YOU

I LOVE YOU

LAURA DOCKRILL

ONE PLACE. MANY STORIES

HQ
An imprint of HarperCollins*Publishers* Ltd
1 London Bridge Street,
London SE1 9GF

www.harpercollins.co.uk

HarperCollins*Publishers*
Macken House, 39/40 Mayor Street Upper,
Dublin 1, D01 C9W8, Ireland

This edition 2024
1
First published in Great Britain by
HQ, an imprint of HarperCollins*Publishers* Ltd 2024

Copyright © Laura Dockrill, 2024

Laura Dockrill asserts the moral right to be identified as the author of this work.
A catalogue record for this book is available from the British Library.

ISBN HB: 9780008586911
ISBN TPB: 9780008586928

MIX
Paper | Supporting
responsible forestry
FSC
www.fsc.org
FSC™ C007454

This book contains FSC™ certified paper and other controlled
sources to ensure responsible forest management.

For more information visit: www.harpercollins.co.uk/green

This book is set in 11.5/16 pt. Sabon by Type-it AS, Norway

Printed and Bound in the UK using 100% Renewable Electricity at
CPI Group (UK) Ltd, Croydon, CR0 4YY

For Jet. One day you will ask about our story
and my reply will be something like this . . .

Chapter 1

Now

If you were to press pause on the dancefloor of my life, this is where you'd find me: in sweet desperation, flinging myself across a room to rugby-tackle strangers, in an attempt to catch the bouquet (of a bride I haven't seen in years) to Gwen Stefani's 'Hollaback Girl'. Screaming.

Fucking weddings.

I know the superstitious tradition. I know what it means. But you know, I've surprised myself by accidently having a gorgeous time, and everyone else is trying to catch the bouquet, so why not me? I should know better than to follow a crowd. I can hear my mum now: *If everyone else jumped off a cliff, Ella Cole, would you?* Maybe I'm doing it for all the times I've said *things like this don't happen to people like me* and sat on the sidelines of my life eating Flame Grilled Steak McCoy's instead of taking a chance? Probably, most likely, I'm doing this because – well – I've drunk about 17,000 units of various cheap alcohol and I don't know who many of these other people are. So, it's fantastic really. I've got a free pass.

Right now, I'm *that* champ. *Why,* it's as if since doing those three yoga classes on YouTube, I've become some next-level athlete and my best friends are cheerleaders. Aoife, Ronks, Bianca – all lovely losers like me – proudly clapping in an enthusiastic semi-circle, egging me on. And I'm the clumsy, unassuming underdog that they're all rooting for to bring Mia's bouquet home. A bolt of spontaneous lightning, a local superhero in a that-bit-too-tight hot-pink Eighties jumpsuit with ginormous shoulder pads and gold buttons.

This is the trillionth wedding (third) we've *had* to go to this year. People we know seem to be busting into their thirties with a bang! Like eggs hatching – once one goes, they all seem to go. They're cracking all over any building they can transform into a function room: warehouses in London, ex-barns in Sussex, ruins in Edinburgh. Our diaries are now punctured with them. Weekends snatched, bank accounts raided. I don't want to *not* be invited because *yes, of course my feelings would be hurt* but at the same time PLEASE DO NOT INVITE ME TO YOUR WEDDING! Where I have to dress up and be fun and pretend I'm not hungover from *another* thirtieth birthday party the night before that I also felt like I couldn't say no to or not drink at because then everyone would ask if I was pregnant or on anti-biotics or having a breakdown. How is anybody affording this lifestyle anyway? Financially. Physically. Emotionally? So, please don't invite me outside. At all. Ever.

And yet, here's me, in the thick of it, sweating, begging to catch Mia's bouquet like my life depends on it. What can I say? I'm a romantic at heart and weddings make everyone go a bit weird anyway, don't they? Unsurprisingly really, when you've been asked to *Save a Date* longer than it takes for a tin of corned beef to expire.

Summer is over and we've been freezing our tits off in a derelict dilapidated ex-biscuit factory where everyone's running around saying 'Can you believe this was an old biscuit factory?'. Mia's parents have dug into the cobwebby cellars of their pensions to hire a half bulldozed building site that, let's be honest, we probably should be wearing hard helmets inside. But once love arrives, draped in lights and hydrangeas, the fairy tale bursts into life: stardust.

My friends and I have been trying really hard to be adults all day. *Bless us*, we acted terrifically sober even though we'd already knocked back two gin-in-tins each on an empty stomach on the way here. Despite Bianca already harbouring that *why does that girl keep looking at me?* energy (nobody was looking at her), we stay calm. Tame. We've been on our very best behaviour, taking it all seriously for our old school friend Mia and her big day. Acting like we are the kind of people that carry a pop-up chemist on their person: tissues, blister plasters, gum, paracetamol, Vaseline, toothpicks.

Aoife, my best friend of over twenty-five years, got her lashes done for this one; Bianca squished her tattoo-covered body into a bodycon dress, today's blue hair slicked into some fraudulent bun; and Ronke, seven months pregnant, still showed up in a heel and goddam fascinator for fuck's sake! Clutch bags replaced our usual reliable rucksacks and bumbags, our everyday trainers and sliders now peep-toe wedges. Except for Bianca, who is making a point of being as stompy as possible in her Doc Martens.

During the ceremony, we whisper politely, shuffling and shushing each other nervously along the charming mismatched wonky wooden chairs – you know those old church ones with the slot at the back for the Bible? We flip our phones to airplane mode and speak to Mia's parents in our best grown-up podcast voices. 'So good to see you,' we lie, even though we're convinced her dad hates us. My face is already aching from its permanent smile because you never know when you'll be caught off-guard in a wedding photo, so to be safe, you have to be beautiful, dutiful, happy all the time at *all* the bits. You don't want to be the only frown. Caught out, doubting the love. Everyone zooming in on your cynical face in the background, thinking it will never last. Glaring into the abyss of existential dread.

So, I am smiling my head off, and, before I know it, the formalities and rituals are giving me the giggles. The ridiculous pomp and ceremony makes me feel like we're kids in a school nativity with inappropriate tea towels on our heads. Or trying to do the Ouija board at a sleepover. Aoife feels me laughing and pinches my arm – 'Ella, shhhh' – only to burst out laughing herself. When I hear her laugh, I know I shouldn't, it's bad – *terrible* – but I begin to laugh harder. Ronks lets out a snort – and she's not even tipsy – and Bianca starts to cry; she can't help it. Our bodies are vibrating side by side, trip-wiring ourselves into more giggles. Trying to hold in the laughter only makes it funnier.

'I can't breathe,' I wheeze, clinging onto my chest. 'It's not even funny – I don't know why I'm laughing so hard.' We already know we're going to be left with a six-pack after today.

When the room is full, Mia's fiancé looks down the aisle for her in the exact same way I look for food coming from the charcoaled grill of Nando's: *longingly*. Something shifts.

The players of a string quartet glance at each other silently, then start to play 'Time After Time'.

And it's got me.

Don't cry. Oh, I'm crying. What is this emotional rollercoaster? Aoife asks, 'Shit, are we unhinged?'

'I *have* been flagging this for a while now.'

Tears involuntarily come, carving through our foundation in zebra stripes.

And we turn to see our school friend Mia, the elegant bride, grace the aisle: a visiting angel, a *J'adore* advert, a Disney princess, Aphrodite. Mia, who I always thought was just as perfectly strange as me but isn't because someone she loves actually loves her back in the same way.

Wait, am I terrified that it will never be me? That I'll end up a shadowy ghoul with a hungry soul, wailing, haunting the earth's crust, picking at the thorny shrubs of the dirt at the end

4

of the world, unloved? Or worse, that it *will* be me, but I'll be marrying the wrong person. Not the love of my life. That the fairy tale will be wrong? Am I crying because I know this is something I'll never have? Unless I settle. Or lie. Or marry myself.

'Mia Bennett,' Aoife whispers into my ear; her breath smells of Wrigley's Extra – the blue ones. 'Who'd have thought? She's a friggin' goddess.'

'That's exactly what she is,' says Ronke.

'She's made it alright,' Bianca agrees.

We take our seats and watch two people in love make their promises. I take photos on my phone because that's what everyone else is doing. Even though we all know the photos will go nowhere, just sit on my phone until I am free of guilt enough to delete them. At the *you may now kiss the bride* bit, Aoife elbows us in the ribs to offer a crumbled cereal bar that she'd split into quarters. 'Weddings need safe spaces' – she nods as if it's a gap in the market – 'just a darkly lit room with some beanbags and soft cushions, you know, somewhere at the back, to run to and cry?'

At the reception, I pick up yet another glass of the cava they keep calling champagne from the little round trays, overly thanking the waiter like they've just resuscitated me.

'I'm saying Yes to everything tonight!' I announce, and this decision cheers me up enormously.

'*Everything*?' one of those annoying drunk and sloppy NOBODY-ASKED-YOU-ACTUAL-*DAD* dads pipes up.

'*Ew*. Do we know you?' Bianca turns her back on him.

'Ooooo canapes. Well posh.' Ronks grabs a handful from a tray. We tip the tiny squares of toast carrying cress into our mouth like oysters but they dissolve disappointingly like Skips.

'They aren't as good as my ones,' Bianca says, already unhooking her blue hair from the flowers and pins.

'Don't,' Aoife warns, holding her throat.

'What you do is you take a Mini Cheddar—'

Ronks puts her finger to Bianca's mouth. 'STOP. IT!'

'Chew it but *don't* swallow; instead *regurgitate*, spread the mixture with your tongue onto the next Mini Cheddar.'

Aoife retches.

'Why does it sound worse because your tongue is pierced?' I ask.

'Like a little spoon for spreading, innit?' Bianca cackles, biting the stud of her piercing between her teeth like a bullet.

We are directed to our *the only girls from secondary school that Mia likes but not enough to invite partners* table of eight, which is very close to the toilets and fire extinguisher. The four other girls, already seated, who we know – vaguely – wave at us politely as we find our places. *Love your jumpsuit, Ella; that vintage?* If having something in your wardrobe since you were twenty-one means vintage then *yeah* I guess it is.

They begin taking control by passing around a basket of bread, far more Teddy Bears' Picnic than I'm sure they'd like. I wolf down a seeded stale bread roll, fork at my mushy vegetarian main and gulp back white wine, exhausted, already, by the continuous quiet stress-drip of small talk from the girls – sorry, other *women* – playing show-and-tell with photos on their phones of babies, dogs, cold-water swimming and house renovations. I swear this is what Facebook is for? And why I am *not on* Facebook. It's like a school reunion where everybody seems to have established actual successful lives. Charity CEO. GP. HR. PR. PA. Masters upon masters. *I'm a consultant. Cool*, I say, *consulting in what?*

Bianca drains her glass, grabs her handbag and hisses 'Fuck this' in my ear before clomping off towards the giant doors to smoke. I'm so jealous of her escape. My yearning glance is interrupted with a: *You still writing, Ella?* I look at the girl/woman asking, like the word 'writing' is one I don't understand, and I have to catch up. *Yep, still at it,* I say, then comically raise my fist to the sky like the woman with the red spotty bandana in that American wartime poster. I ask, to be polite, *Are you still . . . lawyer-ing?* And she looks at me like *ARE YOU <u>HIGH</u>?* and says, *Yes, I'm <u>still</u> a <u>barrister</u>; I only worked my whole life for it.* Like I haven't worked my whole life to lie about in my pyjamas making shit up all day. *A writer* is a pointless job that absolutely nobody needs. I'm not academic or, let's be real, *relaxed* enough to earn the title. My imposter syndrome, chronic. *Published, right?* People always have to check you're solicited. Absolutely *nobody* likes the terrifying thought of you running around being creative off your own back: delusional, barking up wrong trees in blind faith, debt mounting, ripping through binbags at midnight to eat rotten chow mein like a starved, wild racoon whilst having all these big 'dreams' and great 'ideas'.

I published a book of poems when I was twenty-one. A book I can't even look at now without cringing. I got a lot of press at the time: *POET FOR THE iPOD GENERATION. ELLA COLE IS A POET WHO <u>DEFINITELY</u> DOESN'T KNOW IT.* The press cuttings, once sun-drenched, are now in a plastic box under the bed, my plaudits no longer relevant or valid, my press shots terribly dated. I've been living off royalties ever since. Not from the book, unfortunately, but from some adverts I wrote in a day and a half, back when all the brands decided they loved poems. A piece for TV and radio about how a fizzy drink can bring people together has been my greatest earner. The message being: *if you don't drink this drink, you'll die alone.* My soul, sadly, sold to the 'Dark Arts' bit of the arts. I do a lot of that now to make a living – freelance, helping adverts with words.

I don't tell any of this lot that though, just say, *Yes, I'm pub-lished.* When they ask, *Anything we might know?*, it's like *Yes, probably quite a lot if you switch on the TV.* But I shake my head and say, *Doubt it. Oh.* Disappointment for me and themselves. They thought they were about to meet a famous person.

Aoife kicks me under the table with her espadrilled wedge like *don't do yourself like that,* so I clear my throat and offer, *I've actually just finished my first novel . . . Lol.* Because *lol* is what you say when you actually want to cry. *Oooh.* They perk up. I'd made a promise to myself – annoyingly out loud and in front of Aoife – that when I turned thirty I would submit my first novel, which I've only spent the past four years writing, to my agent. But now that I actually am thirty, I'm scared to let it go because everyone will know I've *tried.* It was fine when I was twenty-one. Now, it's exposing, embarrassing actually. It takes a lot as an adult to say, *I've written a book.* It's presumptuous – the hours, the effort, the sacrifice, the discipline, all those words. Then comes the hard bit – the reviews, the judgement. I want the whole world to read my work except anyone who knows me.

What's it about? one of them asks. *It's a romance.* Calm down, Lord Bloody Byron. *But without the . . .* I pull a face to mean sex scenes.

One of the girls bangs the table with her gavel of a wedding ring and demands, *Have you ever heard of . . .* and goes on to only name the No.1 romance novel that sits on the whole world's bedside table and is now a major Hollywood movie. The table reacts with a gush. *Ow. I LOVED that book.* She clutches her chest. I smile like I'm so delighted that they're all reading this big famous book that isn't mine. Aoife tries not to crack up with laughter at my suffering; Book Club has begun and I'm somehow the host for a book I've not read. *I've always wanted to write . . .* one of them confesses, as if I've never heard anybody say *that* before . . . *I feel I've got a book in me.*

'Everyone's got a book in them,' Ronks replies, 'but not everyone needs to read it – do you know what I mean?'

The table laughs. Ronke winks at me. I love her for it.

After pushing creamy loveless dessert around our plates, the others get up to *mingle*.

'Is it time? Are we allowed yet?' I ask Aoife with desperation. And we both undo our belts and zips, letting our bellies flump out, and breathe a sigh of relief.

'I honestly thought they were never going to feed us; what kind of nasty endurance test was that?' Aoife complains. 'I'm too old for mind games.'

We slump back into our chairs with ecstasy as our dislodged organs find their natural resting places.

'Why do I do it myself? I'm two sizes bigger than when I last wore this dress; I need to accept that. Look at my poor belly . . .' Aoife points at the crimped grooves from the seam before rubbing her skin with affection. 'I think I was going a *bit* mad. I said *fabuloso* earlier.'

'I'm so sorry to hear that.' And we crack up laughing, looking out at these people we barely know *mingling* around a red velvet cake (my worst – but I'll eat it) to The Killers. How soon is rude to leave? Then *ting ting* it's time for more cava in champagne flutes, cava we don't seem to have been given because we're forgotten stragglers at the back so we scramble for the dregs in our finger-smudged glasses.

Mia's husband steps up to the microphone. 'I'd like to make a toast . . .'

Shit, best do my buttons back up already.

'Mia,' he begins, 'sometimes I wake up and think I must be in a dream to be with you. And if I am dreaming – sleeping or . . . in a coma – then please, never wake me up.'

The room yelps and swoons. Applause. Tears bubble in my eyes.

'Bad News,' snorts Bianca, appearing from behind us, stinking of the 600 Camels she'd smoked. Where the hell has she even been? 'They're making us pay for the bar now.' Her fake eyelash hangs off. 'What a piss-take. Some of us are on probation here! It's not like I haven't had to sell my clothes to be able to even afford a new dress for today! *Then* they'll want money towards a honeymoon.'

I haven't told her that the 'honeymoon' money is going towards the deposit for a flat. Mia told me. Turns out, if you want to get a deposit for a house *fast* – throw a wedding and invite three hundred people.

'I feel like I've been mugged.' Still Bianca fumbles for her bank card in her splurging handbag, which vomits tampons, a loose mascara wand and a weed grinder that rolls out like a circus act across the biscuit factory floor. 'Shots?'

Tequila. Sambuca. *Café Patrón.*

Cut to me in the designated smokers' area, *cigarette* hanging out my mouth (WTF?) – telling Aoife, Bianca, Ronks (anyone who will listen) – that *Jackson* – my boyfriend – *and I don't have sex any more; is that normal?* We haven't in ages and I'm fixated on it becoming an issue; we're flatlining and I'm taking it personally. Bianca's livid: *Just pounce on him tomorrow morning,* she says; *that's what I'd do.* No shit, Bianca, but Ronke agrees: *It works both ways,* she says; *you have to make an effort too, Ella.* Some girl begins to give me advice. It might be golden but I can only make out one in every seven of the words she slurs.

Enter the siren's song of Britney's 'Toxic' resounding like a choir of angels, and we kick our shoes off and run to the dancefloor. Turns out that hours of being nice and patient to everyone without one sip of water takes its toll. Like Gremlins that *did* eat after midnight, our true selves come out. Hair comes down or scrapes up into topknots. Abdominals relax. Lipstick smudges and skirts hike. *We did good today.* We pat ourselves on the back. We're the life and soul, turning it up. And it's to Destiny's Child's 'Lose My Breath' that I lose all sense of dignity and pride.

So, when it's time to 'throw the bouquet', who could have known it would be me, in the thick of it, elbows out, ready to catch my fate?

The flowers take me down with their weight, heavy and wet,

knuckles kissing the dancefloor as I bow like the branch of a tree to catch them. Surprise, gasps, laughter, the room applauds. Aoife and Bianca scream; Ronks films me. My shocked face is apparently *priceless*. I never catch anything. I never win anything. The photographer snaps photos – bedazzled . . . stunned – a halo of silver stars around me like I'm Miss World.

'Congratulations!' says Mia's nan with a grip so hard she could kill a minotaur. 'That'll be you next to walk the aisle then, love. Got anyone special?'

It could be a coincidence (it's definitely a coincidence) but it feels like a targeted attack when the DJ plays the next song. I know it by the feeling; the feeling always comes before the sound. I feel it before I hear it. It's my 'friend's' (the '' are important) band, True Love. It's *him*. Lowe. The guitar line, the melody in those recognizable chords, his voice, warm syrup over sponge, always collapsing me to mush. And I shove it down, just like I always do, and excuse myself.

In the toilets, Book Club are doing coke off what I'm pretty sure is a nappy bin. They look at me with an *oh, it's just you* and get back to it. No one ever offers me drugs. Do I just give off that *boring* scent? The irony that now is the one time I could probably really use a drug. Some sort of pain relief. A droplet or two of Rescue Remedy at the very least. The acoustics of the bathroom make his voice jump and vibrate off the walls. I find a cubicle, sloppily slam the door behind me and slump on the toilet with my jumpsuit round my ankles. It's fitted, so I am not wearing a bra, which feels extra exposing but also *fun*. A one-piece is great until you realize you will spend a lot of your time sitting naked on toilets. Boobs hovering above spread thighs in contemplation.

I think of him.

Of course I do. He lives rent free in my head. Does he think of me? I want him to be doing something, somewhere and stop. And for that one second think of me. Let that moment of his be mine. Let his hairs stand on end in some contagious shudder of ET telepathy. I have the urge to speak to him. I *should* know better, trust that I've been here a million times before, that the feeling always passes. Find the wisdom to remember that another passage of time will go by where I won't even think of him and I'll be grateful that I didn't send that impulsive message.

I take my phone out . . . I search for his name in my phone book, heart beating – I'm going to do this tonight. I'm going to text him. It's a great idea . . . isn't it? *Isn't* it?

But then the cubicle door flies open with a bang. *Shit, the lock.* I leap up to slam the door shut. 'Sorry!' I shout out even though the door-pusher should be the one apologizing. But it's too late: Mia's father-in-law has seen it all. Mainly the hovering boobs.

He's so angry with embarrassment, I hear him muttering something prehistoric about 'the trouble with unisex toilets'. And, as he storms out: 'I'll take a piss by a tree!'

Well, that was *sobering*. I put my phone away.

The door barges open again and I hear Aoife's familiar voice: 'They're playing "Young Hearts Run Free"! Where is she? Ella! You in here?' Aoife kicks the cubicle door next to me wide open.

'Yeah,' I call out, 'I'm here!'

Followed by Bianca: 'Did Mia's dad-in-law just see your tits?'

But I don't answer because I don't care. Because I'm not here; I'm back there, back where it all began.

Chapter 2

Then

It's the year 2000 and summer here in London is almost over. I'm fourteen. I'm trying really hard to be a grunger right now but I look like an uncooked meatball in a Foo Fighters t-shirt and a spiked choker. Probably because I'm addicted to Dairylea Dunkers and those waxy orange rolls of Bavarian smoked cheese. (I'm also trying really hard to grow out of my lip-sniff habit and everything has to be an even number otherwise we die, but that's by the by.) My soft little universe is meant to be opening up, only just getting started and yet, because of the millennium, there are rumours that the world is going to end (in which case my lip-sniff habit really isn't that big a deal). It hasn't as of yet but I still have reasons to believe it's true.

We've spent the weeks not on a beach in Spain or camping in the New Forest like the other girls in my school but packing up our life into boxes. We've just left our cosy cocoon ground-floor Brixton flat, where we were all 'living in each other's pockets' happily, or so I thought. Apparently, it wasn't big enough for three kids. Violet, Sonny and I have outgrown the overflowing cupboards and beaten down, Biro-doodled sofa, frame buckled from being tickled, performing shows and playing dens. It was noisy and restless. But it was ours. Now it's time to break free and become butterflies but I miss the flat, terribly. I don't like change at all.

My parents decided to take a gamble on a doer-upper, only without any money to doer-up: 251 Palace Road. The house looks like Count Olaf's (only, the series of unfortunate events is now my life.) My mum, Antonia – as if carved from stone, with the physique of a shot putter, almost tall enough to block an entire doorframe, loves the three of us fiercely – is a practical person in need of a project. My dad, Rod – a two-pints-after-work mechanic, who listens to Motown all day long and *never asked for this* (meaning how his life has panned out) – just wants an easy time. Up until 251 Palace Road, they were a team, a force against the world – Bonnie and Clyde, Barbie and Ken, Kermit and Miss Piggy – though maybe now Mr and Mrs Twit would be a more accurate comparison.

But let's not make things depressing. It's actually quite a good time to find me because I have a boyfriend. Or that's what I'll tell anyone who will listen on our first day back at least.

'Hey, guys, so, if you've been wondering why I've been quiet this summer holiday, well, I'm not exactly sure how to say this without making you seethe with jealousy but I now have a boyfriend. So if you notice any elevations of maturity in me, that'll be why.'

The reason I can say *I, Ella Cole, have a boyfriend* is because I now have 'proof', in the form of a photograph, AKA gold dust. Said photograph was found – hear me out – in the bottom drawer of a rickety old dresser that Mum picked up on the roadside saying TAKE ME. The photo is of a teenage boy – maybe seventeen – I KNOW! – with blond curtains. The photo is of a total stranger but *he'll do*. I stuff the photo into my hoodie pocket. In the photo he's sleeping, almost like I took the photo with my own disposable camera one lazy morning in bed and got the photos developed at Woolworths, paying extra for the twenty-four-hour service. Even on the grainy matte Kodak print I can see how juicily surfaced and poppable his spots are – like heads of seals emerging from the ocean. But imperfections are good; they make my boyfriend obtainable, realistic. The brutal *reality* that I've not even had one snog in real life is quite irrelevant. I guess what I'm saying is: he's a lie. I suppose it's quite sad if you look at it like that, so let's not look at it like that.

My journey to the local girls' school is a lonely half-hour walk down the Brixton back roads, ample time to fixate on my phantom boyfriend (his name is Jason now) and invent our summer love story in preparation for this morning's recital.

Me and Jase. Jase and me. We are so in love. Yes, I know I never mentioned him before but that's because I met him on MSN messenger, silly billies, and he lives in Slough. His great-grandad owns the Cadbury chocolate factory so when we get married I'll get unlimited Crunchies. He's going to get me a gold Argos ring with our initials engraved. We go to Thorpe Park and queue up for the teacups and people are jealous of our young love as we inch along in our spotless matching shell toes. Tongues tied in a red-hot lasso of Dr Pepper, Carmex and sour pineapple gum. He wins me one of those massive teddy-bears holding a heart in its paws with the words stitched I LOVE YOU. We plunge down the log flume together and I sit in-between his open legs, leaning back, casual, as we splash down the ride, blinded by the flash of the camera – but still posing – so we can get it printed onto a keyring so I can tell everyone that's my boyfriend, Jase. We go to the cinema and I get fingered. Pretty easily actually because in the fantasy I am wearing those Adidas tracksuit bottoms with the poppers that Mum won't buy for me. We celebrate in KFC. After that great day, I get to lose my virginity to K-Ci & JoJo's 'All My Life'.

But alas, my fantasy takes an unexpected turn. I fall pregnant and have to quit school, but I'm happy at first because I hate school anyway. I work in Shoe Express, which is a dream because it is my favourite shop of all time, but it's not easy with our baby – Topanga – strapped to my chest, which is especially annoying when it comes to sizing people's feet and eventually the novelty of employee discounts on sexy-ish school shoes wears off once I realize all the shoes at Shoe Express are made in the back room with a glue gun by a man called Keith and I have no reason to wear school shoes because – oh yeah – I don't go to school any more so Jase could follow his dreams of just going to the Go-Kart track all day long until one day a girl with a push-up bra is having her eighteenth birthday party there and he fancies that girl instead and I'm left alone with Baby Topanga.

Eugh. I hate it when a fantasy goes off-piste.

I scrunch the photograph up and throw it in the bin. Those are minutes I'll never get back. I hate Jason. I feel so used and dirty. Like I'm wearing someone else's knickers. That's the thing about lies – annoyingly, you just can't lie to yourself.

I look at my mood ring to access my feelings. It glistens a yellowy amber, which can 100% only mean absolutely one sure fire thing . . . mixed emotions.

Oh.

The symptoms: uncertainty and nervousness.

Classic.

At this highly academic girls' school I am in bottom set for everything from English to Science, which does absolutely nothing for my self-esteem. I know I only really got a place because Mum wrote some convincing sob story letter about how *good* I was at creative writing and stapled some of my scruffy handwritten poems to the admission form. One was about a fading beauty queen with feet like dead dormice. The other was about imagining if I had cancer.

I am exhausted by the teachers not giving me extra time, not making *me* their passion project or being excited by my potential. For all they know, I could be the expert they never knew they had who fosters a particular skill for finding rare fossils or accurately counting how many sweets there were in a jar just by glancing at it. Turns out, nobody wants to see my doodles and drawings and letters. My – don't laugh – *designs*. One, a skin-tight white boob tube dress with a barcode down the side reading 2 XPEN5IV3 4 U. *Cool, right?* Or if somebody invested the time to teach me the guitar, I could turn my poems into songs for my band, 'Skipped Disk' (which is a hilarious and clever pun on the spine-injury slipped disc, and on the CD itself will be an X-ray image and of course the disc will inevitably skip – as all CDs do – and then the joke will really pay off. It's really fucking cool actually).

'We cultivate *talent*,' they say. Only they don't mean *talent-show* talent; they mean please be a genius at stone-cold maths or create something 'outstanding' like an entire grandfather clock or a 3-D printer you designed on your lunch break that goes on to make a chamber to slot inside somebody's dying heart. Being great at chemistry, cricket, gymnastics, classics, choir or painting a still life of fruit tumbling out of a goblet also counts as talent – not, spending all of double science giving the girls a manicure with a pot of Tipp-Ex. Well, they'll be sorry when I start my 'collective' and earn critical acclaim by creating gigantic, distressed canvasses with progressive art upon them, which will basically be a blank canvas with a word like BITCH scratched in massive letters and I can charge twenty grand for that one. No doubt they'll be begging me back to give a motivational talk on Careers Evening and I'll say no.

Aoife, my best friend, is the smartest person I know and for Aoife there is no telling where school stops and home begins. *Living* is education. Her interest for life is infectious and inspiring. All lethally supplied in heaped unfiltered doses by her South London hippy parents, who hide *nothing* from her. This level of honesty is refreshing and I appreciate it, as my own parents seem to be in on some *hilarious* in-joke of despising each other for the past year whilst plummeting us into debt and despair and not uttering a single word about it. I reckon the only reason they've got the bigger house is so they don't need to be near each other. My dad always scuttling off to sleep on the spare bed in his hideout. Separate from Mum.

Instead of passive-aggressively slamming the door off the hinges, Aoife's parents discuss everything from politics to psychology, the economy to engineering, sex, drugs, to the plot of *Eraserhead*, over reheated sweet potato at the dinner table, where Aoife's point of view is regarded and valued. Her parents actually *listen* to her as she holds the floor, debating, laughing at in-jokes about politicians and passing around a witty short story in the *Guardian* she'd scissored out over the weekend. Even The Lodger joins in, pulls up at the table to throw in their twopence and I watch on in awe as it all sails over my head and wonder why my potato was 'sweet' and orange and not white. I stay the night, brain beating, absorbing, learning about Mad Cow Disease and the Labour party and Flat Feet. And in the morning Aoife and her whole family (+ Lodger) are off on the 159 bus with a packed lunch (including two-litre bottles of carbonated water), to visit some free exhibition at an art gallery on Human Rights, eat a slice of vegan gluten-free cake at the Buddhist café, swing by a feminist protest outside the library and make it home in time to watch *Buffy the Vampire Slayer*. But was Aoife our school's kind of smart? Probably not.

Ronks is book smart; often we need her to explain to us in slow-motion what the teacher just said. She's clever enough to go Cambridge but she brushes me off and says, 'Ella, don't be *mad*.'

Bianca is the most rebellious of us. She's the oldest and third tallest in our year group; I'm not sure if this fact is related but she also started her period a year before everyone else – so, like in a cavewoman sense, she's the leader of the pack. And her surname starts with the letter 'A' so she's first in alphabetical order for everything at school, and because of this, she gets whatever she wants. However, Bianca's a bit too weird for her own good and rather than being the boss of everyone, she chooses to only micromanage a small group: us. And we let her because we are scared and weak. Bianca is constantly in detention for dying her hair different colours and getting extensions, wearing her skirt too short, not covering her nose piercing with a plaster and smoking the cigarettes she steals from her dad's duty-free cartons, whilst the rest of us are eating Flumps. Bianca lives with her dad, who will always buy us a takeaway if we annoy him enough – but he's also the strictest of our parents. Then again, I would be strict too if my daughter was Bianca. But Bianca says it's the other way round; he *makes* her act out *because* he's strict.

Then there's Shreya, who says her insides are glow-in-the-dark because when she was a baby she drank a glow stick. Sometimes she has to run out of class crying – mostly during tests – because her parents died tragically in a car crash. But I saw her parents at her fourteenth birthday and they looked perfectly fine. She then said the car crash was just a premonition.

And The Twins. Who are, you know, posh and twins.

And apart from each other, we are ignored.

The girls at school really aren't our species anyway.

On the plus side, there are no boys, which, at fourteen, is probably a good thing for us because we really fancy them. So that means we can sit back with our skirt buttons undone and eat as many KitKat Chunkies as we like.

The art of 'self-defence' is very much a part of our curriculum, taught in the sports hall by a teacher called Miss Eugenie who presents herself as a handsome fairy-tale prince. Basically, she is lanky with a Leonardo DiCaprio jawline, razor-sharp blonde haircut, piercing green eyes and a love for Eighties rollnecks.

Miss Eugenie tells us not to walk down alleyways alone, not to sit on the top deck of a bus alone, reminds us that perverts could *even* look like old women, so now on top of being scared of every passing person we must also not discriminate or underestimate our abusers. Must trust *no one*.

She says, if we're ever threatened in public, we are to stand up like a Girl Guide and shout at the top of our lungs, 'EXCUSE ME THIS PERSON IS BOTHERING ME!' Or better still, 'FIRE!'

'Passers-by might ignore a girl crying out for help, but they *won't* ignore the threat of a fire!' She holds her finger up and looks at us *powerfully*. 'Trust me.' She winks, like she's had to shout 'FIRE!' more than once in her lifetime.

One time, there is a man who flashes at us. He sprints manically across the field, letting his liberated willy flap from side to side, wagging and spirited like an Alsatian's tongue out of the window of a back seat of a car speeding down the M23. And we are instructed to *get inside, girls!* and the doors are bolted. Despite the squealing, we are not really scared of this man, because he is just one quite small naked man, and we are 700 girls in bottle-green uniforms with facts about the periodic table that would bore an erection to smooshed banana quicker than one could say titanium. Instead, we are kind of thrilled by the experience, excited to be out of maths. We wait in the hall to *quieten down*, where the view is of a different organ altogether – that being . . . an . . . actual organ.

The whole thing feels very olden days, like nuns flocking inside some church hall, waiting for Dracula to pass. The organ makes that visual really *pop*.

Instead, we talk, we rehearse the 'Macarena', try to master the *CrazySexyCool* of TLC's 'Waterfalls', braid each other's hair, take turns to try on Zeniyah's new Baby-G watch. We learn that a sneeze is one eighth of an orgasm and then try to make ourselves sneeze by pinching and sniffing the dust under the stage curtains. We scrounge, like gulls, smoky bacon Wheat Crunchies and gulps of Apple Tango and squabble over which of us the man was looking at, flattered (wait... annoyed? Confused? Sickened?) that *any* man *ever* even recognized us as girls.

'*Apparently,*' says Cherise, 'the flasher left a porno mag in the school field with a yellow Post-it note attached to it saying if any girl wanted to "show themselves" to him, he'd give them ten pounds.' The magazine was a 'brief'. *Stage directions* – this is what he had in mind. I never get to see the magazine or the note but I do wonder how the transaction would work, in a practical sense.

Would he really just hand a £10 note over?

Miss Eugenie ups the self-defence classes after The Flasher. She does spontaneous routes of the school, working her way down the corridors like a hound, pressing down on the metal handle without a 'come in' from whichever teacher is teaching, and begins instructing an impromptu combat class to catch us off-guard. She is always hovering, switched on, like an avatar on stand-by in a computer game. Chest heaving, blood pumping, on the look-out for danger . . .

'Girls, a fox has regrettably sniffed out the henhouse and it is only a matter of time before he *strikes*.'

We shriek and flap about on cue like the flustered hens we are.

Oh, she can't *wait* for this fox of a man to strike so that battle can commence. But he never returns again.

Once, a boy called Maximilien, a name meaning *The Greatest*, is brave enough to take part in an exchange programme and comes all the way from classy France to be a student at *our* girls' school. For two whole weeks a real-life actual boy takes RE with us. Geography, History, Science. Even PE with us. One boy versus hundreds of *us*. It dawns on me that if Maximilien tried hard enough, he could possibly potentially get ALL of us pregnant and we could recreate a whole community without ever needing another man ever again and that is both a startlingly scary and powerful thought. How far can sperm *stretch*?

Maximilien is just a boy, any boy, and we perve the absolute life out of him: gawping, winking, pecking, poking, frothing at the mouth. All every girl in our whole entire school cares about is which one of us Maximilien will choose to be his bride. We aren't sophisticated enough at this point to understand that attraction comes into it, that actual consent comes into it. That girls might not even be his preference whatsoever. Because for us, this isn't about Maximilien; it's a case of: whoever gets chosen to be the wife of the exchange student is, by default, *Queen of the Fucking School*. All hail.

It's easy for me. One of the perks about not being pretty is that Life Olympics such as these seem to simply pass me by. I don't have to enter them. Like, there is just NO point. I can hold my hands up from the start and say, *I'm out* and just write about the chaos I witness in my notebook instead.

Total pandemonium ensues. The popular girls start wearing gloss on their lips as thick as mayonnaise, rolling up their skirts, stuffing their bras with balled socks and pads of tissue. This Maximilien must think he's died and this is his heaven – if angels all wore bogey green and had greasy fringes and retainers they had to take out before they ate their tuna melts. At first he rocks it. For a minute Maximilien, the boy with the name like a new chocolate bar, lives up to his namesake – he must really feel like The Greatest. But then the pressure, prowling and, let's be honest, *harassment* clearly overwhelms him. His once almost-starched popped collars begin to droop, his shoulders to cower. Towards the end of week one Maximilien lunches by himself or with teachers who shield him and his panini like bodyguards. Maximilien is a trophy. A sword in the stone. And the girls are on odysseys driven by throbbing hormones and hysteria. He begins to creep, sheepishly, around the corridors like a quivering lamb, avoiding the growls of hungry lions (I am an alpaca) to the safety of the accessibility toilet – the only toilet he can use without fear of being spied on and terrorized. The door pounds, the handle jiggles, perverted whispers smoke him out through the gap in the door, or a girl just bursts out from behind the hand-drier with a 'gotcha'.

I mean this is not OK. This is fucked up.

He counts down the days before his release and then he RUNS out of that school, boy, probably not breathing a single sigh of relief until his plane zooms off into the sky and the drinks trolley is coming round.

Some girls have boyfriends who hang around outside the school on bikes. Or *even* inside cars. The teachers do not like this. Boys are a DISTRACTION. And girls like Aoife and me, *The Unchosen*, walk past Boyfriends like they're a road accident, minding our own business, *but* craning our heads to steal a look. The Chosen girls look at us with screw-faces like we are after their parking space or table by the window at Pizza Express.

Some of the girls aren't interested in boys. Yet or at all. Some hold hands freely with other girls. Sometimes, I hold Aoife's hand too, but I don't get any fanny tingles.

As I walk out of the school drive towards the gates and I see the boys, I can almost trick myself into thinking that maybe the boys are waiting for me. It's a sad fantasy daydream game that occasionally my dad wakes me out of with the horrible honk of his battered old Saab.

Or worse – The Vespa.

Nothing wilts my heart at much as Dad arriving to pick me up from school with his Vespa. It means having to lift my *actual* leg *up*, flashing my bobbly knickers enveloped with potentially a sticky sanitary pad, wings spread to the entire world, my heavy book bag digging into my bum, a badly fitted helmet rattling on my head and quivering all the way back home with Dad ordering me to 'lean in' with him at the corners.

You mean lean in to death, Dad. To having my face shaved off by a pavement. And he wonders why he has a hernia.

I come home, leg hair windswept, muscles taut and tense, eyes streaking, freezing cold and needing a hug.

On Fridays I walk home, taking my time winding down the

back roads, sometimes with Aoife; then, in my freezing cold attic bedroom, we talk about boyfriends.

Aoife thinks boys are *terrific*. We say *terrific* because it's the one word my little sister Violet's Barbie doll says when you push the button in her spine: 'terrific'. It's terrific that Ken has cheated on her with the Pocahontas doll, that she's been trapped in the shoe cupboard or dragged around by her hair by Sonny. '*Terrific, terrific, terrific*,' she announces like a psychopath.

'Something in the Way' plays on repeat and Aoife lies on her back staring up at my DIY wallpaper: cut-outs from magazines, printed song lyrics and photographs. Her glasses steam up and she sighs, 'Ohhh, Elbow,' her nickname for me because once a teacher asked me what Ella was short for and Aoife said, *Elbow* and now it's stuck. 'I just *really* want a boyfriend BADLY. Don't you?'

'So bad,' I say to fit in, but secretly I'm frigid as hell. I miss Hibjul, my boyfriend from nursery. He was such a decent bloke.

In truth, I don't think a man or intimacy is what I'm after right now, given that my idea of great physical pleasure is diving into the massive rolls of oversized carpets that hang like a giant's mangle at Carpetright (because obviously an entire pixie universe is to be found back there). That's the kind of out-of-body utopia I'm trying to get to but I'm worried that if I don't at least *meet* a boy up close and personal any time soon that I'll be like this forever. Rolling into carpets whilst my mates are getting married.

'How the hell do we get one?'

'Maybe our blood isn't sweet enough?' I offer.

'Go on . . . ' Aoife takes it like I've only gone and cracked it.

'Mum says the reason mosquitos don't bite me as much as Violet is because I don't have "sweet blood". Maybe it's the same with fit boys? We *repel* them? Maybe my blood's just too – you know – *savoury* from eating all that smoked cheese and turkey wafers?'

'True. So, what you're saying is that we just need to eat more chocolate biscuits?' Aoife takes on the Old Wives' hack, until she remembers: 'Oh no wait, I always get bitten by mosquitos.'

I won't lie, my heart wilts at the thought of Aoife's blood being all Snapple sweet. I bet mine's all briny like the gross juice they put around tinned tuna.

'Where are all the boys?'

Where is the boy *zone*?

Boys cut from the metre rolls of Boyfriend Material are scarce. They hang out by the ice rink. By the Odeon Cinema. By the chicken shop. By the bus stop. Sometimes by the train station. A lot in the park.

Usually in packs. Unapproachable. Eating. Smoking. Riding. Skating. Laughing. Walking. Talking. *Breathing*.

So how does one go about *catching* a boy? Hmmm. This is tough.

All of the suitable boys ignore us. It's like they think we don't exist. They don't even *acknowledge* us – their eyes glide over our heads like they're looking for their train on a timetable behind my face. Like we're getting in their way.

As an experiment, I try crushing on Mr Paul – the IT teacher, who we all think is hot because he's not ancient like the others and lets us call him Mr Paul. If you squint, he looks like Beppe di Marco off *EastEnders*. But Grace says she once saw him lift up his balls and dollop them over the back of Angelica's chair like two tinned plum tomatoes. So it's a no go.

It's bothering me now; it's grinding my gears that since leaving primary school – other than my baby brother Sonny (who's six), Kurt Cobain and AJ McLean from Backstreet Boys fame – two of whom I have only met in my dreams, both of whom I reckon live in America and would definitely know that, if they were to ever fall for my unobvious beauty, they would instantly be pinned as paedophiles, and one of whom is sadly dead – I know NO boys, not even to test the water with.

My view becomes skewered; I try to broaden my mind. Why do I have such a *block*? Really *try*. I kiss Bianca in her bed but feel only that same warm satisfying gooey feeling as sharing a whole tub of strawberry cheesecake ice cream with her. The girls' school has left me with a warped unrealistic altered view of the world. I no longer know what is attractive to me. I'm underdeveloped, like a half-baked brownie. I don't know who is handsome or who isn't. I don't know who to fancy or even *how* to do it. How to go about measuring my desire in appropriate doses so it doesn't come out in one big pour. I don't trust my love compass or radar. I start to fancy everybody – Donatello from *Teenage Mutant Ninja Turtles*. Sonic the Hedgehog. *Help me, I fancy a hedgehog!* The tiger from the Frosties box – yeah, Tony. The rabbit from the Cadbury Dairy Milk Caramel advert. Rufio from *Hook*. I fancy one of my Barbies. At one point I fancy a member of Slipknot. A mask. No, not the willy-nosed one, but still. A mask. Great – now *I fancy a horrible scary mask.*

At one point I fancy Moe, the grey-haired barman from *The Simpsons*.

Do I fancy *Outlaw*, the shiny black horse at the stables at the top of our road?

He's so muscly. Rebellious. Commanding. Is he *sexy*? Do I fancy Outlaw the horse now?

A touring Theatre Company visits our school. I whisper to Mia Bennett, a girl in my form who I mistook for a comrade, that I *a bit* fancy the woman playing Peter Pan. But 'like *as* Peter Pan though', I make clear, even though it isn't entirely true: I like everything about her, *especially* that she is a woman playing Peter Pan with her shimmery tights. But it's too late; Mia's face fires up like a fruit machine, *oh for fu*— She's hit the jackpot with this one and before I know it a lazy unoriginal rumour is spreading that I'm 'lesbians with Aoife'.

Oh, of course I'm 'lesbians with Aoife', Mia. There has been a rumour going around that I'm 'lesbians with Aoife' since I was about seven years old. Plus none of us, Mia included, is very popular so nobody really bats an eyelid.

Anyway, that boat sails, and I watch the Peter Pan tour bus fly away to the next lucky school on tour for Peter to break more hearts.

I need to realign my standards if I am ever going to get lucky in love. And that means: get realistic.

Even when practising the art of fancying in hypothetical scenarios – *in fantasy* – I focus on keeping it *achievable, even* when I'm pretending, to avoid disappointment. I never set my sights on a lead singer or main character. I leave the heart-throbs to the pretty, popular girls. Perhaps it's also a snobbery of mine about not wanting to go with the crowd and to be alternative. A self-conscious way of carving my own lane. My subject of desire has to be the underdog, the odd one out, the weird cute one, the dark horse. (Or, failing that, an actual horse.)

It doesn't take the smartest cookie in the cookie jar to know this all stems from a fear of rejection. A fear of humiliation. I have this quite cool way of switching off my attraction and attention to anybody if they aren't interested. I can make myself immune to boys if I choose, like a puppy without a scent. It's a way of protecting myself whilst keeping up with the pack.

There's a new thing going around at school where an attractive person, instead of 'fit', is described as 'spicy'. It's gone one step further where there now seems to be a grading system, where good-looking-ness gets ranked. 'Saffron' means the most smoking, because saffron is the most expensive luxurious spice of all.

'They are so saffron.'

Well, if this is the case, label me 'mixed herbs'. I pretty much decide that, for the time being, it's probably safest if I just forget that I own a fanny at all. And so that's what I do. I try to pretend my vagina doesn't exist, in the hope that, if ignored and neglected long enough, the flesh down there will politely sort of seal up completely, scab over, with fresh skin, in its own time, like a doll's, with just a simple small round 'O'-shaped hole for wees.

Chapter 3

My first proper kiss is in Ireland. We're there for Aoife's great-grandma's eightieth – a dark function room with a giant cream cake and loads of pissed-up adults. We sit there, awkward as hell with our sleek fringes, nursing our lager tops to fit in and eating 500,000 dry-roasted peanuts. Aoife anxiously picks her spot scabs. I pick my fingers. We were hoping boys our age would be here. But it's just Aoife's cousin – who has a diamond earring and is quite fit but he's brought his girlfriend, who has streaky fake tan. The kiss takes place the next day with a boy called Connor who works on the miniature steam train opposite our hotel. He has a Nike tick shaved into the back of his head. He's Irish and calls kissing 'going away'. He says, and I quote, 'Do you want to go *away* with me?'

'Where to?' I ask innocently looking at the nearby lake and wondering if he owns a rowboat, anxiously biting the dead skin around the edge of my thumb until blood comes. But with a twinkle of his lazy eye, *oh I know where we're going alright*. On a fast ride to Adulthood, that's where alright. This is my chance. A crash course in snogging. If it goes badly, nobody has to know. I may as well get it out the way. And so we agree.

The Kiss takes place on a grassy shrubby hill in the playground by the tree next to a windswept carrier bag, a twist of dried-up dog poo and the hipbone of what I'm pretty sure is a rat. I press my bleeding thumb into the sleeve of my hoody to soak up the blood and the soft locked bruise of a kiss. For a minute, the electricity of oxytocin surges through me but actually I think I just got a static shock from Connor's shell suit rubbing against my thigh.

The *going away with me* is a contract. One of those spit pacts they make except with our actual faces. When the painful everlasting seven seconds are up, THANK GOD, I unashamedly wipe my mouth in victory in front of him. Right there on my sleeve is the evidence. A snail trail of saliva that snaps back at us like snot. The deal is sealed. I am no longer a *real* snog virgin.

Thanks for that, Connor. Thanks for that, Ireland.

And away I go back to grey London feeling like I'm made of gold. Like I've been invited to the Ambassador's Reception off the Ferrero Rocher advert. Like people will notice that something about me has changed. My boobs that bit bigger, my hair that bit shinier in a swingy pony-tail. At last, I stand, a woman.

It seems I am on a roll. More mosquitos want my savoury blood. Now that the seal has been broken, my second snog follows swiftly after. Lex goes to the Steiner school behind mine that has an intake of about fifteen students between the ages of toddler and teenager, with a sheep ratio of about seventeen to every child. He has impressive acne and wears it confidently – a constellation upon his bum-fluffed cheeks. I admire this about him. His hair is bleached like Eminem's – FIT – and gelled into stiff spikes like snowy mountains, and, better than that – Lex is a *skater*.

I 'meet up' with him one weekend at Brixton Bowls, where we ignore each other for the entire day and only when it's time to say *goodbye* do we finally say *hi*. We go ahead and do the snog over a hip-height wall, him on one side, me on the other, his skateboard in-between as a metaphor of why it will never work. How a money-grabber kisses someone for their debit card – poor

Lex must know that, deep down, the only reason I like him is because he skateboards. I'm such a skateboard-grabber.

It is the driest snog of my life, like licking the seal of an envelope. Like I've been dared to eat all the salty maize snacks from the shop. Still, there is much to celebrate: I've just snogged a skateboarder on home turf, which feels ten times more legitimate. I race for my bus home, tingling. Feeling like I want to do something *crazy* like . . . Oh, goodness . . . I don't know . . . get the top bit of my ear pierced or something. But I just press my face into a pillow and squeal.

Then once again: drought. Like when the hyenas take over in *The Lion King*. There is a thirst.

At school we ignore it and get on with eating Wispas and toasties, fattening up for a feast of some sort. Great if we're to be the main event of the feast, like the glazed pig in the centre, but boy, as the measurements on our skirts go up – we are somehow STILL hungry. Starving for that sweet treat that just can't be found in a secondary school tuck shop.

LOVE.

But no new boys will ever find us here behind the bolted gates, so we are entirely reliant upon chance, fate and luck until eventually our prayers are heard. A few weeks into the school year, Mia abruptly leaves our form to go to a *mixed* school closer to her new house. We take turns to warmly hug her goodbye whilst hiding the fresh livid bitterness of seething jealousy, reminding her of our closeness so she remembers to bring us forth into her new life of being at school, every day, with *boys*.

Given the circumstances, I *suppose* I can, just this once, forgive and forget the rumours she spread about me. 'I'll miss you so much,' I bleat like the others.

Mia is awaiting a transformation. From kiwi-eating, fluffy-pen-carrying, *Trolls are my best thing*, rumour-spreading, shit-stirring Mia, to a *New Girl*.

And down she she'll go like blood in the ocean to a classroom full of sharks . . . and jellyfish her newness everywhere and see what they make of her.

Mia has a chance to start again. An opportunity, just like Maximilien, to be hot.

I mean, *spicy*.

Chapter 4

Understandably, Mia wants to introduce us girls slowly, like Bisto gravy, bit by bit, so as to not overwhelm her mix by having unwanted clumps. Mia wants us to *blend*. *Smooth*. And I am, luckily, in the first batch. As it's half term we have to be prepared for drop-of-a-hat-parties where parents are at work so you have to be ready to be drunk by 11 a.m. just as your Shreddies are digesting.

None of the popular girls are invited. BOO HOO. SOZ. *Good*, I think initially, *thank God*. Closely followed by: *what if there isn't enough incentive to make The Boys stick around?* One or two hot friends within the pack is enough to trick the untrained eye into thinking we are an entire unit of *Spicy Girls*.

And then: *you know what? FUCK THOSE GIRLS. They were never nice to Mia at school so why should they get in on the reward?* As though The Boys are an inheritance left behind for us to fight over.

And I am glad because us lot are pretty and confident in our own way too, and The Boys will have the space to truffle out our hidden natural beauty without the distraction of the hot girls from school and the way they get away with train track braces and wear their hair in *un-messy* messy top buns, the way they somehow came out of a five-star womb with a manual on how to overshadow us.

So, rather than make myself hotter, I double down on my insecurities because THAT MAKES SENSE and opt for wearing my little sister Violet's hoodie, which on me fits tight, flattening my boobs and coming up short on the forearms. I use the puffy bulging front pocket to bundle my stubby hands inside like a Victorian muff so that I can anxiously pick away at my fingers to my heart's content without being disturbed or judged. I know it's not a good look because when I see my younger sister, Violet, on the stairs before leaving, she just looks me up and down and says, 'OK.' I wear, always, the same pair of washed-out light-blue denim baggy jeans where the bottoms are matted and drenched up to the knees in dried puddle water and city scum. You'd think my friends and I were employed by the council, responsible for mopping the gutters of South London with our strides alone. In case we don't sound boyfriend-trappable enough, the jeans are also an extra size too big, making me look like I come with a parachute attached, and I always insist on jamming a thousand things into my pockets like one key with 4,000 keyrings, Tamagotchis, squeezy gel pigs, little notebooks, lip balm and, of course, don't forget, my collection of rape alarms, which for some reason I'm too afraid to *test* in case they *don't* work and then I'll have anxiety that my rape alarms don't work all the time which defeats the object of having a rape alarm at all.

It is a chosen few: Aoife, Bianca – our greatest asset in breaking the ice – The Twins, Ronke, Shreya, Zeniyah, Holly, Georgie and me.

'Well, get on with it then – press it,' we bicker by the doorbell, batting each other's hands away, giggling and snorting.

'Jesus,' Aoife mutters. She puts her finger out on the bell and presses . . .

Ding-Dong.

AHHHHHH!

Aoife quickly takes off her glasses and shoves them into her pocket.

'Is that a good idea? Can you even see?' I ask.

'Blind as a bat,' she whispers. 'Link my arm, Elbow.'

'Oh, for fuck's sa—'

Mia opens the door how one would when they have something of particular intrigue hidden inside their house, like a litter of new sleeping puppies. *Shhh!* She quietens our excitement but gives us a wink to keep the buzz alive. We are like the frothing neighbours in *Edward Scissorhands* with the bowls of purple coleslaw. Mia's wearing eyeliner, her eyes – quite rudely – say, *don't mention the eyeliner* – as if we would do her like that – *I mean it*. We respect almighty Mia, for right now, if there is a queen, it is her. We obey, speaking softly, kicking off our try-hard skater shoes that have not once touched the grip paper of a skateboard in their lives.

Already we can't help but feel disappointed. We had hoped to see size 8 and 9 – maybe EVEN 10 – skate shoes here, *boys'* shoes, the scent and heat beating off them, battered, stickered, skateboards mindlessly leaning up against the wall . . . proof The Boys are real. That they exist.

Where is Mia hiding them?

This better not be a sick joke, Mia.

We've come all the way to Wandsworth for this, Mia. Bunked a train for this, Mia. Risked a fine for this, Mia. It was NOT a normal walking distance, Mia; it better <u>not</u> be for nothing.

It's the middle of the day. The house is cold, empty. Full of dark wood and rugs. Astrology and philosophy books and a smell like boiled vegetables. I notice a telescope. Grown-up marbles. It's quite clear Mia hasn't told her parents she was having people over as she's shoving us outside in October.

Mia, with all the power, sashays us into her back garden. And there they are – The Boys. Shoes on their *feet*.

How dare she make us all take our shoes off and not them?

And now we feel enormously stupid in our cupcake and animal socks. Me, even worse, in *my dad's*.

Cheers, thanks a lot, Mia.

Literally on the back foot, we step outside into the turning air, pricking our skin into goosebumps; we really should be wearing jackets.

The first job is to count them. This is The Twins' idea. 'Count them,' one orders through gritted teeth, 'so we can be sure there are enough boys to go round.' Like the boys are a tray of biscuits. 'We don't want anybody getting, you know, *left* out.' This is such a Twin thing to count the boys, to make sure everything is fair.

One, two, three, four . . . They won't keep still; I'm trying to tot up the head count but they're just so . . . *busy* . . . they roll on the ground like cubs, playing, jumping off hedges and spraying beer at each other. But when they are standing, a couple of them are big. *Big.* Big. Giants. *Men.* But with rollercoaster voices that go up and down and twang like tuning forks. I see no love of my life here. I can happily sit this one out. My friends are ready, their glances *changed*, their looks *fixed* – then again, Aoife can hardly see. The Twins have the nerve to pour Lambrini into picnic cups like we're sophisticated adults. When we're really a joke. Bianca's bright shock of dyed-red hair and wonderful boobs smothered in roll-on glitter are delighted with themselves, plunging buoyantly. She twists her nose stud; it winks with power. Aoife readjusts her sparkly butterfly clips. Ronke is already accepting a spliff from a boy! *Ronks?!* What the hell? That is very advanced. Meanwhile my fanny origamis in on itself, never to be seen again.

And it's as if my eyes are lasers, red beams cornering off the Crown Jewels. I score a square in the air and friend-zone myself. Mentally, I see the red lines clearly, like in that film, *Entrapment*. And, here, in my zone, safe. Immune from romance. Immune from rejection. Untouchable. A chair. A brick. A cabbage.

Bianca confidently passes to the boys a bottle of clear hard cheap booze that smells like nail varnish remover. They take turns to swallow it down in bold mouthfuls, like they do this all the time, dragon breaths burning. They hand out cigarettes like sparklers on Bonfire night. Bianca never shares her cigarettes with amateurs. *If you can't inhale properly, it's a waste,* she says, monitoring under her shaved brows to make sure you don't spill a drop of her cancer. There are some Monster Munch crisps in a bowl as a gesture, which The Boys tear into, so now they smell of E-number Roast Beef, rip-off alcohol . . . and—

Wait. *Is* this *what teen spirit smells like?* Like Roast Beef Monster Munch?

Mia is cool, casual, umpiring like the Great bloody Gatsby, honoured to be the host. It's her free house, her territory – her alcohol, her Haribo. With her generosity, her social importance soars to such a dizzy height that she could nominate herself for Prime Minister and she'd have the vote. 'I've made punch!' she announces, raising her ladle to the sky.

Said punch is a bright orange witch's brew. With jelly babies at the bottom that have swollen into bloated distorted pregnant goblins. The mixture tastes like Panda Pops and sticks to the back of the throat like cough medicine. 'EUGH! THAT'S GROSS!' Someone wretches.

Mia laughs the critique off giddily but I can tell she's hurt. She plays harder, as if that was the reaction she was after – 'Yeah! My punch is *lethal*, man!' – as if it's a family recipe that goes back centuries. She pours an old white bottle with a palm tree on it into the bowl, the metal cap crusty, and swirls it together, whilst everyone makes a noise about this: 'You're crazy, Mia.'

And Mia glances at me like, *I'm not sure I want to be crazy, Ella; is crazy a good thing or a bad thing?*

And I nod with reassurance like, *don't overthink it. Crazy's fine, I think. I dunno.*

When this is my brain: FUCK! THEY'RE CALLING HER CRAZY!

I'm completely sober. I have a responsibility, a job – the role of The Goody Goody Parent Pleaser. Every group needs one, especially at gatherings: somebody sober, who, in case of an emergency, can hold the fort, calm The Worried Parent down, reassure them that we're not as drunk as they think: *see, look at me? And we all drank the same amount!* Tell them that I'll be the one to text when we get there, to order the taxi, to make *so and so* some toast to sober up, to listen to The Worried Parent's problems whilst the kettle boils. To distract, whilst your friend is throwing up, or crying, or getting fingered in the Treat Cupboard. It really helps.

We listen to music; we talk over each other, parading, showing off. We are loud and boisterous. Aoife is already snogging some guy, and Shreya has disappeared into a bush with someone somewhere (and they both have braces, very weird) but this is what we came here for, right?

And I have a feeling in my belly when I look at Mia, a shove of envy but mostly pride. She's done it: she's broken free. She is reinvented as *cool*.

And suddenly, what feels like just moments later, we are covered in it: thick coral vomit. It pounds down from a height, like gunge from that show *Get Your Own Back*. Galloping down from the open bathroom window, ploddy sick cascading down like a veil of sweet and sour cake mix. *Oh, Mia.*

WOAH! The Boys dodge the vomit dramatically; screaming, shouting, laughing, pointing, hopping onto the wall. Complete overreaction. Humiliation.

We turn to run towards the house to get Mia but OH, RIGHT, she's already here, trembling in the garden, eyeliner streaking down her face like a Batman villain, her face like a Rorschach test in mascara. We rush up to her, put our arms around her, half-giggling, thinking, hoping, praying she'll see the funny side. She does not. There are no *sides* to vomit.

But we all want to save her. I *really* don't want to have to go home.

I run inside, into the kitchen, scramble for a pint glass, fill it with water and hand it to her. 'Drink this . . . ' I offer, trying not to show I can smell the tang of sick.

'FUCK YOU!' Mia dribbles back at me in a demented roar. *OK, rude.* And she throws the pint glass at our baggy jeans and the water soaks into our socks. Mia orders, 'GET OUT' and that she 'HATES' us. She razors, 'JUST GET OUT MY FUCKING HOUSE I SAID, I FUCKING HATE YOU ALL!'

Maybe she does? Maybe she does fucking hate us?

The boys make comments about her, that she's *lost the plot*, that she's a *psycho.*

Psycho Mia. It doesn't even have a ring to it.

And – oh shit – suddenly her dad is there, her *dad*, still in his black real-life-actual-job overcoat and briefcase in hand, shock and panic in terrified graphs all over his blank face, wrestling with his drunken daughter across the kitchen floor, ordering us all to leave, with *immediate effect.*

And as a group, we are kicked out from this house of horrors, onto the streets. The sky seems to be darkening in that impending doom way that always germinates dread. Like Sunday nights before school. It begins to rain, *hard.* Typical. The cars rush by.

Mia has peaked too soon; these are her new school friends and this is what she's done and it's hard to come back from an act like this. And we can't pretend we're just kids and say we 'didn't know' because we know right from wrong. And I feel bad about it, proper guilt, that it's somehow our fault, that I didn't spot she wasn't OK. It *almost* makes me want to go home.

And then I hear one of the boys ask:

Where to now?

Chapter 5

The Twins suggest, 'We could always go back to ours?'

The Twins' house is a great idea. The Twins have a ginormous trampoline and a lovely calm supportive grandma dog. The Twins have alcohol, always. Which their mum buys *for them* because she's safe like that and what's better, they never drink it, so essentially their mum buys alcohol for everyone. The Twins have a bounty of supplies. Cookies, bagels, endless toast and multipacks of crisps. That bad ham in the shape of a bear's face. Sky TV with, like, five remotes. And a house phone that you can use to your heart's desire and a plug for everything and spare batteries and internet and no mention of a bedtime. The Twins have bags of unused untouched still fresh-in-its-packet make-up, wet-wipes, a selection of perfumes like a counter in a department store. Quality sanitary towels, tampons in all sizes. They have clean folded t-shirts in not-overly-stuffed drawers to change into that smell like washing powder, that you don't even have to give back if you don't feel like it.

'Hey,' one of the boys says on the walk, 'that's Sam's house.' *Who's Sam?* 'Let's see if he's in.'

OK, let's. We all begin to chant, 'SAM! SAM! SAM! . . . '

Sam is quite a fit name actually. Sam sounds fit. Underplayed. Underrated. Subtle. You can't go wrong with a Sam.

Ella 4 Sam 4 EVA.

And before we know it, we are standing at this Sam's door knocking for him.

We all peer inside the small peach-coloured house, where everything seems incy wincy and matching and adorable like a mouse-house in a shoebox. The central heating blasts out.

'SAMUEL!' his mum shouts up the stairs. 'DOOR!'

We await our destiny on the doorstep, us damp kids, nervously breathing in the body heat of each other. *Come on, Samuel. Please be medium-to-quite-fit, not too-intimidating fit. Be just right. Maybe Sam will be the love of my life? Then this can be my in-laws' house. Maybe Sam will be the one who reverses the evil spell cast against my poor fanny, who makes me realize that I do in fact have a pulse down there?*

We await his reveal like a blind date.

Sam appears and a grin washes over his face like he's about to bust up laughing at the state of us. He looks young. Small. Sweet. With big frenzied scatter eyes that are untrusting. He descends the stairs, but he's not *The One*; I don't get *the burn* I was looking for. But he isn't alone.

There's another boy too. He's wearing jeans, a hoodie. And a cap.

They both take a seat on the stairs, the *new* new boys. Sam and this other one, they ask us *where we've come from, why we're roaming the streets soaking wet* and as one of the boys fills them in, I watch this other boy taking the story in, this quiet thing, nodding along at the right beats. I look at him, zooming in close now, my eyes are microscopes, closer and closer . . .

And it's almost like I can't believe what I'm seeing.

This *guy*.

Sorry, who is this beautiful stranger? OMFG, this lovely face – plump lips, cupid's bow, swollen and red like he's just eaten a reaper pepper whole. Chubby cheeks. Smiling eyes. He's delicious. My God. I go inside myself, through the willow trees of my childhood. And that's when the world around me drowns out and all I hear are the rising power chords of Lenny Kravitz's 'Fly Away' . . .

And the boy better run for his life. I am ON.

With just a look, I fall through the ground where I split, come undone like a seed and burst from my shell. His eyes trigger a network of roots and shoots that tangle and connect with a force strong enough to light up a city with full power. *PING. PING. PING!* My walls, with a wrecking ball of a look from him, pound down to grit and I am lost in the thunderous dust, inhaling only this new person. This starburst galaxy. This rip tide. This hurricane. And yet as sweet and delicious as crisp cherryade.

HE. IS. SO. FIT.

Everybody around me is talking but I'm in my head because see, *he* is there now, waiting, chill as hell, like he was there all along with an ice-box of snacks and beer, camping out in the canyons of my mind. Him and those browny-green confident eyes that swirl like my mood ring, carving promises, sparkling like fool's gold, glinting to make a deal, twirling hypnotic, like the tip of a spinning rainbow umbrella and I follow him down to the meadows of his eyes.

So clichéd. So obvious. I can't. And for the first time ever I am the chosen girl in the lift for the Soothers advert who gets kissed on the neck. A love bite. My blind spot. I've been bitten. *Ouch.* Can nobody see this blatant crime? Is everyone just going to sit back and let me get hijacked like this? Does nobody care that I'm clearly on fire?

'This is Lowe,' Sam says like it's nothing, elbows on the stairs behind him. Knowing that's the coolest name he's ever said out loud before and he's definitely the only 'Lowe' we've ever met. Jammy git. We don't know how to respond to a name like this.

'And what's Lowe short for?' Bianca barks, tossing her devil-red hair to the side. Oh no, she twists her nose-stud like stirring sugar into tea. *Shit*, she's suddenly a tigress. She likes him.

'It's just Lowe,' Lowe says.

Oh, IS IT now? THE FIT AUDACITY.

Lowe. Like 'low.' Like 'low' down. I find myself muttering it under my breath. Feeling my tongue press my teeth.

Lowe.

On cue, soft cheeks blushing, Lowe stares down at his bobbly socks, and just when he's about to overboil, he catches himself, he looks up at me with those huge eyes and I fucking die.

Blood thumps, clangourous, somewhere new and deep. I look away. *He's just a boy, for fuck's sake.* But what a fucking lovely face. He's got vampire teeth, but then they are too kind to be inside the mouth of a vampire; they are here in this mouth. How dare he?

'Right, we'd better get going.'

I cut the chat short. Can't be doing with any of this love stuff, so *bye bye now*, thank you so much. I lead the way, disciplining myself like some martyr, a mean old spinster Sister running a convent. I won't allow myself the joy, the privilege, the luxury of liking somebody, especially not a subject like *this guy*. It's like throwing a blanket over a parrot cage; I shut out the light and plunge into the darkness. SHUT UP, BRAIN. SHUT UP, HEART. YOU TOO, FANNY. *How dare I fancy somebody? Oh this is a nightmare.*

WHY IS MY BODY BETRAYING ME LIKE THIS?

'OK, we'll just grab our shoes,' Sam says and Lowe is already grinning again, reaching for his Etnies trainers (a fit boy MUST) like he knows he's got me, *just like that*. Eyes flash, up and down, down and up. He hoists up his loose-fitting jeans.

'Hey?' I say with a question mark like *can I help you?* and find myself saying, 'I'm Ella,' even though no one asked. To which he nods. Like he's letting it sink in.

I've just handed over my *name* and he says nothing in return.

This *Lowe* begins pushing out the front door his red BMX that's been standing up by the radiator, leaning, equally as cool, as if it's another friend that's coming too. I mean, even if the *bike* became my boyfriend I'd be chuffed; it's covered in stickers of all those Extreme Sports brands we look for that signpost us to hot boys. I can't stop looking at him: the geometry of his hands, obsessing over his raw knuckles clamped around the handlebars, split and rough, his nails short and smooth with a slug of just the right amount of doing-stuff-grub, the way the ragged sleeves of his hoodie bunch around his elbows, his veined arms . . . I was not prepared for this.

And so, I do what I know best.

I mark up the friend-zone borders immediately, scoring the line through the air quicker than I've ever drawn it. And I place myself firmly inside.

Locked in. Where I'm safe.

Where nobody can call me sad or weird or annoying or fat or ugly or embarrassing or strange.

Where nobody can say *No*. Or *I don't feel the same*. Or *Sorry, no*. Or *Just friends*.

Where I can't get hurt.

I ignore him on the walk up to The Twins' house in the rain. Over the stones of their front drive, past their spotless seven-seater and twitching security camera. I imagine my gooey-Meerkat-eyed self, lovestruck through the CCTV screen in night-mode, pixilated in black and white, the infection of him showing up in ultraviolet blobs all over my body. I ignore him. Even when we slosh past their granny Labrador and through their brightly lit show-home kitchen. And out into the garden which backs onto the common, with the epic dripping trees hunched over the great fence behind. I still ignore him. Even when we all kick off our shoes into a heap and climb up onto the huge trampoline. Even when Bianca deliberately takes turns to fall onto the boys' laps and laughs and squeals and then accuses with an 'OI, DICKHEAD? DID YOU TOUCH MY BUM?' And this one boy Nas just puts his hands up in the air in surrender and says, 'Not me!' Even when everybody laughs as she rolls off, arms and legs everywhere and onto the next set of knees.

I still make no eye contact. I still ignore him.

Even when we all sit on the damp padded spring covering of the trampoline, in a circle, and I can feel the vibrations of everybody in the elastic, and people switch places, shift and swap with a *budge up*, *move over* and now I'm next to him; *OH SHIT*, chemistry – we seem to be static, hyper-charged off the electricity of meeting for the first time. Us with our soaking wet jeans with puddle water up to our knees – we don't seem to feel the wet, the wind, the cold at all. Only sparks. Against plastic. Against rubber. And skin. There is shock. And I have to get up and do something or I might actually explode . . .

Music.

I run up to get the girls' stereo, to The Twins' lovely clean bedroom with their twin beds and Beanie Babies – I have this moment to myself to stop and breathe.

LOWE. Fuck. Who *is* HE? Where did he come from? My pulse quickens as I pick up the CD player. They have a good one with a CD *and* tape deck with speakers on long cables so you can really stretch them out. I grab my sacred fluffy rainbow bible of a CD wallet, which comes everywhere with me, and carry the whole thing under my chin, careful not to drop anything.

I avoid eye contact with The Twins' mum as I plug everything in; I don't want her to stop my scheming or be annoyed as I unplug the giant lamp with its fancy cream shade and possibly the goldfish water filter too, but I check for signs of life bubbles and they appear, so Beans and Hashbrown are *absolutely* fine.

In my mixed CD goes and that's me thrown out for everyone

45

to see – my taste in downloaded music (which definitely gave my family PC a batrillion viruses) up for judgement.

A few voices whoop, begin to nod along, mouthing the words to Green Day. Bianca takes this as an invitation to dance, thinking she looks sexy like a girl in the video but just *no. Do not dance sexy to Green Day.*

Out of the twenty new faces, all lit by one brilliant white garden floodlight that makes us look like a football crowd on TV, the sky spitting down, his is the only face I see.

'Nice,' he says.

I get this tightness in my throat. My chest heaves with a crushing feeling and I think I might be dying. Or maybe, just maybe, this is love?

Don't engage, Ella – ignore him. And so I do. Even when cigarettes are handed around and vodka bottles with labels wet from the rain and beers, plastic bottles of cider which go down like lightning, crackle as they hollow out. My eyes gaze over Lowe. Stealing looks when he's not looking, each micro-detail, *hunted.* Fingers. Lips. Eyes. Hair. Nails. Skin. Throat. Ears. *Watching.* Everything this goddam guy does. I see it. I take note. I absorb. Waiting for him to slip up, to do something, to reverse this *want,* to make a move with somebody else so I can be released from this grip.

And when it comes to the end of the night, when it's time to say goodbye, when The Twins' mum is politely waving everyone out the door like she *wanted* us to eat her out of house and home, Lowe smiles at me. He runs his hand around the rim of his cap and I see his wrists and clench my jaw involuntarily, so hard my teeth crack like almonds. He says, 'Night, then.'

And I'm smiling so hard I forget to say it back.

I am thinking of the child in me and the adult in me too and where they both are at this point. *And which one of them is in charge here please and who is going to deal with this?* I'm thinking of Kurt Cobain and the Slipknot mask and Moe from *The Simpsons* and the tiger from the stupid cereal box and – whilst we're at it – the footballer Ian Wright too. I'm thinking of the sound of a trainer squeaking on a school hall in a basketball game, electric guitars fusing, *explosio*n, blowing the fronts off speakers. Lying on the grass. Touching his face. Trying to hide how in love I am with somebody I've only just met.

My heart is a harmonica. South London is a valley. World, hear my song.

Chapter 6

Now

It's 6 a.m. and it's awful. I lie – a defrosting dead person – in the grave that is my side of the bed and try to sleep, but how can I? When my mind, like a TV, automatically switches on and every channel plays a montage of the worst moments of my life. My thoughts, like a radio, crackle awake, spilling gossip about my biggest fears: abandonment, loneliness, rejection. *PS everyone hates you. You're so shit.* My wardrobe doors fly open, a theatre, *oh no*, the hangers like hands, peel last night's wine and cigarette smoke-stained bright-pink jumpsuit up from off the floor. How are the hangers doing that? The sight of last night's outfit makes me want to dry-heave like the return of a meal that was the culprit of food poisoning.

The jumpsuit acts out a puppet show of me from last night. A horror, of course. Mia's wedding where I play The Fool. Thanks a lot. I can never listen to Gwen Stefani ever again now. The veins of my eyeballs are tangled chicken wire, sockets, screws, the palpitations, blinding, the dry tightening in my tomb of a throat, the dread, the sickness, the way my hairs stand on end. My pounding head is a wrecked junkyard car, begging to be crushed by a demolition monster truck to be put out of its misery. I'm *such* a terrible person; I get drunk at weddings and make it about me. I'm not a good person. I can't even take care of house plants. I don't call my nanna enough. More bad-karma debt racking up.

I look for the horned master of this hell to make a deal with, slam to my knees and beg: *I'll change, I promise; I'll never drink again. I said it before, I know, but this time is different. I don't need alcohol to have a nice time. I'm sorry.* But *NO!* bellows the demon king; *it's too late; you had your chance and you blew it, bitch. It's over.* Mia's spoiling bouquet is on the other side of the room, balanced on the washing basket (where I put anything that doesn't go in the bin) and yet the weight of them is on my chest – flowers for my grave. I can't look; I roll over, bury my face into Jackson's sleeping shoulder blades, cling to his t-shirt to anchor me before I'm dragged to hell.

'Jackson . . . ' I whisper, cuddling into his back. We've just bought this little flat, our first place together. It hasn't been touched since the Nineties; it's brown, depressing and scary. I'm still not used to it, its new shadows and clanking pipes. 'Please can you wake up?' I forgot to put my gumshield in last night and I've grinded my teeth to sand. The pain of a clenching jaw shoots up to my temples – the anxiety about why I clench a pain far more severe.

'Jackson?'

He turns to face me, eyes still closed, brows frowned, clinging to his peaceful slumber where me and my festering Hangxiety aren't welcome. It's the weekend; he deserves a lie in and I've disturbed him. I'm so selfish. Mean. I'm dirt and he's so clean. He just went to the pub with his friend last night. They had a burger and a pint and called it a night. He barely drinks. He would have showered, brushed his teeth and watched some documentary on his laptop in bed. He's an angel. I want to rub his goodness all over me. I burrow under his arm for protection; he smells of his usual 'aftershave', *Deep Heat*. His long arms octopus around me.

I feel an overriding sense of love and gratitude for him. Thank

God he's here. When he gets up, he'll know what to do. I'll see his hopeful, optimistic fresh-water eyes, his new-day-*A-OK* smile and feel better. At thirty-five, the growling silver fox in him is already threatening a thrilling presence. Then, apparently, Jackson will look like, in his own words, 'a *GQ* cover'. He's getting handsomer behind my back. I will start paying more attention.

Before the inevitable diarrhoea, I think about instigating sex, *pouncing* like the girls said to. But I haven't trimmed my pubes in so long they look like pickup sticks. A bonfire before it's lit. An upside-down sleeping fruit bat that would prefer not to be woken. It's only because I'm hungover and needy that the weight of six-foot Jackson on top of me would feel better than the crushing weight of my own demons. But there's no point: my legs hurt from all that unnecessary winding in heels and, besides, my mind would stray; I'd just be lying there trying to solve the mystery of the Upside Down in *Stranger Things*. Thinking about how Fergie spells out the word G-L-A-M-O-R-O-U-S. And you know what I haven't had for ages? Weetabix. I don't want to put either of us through that when we'd both rather be eating Weetabix on the sofa than getting *pumped*.

I replay the conversation from last night. I said out loud that we didn't have sex. What did I say *exactly*? It feels deceitful.

'Am I bad person?' I ask Jackson, as if he can magically dispel my anxiety when he wasn't even there, the jury lingering in the air around us.

'Don't be daft,' he grumbles in his comforting, nonchalant Midlands accent, barely moving his lips to considerately mask his fish-tank morning breath.

'Unstable then?'

We share the same Spotify account; he knows I pendulum from Kate Bush to Busta Rhymes to UK garage within ten minutes. It's worrying.

'You're just hanging.'

He's right. I know that, but in this nest of paranoia I don't believe him. I'm due on my period so my anxiety is ramping up. *Then* I'm a fucking bitch whilst I'm on my period, so basically there are only twenty-six weeks in the year when I'm a nice normal person.

'How do you know? You might be too close to see the signs?'

'I just do.' He sits up, *at last* – this act alone enough to improve my mood – his shoulders pressing into the headboard of our bed. He takes a sip of water, straps his Apple Watch on and reaches for his phone to look at BBC Sport. Without looking up, he says plainly, 'You would have just chatted a lot of shit and danced. Dancing is good because it stops the chatting shit.'

My God, is he psychic?

'It sounded like a normal, fun wedding – even if I wasn't invited,' he jokes. *Still* joking, he says, 'Mia better not expect an invite to our wedding, that's all I'm saying.'

He *never* talks about *our* wedding. He's a d*on't need a piece of paper to say you love someone* type of person. Weddings are a waste of money. A scam. A hullabaloo.

'I thought you weren't getting married?'

'*IF.*'

IF is new.

I'm too sensitive right now to question him, so I sit up too and brave my phone. We scroll in silence.

I see good old Ronks has taken it upon herself to missile the video of me catching Mia's bouquet across to our 'Friendship Never Ends' WhatsApp group. I don't want to watch it but the idea of them seeing it and me not cringes me even harder. I turn the volume right down so Jackson can't hear. The look on my face though: lipstick – smudged. Hair in a high-pony like a Nineties WWE wrestler. Sweating like one too.

This isn't exactly what I saw for myself at thirty to be honest, but here we are.

Thirty. FUCK. How did this happen? It's really taken me by surprise, like a bath that runs too quick in a hotel room and is about to overspill and flood. I've woken from a long hot summer of twenty-nine years and suddenly a brutal everlasting winter is coming and I didn't prepare for it because I've been dicking about, thinking I was immortal and that life had no consequences. Suddenly I'm scrambling around for miracle eye creams; am I meant to be making collagen bone-broths or to be vegan? Why did nobody warn me that UNLIKE ALL OTHER BODY HAIR if I plucked all my brows off as a teenager they'd take an entire lifetime to grow back? And now I'm just desperately waiting for the day they announce that skinny/bald brows are back in fashion. Why didn't I drink more water? Gallons of the stuff. Why did I drink all that tea and stain my teeth? Nobody needs that much tea in one day, ever. Why didn't I exercise and tone? I did eat two fistfuls of food as my portion sizes, but my fists were inside generous oven *mittens*. Or BOXING GLOVES. Why do I still wear the same bobbly bras I wore when I was nineteen? Why do I sleep in a massive oversized t-shirt for a marathon I definitely didn't run? Why do I own so many fucking tote bags for corporate events I definitely didn't go to? Why is my whole wardrobe full of clothes reserved for a Cinderella ball that I never get invited to because it doesn't exist? Why am I excited to go to the Big Supermarket? Like it's a day out. Only to find myself crying in that Big Supermarket, panic buying, my basket full of dark green leaves, vacuum-packed mackerel and Yakult. Overwhelmed by the vitamins. It's time to take evening primrose, isn't it? Burp up repeats of cod liver oil. I could have sworn that yesterday, when the cheap semi-permanent 'chocolate' box of a home hair dye kit hit my basket with a hopeful plop, the woman on the front of the packaging, with her perfectly shiny dark chocolate wig, jeered at me through her white-toothed smile and said, 'You silly, *silly* girl.'

Oh, NOW you tell me I was meant to be taking care of my mental health the entire time too? *Oh, for fuck's sa—*

Thirty years spent as an optimistic feminist and now I'm deemed an adult purely because of my age. I still secretly look at emerging girl bands and, honestly, in my head, I believe with my whole heart that I could slip in as a fifth member and the general public would be none the wiser. I thought that by now I'd have everything sorted and be a millionaire mother of five happy gorgeous children with reels of Super 8 footage of me looking glorious in a big floppy hat at the beach to play as a montage at my funeral to Spice Girls' 'Viva Forever'. I thought I'd be living in a mansion, CEO of some ginormous company, and have travelled the world. I'm not and I haven't. What made me think that taking out that student loan was for *fun times*? I thought I'd be elected the next poet laureate and I'm not even on the poet laureate choosers' radars. I thought I'd have a pierced belly button, for crying out loud! At the very least I thought I'd like the taste of anchovies, but I haven't even become sophisticated enough for that. Even if I was a millionaire, turns out that in London, a million gets you a *normal* house. Not the house in *Home Alone* that I just *assumed* I'd be living in aged thirty. Put it this way – the thought of a child drawing me now scares me. Would they see me as an old woman? And why am I the only one with wrinkles anyway? Oh, because all my friends are secretly running off and betraying me by getting Botox and pretending it's just 'good foundation'.

I'm not being ungrateful; I'm just saying it how it is: thirty is the biggest disappointment since Sea-Monkeys. Look, I know I'm not old. I know thirty isn't old. I get it. I'm just not *there* yet. I still have to make an 'L' to show me the difference between left and right. I still think I'm in a music video when I walk to the train station with my headphones in, listening to the same songs I always did with lyrics about our 'thirties' thinking thirty was *so old!*

And oh, now I'm just still listening to that music without a shred of irony like nothing has changed, *oh ha, ha, ha*. Songs from my youth are making comebacks as *samples*. Kings of Leon's 'Sex On Fire' probably counts as Dad-Rock. It's DE-PRESS-ING. Sometimes I find myself googling how old actors were in films who once looked *old* to me to find out that they were in fact *younger* than I am now at the time of filming and they look like my friends. The dads in the films I used to watch as a kid look hot, like I'd be *lucky* to get with them. Fancying the boybands I used to like makes me feel like I need to hand myself in at the local police station.

I don't feel old in my soul – that's why it takes me by surprise that my knee cracks when all I'm doing is climbing a singular stair, that my back hurts for no reason other than I laid in a bed and slept. That if I were to ever have too many tequilas and perform a spontaneous roly-poly in a friend's living room, I'd have to retreat for a week afterwards. That I have to listen to an audiobook so I don't have to be alone with my thoughts. That I'm still gobsmacked at the price of a Freddo. It's in the way teenager's eyes pass over me like I'm nobody; they no longer want to mug me in the same way, never mind chat me up. And all those things I always said I was so sure would come back around . . . have not.

I message back: **ahaha**

Even though my face is not smiling one bit.

Ronks replies with a laughing face and sends back a photo of herself glowing at pregnancy yoga. And **oh, and here's that pie recipe I was telling you about.**

See? We're OLD.

Thanks Ronks x

I hope I didn't tell Jackson I caught the bouquet last night? Cheesy rituals like this annoy him. They're gimmicky. Tacky. Uncool. He hasn't mentioned it but he's obviously seen the massive bouquet of white fucking roses in our bedroom. If he asks, I'll say I was *given* them. That they were left behind on the table at the end of the night. I can't say the truth: that I chased, hunted and killed for them. It's embarrassing, desperate. It's out of character. An act of madness, maybe? A cry for help?

He comes up for air. 'God, got sucked into a vortex there, hate this stupid thing.' He throws his phone into the blankets. 'Right.' He springs up. 'Coffee?'

Jackson works (long, stressful, boundary-less hours) at the ad-company KTPLT (catapult – don't ask me why they've spelt it like that) – where I met him, just over five years ago, after they commissioned me to do some writing. It's now where I continue to help out making their pitches and treatments *poetic*. I work from home, occasionally going into the office for a meeting (enjoy free snacks, feel sense of community). I remember the first time I met Jackson, this gentle giant, ducking down to shake my hand. The eye contact – true and deep. *Snap.* Talking in the meeting room with his colleagues, all strangers to me, Jackson made me feel so relaxed, his hands animated and open. I actually thought, at first, he'd be PERFECT for Aoife. The two of them would get on so well – they're both kind and funny, with that nonjudgemental frankness that I subconsciously always look for in a person – but when I spoke, it was like I was reading on stage and he'd paid for the best seat, his elbow on the meeting table, his fingers twisting his ear, hanging on his lobe. He was *flirting*. I remember sharing an idea I had for a trainer ad that was so far-fetched and ridiculous (based on a folk story about how shoes were invented and involved covering the ground with fake-leather) and – for some reason – it tickled him. He laughed easily and freely, his face scrunched up, tears rolling down his cheeks, which obviously made me laugh. The rest of the room like *what is going on here?* His arms hugging his belly, how a child might, like I'd shot him in the stomach with an arrow of joy and he was protecting the wound from further attack. Every time I went to speak he'd surrender, *no more, go away, I can't take it.* I knew I liked him and his Robert De Niro mole right then.

He never laughs at my stories like that any more.

'You should have seen Mia yesterday,' I say, grabbing my granola, shoving a handful into my mouth. 'She looked so *happy.*' So happy it was spooky.

'Well, it *was* her wedding day?' Jackson plunges the coffee.

'It must be hard to be yourself though? With everybody watching. You must feel pressure to put on a show to give people a good day.'

'Do people do that?'

'You know what I mean.'

He does not. 'Then they're getting married for the wrong reasons.'

'Why are you being so stabby?'

'I'm not.'

'She just looked . . . they *both* looked . . . so happy and in love. That teenage, electric, young love. You could feel it; it was contagious. I thought everybody lost that when they've been together a long time and they're older.'

'But a wedding is *meant* to be a celebration of love, so if there's ever a day for it – it's then, surely?' He sips his black coffee, starts building his little protein shake. 'But I can't see why anybody feels the need to do a whole *spectacle.*' He still hasn't mentioned the flowers.

'No, I can't see why Mia would want to look absolutely princess-divine with the love of her life when she could be slobbing about in a just-shy-of-six-hundred-feet South London granny flat, in a bobbly jumper saying CARBS CLUB.' I point at said jumper to make him laugh.

I load my spoon. 'When you turned thirty, were you, like . . . *happy* with where you were?'

'Are you crazy? Course I was. I had just met you,' Jackson says matter-of-factly. It's kind of hot actually.

'Very cute. But you'd just split up with Nicole? And you'd been with her for ten years, so obviously you had a *bit* of a freak-out?'

'I didn't have a freak-out, Ella. Nicole cheated on me.'

'See? *Nicole* had a freak-out about turning thirty.'

'Sorry, why are you sticking up for my ex? Defending her for cheating on me because she turned thirty? I don't think so.' When Jackson is pushed, he shuts down and goes into a silent strop and sulks. We're in the Red Zone. I have to win him back around.

'I didn't mean it like that.' Even though I do feel there is some truth in my theory. 'Sorry. That's horrible,' I add.

I try to change the subject to something more light-hearted.

'I can't believe you liked me though – twenty-five-year-olds are so annoying!' But I'm doing more damage than good here because I'm still quite annoying, so I stupidly dig further. 'I can't imagine fancying one now.' Which is obviously offensive.

Jackson, instead of biting back, throws it back to me. 'Why are you so obsessed with age right now? You're sounding ageist.' He does that laugh as he says it. The soft laugh he does when he's saying something contentious.

'You can't be ageist against yourself.'

'It's just a number, El – get over it. Thirty-five isn't old, so thirty *definitely* isn't.'

I think about the way Aoife, Bianca and I used to cuss out *old* men who used to chat us up: 'Ew, no way, you're like *thirty-five!*' That was literally the beginning and end of the entire cuss. And that's now my appropriate category of men. That's my genre. That is actually my boyfriend's age. I want to write all those men an apology.

He adds, 'If I was a footballer, I'd be washed up by now and I've made peace with that.'

'No! You'd be one of the ex-players in the expensive shiny suits in the studio at half-time saying things like *that goal was stunning.*'

'Haha.' He likes this. 'Anyway, I'm looking forward to getting older.' His back to me at the sink.

'Do you think we should have more . . . ' *any/some* (?!?!) sex, is what I want to say. But I'm not even sure I do want more/any/some sex with Jackson. It's the rejection/neglect bit that worries me, not the lack of orgasms. Is that bad? I want to be *with* Jackson. I want to be close to him and *do* life with him. Course, I'm not going to lie, it's not *ideal* to not have sex with my partner, creeping off to bed each night with a Sarah Waters novel under my arm, popping my head round the door like how someone might let their boss know they're leaving the office for the night. But not everyone has everything. And not everyone has what we have. Companionship. Understanding. We're a team. We have one another's backs. It's someone to sit up with in the dark when you can't sleep. Someone to root for you. Someone who knows what to order for you from any menu. Someone to face the world with – the bills and bad news. You're invested, in each other and the big dreams. Each day, we go off on our individual life trails and we meet back up at the end, pockets full of pebbles we've collected, and we pour them out on the kitchen table. *Look what I found. Look what I did. Listen to what happened to me today.* Someone to run weird paranoias past like if I've left back door open, or the iron – that I never even use – on. Or if a friend doesn't reply to my text and I immediately decide they've broken up with me.

But I finish my sentence with ' . . . dates?'

'We've just bought the flat,' he tries. 'Give us a minute.'

At risk of sounding like a nymphomaniac, I say, 'You never try it on with me; you never *feel* me up.'

And he snaps right back, 'You never try it on with *me*! You NEVER feel *me* up!' Still at the sink, his back still turned.

Can't really argue with that.

'Still wouldn't mind getting shoved against the wall and getting absolutely railed from time to time though.' I smile.

I've got his attention as he turns at this, drying his hands. We both splutter with laughter. He twists his ear. Flirting. He leans against the kitchen counter, folds his arms across his chest, thumbs under his pits in that casual way I like. Tips his head to the side like he's properly considering shoving me against the wall, like he might actually *do* it. He's playing out in his mind what an act like that might look like. His eyes lock onto mine – PING! – a little side smile. There he is. *Fit.* In the background Absolute Radio plays The Cure and has the nerve to call it 'new music'. He staggers towards me, ducking down to kiss me, those long arms pulling me in, hands looped around my seated bum. He pulls me closer in the chair; the legs grunt across the wooden floor. Jackson always holds my face in his hands when we kiss. Like in *The Notebook*. I try to concentrate and be in the moment but can only think of the onlooking houses that can see directly into our kitchen. I found that out the hard way whilst twisting in a forkful of spaghetti only to find I was bolted into awkward eye contact with the choir teacher from across the small garden who was, at the time, eating what looked like a battered sausage.

Jackson bends down before me, his forearms resting across my lap. He butts his forehead into mine with a romantic force. Our faces so close our noses touch, eyes to eyes. He smiles and points out my freckles. They always burst out after the summer. He begins to count, laughs and says, 'I've lost count.' He dips his nose on the end of mine, nuzzling. Digging his jaw into my neck for what we call *nibbles* – minutes of teethy animal biting that make me contort tensely and squeal. Jackson's bites are just the right pressure. Not limp or pathetic. They're full of intent, accompanied by indistinct murmurs. Strong. He's like a giant fit lion right now; I'm wanted in his grip.

I love you, he says.

And I love you.

We kiss again.

And that's it. He's off on his routine. *Oh.* I can already hear the electric toothbrush purring. Him spitting in the sink. Returning in his offensive costume change: running stuff. Oh, the betrayal. He plops his exhausted trainers on the floor, sits at the table next to me and rolls trainer socks onto his very long feet. He knows he's annoying me with his cleanliness and gumption. Smug little shit.

'Coming?'

'Do you really want a breathless pug snuffling next to you?'

He laughs. Too loud. And doesn't even say anything to make me think I'm not a breathless pug. Then he downs his coffee, bangs the empty cup assertively on the table and zips up his windbreaker. With that 'right' again, slams his hands on his thighs and stands to leave.

'Don't you want to just go to the café and eat a fat breakfast instead?'

'Nope.' He pats his belly like just the idea has put half a stone on.

'Have fun.' I pour out more cereal.

'Do some writing?' he says caringly. 'That makes you happy.'

'Yeah, maybe?' I say. Knowing the only one of us that work makes truly happy is Jackson.

The door slams and I'm alone in the granny flat with my laptop. It's a horrible place here: a chaotic desktop of KTPLT campaigns I don't believe in and unfinished projects. My inbox now just a squat-den for barking estate agents, newsletters I swear I never signed up for and links to reset all my forgotten passwords. The blank page is so *threatening*. And there's my book, waiting for that final tidy and sprinkle of magic. 99,081 words. I can't open it today; what if I think it's shit and make irrational edits? I have to protect my work from myself.

Instead, I type into Google: *is it OK to be with someone your whole life and not have sex?*

Great, that will be Viagra adverts for the rest of my life then.

I type: *I love my boyfriend but I'm not sure I'm IN love, advice?*

The *advice?* bit is weak.

Links pop up for therapy and intimacy counselling. A holiday – *yeah, no shit, thanks*. Role play. Bedroom *kinks*. Maybe *this* will reignite our bond? Lead to our path of tantric sex and roly-poly sixty-nines. I begin to slide into a rabbit hole. Does this count as *porn*? What if I click onto an illegal advert by mistake and see something I can't unsee? Will the police come? Or will my bank details be suddenly leaked? Or what if a pimp gets ahold of my pictures and puts them on the heads of porn stars and then uses them as collateral and wants 50k to take the pictures down? I don't have that kind of cash.

I slam my laptop lid shut.

I know. I'll tidy the flat. Win back some control. Something productive. *Fresh start. As of right now.* No drinking – I'll get an app and everything. DAY ZERO. Pledged. Healthy eating. Get a Filofax.

I *should* probably face Mia's browning flowers. What am I meant to do with them? Put them in water? Hang them upside down to dry them out or dash them in the bin? Is it unlucky to throw out wedding flowers? Will I get cursed?

The second the stems touch my palm, it happens. I think of him. His name, an apple that falls from the tree in the garden of my thoughts, the heaviest, dustiest book from a shelf in the library of my mind. LOWE.

My heart stops. I swallow the feeling. He does this – occurs to me from time to time. It always makes me feel the same: sad for myself and bad on Jackson for even thinking of another guy. But hold on, did I *text* him last night? What was I *thinking*? *Oh, God, where is my bloody phone?* I throw clothes and towels in the air without strategy. Pins and needles shoot through my hands. Heart rate rises. Found it, right on the drawers where I left it, of course. I check to make sure I didn't send a message. *Please. Please. Please* . . . Nothing. Thank FUCK.

My phone pings in my hand. It's Dad; his texts read like Post-it notes.

Vi said caught bouquet!? New suit?

Bloody Instagram!

I text back: **no, Dad. You don't need to get a new suit.**

Chapter 7

Then

The day after and he's still there, a dart in my brain. I'm like Peter Parker the morning after he realizes he's been bitten by a radioactive spider. *Infected*. And guess what happens to him, guys? He becomes Spider-Man! What is going to happen to *me*? I find myself doing stupid stuff like blasting Mariah Carey's 'Fantasy' at full volume and saying inside my head, *Imagine if Lowe walked into the room right now; what would I do?* My pen so badly wants to write down his name in loopy writing, in bubble writing but I'm scared that writing his name down will jinx us. As you can imagine, I'm pretty pissed off about it, but I just can't help myself: I doodle him from memory, get him *down* on paper. Capture him in my Groovy Chick notebook; sketch his shoulders, his arms, his eyes. I draw me next to him, us holding hands and—

Ella, did you just draw yourself as a bride?

Every song I listen to I can't help but see his face, think of his hands, his smile, his voice. I am completely intoxicated and I hate it about myself. I can't tell anybody about this *illness*.

OH ME, OH MY, OH HELL.

I should just clear my diary and cancel all plans for the remainder of half term. This calls for total wipeout because I am *otherwise engaged* in being completely and utterly obsessed with someone to the point I'm almost begging for school to start again for the distraction. I try and recite my calming mantra, '*Dance as though no one is watching, love as though – err—*' but I can't remember the rest. See, he owns my thoughts now; he's wiping out my brain cells. It's only matter of time before he's completely reset the entire thing.

The next day we get the scent of a free house, with a party happening inside it. We're getting ready at Aoife's. Her dad doesn't let her have CDs and the few second-hand ones she *did* own he's hung up outside in the garden as 'entertainment' for the birds. 'I've got so many brilliant vinyls – why don't you explore those?' The *brilliant* vinyls he's referring to are the experimental bootleg records he picked up at Brixton Market. We listen to the radio and take turns to bathe in her small tub with the rubber hose and the mango scrub that is 100% enough to make us get called 'spicy'. With blobs of toothpaste on our spots, we talk about our insecurities out loud, complaining and comparing – 'Why am I so spotty?'; 'Your boobs are so much bigger than mine'; 'Why am I so chubby?' – and then we reassure each other: 'It's good to be chubby; at least it means you have hips and boobs.' And her little brother Sean shouts up, 'You're both BUTTERS!' And we scream down, 'WE HATE YOU!'

And we brush it off but it does bruise us. Our brains are soft fruits, peaches and plums, and every knock makes a dent of some kind, no matter how small.

After that, in front of the full-length lightweight mirror – the same mirror we unhook from the wall and take turns to lie down underneath wearing just our knickers, so we can get an idea of the realistic view of our bodies that someone will have in the future when they are having sex with us – we do our make-up. I sit on an orange blow-up armchair; Aoife leans over my head. First things first, we pluck our eyebrows accidentally completely bald. Then, we share our shared collection of Barry M's dazzle dust – little glass screw-top lids full to the brim in every rainbow colour and shade you can imagine. To us, these little eyeshadow tubs are the most precious things in the world. If we were to lose the tiniest sprinkling of dazzle dust, we would be on the ground scooping it up like it was cocaine, sobbing into the carpet as if someone had tipped over our mother's ashes. No colour is too much, no look too dramatic, no eyelid too small for a cosmic space scene, an underwater theme – blue, pink, green, purple, glitter, *glitter*, GLITTER! Sparkle and iridescent shimmer, right up to the eyebrows we go. We take turns dabbing from the tubs, blowing our fingers like the end of a snooker cue, ready for the next hit, puffing through the air like a fairy's fart.

We drown ourselves in Impulse body spray. We tease our limp hair with coconut dry shampoo and an old nit comb because it gets to the roots. Drag purple hair mascara though the layers. Shower ourselves in sparkly talcum powder. We smell like Disney and popcorn, tropical bubblegum and apricot sour sweets, chemicals and period blood. We snake our hot-pink thongs (99p!) up our hips, making sure the straps are hanging out the top. Aoife's hip bones jut out like shoulder blades, but my thong digs into my side squidge like the candy-cane-striped string on a joint of beef. We slide on our heavy dirty baggy jeans, so crusty they *crack,* and wear tight tops which suck in our waists and plunge out our misshapen boobs. Then we add as much jewellery as we can find – mostly 'shag' bands which we pray will get snapped by someone fit. (But not *actually.*)

After Aoife and I have convinced each other that we look *just about* nice enough to get a boyfriend, that it's everyone else's fault we're single, after we take turns to say *I fancy you, no I FANCY you,* we trundle downstairs to get *judged* by Aoife's opinionated hippy parents. Then, and only then, are we ready to go out.

'Oh no you don't . . . ' says Aoife's mum, Elaine. That stops us in our tracks and we have to sit at the dining table surrounded by the Moroccan tea sets from their travels and eat half a freezing cold jacket potato each, with a slab of ice-cold butter and a stalk of raw broccoli, washed down with a pint of tap water. But it's not *all* bad. We are allowed as much E-number tomato sauce as we want. That's the thing about hippies: they're hypocrites.

And it's *then*, and *only then*, that we are allowed to leave.

'Don't go the shortcut way.'

'We won't, Elaine.'

But we will, Elaine; we will.

We meet the others at the station. (We would never head into a party on our own – we are not *clinically insane*.) Bianca is wearing her thong *over* her trousers. Yes, you read that correctly. She's already smashed, giving a speech about how everybody in Balham is a perve. She stops to light a cigarette. She smells medicinal, of vanilla ice cream and marzipan. She shifts her dyed-red hair over her widow's peak to try not to look as much of an evil stepmother as she already does. Aoife races into the newsagents to buy a small bottle of gin and a ten pack of Marlboro Lights. All I truly want is a Toffee Crisp. But I buy a watermelon Bacardi Breezer because I probably *should* and a packet of gum. When I come out the girls are talking.

'Lowe? He's cute,' one of The Twins replies to Bianca. *What's this?* I try not to ping my head back and forth. Why are they talking about *Lowe*?

'Which one was he again?' Shrey asks.

'Cap, hoodie, big eyes?' one Twin says.

'Always smiling,' the other Twin adds.

'Ooooh myyyyy daysss, his smile is *so* cute.' Bianca presses her hands to her chest like she's the Virgin bloody Mary.

Oh no. I become dry-mouthed and panicked. All boys love Bianca too.

'You haven't spoken about him before . . . ?' I can't help but interrupt.

'Yeah, that's cos I didn't know if he was coming tonight but apparently he is.'

Oh, so you like to keep your options open by stealing the man of my dreams but also SHIT – *he's coming tonight?*

'He looks kinda young,' Ronke intervenes. 'No?'

'No, he's just short,' Aoife says, her mouth open like a fish, picking glitter gunk out of her eye and squishing it into a ball. 'And shy, poor bubba.'

BUBBA?

'Bless,' a Twin swoons.

'You don't have to be loud like that dickhead Jonas to get noticed,' the other Twin defends.

No idea who Jonas is. I don't seem to recall any guy that isn't Lowe.

'He's quite *mysterious*, don't you think?' Bianca snatches a pocket mirror straight from one of The Twins' hands and begins to check her reflection, slapping more lipgloss on top of her already dripping lips. I know she thinks the word 'mysterious' counts as a complicated word.

'Oh very *mysterious*. He's chilled and laid back, just like really comfortable in himself?' Aoife adds dreamily.

'—and very cool. Effortless actually,' says Shrey.

'OH, he's so cool,' a Twin pipes up.

'And he's got this great big cheeky grin!' says the other Twin.

'Adorable,' Aoife concludes.

Bianca lets a demonic snarl spread across her face like she's a very powerful womanly person, like, I don't know . . . Cher or someone, and announces, 'I think he's buff, you know?'

My body shuts down. She's taken her pick. She's *chosen*.

'Yeah, he's fucking hot,' Aoife blurts. *You alright there, Aoife?*

'But, Aoife, you like Oli, right?' Bianca double-checks.

I swallow, but it's like swallowing a ball of discount socks from Sports Direct.

And then it gets interesting.

'I think Lowe likes *you*, Ella,' a Twin offers, linking my arm sweetly.

I gulp. *Panic.* Is it *that* obvious and she's trying to make me feel better? OK. I have to stop this. I don't want the attention on me; I don't want to begin the *Ella fancies Lowe* campaign only to get publicly rejected.

'No, he doesn't. What makes you say that?' I ask.

'Errr . . . it was kind of *obvious*,' the other Twin backs her sister up, like they've spoken about it in their marshmallow-soft pyjamas at night.

'I don't think he does,' I say. 'We just have things in *common*. That's all. We both like music.'

'*Everyone* likes music, Elbie!' Aoife cackles. (Not everybody classes *NOW THAT'S WHAT I CALL MUSIC!* as being *into music*, Aoife, but anyway.)

'Not *their* kind of music,' The Twin (it doesn't matter which one) states, as if Lowe and I are into the friggin' pan pipes.

'So do *you* fancy him, Ella, or not?' Bianca asks, really needing to know. Everyone zooms in. Shrey and Bianca stand there, blinking.

'I . . . dunno. I didn't really see him like *that*.' Could I try lying any harder?

'The dude looks like he has no pubes,' Ronke cackles.

'Truuussstttt me, Ronks, the boy's got pubes!' Shrey blurts and everyone laughs.

'No, really, Ella, for real, so who *do* you like then?' Bianca demands.

' . . . Errr . . . ?' On the spot, my mind Rolodexes through all the boys I can think of like an emergency game of Guess Who? on fourteen Pro Plus, hoping it will all go away if I just say a name: *say someone, Ella, anyone.* ' . . . Er . . . ' They wait – blink blink blink – but once I've said a name, that's it, Lowe is up for the taking. Bianca looks impatient, Aoife unconvinced. *Just say a bloody name.* ' . . . Sam?'

'SAM?' they chorus like his name has come completely out of the blue because *oh yeah it has.*

'Yeah?' I say, making my face force a blush like a 'lady' in a Shakespearian play might when she's confiding to the chicks about how besotted she is with her new beau. 'Sam's alright?'

'Sam, you say? Oh yeah, Sam's nice alright.' Shreya proceeds to dry-hump a lamppost. We all laugh. 'Sam is FITTTTTT!'

But Bianca's not done with me yet. 'So, I can pull Lowe tonight, yeah?' (Like the guy doesn't have a choice in the matter.)

I look down at my hands, my stupid ambitious shag bands, my chipped blue varnish and ugly bitten nails.

'Yeah, course,' I say, 'go for it.' Which is an anagram for SHUT THE FUCK UP!

'You lot better set me up with Lowe tonight then . . . ' Bianca threatens. 'C'mon, Ella, you're good at writing love poems. Tell me what you're gonna say?' She looks at me, begging to role play.

Why me?

'Come on . . . practise.' But instead she sends herself into some frenzied hysterical squeal: 'Oh, just tell him I said he's *fit*,' she orders, landing the word 'fit' like a swear word. Then she untucks her boobs from a sticky underwire, reapplies more marzipan perfume – which comes in its red little devil bottle that looks exactly like the bloody boar's heart that the Huntsman gives to the evil stepmother instead of Snow White's – sucks her cheeks in and says, 'OK, let's go.'

The party, sorry, *gathering,* is at a new house. Mia was invited, *apparently*, but she's busy, *apparently.* I haven't spoken to her since the exorcist showdown at her house. I tried to call her house phone but her dad said she wasn't in. I didn't push because he clearly hates us now. We reckon she's grounded.

The host's name is Dean. And Dean has walked fresh out of a Nineties R'n'B music video. He has greased-back hair and wears a fitted ribbed woollen polo-neck jumper and too-tight white jeans. He meets all the girls at the door of his parents' double-glazed-windowed house, with a plastic stemmed rose with fabric red petals – the petals are adorned with fake droplets made to look like dew, which have clearly been stuck on with a tube of UHU – until he runs out and has to 'grab back' the roses he only just handed out. When Dean introduces himself, he holds his hands over his chest in prayer position, asks us our name, repeats our names back at us to sear them into his brain and *thanks* the heavens, as if we're fallen angels.

'Where'd he learn this crap?' Aoife whispers.

Dean's house is full of shiny black marble, flecked with shards of silver and mother of pearl, black leather couches and flashy trashy gold ornaments of dolphins and elephants. There is a cream marble fireplace with ceramic statues either side of frosty livid-looking snow leopards with painted gold eyes. On display, a tacky black-and-white pro-studio photograph of Dean and his family, barefooted, arranged in the most awkward position you've ever seen, like they were playing Twister and the mat was removed at the last minute. Dean has ice buckets filled with Smirnoff Ice, speakers muffling badly downloaded hip hop, snack bowls filled with salt and vinegar Chipsticks and pastel Love Hearts – 'sexy' and 'be mine'. Dean himself smells of CK One, Febreeze and an impenetrable desperation to lose his virginity on a bed of rose petals ASAP. He's definitely been carrying a *just in case* condom in his back pocket since he was twelve.

'No smoking inside and no going upstairs,' Dean reminds us.

We head outside so Bianca can smoke. It's still light, the sky like sherbet. I am extremely grown-up tonight. Maybe it's my turquoise flicks; they really came out good. Maybe it's my body?

The way it fits into this snug pink top? Maybe it's because I'm excited to see Lowe again—

'OH, MY FUCKING DAYS, ELLA – your belly button looks fucking HUGE!' Bianca screams. 'You can see it sooo big through that top; it's absolutely massive!'

I laugh it off. But no, the red rash is there, creeping up my chest and throat. I think of Bianca's pierced belly button. A perfect noodly twist. A cockle, a piglet's snout with its Britney Spears diamond underneath her massive boobs. *Fuck you, Bianca, for being a bitch about my belly button, for choosing Lowe when you could have anybody you wanted.* I'm Dolly Parton, wanting to beg Bianca not to take him just because she can.

I decide to head inside with my *wishing well* of a belly button and get some water so my rash can calm down. I might be able to get away with secretly slipping my trainers off and letting the soles of my feet cool on the kitchen tiles.

Dean's glasses are all champagne flutes with gold-leaf rims. I use a Garfield mug, like the fat cat I am.

And it happens so quickly I don't even have the chance to breathe.

'Hi!'

It's him. *Lowe.* Oh God. He's wearing the same-but-different blue hoody, jeans and cap, this time, cocked up playfully. And he makes me *dizzy.* In one move he uses his arms, alone, to launch himself up into the sweet spot next to me on the counter, simmering, so *shiny* and twinkly.

And I am a magpie.

Once again, I am rushing from the BOOM-BOOM-BOOM of my own heart.

I melt down, like one of those thick trickling church candles, the way wax would drip like tears.

' . . . Ella?'

He says my name tentatively, because he's cool, or in case he's got it wrong, or is that his way of making out he doesn't care? Or maybe he truly doesn't remember my name. His voice is so low, uttered into the neck of his jumper, as smooth and sweet as caramel.

'I didn't think you'd be here,' he says.

I tingle. 'Yeah, those boys from your school invited us,' I say. I blush again, my cheeks all hot.

'So where are your lot then?' he asks. *Great, here we go . . .* only moments before he finds Bianca and her great boobs and storybook wicked-witch beauty sucking cigarettes under Dean's little olive tree.

'Outside . . . ' I look out the window behind the sink, where I can see them smoking on the patio.

'I didn't meet any of them properly the other night,' he adds.

My belly tenses; I'm used to this, this gut-punch. Now I know he wants to meet my friends and not me, it makes things easy, gives me permission to move on. I point through the fake Tudor diamond effect on the double-glazed window.

'That's Aoife – my best friend; we've been best mates since we were three. That's Shreya – she's the funny one. Ronks – she's basically a genius. The Twins – Louise is the one with the mole – that's Bianca – she's the wild one that—'

'Which one are you then?'

I look at him. 'Huh?'

I laugh, realizing I was introducing us like characters in a TV show. He dips his head closer to me, and I can smell him now, washing powder, outside air and adventure.

He says, laughing, so throwaway it could be a joke, or *even* an insult, I can't tell, it just rolls out, 'You must be the *pretty* one, then?'

The *pretty* one? I don't think so. All the blood swims to my face. 'Ha! No, I really don't – think – I – am, no . . . ' I'm obviously not *so pretty* anything.

He nods, like he's absolutely certain of it but then bursts out laughing. Is he taking the piss? He's winding me up, isn't he? Or is he for real? This is heftily reminding me of the time a boy once said I looked like Cameron Diaz – I don't, given that she's blonde and a model – only to later find out later that what he actually said was that I looked like 'a fat Cameron Diaz'; even then, nope, still don't see the similarities. But maybe I'm just traumatized from that encounter? Bleugh, this is so AWKWARD and ADDICTIVE in equal measures I can't cope. I don't know where to look or how to be; my body is pancake batter and with the heat of him, jeeezzzz, I'm *cooking* crepes over here. The chemistry is . . . WHEW.

He nudges me gently with his shoulder, so I laugh back and he laughs more and I laugh more and *oh GOSH I can't tell if this is sarcasm or a joke.* Our eyes up and down, and he tries to catch my gaze so we can Velcro lock in, but I just look shyly at my hands. I realize that he probably thinks I'm not taking his compliment seriously, and that it might have taken a lot for him to even say it. But nobody has ever really said I'm *pretty* before other than my dad, and of course he'd say that because I look exactly like him just with eyeshadow. UGH, it's such a nice feeling that I wish I could bottle it and micro-dose like some mad vitamin with powerful propellant properties for the rest of my days. The things I could do with that in my system. I'd be unstoppable.

'You are,' he says, again.

AHHH! There's nowhere for me to *go.* I've outgrown this body of mine. I want to burst through the ceiling of myself, and run rings around the planet.

'You're cute,' he says.

Cute? I don't want to be *cute*! Cute means *friend.* Means *little sister.* Means *hamster.*

'Well. OK,' I say. '*Thanks?*'

Bianca is at the window now, pointing at *us*, hurrying me along, ushering me to slip her name into the conversation. She doesn't

73

care how indiscreet it is, so long as the job's done. I need to be a good friend to Bianca and make a speedy U-Turn, reverse my feelings by focusing on all the things I *don't* like about Lowe, of which there are none. He rolls up the sleeves of his hoodie and I catch his arms and wrists, which are strong, square and elegant. Veins bulge, his beauty drip-fed. He's looking into my face again. My eyes sparkle on demand – *bitches*, betraying me like this; my eyelashes bat, flap up and down like Betty Boop and I just say, 'So, you know my friend, Bianca? She really likes you.'

'Who?' Lowe says, surprised like *why would you say that?*

I feel ashamed. He probably thinks I don't like him back given that he's just called me pretty and cute and in return I've told him that one of my friends likes him.

'Who's Bianca?'

He really didn't know who she was, did he?

'The tall one standing there, smoking, with the red hair and big boobs.' Just like all the other times I've had to point her out to boys.

Bianca waves on cue to us, like the window is a TV screen and she's a singer on the Eurovision Song Contest trying to encourage us to vote for her by telephone.

He nods. Waits for me to change my mind, or take it back. He opens his mouth, like he wants to say more, looks puzzled and just says, 'Cool.' Nodding. Brows furrowed. Confused. *Hurt*, even? He lifts himself coolly off the counter and loses himself in the faces of the party.

And that, right there, will be the worst decision I make for a really long time.

Chapter 8

It doesn't take long for Bianca to pull Lowe.

Well, for Bianca to instruct Lowe that this is what is happening.

And it doesn't last long because Bianca throws up in a frilly silk pillowcase and gets put to sleep in Dean's mum and dad's bed.

Under a shrimp sky, a breeze sends crisp leaves crowding under Dean's family barbecue. The temperature dips with the sun, naturally forcing Lowe to sit up next to me close on the wall outside. We pretend like nothing has happened, like he hasn't just kissed one of my best mates. It's actually a *good thing,* I tell myself. It means we can begin again, start over, as friends. It means I can talk to him without it being anything more than a friendship. To be Lowe's friend means to be close to him, as close as I can possibly get without ever having to be rejected or forgotten or looked past. Being his friend means that we can have something different, something far more special. Something that never has to end.

'So, like' – we have to say *like* as much as we take oxygen – 'what are you into?'

'Music,' he says. 'I dunno . . . riding my bike?'

Fit— *STOP IT, ELLA!* He's obviously betrothed to Bianca now, off limits, out of bounds.

'Do you have a bike?' he asks me.

'What, like' – see, told you – 'a bicycle?'

'A *bicycle*, haha, yeah, do you have a *bicycle*?'

'I have a Legoland driving licence? But the older I'm getting, the more the novelty of even an impressive accolade such as *that* is wearing off.' We laugh. 'No, I haven't been on a bike in years . . . '

'Well, I'm very sorry to hear that,' he says with a smile, meaning to be funny, but with a hint of *that's a real shame and the real reason why we won't ever be getting married*. 'Why not?

'Ummm, because they're . . . dangerous.'

'How is it dangerous? Riding a bike is like . . . a car but better. It's like . . . I dunno . . . having *wings*.'

Cheesy. But no, he means it. I see his feathered wings. And then I think of Bianca and that sloppy toffee gunk she basted all over her lips before she kissed him. I look down.

'It's true,' he says. 'Everyone needs a bike.' I can see he's conflicted; he's shy but he wants to talk more. He's pushing himself. 'We have this boy who lives near us who didn't have a bike and wanted to ride, so me and my friends – we made him one.'

'You *made* him a bike?'

' . . . Yeah.' He bites his lip.

I have to lean in close to hear him.

'We all donated towards it. Most of us work Saturdays at bike shops and get paid in bolts and brakes, and, well . . . it's a bit of a Frankenstein bike, but now he rides with us.'

He's got *layers*, boy. I like him so much.

'In art I actually made my friend Aoife a shell out of clay for her jewellery but when it came out of the kiln it just looked like a Cornish pasty.'

Lowe tries not to but once he sees I'm laughing he can't not.

'So what do you like?' he asks.

YOU YOU YOU!

'I write?' I offer apologetically.

76

'You're a writer – that's cool.'

'Well, I'm not a *real* writer,' I say. 'You kind of have to be a dead man to be a writer and I'm kind of . . . an *alive* girl.'

'Writing's cool,' he nods. 'You can be like Bob Dylan.'

'Yeah see, a dead man?'

'Bob Dylan's not dead!'

'Oh. Sorry.'

'I'd like to learn the guitar, really,' he confesses. 'Be like Bob Dylan. That's what I'd *actually* like to do.'

'What? Like on stage? We listen to more punk in our house. I don't know much Bob Dylan.'

'Whaaaattttt?'

And then, shy quiet Lowe begins to *sing*, like he has nothing to prove, his voice so natural and yet perfect in its own way. He can't help but smile as faint words fall out of his grin, delicate notes, so gentle and sweet. He smiles as though he's aware that singing at me like this *could* be an awkward cringing serenade, but surprisingly, it's unvain, appropriate, instinctive, like a lullaby to soothe a baby. If that is how Bob Dylan sounds then I'm angry at my parents for never showing me him.

'When you get famous, don't forget me, yeah?' I joke out of awkwardness.

'I think you're pretty difficult to forget.'

He reaches inside his pocket for his inhaler, the blue one, and shakes the Ventolin.

'Ooooo my dad has asthma,' I announce like it's our common ground. *Really cool, Ella.*

'Ah, well, see, I've actually got a *very special* type of asthma.' He puffs on the inhaler twice, holds it up like an asset. 'So, if we're gonna start hanging out, you'll be seeing a lot more of this cool little guy,' he jokes sarcastically.

But – I'm sorry – *hanging out* – what does THAT mean?

'Fine by me,' I say in probably the most 'chill' tone I've ever used.

BOOM-BOOM-BOOM! says my heart, in a very unchill tone.

'Hey, I could make you a mix tape, if you want?'

Are you serious? The act of him physically making something for me is too much.

I find a Biro (I've never found anything quicker in my life) in the kitchen drawer stuffed with all the takeaway menus in Dean's house, and write my address on the back of his arm in blue. PRAYING Lowe never takes it upon himself to *hand*-deliver a letter. He wouldn't, would he? I don't even want to imagine him dealing with our rickety gate, walking into our overgrown front garden, stepping over the old bath filled to the brim with a swamp of spawn and algae with his fresh trainers, to reach our front door. Can't think of him rapping on the bull's-jaw door knocker, oxidized turquoise; weirded out by the rusted chainsaw that's been strangled by the poison ivy – like the plants have *won* – and the Eighties hoover with a puddle of fox wee in the motor; freaked out by the spiders' webs as big as bedsheets, sweeping from door to window, hosting a buffet of dead flies. The huddle of opinionated, chuckling stone gargoyles that stand about like smoking bouncers.

'I *will* send you a tape,' he warns, watching the letters appear on his skin. 'I'm not joking – I will.'

And I melt like a gooey chocolate fondue. 'Good,' I say. *Good.*

I don't say . . . *Maybe I love you.*

Whilst the others are picked up in The Twins' mum's bloody coach, Aoife and I have to waddle Bianca back to Aoife's in the pitch black because she's too pissed for their spotless interiors. After a couple of minutes, Bianca gives up to dry-heave on the banks of grass, then slops her body down on a creepy backstreet, groaning, 'Let me sleep.'

I begin to panic that someone might attack us like we're wounded deer. 'Get up, Bianca, *please* . . . ' I plead.

Up again, her drunk arms around Aoife and my shoulders, her

trainers twisted, tripping up on the ragged shreds of her scuffed jeans. She's so tall, a drugged giraffe, towering and tumbling, demanding more alcohol, a kebab, chips in pitta and a cigarette – which she scrounges off a stranger, putting it into her mouth filter-first – going on and on about Lowe and how much she *loves* him and she didn't even get to say goodbye and do I think he loves her back? *Yes,* I say, *I'm sure he does,* thinking of my address spelt out on his forearm.

Anything to get her to walk home quicker.

We wouldn't normally stay at Bianca's – her dad is stricter than any of our parents, and she's *so* drunk – but her house is closest. We beg for a taxi we can't afford at the cab office, all of our gold and silver coins on the booth counter. The operator is considering it as it's quiet and only a short journey until Bianca decides this is the moment to allow her eyes to roll completely back into the depths of her skull. Classic. The drivers clearly don't want to transit a drunk teenager.

'Come on, you . . . ' I say to Bianca. 'Let's get you home.'

Inside, we skulk about so as not to wake up Bianca's dad. We have to act sober. We sit by the toaster and eat nearly a whole loaf of bread between us – even the back ends get destroyed; any piece of carbohydrate we can find gets shoved in that toaster. We make tea after tea and Bianca dreamily scoops teaspoons of salty sweet peanut butter onto her tongue straight from the jar and tells us once again how in love she is until she instructs us that 'she's tired' and orders us up to bed.

Bianca stumbles up the stairs, aggressively *shhhhhhhhing* us past her dad's room, and we giggle as she flashes us an angry look, comical with her smudged make-up and the sick stains on her t-shirt, to only then make the most amount of racket you've ever heard in your life by accidentally rolling down the ladder to the loft, which thunders towards us like some robotic Jack-in-a-Box guillotine, taking us all out in one swipe.

We lie on the futon bed in her room, all three of us on two pillows, and I gaze out of the window into the London night, like I'm shooting a new video for Savage Garden's 'To the Moon & Back', wondering what it was like for Bianca, kissing Lowe, and how I can't ask her, because it would suggest I liked him but, also, there's no point, because she was probably too drunk to remember.

What a waste.

Chapter 9

It's sometime in the week, just as I am trying to revitalize a few bits of stale baguette into lunch of some kind for my siblings and me, when the letterbox flaps.

And there it is. Lowe's letter, on the hallway floor of 251 Palace Road.

It's a regular envelope, one of those plain ones and it's an outsider – too clean to be in our house – a feather from a dove that has found itself in a circle of fresh cowpat. My name heavily drawn in pencil lead, all in capital letters, at a slant, scrawled with a certain flare that suggests Lowe would maybe quite like to spray his tag on a railway bridge.

I know what's inside by its rectangle edges and the way it rattles: the tape.

And *so much promise.*

This is what Sugababes meant by *overload*, isn't it?

My stomach lurches as I hold the letter close to my chest. My beaded bracelets *tremble.*

I forget about food for maybe the first time in my life and hurtle up the stairs to my messy attic bedroom and close the door behind us. Us being Lowe's letter and me. My first thought is OH LORD. My second thought is *Bianca*. This is wrong. I shouldn't be receiving a letter – OK, let's go ahead and call it a *love letter* – from Lowe. It would make me a really awful friend. But so far everything has been very 'above board'; the lines are clear. I just have to make sure I stay firmly in the friend lane and *not* get carried away with the idea of it evolving into anything more. I'm pretty sure I can rely on my own insecurities to make sure that happens anyway. And my last thought is *my mum would be so mad if she knew.* Not because I'm talking to a boy but that I'm allowing myself to get caught up in the romance of it all. Writing to a guy who called me *the pretty one.* And then laughed. Who called me *cute.* Who sang to me. And sent me a mix tape. *Pathetic,* she'd think. *Shallow,* beneath me. *Who wants to be called pretty? That's not a compliment. Boys that age only want one thing.'*

I see him buying the stamp, licking the envelope down with the dots on his wet pink tongue, walking to the post box and pushing my letter inside with all the bills and birthday cards. The thought of him taking the time out of his day for me flips my stomach over a thousand times.

The tape isn't in a box. It tumbles out onto my lap. I leap back like it's scorching hot.

I stare at the greying plastic case, the shiny ribbon and spirals. I feel absolutely sick. I've never seen an object so beautiful.

'ELLA!' Violet shouts up. 'What the hell are we doing with this bread then?'

'I'M COMING, JUST WAIT!' I roar.

'WE'RE STARVING!'

After barging down the stairs, storming into the kitchen, slamming the stiff loaf onto the table with a tub of butter and a block of stale cheese that has cracks like Dad's heel after football and blue bits that *also* don't look that dissimilar to Dad's feet after football, I say 'There!'

I charge out again towards heaven . . .

'GAWD, ALRIGHT . . . ' Violet digs, 'Has this got anything to do with why you're playing Jennifer Lopez on repeat?'

'GRRR! SHUT UP! And I DON'T listen to J.LO! AS IF!'
I definitely, definitely do.

The letter itself is folded into three sections, neatly, like Lowe's taken his time and really thought about it. It's all on blank A4 paper. I rip it open it too fast. I wish I could have slowed down but I have terrible patience. My jaw is slack. I become hot and cold. Very clammy. Very un-calm. Inside are more of the gruff silver lines from the pencil, which makes me think he might have had more than one go at it – a practice letter; aw, he *rehearsed*. I try and discipline my eyes to not read a word. Not yet. I want to savour every bit.

The first thing I do is *smell* the letter, of course, to try and capture some kind of essence of *Lowe*, to breathe him in. I want to get to know him, who he is, what his house smells like.

Cold office paper. Zero giveaways.

It opens *TO ELLA* also in pencil, so he could rub out mistakes. My name underlined twice. And a firm full stop.

The letter begins with the fact he's left-handed. *Probably dyslexic,* he adds. And *new* to letter writing. He goes on to say that – as promised – here are the songs on the cassette, with a track listing. I want to read that section slowly, for maximum impact, song by song, whilst listening to the music to see if there are any clues about his feelings, why he chose each song – the lyrics, the order, the story he's *telling* through the guise of music. Then I will, like a scientist, analyse the hell out of every single damn bit of evidence before me. Hunt for love like a hound.

He says *it woz really nice meetin* me and *c'yin* me again and *dat* he hopes to *c* me again soon.

OK, all of this can be forgiven. It's just to look cool.

From Lowe and a definite X

At the bottom corner, he's written his own address: *Orchard Road*. Which I let my eyes feast on. A garden of fruit trees grows in my mind.

On the tape is a thin white sticker saying *FOR ELLA x*.

I run my stubby, bitten-down finger over the letters E-L-L-A and put the tape in the player. It's a fresh tape, one he's bought maybe? No box though? Risky. He's too cool for a box. Side A, first. I push my finger down on the Play button, slowly. It crunches robotically, clunks into gear and I hear the muffled sound of something starting . . .

Ecstasy.

All day and all night I listen to that tape: Side A, Side B. The stereo my life support machine. If the tape ribbon comes loose I panic, like my own heart has stopped beating, and resuscitate, perform emergency open-heart surgery, winding the ribbon back with the end of a pencil. Some of these songs I already know and that must mean we're destined. It is fate, see? I identify every instrument, meditate on every lyric – I write them out like I'm revising for an exam about them, pressing pause-play-rewind. If the words are unclear, I make up new (probably better) lyrics and sing them out loud. Some of the songs are not about love at all yet it doesn't take much invention to crowbar myself into believing they actually are. I use association techniques, bleeding the metaphors *dryyyyy* to make it relate to us. Time – *us*, home – *us*, travel – *us*, nature – *us*. Death – Duh! *Us*. Us. US. I bangarang that tape around the cracked walls of our house on repeat. I wear that tape to death.

I dress up. For who? Me. In the mirror, I lip-sync the life out of every word. My bedroom is a stage. My books and the posters on my wall, the crowd.

'Gross. Get a life,' Violet sneers but she doesn't get it. For she isn't in love.

I know the tape off by heart – the gaps of quiet between each song, the way the music lifts up and dies down.

I FUCKING LIVE FOR IT.

He didn't ask but it's my turn to make a tape now. Where to

begin? Dad usually has loads of blank tapes. I knock on the door of the downstairs room he hangs out in. With no response, I turn the screw-driver door handle and I'm quite surprised to see he's created his own little bedsit down here. Maybe because my little brother Sonny sleeps with Mum most nights like a child shaped cock-block I didn't realize how out of control it'd become? Now it's the only place in the house that feels tidy and neat – it's like Dad's quarantined from our infection. Like an older brother or a down-and-out uncle.

I shouldn't *really* just take a blank tape from Dad's shelf without asking but what better purpose for a blank tape than for his eldest to record her deepest, innermost feelings and then post it to a boy she hardly even knows? I take a few CDs too. This blank tape is really great because it's in a clear Perspex box with a piece of lined and numbered card to write your track listing on like a legit musician. The other thing I love is the spine. You can make a name for your playlist, so if it was lined up with real tapes, you would see it. *Certified.* I only have one shot – this is my big gig, these songs my weapons of choice. What will I open with? I don't want to peak too soon. How do I balance the humour with the emotion? How will I close?

The tape results in a messy collage of Dad's punk, soul and Motown, my grunge and rock, plus some cool-ish pop (for comedy and irony). Fortunately, I have all the compilation CDs that come free with magazines too to chub it out to make me look eclectic. Some of the songs I haven't even heard, but I know the band names and maybe they'll make me sound cool? Other songs, like I imagine him doing, I choose deliberately, with lyrics that will stir something, make him think of me. There's one song on there that says everything I want to say, the simplicity and the complication. Will he find it? Will he even get that far? Will he listen to the tape with the intensity that I've used to make it? (Impossible.)

Now comes the easy bit: writing back. We don't have a stack

of fresh A4, so I tear lined paper from my school ring binder at speed, which takes off half the spring with my eager ripping. I would have *preferred* a fancy fountain pen but I don't have one and I'm NOT about to use my *school* Parker pen, am I? Ew. Not after he's used this lovely pure pencil. So, I take Mum's green Biro (Mum's the only person in the world to use green Biro) and begin.

I make sure not to write anything too cringe or revealing so he can't use it against me in the future, in case we end up as bitter exes. I draw little cartoons of me listening to the tape and speech bubbles saying words that might sound cool. I tell him some facts about myself – that I ate superglue as a baby, that my favourite drink is Strawberry Ribena. I write: *Some people think grunge music is about feeling sorry for yourself but I think it's about sticking up for yourself.* Sorry for being a philosopher. I sprinkle in a *flavour* of my poetry – Rossetti or Dido could *never*. I add my phone number at the bottom with an *H:* for house phone and an *M:* for mobile like it's a business card. And then, I spray the whole thing with perfume. I don't use the *Jennifer Lopez* perfume because I want this to be a classic romantic love letter – one that will be showcased in museums to celebrate my life once I'm a dead author – Body Shop 'White Musk' it is. But the perfume leaves oily marks on the paper as though I've reread the letter back whilst eating a bag of chips. Fuming.

I rewrite the entire thing, ensuring I retain the same spontaneity the first letter had. Trying not to sound forced or repetitive. This time I spray the tape *case* in the White Musk instead.

Then I realize we don't have a stupid envelope. Or a stamp. *Drat.* I try out the word to sound like a Victorian poet but no. *Fuck* is better. I scrounge for coins down the back of the sofa, fruit bowl and in my school blazer.

And by dusk, yes I said *dusk*, my first love letter is ready to go.

But it won't be my last.

Chapter 10

Hey ☺ Ella. i jus got ur letter x

He then texts again: **it's Lowe**

Like I didn't already know. Like I wasn't begging for this day to come.

Rapid, we move from texting to speaking on the house phone and the hours rush by like seconds. I am floating in space. He has a cordless phone; he moves around on it loads, like even into the garden. I wish we had a cordless phone. We have two phones for one landline, both with their own issues. The upstairs one is bright yellow and more reliable and better because I can phone Lowe in private, but it's annoying too because it's harder to tell when Violet and Sonny pick up the phone and listen in on my conversations. I could be midway through opening up about how much I wish I didn't have red bobbles on my arms to Aoife, only to hear my sister honk down the line, 'What you gonna do about the red bobbles on your bum?' The other phone is in the living room where everyone can hear you.

On the landline we talk about music. He talks about his dreams of being in a band. I tell him about the books I'm reading. I read him poems and he actually *listens*.

Bianca calls me up and guilt casts its ugly shadow once again. She wants to know why Lowe isn't asking her to be his girlfriend. What's *wrong* with him? (She never considers that it's something she could do herself, or that it's anything to do with her.) 'He's such a dickhead,' she says. 'Why's he being so slow for? I could have anyone.' And then she says, 'Can you talk to him for me?'

I want to be a good friend. I don't want to be sneaky or two-faced.

'So . . . ' I begin, dutifully, 'how do you feel about Bianca?'

'Errrm.' I can tell he's blushing. He speaks close into the mouthpiece; his voice makes my hairs stand on end and my body do a wobbly, like when someone's treading over your grave.

'What?' I giggle. My teeth are dry from smiling so hard, like I've dissolved a powdery calcium vitamin on my tongue. The wire between us is alive. We hold on so tight. I push the phone to my ear so hard it gets all hot and my wrist cramps but it's worth it. I don't want to miss anything he has to say.

'What *yourself*.' He laughs back, so warm like hot fudge sauce, sliding down the walls of my house. 'I do *like* her. It's just . . . I dunno . . . ' He hesitates, looming. 'What do *you* think?'

What do *I* think?

This could be my chance. Surely he's passing the ball over to me? He's giving me an opportunity here to say something. To take it all back. To start again and say how I feel. Or simply be a manipulative bitch and fuck it all up by backstabbing Bianca. But I can't. She's my mate. And also. I just can't. I'm too afraid.

Dad picks up the downstairs phone suddenly, acting like it's not one tiny bit weird that I'm now having an INTIMATE three-way call with him and the love of my life. Not even to call anybody but to just *talk* to me. 'Do you know what time your mum's back?'

'*DAD*! I'm on the phone!'

'You're always on the phone, Ella. It's the only place I can speak to you! Now get OFF it so I can find your bloody mum!'

And he slams the phone back down in its cradle.

'Um. Sorry about *that*.' I am BURNING. 'I better go . . . but about you and Bianca.' I stagger, 'I think you're both great,' which is true. I leave out the bit where I say: *Just not together. Because that kills me.*

'K,' he says. 'That's not really what I . . . but K.'

'K.'

'K.'

Chapter 11

Every weekend Lowe and I are together *somewhere* at something. Mum asks, 'Why don't you do a lil' party here, Elliebellie?' But she says party like PAR-*TAY* so *that's* why. The house is embarrassing and I don't need Mum making conversation, getting my friends to lift bags of concrete and soil, taxing for weed and dropping words like 'bodacious'. I really don't need my parents fighting like Punch and Judy IN FRONT of an audience. No, thanks.

So other people's houses have become our restaurants, bars, cinemas, cafés, nightclubs, where we spread out like sixth formers in a common room and take the piss. Any room in any house where an adult is out or doesn't care will do; just give us an address and we'll be there. One of these parties happens to be one of the *very best days of my life* as Dean tells Bianca that she 'could be a model' and they kiss. Well, I'm so happy you'd think Dean was my forty-five-year-old bachelor son who just secured an engagement.

When we're together Lowe and I sit on sofas *close*, on our own 'whole new world' magic carpet ride, tempering the sting between us like we're under a spell, giving off charge and heat. In my head there's always a force field around us, a bulb of golden light, and we are the filament inside of it, sparking. Sometimes our fingers touch and we leave them there, skin melting, the hairs on our arms standing to attention. We are magnetic. Sometimes our knees brush past each other, deliberately, and we don't move one bit. I want his fingerprints on my clothes, my books, my CDs. Once, we share from the same carton of Mango Rubicon, and that feels like an open wide-awake kiss that's passable, allowed in public. His taste in my mouth. I want to not know where I end and Lowe begins. I want him to know what my house keys look like. What book I'm reading that week. My earrings. My pen. I want him to be able to pick up my jumper and know it's mine by the smell of my perfume. I want him to know what I'd order from a café. I want him to see something and think to himself, *Ella would like that.* I want him to look at my shit phone and think, *Who does she text before she falls asleep? Who does she talk to on the phone at night?*

He points out funny things; he admires the view. He stops to pet street cats and swerves his bike to not alarm passing dogs. He occasionally spits on the ground – only when he's out of breath – but never litters. He throws his sandwich crusts and crisps to the birds. He halts the traffic once with his bike to let a senior man cross the road. People comment on his smile, say he has an aura, a good energy. He has perfect manners. He listens. Is a nice guy.

We know all the rap bits to songs. Guitar breakdowns. We laugh at the same bits of TV programmes. At just a glance we know the same people annoy us. We can't believe how similarly our brains work, how alike we are. We're like twins. Geminis. We come as a pair. Knife and fork. Pepper and salt. A set of gloves. But nothing happens between us. EVER. Maybe it would if we saw how the night played out past midnight but Lowe is not a late-night kid. He's a summer day, excitable, energetic and playful, far more suited to flying down the road on his bike in just a t-shirt. He's sunshine and mint toothpaste. Alive with the birds. Unashamedly eager to get home in the evenings. And I like that about him. It's attractive that he likes his home. That he's secure. And although he's quiet, once he's gone home, he is missed. There's a space in the room where he should be. People always leave pretty soon after him. He's one of those luminous, upbeat people who can turn any old day into an event just by sticking around.

We write our way through autumn, snowballing towards winter. When the trees strip and the wind blows. Shorter days mean it's dark by 5 p.m. Writing letters to Lowe is like delightful homework, the only extracurricular hobby I'll take forward with me into my future – the writing more elaborate, detailed. We flex our creative muscles, let our guards down.

But winter comes for us and 251 Palace Road hard. Count Olaf's is subsiding. Cracks ladder their way up the walls. The rooms tilt like a sinking ship. Dad gets a hernia and Mum can't stand him moaning about it. (I mean TBF I've been cursed with an in-growing toenail and I don't go on about it.) Mum smokes weed. Dad puffs on his inhaler more than ever. The two of them are like Thomas the bloody Tank Engine. Mum decides she wants the attic room as her bedroom so we swap rooms. Could she want to sleep any further away from Dad in his ground floor bunker? It's fine, except my new room is opposite the railway line and I STILL don't have a curtain because I don't want to use the second-hand moth-eaten dirt rag that Mum's supplied me with so I have to duck to put my scrubby bra on. There are no shelves so Mum builds me a shelf from a plank of wood and some bricks from the garden. Whenever I need more shelves, I just take planks and bricks and continue to stack them up like some dangerous escape route someone might have built in secret to flee a dungeon. Traumatized disorientated woodlice scuttle into my wardrobe, burrow into my clothes. My bedroom rumbles when a train gushes past. Items wobble off my brick shelving unit. A love-heart snow globe filled with a cut-out from a magazine of the killer boyfriend in the movie *Scream* (that I somehow think my friends are gullible enough to believe is a real life legit photo of my ex-fiancé) smashes. An omen of my love life going bad to worse.

Suddenly, it's the lead up to Christmas; the buzz, the ride, the waiting, the constant glow. Like I know that *something* is going to happen. We *even* speak on Christmas day – much to Violet's disapproval in the way of passive aggressive deep sighing and oven door slamming. We continue to roll out this way, speaking in those in-between nothing days that follow after Christmas. He's away visiting family but is the first to text on New Year's Eve and I'm so happy that the world didn't end so I get to see him again in 2001. There's no *new year, new me* going on here; no, I just want this break to be over as quickly as possible so I can jump back into our routine. And now that Bianca and Dean are hanging out, I'm free to feel like I have a boyfriend even though I don't. I'm secretly falling in love. I pretend I'm *same old, same old* when meanwhile I'm running around like Björk in the 'It's Oh So Quiet' video.

We don't tell anybody about the amount we talk but it couldn't be possible to know somebody so well, to have achieved as much groundwork as we have in such a short space of time. We refer to our phone conversations and letter exchanges and our friends are gormless, out of the loop. They just think we've hit it off. That we really are *just* friends. But we operate on a whole other level. We have long, thick, strong magic roots – a deeply complex jungled network of flowing information in the undercurrent of our nuanced understanding.

We send more music, getting more confident with our song choices, saying that bit more as our feelings flourish. Every weekend, whenever, wherever we are, I say, 'Bye,' and Lowe says, 'See you soon,' and we hug, just like everyone else, knowing full well we will be speaking the entire week like Robert Browning and Elizabeth Barrett. Lizzie wrote 573 love letters to Bob, and no, you don't run out of things to say. There are always more mix tapes to send. Funny things we find. Sweets. Balloons. Photos. Old postcards. Stickers. Anything light and postable.

'I feel like I've known you my whole life,' he says. 'You're not like anybody else I've ever met.'

'Yeah, I am,' I say. 'I'm like you.'

I could definitely write the inside of a Clintons Valentine's Day card, or an episode of *Hollyoaks* at the very least.

Once, after Aoife, Bianca, Ronks, Shreya and I have invited ourselves down to the skate park (*conveniently* located slap bang next to Lowe's work at the bike shop) to do nothing except fancy people and pretend we're not freezing, Lowe glides over on his bike, sweat beads on his forehead. 'I was thinking, we should make a handshake – a *secret* handshake.'

I can't help but look behind me to be sure he's actually talking to me. 'YES!' I say excitedly. God, *chill*. 'I've never had a secret handshake – it's one of those things I've always wanted.' We slide our hands together and his skin is AMAZING. Even the rough callouses from gripping the handlebars of his bike are sexy and lovely to feel. *In. Out.* We find a rhythm. *Link, grip, grab.* Our eyes meet as we start with a thumbs up and *lock, twist, press,* clutch our fingers, twirl our hands into a fan – my idea. 'Nice,' he says, the condensation curling from his breath; it's smooth, eye-to-eye. This feels more intimate and romantic than any kiss – this is *touch* – synchronized. We rehearse over and over until it, like us, becomes muscle memory: *clap, clasp, twist, link, thumb to thumb, spiral, spud, punch, hug.*

Something only *we* can do, that our drunk friends try to copy. Even if mastered fluently, they'd never have the chemistry required to make it zap like us.

It is always us.

But protecting my feelings towards Lowe is constant maintenance. I have to guard him from the snooping prey of other girls but also not *squish* him to death with possessiveness. He is not *mine*.

'*You like him!*' the girls say but I deny it. Why? Because I'm scared. Of getting it wrong. Of looking a fool. Of rejection.

'We tried to work out your love score and the percentage was *literally* so high, it actually *broke* the test,' Shreya enlightens me. 'Even The Twins were confused by it.' And The Twins love maths.

'It's true,' one of The Twins admits, ashamed they'd been sneakily doing my love sums behind my back. 'You guys scored like four hundred and one per cent!'

'I've never seen anything like it,' adds the other.

Lowe and I throw the tired theories of love out of the window. *Our* love is shaming the textbooks. Making a fool out of science. This is love in real-life. Love in 3-D.

I laugh it off but, really, *401%*? WOW. Our love *broke* maths. Even though I'm pretty sure if you add up the four and the one it would make 50%. 50% is a terrible love score. Possibly the worst.

'Try it again. Did you use our middle names? You lot didn't add it up the right way anyway; which version of the love calculator are you even using?' I interrogate. Trying to conceal my desperation.

Shrey and The Twins whip out their fluffy pads and do the *alternative* version of the love calculator and the score is even worse – 18%. This can't be.

'I'm willing to bet every penny in my bank account that you two end up getting married one day!' Shrey says.

I blush, knowing full well that Shreya, like all of us, doesn't even have a bank account to bet with. '*Guys!*' I roll my eyes. 'You're so immature. I honestly don't like Lowe like that.'

I lie again. I lie so hard that I begin to lie to myself. Like the way I say that 'Teenage Dirtbag' isn't a good song. I find different people to fancy, substitutes and distractions. Guys I don't pay any attention to who pay me none back. Guys who don't even know I exist, to ensure there would never, *ever* possibly be a way of us getting together, but enough to stop the allegations and prevent the rumours and suspicions of me liking Lowe. It's especially hard to dodge when Lowe calls the house phone when the girls are at my house, and their stupid eyes bulge out of their brains like *wait, Lowe's phoning YOU?* At home, on a Thursday, like it's no biggie. (Yeah, and our last call was two hours forty-eight minutes long about ABSOLUTELY nothing.)

And I'm like, 'Yeah, we're *best friends*, remember?'

Even though they look at me like *whatever you say*. Even though Aoife's standing there twiddling our friendship bracelets like *I thought I was your best friend?* As I try and steady my excitable face to take Lowe's call.

I lie in my own diary. I actually write how 'fed up' I am of my friends accusing me of fancying Lowe. That I don't see him like that, *ew*, it would be like fancying my own brother. Why can't they see that we're just friends? *Best* friends. *Have a boy and girl never been best friends before? Can't a boy and a girl just be best friends, for crying out loud?*

This constant lying cannot be good for the soul. I reckon if I don't grow a Pinocchio nose, I'll get a hunched back from the guilt instead. A cyst of some kind from carrying all that built up denial and deceit.

One time, after the trillionth interrogation, Aoife jumps to my defence and says, 'Look guys, I've known Ella Cole since I was three years old; she's a lot of things' – alright, Aoife, *like what?* – 'but she's *not* a liar, just leave her alone, OK? And if Elbow *does* fancy him—'

'Which I *don't*.'

'Which she *doesn't*,' Aoife acknowledges and repeats, 'don't you think something would have happened between them by now?'

Aoife's right. Lowe and I are both single. Nothing is stopping us. Does he lie to all his friends in the same way I do? Is he also too proud and trying to save face like me? Or maybe he just doesn't feel the same. Maybe he doesn't like me back? Maybe he has nothing to lie about.

And looking around, after Aoife's supportive line, it kills me seeing my friends' convinced faces like, *maybe they are just friends after all?* They feel bad.

One lunchtime, we're smoking in the woods behind school – well, I'm keeping Bianca company whilst she smokes – I'm just pretending to with the condensation of my hot breath on the cold air. We're both sitting on the stump of a dead tree, shivering, in our bright green lab coats over our school uniforms, to mask the smell on our jumpers and coats – plus it's FREEZING. Even Bianca manages to be humble.

'Ella, I'm – like – really sorry. If I had known you had feelings for Lowe – in *any* way – I would never have pulled him.'

'I don't know what you're talking about, Bianca.' I hit back with a lie before I can even think. 'We're just friends. I don't even really remember you *pulling* him, to be honest.' Which is another lie because it's all she spoke about and every time she did, it felt like I'd had my organs looted.

Bianca looks at me, confused. Like she knows me better than I ever could. Testament to our albeit obscurely competitive/ twisted/fucked up but actually quite comforting sisterly teenage friendship. 'I'm still sorry anyway.'

And I squeeze her arm as if to say, *Thank you.*

Thank you for saying sorry. Thank you for being there. Thank you for maybe secretly seeing I'm lying – badly – all day long, and thank you for not calling me out for it. Thank you for being my friend.

In all honesty, it is such a burden liking Lowe the way I do, I'm battling with it. I don't want to any more. And I really have no idea how he truly feels about me – he's so hard to read. How I see it, if he liked me like that, he'd say so? And I don't want to be the one to make a move in case I get rejected or spoil what we have.

Even if we managed to become friends again I'd always be that friend who was a little bit in love with him. Gross. But maybe he's doing the exact same thing as I am and we'll just go on forever like that, saying nothing. Maybe he did once-upon-a-time fancy me and my feigned lack of interest fancying him back just put him right off. *He* felt rejected. Maybe over time he's begun to truly genuinely appreciate and value me as a friend and doesn't want to ruin anything. Oh God, I've dug myself into a right old hole. And I dig myself deeper and deeper. Cornering and trapping myself into the friendship zone forever. When really, I don't just like Lowe, I don't *like* him at all – I one hundred per cent madly truly deeply purely absolutely wholly *love* him.

I am in love with him.

True love.

January and February seem to never end. The sparkle of Christmas is now just reduced to the odd bit of leftover glitter in Dad's eyebrow. A pine needle in the floorboard. Mum has to work, but Dad can't care for us with the pain from his hernia. The NHS waiting list is so long that Dad has to go privately for his operation, which bites a hole out of our last chunk of money, sliding us into even more debt, and then the unworking *git* of a boiler has the absolute nerve to *blow* up. Dad has to buy some electric heaters, which are a MASSIVE investment. Violet, Sonny and I sleep in the same bed to keep warm. I tell myself that I actually got chubby on purpose, *deliberately*, because I'm smart, like how a walrus needs its blubber to insulate itself against the cold harsh arctic winds. Well, I needed an extra layer or two to warm me up in Streatham. We fight over the heaters from each other's bedrooms, unplug them out of spite, yank them out of the power sockets mid-argument and primitively slam doors with a kick, all whilst hugging a boiling hot convector heater. It's a health and safety nightmare.

And I am so, so homesick in my own home. For when we used to be happy. I'm a mess of pain, transition and contradiction. A teenager acting like a child, sick of trying to be a woman, in a training bra, listening to the Backstreet Boys, sleeping on a mattress on the floor that somebody has given us to be closer to the heater, shivering, under the naked lightbulb, into brittle adolescence. My parents continue to slam doors and chase each other up and down staircases with raised voices and every other word is 'fuck!' And Dad doesn't get to recover on the sofa after his operation like he needs to because Mum says he's lazy and that makes him resent her on top of her already resenting him. And Mum goes out more and doesn't come home and when Dad tries to call her, she picks up the phone only to hang up immediately and Dad, so primal and bear-like and simple, doesn't get the mind games, can't *stand* them. 'Bloody Nora!' he yells to nobody, and my gut clutches, as she works him into a frenzy. He picks the yellow phone up in his hand, and smashes it into his forehead with Homer Simpson rage – over and over – showing his teeth. I see my dad is broken.

And now the phone is too.

Its guts, all wires, on the floor.

My heart strings yelp as my major lifeline to Lowe is severed and now we'll have to rely on texts until my parents scrounge enough together to replace it.

I take my brother and sister upstairs; we put on the TV and laugh like nothing has happened and very quickly forget. It's wonderful being a kid like that. You think trauma is just sliding off your skin, when really it is the opposite; it's sinking in deep, like the most painful tattoo ink of a word or picture that you absolutely hate, directly into your nervous system, that nobody else will ever see unless you one day are loved or desperate enough to show it.

I sit at the top of the stairs, with one of Dad's oversized t-shirt on like a nightie, listening to the nightly rows with a *here we go again*. The house. The bills. The kids. I pull the shirt down over my whole body. 'Pssst, Violet,' I say, pointing at my knees, 'boobs.'

She laughs and tries to do it herself. We haven't had an adult hack like this since Violet realized if you hung the Christmas decorations over your ears they make convincing dangly teacher earrings. I shouldn't really let Violet and Sonny listen to our parents fight like this, but I want them to hear, I want them to know, because I'm scared of going through it alone. This is what siblings are for – to help parent your parents.

I hear Dad threaten to leave. *Ha! Good one, Dad.* He wouldn't *actually* though. It would be like the times I threatened to run away – you never do it and if you do, you always come back. Still, I find myself worrying about *all* the little things my parents don't seem to: how bills will be paid, who will pick us up from school, make sure there's milk? And this makes me anxious. I'm so scared of us falling apart that I hold on, tighter and tighter.

I try to keep a diary but everything seems to go wrong whenever I do. It's almost as if creating a diary in the first place is an omen to make my family hate each other. Instead, I fill pages with things that make me happy: drawings, poems and stories. I write using the orange glow of the streetlamp outside as a nightlight. I write long letters to Lowe that I will never send, saying how great my life is, how happy I am, spraying the pages with dozens of Biro hearts. Writing our names out and adding up the letters to tally up our 'love score' again and again, finding ways to make the number soar. Ronks says, *The letter the ring-pull comes off at on a can of drink is the first letter of the name of your future soul mate.* So I bend those ring-pulls backwards, forwards, backwards, forwards on every can of Sprite I drink, until the ring-pull snaps (I yank it) off on the letter 'L'. I find that the word Lowe is one letter away from the word LOVE. His name hidden in the word sunflower which is my favourite flower. I can't help but think it's meant to be.

One night, I play architect with a bottomless budget, scribble us a house from a bird's eye view. All straight lines and boxes. A huge living room with giant sofas and a massive TV. A great big kitchen with a dining table to seat sixteen people. Hot tubs in the bathroom and mirrors with lightbulbs like Hollywood film star dressing rooms. Outside, a heated swimming pool, hammocks, a secret garden and a thriving orchard, with hundreds of fruit trees that you can reach your hand out from any window and pluck peaches and plums and pears from, oh, and fish in a pond, sleeping hedgehogs, leaping rabbits and peacocks. And house phones all over, parked at their own little stations. Even though there's nobody I would want to call except him.

I give Lowe and me separate bedrooms to not be presumptuous. Maybe over time, when we're older, once our relationship has developed and grown, one night, after work, when we're making pesto pasta, he'll bring out of a bottle of Chardonnay and say . . .

Ella, I think I'm in love with you.

And then we can knock through a wall and push the beds together.

On the phone one night, I tell Lowe my parents have been fighting a lot.

'Do your parents fight a lot?' I ask.

'No, my parents never fight,' he says.

'Do you think your parents are in love?'

'Yes, they are very much in love.'

Very much cuts *deep.*

I haven't told anybody that I think my parents are breaking up, so used am I to them arguing now. It's normal not to be in love; no parents are in *love* love. Aoife's parents seem to just about stand each other. I don't think I've ever seen Shreya's parents kiss. The Twins live with their mum. Bianca lives with her dad.

Everybody is different. Actually, now I think about it, Ronke's parents do seem kind of in love. It's on my mind and it must be beginning to show.

Once, a nice teacher catches up with me before break and asks, 'How are things at home?' A girl in my class called Celine who I hardly ever speak to leaves a postcard in my locker – it's of some lips saying TALK TO ME and she writes, with care and empathy in her unreadable handwriting, about how I can talk to her if I need to. I never do (not out of choice; she gets expelled for starting a witchcraft cult before I get the chance), but I still keep the card.

It's not that bad though, really. I'm already able to see the buds of pink and white on the naked trees, the spilling daylight shining on my walk home, calling new leaping, friendly shadows to dance with, creating a sky you want to stop and stare at. The clusters of bright yellow daffodils shoot up, the birds sing; they are telling me that it will be OK, that winter is almost over and that spring is coming. That we made it. And soon a field of daisies, as far as the eye can see, will spread like an inviting picnic blanket, outstretched, waiting, for me to dive into glorious idle hours spent, *he loves me, he loves me not, he loves me . . .*

Chapter 12

Now

It's a Sunday and I'm at Mum's for a roast. Roast to Mum is taken very literally. Find anything you possibly can and roast it. And somehow it always tastes alright. I'm here for the addictive *quality* of my family mostly. That fix I can't get anywhere else. Our comforting in-jokes and that cosy familiar same-species likeness that you only get with immediate family that permits you be 100% yourself at all times.

251 Palace Road looks pretty much the same as when Mum bought it with the promise to renovate it all those years ago – not from want of trying. The little DIY was stubbornly refused by the house – the layered paint bubbles, cracking with condensation and conversation, rickety improvised floorboards hammered with the craftsmanship of a Loony Tunes character. Since buying our place, I have so much more respect and empathy for Mum. I remember thinking you could just do all the knocking down walls in a weekend yourself and it'd look fantastic. Turns out no and no.

Mum's headquarters is at the kitchen table, her 'office'. Covered with a bowl of homegrown mouldy fruit and bendy veg, un-opened post, remote controls, expired bank cards, batteries, a gardening trowel, WD-40, lumps of dope and stuff to sell online. Over the years, this table has seen it all. Friends and neighbours come and go. It's a watering hole, a place to plot world domination and butter bread for sandwiches; a confession box. Tea, coffee, *anything stronger* all-year round, an extra plate, room for one more. Mum's kitchen table is a place to take risks, plan revenge, offer unsolicited advice, for belly laughs, bad news and chopping onions. Not the most comfortable and yet it's everyone's favourite booth at a haunt.

Mum sits head of the table now, in her position of power, right opposite the doorway. She doesn't even flinch when I enter. Her callous hands rolling a spliff, muscular legs stuffed into Caterpillar boots, as weathered and intimidating as a cold mountain. Her all-year weathered terracotta suntan on her chest and shoulders from gardening is rich, her long beetroot hair in an unkept scorpion plait. But her wet soulful brown eyes give her away, show me she's happy to see me, as she always is when I'm home.

I can see she's not even started on the roast. When I *gently* hint at that she tells me, 'It'll only take me five minutes'. *Yeah. OK.* I open the cupboard where sometimes, on a good day, Bombay Mix or ginger biscuits fly out at you but today, nothing. Mum's dog, Spy, sniffs around me.

'Where's Jackson?' she asks.

'Playing football.'

'That man . . . I've never met anybody with so many athletic hobbies; it's unsettling.'

'Yooo!' My baby brother Sonny enters, wearing baggy tracksuit bottoms and a vest; his pumped arms hang on the doorframe. He's the only one to have inherited Mum's height. 'What you saying?'

'I'm *saying*,' I answer, with my head in the fridge to be met only with rancid jars and Mum's *marinades*, 'do you not have any food in this house?'

'Do you not have a *house*?' Violet lashes.

'Do YOU?' I fire back. Violet thinks she's able to live at Mum's rent-free for life because she's saving to open a café.

'What else are we meant to do?' She means it.

'The world is crazy out there,' Sonny adds. 'Do you think I want to be here as a successful man in my early twenties? No, I don't. It's impossible to live.'

'Oh, so I see,' Mum interrupts even though this is NONE of her concern, 'I'll just pay for all three of you to live.'

'You HAD us!' Violet argues. 'We didn't ask to be born into this shit world.'

'You're meant to be taking care of me now!' Mum argues. She's wearing a vest top and no bra; her boobs – evidently once blown with warm milk to feed her three babies – jobble.

'That isn't possible by the way, so don't ever retire,' says Sonny. She has to hear this at some point.

'At least stand on your own two feet, then?' Mum begins wiping marmalade off some designer ties she plans to sell on eBay.

'Don't you think we're *trying*?' Violet points at me as though I'm the example of *trying*.

Mum says, 'It's really not that hard: you go to work, you earn money, you buy a house. I did it.'

This boils my blood and I'm hangry. 'Mum, you never even had a stable job in your entire life because it was the Nineties so you could just rip meaningless cheques from your chequebook like a Monopoly-joke that meant nothing because the cheques would just bounce back and now you get to *bumble* about in your fat house that you bought for nine pence and will get to, all thanks to inflation, sell on for trillions, meanwhile we can't even afford a shoebox in a crummy cupboard because you polished off our inheritance in a Martini glass, and will have to cook our dinners of conkers over a friggin' candle! You know I use tampons as a TREAT?'

'That's more because of the environment, though, right?' Violet adds.

'Don't get me started on the fucking environment, Violet,' I snap. 'I just want *love*.' It comes out way more heartfelt than I intended.

'OK-eee,' says Sonny. 'Awkward.'

'Oh, someone give her a hug,' Mum says, not giving me a hug. 'She just wants *love*.'

Violet puts her arm around me and pats sympathetically – 'There, there' – but it comes out sarcastically.

Adam, my stepdad, wades in at this point with wellies on made for wading. Good, because he's just landed in shit.

'Hey, Ella, you look tired.'

'*Thanks*.'

'Anyway, you should be haps.' Not Mum abbreviating. 'You *have* just brought a – well, maybe not a house – but *something*. You're a homeowner, Ella. And that means you can take back your old shit that's filling up my spare room.'

The *old shit* Mum's referring to are my boxes that I temporarily left at the house with the hollow promise to pick up once we'd moved. Identity cargo – school books, photographs, notebooks – that I don't have the physical or psychological capacity for in my own home. Stuff I *can't* bring myself to throw away but also stuff I'd quite happily never see again. I was hoping the boxes would just disappear in Mum's walls, with the other junk.

'Just throw it all in the recycling.'

'Ella? They're your *memories*!' Mum says.

'URRRRR. Fine.'

'I can make you a Bloody Mary if it helps?' she offers.

'I'm not drinking.'

'Since when?' Mum sounds surprised.

I pull out my phone and show them my app, the timer continuously counting the seconds. 'Fourteen days as of today, actually.' Come to think of it, maybe that's why I'm so cranky. I'm not an alcoholic but doing life raw is a lot.

'Mia's wedding tipped her over the edge,' Violet says. 'Well done, El.'

'So can you, please, at LEAST start making food?'

Mum shrugs like *we'll see*.

As I climb the stairs towards the spare room, Violet pushes her face into the banister and says, 'Pssttt. Shall I knock us up some pasta?'

'It wouldn't hurt,' I say.

I slump down before the squirming bag of dust-covered snakes. CDs. A signed school shirt. A Groovy Chick notebook opens with the line *My mum doesn't understand me hardcore*. See? Pure poetry. What purpose will I ever have for my first Barbie or this unbrushed Ginger Spice wig? This red wine-stained *Beetlejuice* costume? Or this embroidered waistcoat I got in Mexico that I can't even do up? But there are photos of us as kids, birthday cards, my nanna's white clay sun brooch, the bracelet my parents got me for my thirteenth birthday, the evil eye necklace I got in Greece, Mum's charm bracelet, a postcard from my sister's summer camp saying *I DON'T WISH YOU WERE HERE, LOVE YOU X* that makes me laugh out loud, school certificates. The receipts of life. Photos from my disposable camera of Aoife, Bianca, Ronks and me. One of Mia and me in our production of *Little Shop of Horrors*. Everyone fought so hard to be Audrey. I just wanted to be Audrey II. She'll find that funny. I snap photos on my phone to send on to them later. The books of poems I wrote as a kid bursting with notes, photos, pressed flowers.

My scrapbook drums like the *Jumanji* game – opening it is alarming. It's like a scary encyclopaedia dedicated to one strand of knowledge: *Lowe*. Wristbands from his gigs, ticket stubs, cut-outs from press pieces in local magazines, a set list. I really kept *train* tickets? Something buried shifts inside. His letters pour out, one after the after, at least twenty. I kept them all. I open one and quickly cast my eyes over the words but it's too much. His handwriting tasers me. And then there are the tapes. More than I thought. We had so much in common. I forget what that's like, being with Jackson; my references seem to fly over his head. He says things like 'They were a bit after my time' about Blink 182. His North Star, Oasis, of whom he takes complete ownership.

I don't even own a tape player any more, and I won't have space for them in the new place anyway. Besides, it's just weird and unfair to keep them in the house with Jackson. Even keeping them at all feels inappropriate. It's not like Lowe will have kept my tapes, my letters. I collect it all and throw the lump down into the recycling bag, where the tape cases clatter. Already thinking about how they'll feel, out in the cold, flecked in rain, sharing a bin with the used teabags and apple cores of life.

After a bowl of Vi's tremendous pasta, I'm feeling more myself and retrieve the soaking wet bag, once again looking for the clues in his letters and song choices.

Wait, did he put bloody Goo Goo Dolls on there? Nirvana's 'Heart-Shaped Box'?

Jesus Christ.

And the guy didn't LOVE me? *Please!*

Too late for that now.

A photograph rolls out, from my eighteenth birthday, his arm around me, cheek to cheek, pure happiness and cheesy grins. I'd tonged my hair that day. I can't help but smile at us. I *could* send a photo of it to him. But would that be weird after ten years? I'd only regret it. Best to not open up that box of us and to keep the lid closed.

Several years ago, just before one of Jackson and my first dates, I was shaken up because some journalist had the audacity to turn up out of the blue asking if I was Lowe Archer's ex-girlfriend and would I be interested in selling a story. This was when he was everywhere and the press couldn't get enough. Lowe had mentioned me in the sleeve of his album, something about us being close, and the press had probably worked their way through the names listed, hoping they'd eventually find a loose brick in the wall who would speak and tell it all. Photos were leaked of us together as kids. I didn't even know he'd thanked me then, although it was a bittersweet surprise, albeit surreal, to find that information out from a greasy journalist. I slammed the door in their face and hid under my duvet.

Flocks of Lowe Archer mega-fans then went through a phase of swarming my tiny book events in bookshops, pretending they liked my poetry but really expecting Lowe to show up to support me. It would be a clever way of cornering him. Easier than loitering at a chance hotel lobby to catch a glimpse. Sometimes they would be so excited and giddy, they'd even convince *me* that Lowe was about to walk through the door of that tiny bookshop in South East London, that damp basement café in Soho, that empty library in Southend. But obviously he never did. Mum said I should have used it to my advantage: *Might help you sell some books for once, then we could do up the kitchen!* But I got anxious. How did the journalist get my address? I worried about packs of crazed fans, stalking me, kidnapping me for ransom. Keeping me tied up in a cellar where I'd have to eat Pot Noodle on repeat and I'd have to sweet talk them to make sure they got me the beef and tomato flavour until Lowe paid up. Then I fretted about how much I was worth to him, even though I knew Lowe would never come – he'd be advised by his team not to pay or else the kidnappers would just keep kidnapping. And so I'd be dumped on the street corner because I'd annoy them to the point of surrender.

Dark times. He's the rich one; he should be paying for my therapy.

I tried to cancel on Jackson that night but he said we could just have one drink and see how it went. Now I think about it, it's kind of Lowe's fault I'm even with Jackson. Then again, it wasn't exactly Lowe's fault that Jackson and I did all that snogging. Then again and again, why am I saying *fault* like it's a bad thing?

Chapter 13

Then

I'm at The Twins' house the night before my fifteenth birthday. Tomorrow my family and I are going to Chessington World of Adventures to ride the Vampire ride and then we're going to Pizza Hut so I can load my bowl up at the salad bar without supervision and eat as much of those bacon crunchies as I feel like, smother everything in thousand island dressing and get to call it greens. Then I'll eat a whole entire (pretty much *fried)* pepperoni pizza – showered with fake parmesan – by myself, before visiting – at least four times – the refillable ice-cream machine. All washed down with four pints of Coke. *And no, you can't say anything, Mum, because it's my birthday.*

But I'm *still* waiting for my dad to pick me up. He's running late. Which isn't unusual; we don't live that close. Maybe he had to get petrol.

I can sense The Twins' mum feeling the nerves – *should she be making me a birthday eve dinner?* The pressure of not knowing if she should be frying up a few rib-eyes or not. *Am I staying the night?* The Twins' mum is never late. She always has petrol. We wait for Dad to call. *He'll be here in a minute,* I say.

Sure, I like The Twins' house, far better than my own, but it's 251 that I want now. It's my birthday; I want my mum and dad.

I'm out of phone credit, so am rinsing The Twins' phone like a babysitter with hot gossip, waiting for Mum and Dad or Violet to pick up the phone, but it rings out for so long I begin to hear new melodies in the simple pattern of it. We watch MTV, self-medicating with snacks, tripping out at Crazy Town's video for 'Butterfly', wishing somebody wanted us like that, until The Twin's mum hands the flashy cordless phone to me. 'It's your dad.' I can smell the relief oozing off her.

'Listen, Ellabell, I'm not going to be able to pick you up tonight, chicken. Your mum and I have a lot to sort out over here . . . '

He sounds drunk. His voice raspy, like he's been shouting. And he's wheezing like he has dried up leaves in his lungs.

'Have you got your Ventolin?' I ask.

'Yes,' he says. 'Don't worry.'

My eyes water; The Twins' burglar alarm blinks every thirty seconds to remind us we are safe here. I can't imagine that kind of security.

'Do you think it would be OK if we came and got you in the morning?' he asks.

'You mean _stay the night_?' I ask, horrified, shaken, fizzing like a SodaStream. 'On my _birthday_?'

I have never been apart from my parents on a _birthday_. And what about Violet and Sonny? It'll feel to them like I have died, _surely_? They might open my presents, assume I'm dead? 'Stumble' across my incredibly powerful poetry, publish it and turn their future children into entitled brats with my millions. _It's what Ella would have wanted._

NO. IT'S NOT.

'If that's OK with The Twins' mum?'

'I'm sure that's fine.' Put me up for adoption, why don't you?

The Twins hold me. They say, 'Let's all make one big bed on the floor tonight!' and drag out the mattresses. We spread out on the living room floor and watch _Cruel Intentions_ and chat shit until we don't make sense any more.

In the morning, their mum – total *diamond* of a woman – lays out warm croissants and jam. The Twins pick flowers from the garden – flowers that could earn prizes – to decorate the table. I take one to press when I get home. *Enjoy today whilst it lasts. Because today is yours.*

So after breakfast, when Dad calls to say, 'Grab your coat, birthday girl, we're going to Chessington!' I say I want to stay here. Where I know there will be cake. And I'll get spoilt all day. The last thing I need is my parents arguing upside-down on Rameses Revenge.

So I do.

Even though it's only 10 a.m. I slide on my sassy choker necklace and zig zag my parting. It feels like we're getting ready for a wedding, like I'm the bride and The Twins are my loyal bridesmaids. Like this is going to be a special day. One I will remember forever. And out we roll into summer, in our baggy jeans and—

OH MY GOSH—

There at the end of the street, waiting.

My one. Lowe Archer.

He's wearing his cap, a grey t-shirt with a blue star on it, a strawberry Ribena in between his hand and the handlebar of his bike.

'My favourite!' I say. But – this is a secret – I'm talking about him, not the drink.

'Happy birthday, Ella,' he says. And he hugs me. *Him.* He props his cap on my head and I feel like I've won an Oscar. Is it just me or is there spring blossom everywhere? Pale butterfly kisses hang from every tree, every streetlamp, sweeping down the road, skipping and slipping into the drains. Is the day not fucking gorgeous? Is it not such sweet paradise here in South London? We walk through the woods where the others meet us with cakes, homemade cards and balloons. We eat those big flat chewy strawberry jelly sweets that get stuck in your teeth, and Dad calls again to say he'll come and get me, that it's *not too late for Chessington?* and even then I still say no. I'm happy under the overcast mushroomy sky – with everyone sitting on the common, singing out our favourite grunge songs like a pack of crying wolves. I am exactly where I need to be. Fifteen years old. And loved.

Lowe pulls out a guitar and begins to play one of my favourite songs that he's learnt.

'No way . . . SHUT UP!' I squeal but he doesn't falter. He's trying to concentrate, trying to keep his hands steady. Tears bulb in my eyes and we all begin to sing, maybe twenty of us now, just kids, perfectly annoying kids, living out loud until the sun sets and our friend the moon is our glowing campfire, our watchful eye.

Lowe pushes his bike up to The Twins' house. The stars wrap around us. I am living in a fantasy where this is my hotel; this is my life.

'You two!' Bianca shouts in her South London commentary. 'Talk about love birds.' (Back there, are we?)

I flush red and slam my hand over her mouth. 'BIANCA!'

And I look at Lowe; it's not as though he's denying it.

'I'm *so* sorry, Lowe!' Bianca jeers, giggling her head off. 'But Ella just *doesn't* like you like *that*? OK?'

Oh, for fuc—

I can't even look at Lowe.

The girls haul Bianca, squealing, into The Twins' house and I linger. Lowe leans against the wall. Is this a *plan*? A meteoroid must be heading at great speed towards our planet. *Something* is going to happen. 'Well . . .' Lowe says at the drive.

Well . . . how about please just kiss me?

'Goodnight then, Lowe Archer – thank you for . . . well . . . everything,' I say.

'K.' He bites his bottom lip. We both giggle.

'K . . . ?'

The brow of a fox twitches. The clench of a fist. The rattle of the sky. The wind sucks back. The plants hold their breath. A bird stretches its wings. A cigarette sparks. I see a living room lamp switch on. Hear a car door slam. Headlights rush and we've still not kissed. I hear an engine purr. A dog's rough bark. The water on the pond as tight as a drum, where a bulbous toad gurgles and nature is on our side. Animals burrow in for the night. It's all on our side, all perfectly timed, all alright and still no. No kiss. A boiling kettle clicks. The shop front yanks down. The train roars by. The kids ride home. The night turns and we've still not kissed.

We both laugh as we feel the moment pass. We escape the trap as the tension lifts. We press the palms of our hands together and do our good old handshake. *Clap, clasp, twist, link, thumb to thumb, spiral, spud, punch, hug . . .*

Ah, well. Maybe next time?

I turn to walk back towards the house with a 'BYE then!'

And then, from somewhere down the road, Lowe shouts, 'Bye then!'

I grin, hiding behind the wall, stick my head out and shout 'Oi, bye!'

He hides behind a tree and pops out with a 'Bye!'

We're both giggling our heads off now. Bye. *Bye.* Bye. *Bye.* The whole way down the road until he's so far away, his voice so small, I'm not sure if it's him or an echo.

When he's out of sight, I still stand on the porch of The Twins' house, shouting 'BYE!', laughing quietly to myself, not pressing the bell until I hear Lowe shout it back.

He calls my phone.

'Hello?' You can hear the smile in my voice.

'Bye!' and he hangs up before I can say anything back.

My heart explodes.

A gargantuan high. An astronomical supernova, right here, inside. Bye.

Chapter 14

The following day, still blissed out from what felt like a holiday in heavenly Wandsworth, I'm tucked up in bed, reading the copy of *Flowers in the Attic* that we've been passing around our class (but hidden inside a copy of *The Hobbit* so nobody can see I'm a dirty bitch), when Dad comes in and nervously drops himself at the end of it.

'Did you have a nice birthday?'

'Yeah, with my *friends*.' I don't look up, keep drawing hard Biro lines in my book. I'm not going to let him know it was absolutely great – that would absolve the guilt too easily. I could get an extra birthday present out of this surely.

'You know, it wasn't our fault; it's not what we wanted,' he tells me. 'Hey, look at me, you know I love you so much, don't you?'

I look at him, just quickly though, nod and carry on scribbling. I mumble, 'And you love Mum too, right?'

He looks strained and hesitates. 'Of course I love your mum . . .'

'What's going on?' I ask. 'I'm fifteen. You can tell me the truth now, Dad.'

By truth I obviously mean, *Please say things are exceptional between the both of you, that you're madly in love and have never been better, Dad. Not the actual truth.*

Dad takes a breath, holds it in his throat, looks at me like *can she take it?* 'Your mum and I are breaking up.'

WHAT? I mean, I knew they weren't milk and honey, but, guys, seriously, this is extreme. They can't break up. That happens on TV, not in real life. They're a team. By having us they made a promise. My mind jumps straight to worst case scenario mode – I see something tragic like a plane crash:

It's more than just turbulence on the jumbo jet of us. Violet and Sonny are reaching for their oxygen masks. I should help them, they're my siblings, but how can I when I can't help myself? When our luggage is flying everywhere? As we nosedive towards concrete. My crazy parents, panicked pilots, battling it out over which one should steer us to safety.

'Me and your mum will still remain best friends' – cos you really sound like it – 'and nothing will change.'

Even I know that's fucking impossible. I begin to cry.

'Aw,' he comforts. 'Bellie, don't cry. It will be OK.' But this makes me cry more.

'Maybe don't tell your brother and sister just yet?' he backtracks. He can see that this news is going down like a wet weekend and is regretting it. 'They're too young to understand.'

Oh. So they were wearing oxygen masks after all then?

I want to say, *But Dad, I'm too young to understand.*

I thought I wanted them to tell me the truth but actually knowledge is not power: knowledge is shit.

Later on, now it's all out in the open, Mum says like it's nothing, 'Your dad's moving his stuff out; he's staying with Brian for a bit until he gets his own place.'

Brian? But Brian's single. And a DJ. That means Dad will be out there on the town again.

'OK,' I reply, in that way you sometimes do when you're a kid. It's a receipt. I hear you. Now stop. And *OWN PLACE?* What does *that* mean? *Chill!* He doesn't need to move out! It feels so detached and separate. Like will wild dogs *eat* him out there on his own? Will he find a new family? Start again – without us?

Then again, maybe his 'own place' would be nicer than 251 and I can live with him instead and finally I can try ham and pineapple pizza without Mum saying it should be banned.

Dad's moving out. But he can't be; he's my dad. We're meant to see each other on the landing. Argue about who didn't push the toothpaste up from the bottom. Accuse one another of leaving the lights on: 'It looks like Piccadilly Circus in here!' I'm meant to hear his whistle.

I nosily peer into Dad's half-empty bedroom and see all the good stuff has already gone. Tears bubble up in my eyes. I have the urge to go into my bedroom and listen to the Lighthouse Family, but thank God I manage to muster up a grain of mental resilience to resist before things get that bad.

Here I am, a teenager, desperate for any excuse to strop about, something to blame for my mood swings, to blast all my angsty fury at, an epic life story to make me have the right to write a masterpiece memoir like Tracy Beaker's. And now it is here and I wish it would go away.

At school, I don't want anybody to know. I don't want anybody to ask me about it. But at home, I use it to my advantage. If they're going to break up, then I'm not going to waste my time revising for my exams, am I? (Pretty stupid, really – joke's on me.) If they're going to split up then I'm not going to tell them when I get to my friend's house *safely*, am I? If they aren't going to take care of us – well, neither am I. At a party I let a friend's mum make me a glass of sangria and I learn to like it. It's delicious as far as alcohol goes, with big juicy rounds of orange – a drink *and* a snack. And I make a whole batch in a washed-out water bottle to take to a house party at yet another really nice house and throw it all up over the white walls. I sick up some kind of knobbly cat food out of The Twins' mum's people carrier's backseat window, and all along her pebble stone drive like some necessary purge. I stink of orange rind and shame. It's now my go to *turn* – and boy have I *turned*. Never this bad before where the room is spinning and every word is sliding and every lightbulb is a disco ball. I am carried upstairs, undressed by my friends and rolled into a bed like a burrito. I really regret wearing a thong.

I hope I didn't get so drunk that I told anybody I loved Lowe?

I start to despise my parents; they've told The Kids that Dad's moving in with Brian for a bit because he has a 'migraine'. HA! *Unbelievable.* Are they actually buying this shit? Get a cold flannel and an Anadin Extra like everyone else's goddam guardians. (*Anything but please don't leave, Dad; please stay at home with us and be our constant.*) It annoys the hell out of me seeing my brother and sister go about life as though nothing has changed, as though life is a perfect, shiny, spinning wheel of Babybel cheese when actually, sorry, *everything* has changed, and they are still in blissful, innocent, ignorant childhood, and I am here in the dark stuff, alone. And nobody even likes Babybel.

I slam out towards the high road on a cloudy day where the air is close and thick. I listen to my Discman really loudly, holding it upright like I'm a cocktail waitress otherwise the CD skips. I decide this summer will be the greatest summer of my life if I can basically locate the skill to ignore anything real that's going on.

We spend it stretched out on The Twins' trampoline, the elasticated mesh now punctured by cigarette-hot rocks. I sit next to Lowe, always. Just having him next to me is enough to make the day go fast, and yet I want it to go on forever. We sit in the park in giant crop circles in the press of the sun until it slinks away and we remain, like statues, under the eye of the swollen moon. The apple-green grass turns rat-grey.

He says, 'I love the way you *do* stuff.'

'Do stuff? What stuff?'

He now wishes he never opened his mouth because he has to explain. 'I dunno what it is but how you move your hands' – I look down my little trotters and think, strange but OK – 'how you tell a story, how you move the hair out of your face, how you give directions to a stranger or whatever.'

'I don't think I've ever given directions to a stranger, not accurate ones anyway.'

'You know what I mean.' He nudges me shyly. 'I even like the way you put your . . . headphones in your ear . . .' he confesses. 'It . . . I dunno the word . . . stop laughing.' He tuts. 'Oh, I'm just gonna shut up now.'

'No, go on . . . sorry.' I have got to stop cracking jokes as a reflex; I straighten my face. 'Please say what you were going to say . . .'

'No. You're annoying. That's all you're getting.' He shakes his head, laughing, looking out to the trees. 'I said it. I like the way you do stuff. That's it.'

'That's sweet of you.' I admit, 'I like the way you do stuff too.'

I could write a book about how much I like the way he does stuff. Like that time I got to watch him eat a chicken balti bake. I mean, *divine*, the stuff dreams are made of. Or that time I thought he winked at me but he was just getting some grit out of his eye. Still, there is an unspoken promise between us, an unsaid vow that says – *you are mine and I am yours*. And everybody knows that now, so nobody dares cross the line. But we are too afraid to make it real on the trampoline with our friends watching.

Just. Kiss. Me.

But he has to get home.

Towards the end of the summer, when the seasons are calling closing time on the party of the holidays, a small group of us are out. The Twins scuttle back for their home tutor but I'm not ready for the warm months to be done just yet. I don't ever want to go home to the inevitable. For the cold to bite at the mushy cracks of my crooked house on Palace Road, where I live as a loose thread on the hem of a skirt. Waiting for the walls to crumble in, for winter to freeze us.

'Why don't you want to go home? What are you avoiding?' Lowe asks me.

'*Avoiding?*'

Nobody had ever used the word 'avoid' to me in this psychological context before. It comes out.

'My mum and dad are breaking up.' I haven't even told Aoife.

He says nothing. So, obviously, I fill the silence.

'My dad's moved out. His football bag gone, his CDs gone, his inhaler gone, his books gone. My dad is gone. I fucking hate my parents. I hate that house. I hate my life. I don't know how to fix it. Everything's going wrong and can you say something now?'

'That's shit,' he replies. Lowe never talks about his parents. His 'deeply in love' parents. Maybe he doesn't want to rub salt in my already quite salty wound? Maybe he's just the ultimate love-child of the most in-love humans on the planet; he wouldn't understand this feeling of heartbreak; he's got nothing to say on the matter.

I try to look like I could use a hug by making my shoulders look *baggy*. Slouching, like I need propping up. Instead, he tears a tag off his shoe, eyes on the ground. He's either the most empathetic person in the world or I've accidently hit a nerve. He clears his throat. 'You've just got to get through it bit by bit.'

I nod. *Great advice. Cheers.*

'You don't understand,' I moan. 'I wish I was like . . . an orphan.'

Lowe laughs.

'It's true.'

'Don't say that; you've got amazing parents, Ella.'

'Selfish parents.'

'They really love you and they obviously did a good job . . . '

He pushes my hair behind my ear. Nobody had ever done that to me before either. 'Because they made you.'

And I seep into the grass.

His phone rings.

'Shit, my dad.'

I jump up as though his dad is standing over us. Lowe steps away from me to take the call. *Yep. Yep. K. Will do. K.*

The call is over in less than thirty seconds.

His mood has shifted. Sometimes he doesn't look like a kid. Sometimes he looks like he has the weight of the world on his shoulders.

'OK?' I ask.

He braves a smile. 'Yeah.'

'I'd better be going home anyway,' I admit. 'It's late.'

The path ahead through the common looks like the artwork for a new horror film. Jagged and murky, the branches of trees droop like hanging animal bodies. A dirty mist.

'Here, stand on the pegs,' Lowe says, reaching for his bike, angling it at me. 'The *pegs*, at the back.'

'I know what they are,' I hesitate with jest. 'I just don't want to . . . *stand* on them.'

'You'll be fine,' he says. 'I'll take you to the station.'

' . . . *Really? Erm . . .* OK?'

It's the bike or be kidnapped. With my hands on Lowe's shoulders, the soles of my shoes find the grip of the bars either side of the back wheel.

'K, hold on tight now.'

'Don't go fast,' I warn.

'I'm not going to.'

He pulls his hood up over his head, zips it right to his mouth. He's obviously an expert at putting whatever is on his mind back into its little box.

'You good?'

'As good as I can be *standing* on a bike.'

'You're funny.' He laughs. 'OK, you can loosen your grip just a *tiny* bit, so I can, you know, *breathe*?'

'Oh my God, sorry.'

And suddenly I'm just on the back of Lowe Archer's bike, a bike he barely even has to pedal because he's just one of those people the earth moves for.

In my pocket, I rummage for the same crumpled up train ticket I've used for pretty much the entire summer, to flash at an inspector on the unlucky days the barriers are closed. Far too much of my life is spent shivering at empty train stations, waiting, with no money, no snacks, no battery on my Discman and no phone credit. We arrive. The gloomy slices of light seem to beat down like some depressing film noir. I feel sick, alone. We both look up at the Teletext timetable screens – no sign of a train going to mine any time soon.

'You don't have to wait with me.' I release him from the obligation. 'One will come soon.'

Lowe slinks back on his bike, arms stretched out, his hands clench, lock onto the handlebar which he swerves, rocking playfully from side to side.

'I'll take you home.' He offers so quietly it could definitely be an auditory hallucination.

'HA!' I push him gently. 'Yeah, alright, that's like . . . *ages* for you. You literally live right here.'

'I know.' He's hardly even looking at me, but on his wheels, a tree behind him shakes like it's laughing at us.

'You really don't have to do that.'

'I know I don't have to but . . . ' He readjusts his cap. ' . . . I want to.'

And my arms are wrapped around his chest, my palms spread over his beating heart; my cheeks are smiling so hard. He needs no direction. He knows the way to mine.

We don't talk, just ribbon the empty pavement under the arrows of stars. I have the nerve to close my eyes, to feel the mild summer breeze on my face as we blow down the hill, to feel *him*. Miles away from Dad's Vespa, I'm like a cool girl on the back of some stud's motorbike, riding the desert. In this moment, well, I'm like any ridiculous trope of a damsel in distress on horseback, galloped away from danger by some handsome knight in a shining tracksuit. And don't tell a soul, but I love every single second of it.

When my chariot arrives at 251 Palace Road, my moth-eaten castle, this princess feels the rising soar of love charging through her belly; I'm so elated by the whole thing that I don't feel embarrassed at all by our falling-down house – it's not like he's going to come *inside*! He lets me off the limousine of his bike; I feel like a movie star stepping on the red carpet. It takes a second to find gravity. Lowe signs off with one of his adorable skids, his face dewy with perspiration and pride. He is still smiling, breathless. He takes out his Ventolin and shakes it before inhaling. *Thank God* for that little blue plastic thing breathing air into his lungs. My GOSH he is so cute. So hot. And so kind. You know what? He is *my guy* – that's what he is. He's *my* guy.

Probably because I'm living in some annoying romance scene in my head, I go over and kiss him on the cheek. Lowe glows, presses his head into his neck. 'Well . . . that was *nice*,' he says. I could be paid a million pounds in this moment *not* to smile, and I wouldn't be able to resist.

'Thank you.' I beam. 'And for listening to me moaning too.'

'You didn't moan.' He shrugs, smiles sweetly.

'A little bit?'

'OK, maybe just a little bit of moaning.' He measures with his thumb and forefinger a sugar cube of space.

'K, night.'

'K, night.' It's meant to be a smooth exit, but then he has to watch me fuck about with the latch of the stupid rickety gate.

Then my knight breezes away into the night, wheels around and his bike reared like a horse.

I know what you're thinking – cycling you home? OK, you've bagged this, girlfriend. Oh, he loves you alright. *First comes love, then comes marriage, then comes a baby in a bloody carriage.* I'm thinking the exact same thing, to be honest. I'll be strutting into school with a swishy high pony-tail, boasting to everyone that I have a boyfriend. For REAL this time. And not just any boyfriend – Lowe Archer.

Chapter 15

But everything changes.

The whole next week Lowe is distant, different.

Lowe's 'not around', 'staying in', 'not coming out', 'busy'.

Is it because I kissed him on the cheek? Did I cross the line? Could he see in my eyes how much I love him, so he knew he had to step back to protect me, to not hurt my feelings? Has he told his friends about my little crush, and they all laughed and said I was ugly and fat and a loser? Maybe it's the opposite? Maybe the cheek was too cold? Maybe *I* drew the line? And now he's backed away? FUCK.

I text: **Hey . . . have I done something to upset you? I don't know what but whatever it is, I'm sorry. x**

No reply.

FUCK. Why did I send that? I'm paranoid, panicky, stressed. I find a frozen cherry pie from Iceland drenched in snow at the back of the freezer and bake it. I eat the whole thing. And then I feel sick. I consider throwing it up in the toilet but I'm too frightened – I've heard not so great things about bulimia. So, I just lie there, relying on my stomach acid to break down the beast of a pie, listening to Usher, crying until I fall asleep.

I wake up in the morning to see his message.

hey ella, I'm goin thru sum stuff at home but it's nuthin 2do wid u or anything u hv done. C u soon. X

(Surely it's harder to text like that than use the actual English language?)

Going through something? Like *what*? And why isn't he telling me? I told him all about my parents breaking up. I fight the urge to press on the matter and simply write back:

k, hope ur OK, miss u x

And he replies straight away with: **miss u 2 x**

I place my phone on my dressing table and leave for school.

When I get home, Mum is sitting at the kitchen table painting doorknobs with her best friend Jackie, who has a laugh like a gurgling plug-hole because she smokes 10,000 cigarettes a day. Jackie carries a beaten-up biscuit tin of weed around with her like it's a treasure chest and drinks tea after tea. I still have my school bag koala-clamped to my back.

'I'm going upstairs.'

'Your friend Lowe's called – more than once,' Mum says.

And I get that same giddy rush I always do when he calls. When I hear his name. Relief.

'Ooo, who's Lowe?' Jackie's ears prick up. 'Your *boyfriend*?'

'NO!' I blush. 'Gross, no.'

Me, in my mind: *yes, we are married with three kids etc.*

His mobile is dead.

His housephone, occupied.

I text him. No reply.

I sit by the phone and wait. And wait and wait. I practically chop off Violet's arm when she tries to use the phone to call her irritating friend Katrin who always speaks in a fake American accent. I eat a satsuma. I pick at the wall. I draw stars and eyes all over my day planner. I do ten sit-ups and then read out the ingredients on the back of the air freshener like I'm the voice-over for an advert. If I make one mistake, I have to restart again from the top or else Lowe will never speak to me ever again.

The phone rings.

'Hello?' There's breathing. A crackle down the line. But not much else. *Is it him?* 'Lowe?'

More silence. 'Is everything OK? Are you OK?'

'My mum's died.'

Stone. Cold. Silence.

He breathes. ' . . . she's been sick for a while and she . . . yeah . . . she died this afternoon.'

I try to speak but nothing comes out.

I should probably say something but I don't know what to say. I am not *trained* in this kind of thing. I didn't even know his mum was ill! He barely spoke about his family. A wave of freezing cold needles sucks me under, spits me out – hot all over – and it all makes sense: the quietness, the constant need to get home . . . of course, his offness was never anything to do with me. It never is when someone is going through something hard.

What the hell do I say? Where do I start?

'I'm here,' I say, somehow. Because it's true. And it's kind. I *think*? I say it again. 'I'm here.'

And he lets himself cry. I can tell how hot and wet his face is from tears, every cell puffed up and sore from crying. He clears his throat, straightening his voice to be practical. 'Will you come with me to the funeral?'

'Of course I will.'

I'm taken aback that he's even asked me.

'I'm so sorry, Lowe,' I add because I mean it.

When all I want to say is: *I LOVE YOU. I LOVE YOU. I LOVE YOU.*

I take the day off school. I don't even own anything black so I have to wear one of Mum's linen dresses with a belt that makes me feel like I'm one pair of wedges away from looking for love later in life in Marbella. Because I own no smart black shoes, I have to borrow my neighbour's great-niece from Birmingham's spare pair of black work heels. Soak up that sentence.

At the funeral, the first thing Lowe points out are the borrowed shoes on my feet.

'Are they *your* shoes?' he asks, accusingly. I didn't think he noticed stuff like clothes.

'Yeah,' I lie. I don't want him to know I'm wearing my neighbour's great-niece from Birmingham's work shoes to his mum's funeral.

Whereas Lowe wears the sort of stuff he always wears. An old holey blue washed-out Fruit of the Loom hoodie. Beaten up Reebok Classics. His eyes are pale and watery, the rings around them dark and deep.

At the service, I'm totally out of my depth. I remain on standby, like a guard or a solider. I'm on duty. But I'm not sure what my tasks are. The polished floor is so slippery under the soles of the heels that every working muscle in my entire body is activated so I don't trip. I'm surrounded by faces I'd never met. Why the hell am I here? I have no place here. This is an almighty privilege that I have not earnt.

Lowe's aunts stand to talk. His mum's sisters: one older, one younger. They have the same sparkly eyes and big smile as Lowe. The three used to share a room as children and tell a story about finding their mum's diary, which she used to write in code as a kid. When they finally cracked the code, all it said was, HELLO, WITCHES. THIS IS NOT MY REAL DIARY. DO YOU REALLY THINK I'D LEAVE IT OUT SO YOU TWO COULD READ IT? HA. HA. HA. LOVE YOU. And the whole room managed to laugh at that, the atmosphere breaking, like that sentiment was an insight into the type of person Lowe's mum was: warm, playful, always one step ahead.

When Lowe stands to read, this was something I was not expecting at all. He holds a small sheet of handwritten paper, his other hand in the back pocket of his jeans. Bob Dylan lyrics

I'm guessing, from what I can recognize, maybe a song I've heard him singing to himself before – but he doesn't say specifically because this is not a presentation or performance. Lowe reads casually, calmly, holding his nerve, his voice almost breaking but then rolling down like waves. He's speaking only to his mum; the words are for her, not for us. He forgets we're even here watching him. *How* is he doing this? How are these words coming out of his mouth? And this just makes me respect him, admire him, love him even more than I already do. I stand at the back but within Lowe's eye-line, and watch the love of my life become a little boy and a man at the same time.

At the burial I find him between the shoulders of strangers. He can't see me but I can see him. That's my only job. To look out for him: my target. He puts his handwritten reading with her, even though I wish she could be with him, by his side, hugging him, saying it will be alright.

How on earth did he deal with his mum's illness without telling us, without talking about it? Without siblings? All those calls and letters. And me bitching about how much I hate my parents. Saying I wished I was an orphan! And he was going through such pain and this slow ripping, this terrifying, awful, painful shock. I was so selfish and naive. *I'm so sorry, Lowe. I'm so sorry.*

And when people begin to filter away, when it feels OK to, I rush towards him and hug him the tightest I possibly can.

There are a few close family members invited back to his house on Orchard Road. We take our time, stagger back on our own, down the backroads, under the buds of magnolias, away from the people he doesn't have the energy to say hi to. I'm not used to wearing these painful heels or the clicky noise they make along the pavement, which might be distracting and irritating for Lowe, so I kick them off and walk barefoot. We hold hands. A V of white birds take off into the sky. Lowe takes out a rollie from his hoodie pocket and smokes it. We don't talk. But I feel like

I should say something. *I'm sorry* again. Or *thank you for letting me be here with you.* Or that I'm proud of him, that he did so well today, but *how can you do 'so well' at a funeral?* Everything seems a *not OK* thing to say given the circumstances, so I just walk and try to say everything I can with my hand in his. I trace the word SORRY and I LOVE YOU in his palm with my thumb.

Please let me take care of you. I would do such a good job.

Today, he doesn't even bother trying to hide the cigarette smell like he usually does in front of his dad. He doesn't stop to buy gum at the shops.

Back at his manicured, restrained, all-clean house I see a printed-out photograph stuck on the wall of the most beautiful woman I have ever seen. His mum. He wants to head straight up to his room, not even stopping to say hello or kick off his shoes. I follow his lead, away from the flowers in the kitchen; adults talking; plates of food, wine and coffee. There are some cards for Lowe by his bedroom door, offerings, which he collects – neutrally – like post. We make our way inside.

Lowe and I sit in his bedroom in the quiet. There is nothing like being in the bedroom of someone you're in love with. Like the rest of the house, it's painted white and practical: shelves and drawers with books and games. Some I recognise from our own shelves at home; I live for these crossovers in our upbringing. One of those metal grip strengthening gadgets boys seem to love. Just right. We say nothing. Lowe gently plays his guitar. He's got so good. I'm transfixed by his hands. And how I wish I was the body of that instrument, being held so close to him.

I watch him play, until it gets dark, when the two cats come purring in through the gap in the door – classy intelligent cats with healthy fluffy bushy tails and leathered polished paws and shining understanding eyes, a mother and a son. *A mother and a son.* Cats that pad around with such sympathetic wisdom like they know *everything.* Even the son cat who Lowe tells me is usually playful and boisterous is totally placid and submissive. They lie either side of Lowe's lap, letting him know that they are here and that they love him. I've never seen animals be so intuitive in real life – like Beatrix Potter animals. It moves me to tears.

Lowe places his guitar down and buries his face into their fur. And I kneel down next to him in the quiet. We both lie into the cat's bellies, like they're pillows. We stare into each other's eyes for what seems like forever. And we say nothing. Just look. Our faces are so close; if we were ever going to kiss, this would be the moment – this would be when the shooting star would explode over his rooftop and rain down magic over us . . . but it isn't right. Not tonight, here in the darkness, as deep and as bittersweet as liquorice.

I lie on the little sofa opposite, in the dress I wore to the funeral. Lowe on his bed. Our hearts are tin cans, a string between us, like old-fashioned walkie-talkies. We speak, but we don't say a word.

When I get home I find Mum in the living room with the TV on low. She never watches TV. She's just sitting there, like she's been waiting for me to come home. I've never been so happy to see her.

'How was it?' she asks.

'Sad,' is all I can think of.

'Poor baby – he's too young to lose his mama.'

'I know.' I kick the borrowed shoes off and hug my knees.

'Nice of you to go. Make sure you look out for him.'

I make Mum a cup of tea and place it on the floor by the foot of the sofa.

'Thank you, Elliebellie. I love you.'

'I love you too, Mum.'

I sit down beside her; both of us cross our legs, hold our mugs with our left hand, smile at the same bits. I am so lucky to have parents I love and to be loved.

Then Mum says, 'Can't imagine if I died.'

'God, make it about yourself then, *jeez*.'

Chapter 16

The funeral changes me. I will take it with me for life. I've never felt death so nearby. I've never trodden so close to the edge of my own mortality either, not even that time those girls called me an emo (I'm a GRUNGER – big difference) and tried to mug me and all they found on my person was an opened unused Super Plus tampon covered in leaky pen ink and crisp crumbs. Or even when I went to that blackhole waterslide in the depths of Penge that urban legends said they put blades inside to slash our arms.

And it changes things for Lowe and me too – and, I'm worried, not in a good way.

He's gone back to being quiet. He hardly calls; he only texts back if I text him more than once and he's never first to message. I'm not expecting anything but it's strange. I replay the funeral in my mind, afterwards at his house. I'm left insecure about it. Was I too much? Was I not enough?

'What are you doing at the weekend?' I ask him at the end of an awkward call.

'Think we're going riding.'

'Cool.'

Sometimes Lowe and these other rider boys he hangs out with go on day-trips to foresty places out of London with trails and pump tracks where they can ride their bikes and forget. These places to me seem as distant and fantastical as Narnia. We hover on the common, killing time until they return, like fisherman's wives. They always come back eventually. Muddy, cold, wet into our arms.

But this time, they don't.

'Call them again!' Bianca orders, but none of us have any phone credit or coins for the phone box. We go to The Twins' house, set up base camp and ping off their mobiles from there. No answer. We eventually wave the white flag and squeeze into The Twins' tiny baby-girl pyjamas, raid the snack cupboard and watch *Cribs*. We learn that they've been hanging out with a new gang – another boy and these two girls and they do *drugs*, which I'd never done and don't want to either. Apparently, one of the girls has a giant house with a pool, an only child raised by her au pair – *typical*. Oh, so that's where they've been; the plot thickens.

The BMX boys invite the new gang to the common one afternoon and we all look the two girls up and down, unable to see what *they* see. Looking for every micro detail, *evidence* of why they are clearly, obviously the devil, split in half and shoved into pedal pushers. For starters, why do they hang around in this little threesome with this stoned guy? Is he their *pimp*? It's odd but – *drugs*?

The guy says, 'Do you have any weed?'

'Sorry, I don't smoke,' I answer politely.

'Pills?'

'I do have *Smints* somewhere.' I pat my pockets.

The girl with the pool has a best friend called Megan; she's a bit older than us, greasy and rude with a real actual weekday job at the front desk of a Holiday Inn, and she is a slimy serpent. She shakes a bag of little white pills and that's all it takes – Lowe is off with her, getting fucked up in the big house. This is where he can escape to a dark place I don't and can't understand. A locked part of him that I will never find a key for. And I didn't get an invite.

I can't take it any more.

'Have you kissed that druggy Megan?' I ask him, in a tone only my mother would use.

'No!' But there's a smile to his voice. Sickening.

'So what, do you like *love* drugs now?' I make sure to sound as judgmental as possible.

'No, I don't *love* drugs. I've *tried* drugs, that's all.'

'Well, I feel like because you think I'm – you know – *anti*-drugs' – OK, I'm making myself sound like I camp outside the Houses of Parliament with anti-drug flags – 'well, I'm not like *anti*-drugs but yeah, I do think they're the worst thing on the planet. Anyway, I feel like you're, like, leaving me out.'

'I just know you don't like them, Ella, so I'm trying to be respectful by not rubbing it in your face.'

'Being respectful would be not doing them because they're dangerous.' *And I have future life plans for us so could do without you depreciating your insides as I really don't want to be a widow and die alone.* 'People like *die* and stuff.'

'You think it's worse than it is; it's not like that baby scene in *Trainspotting*. Look, why don't you come hang with us one time?' No, not *hang*. 'You don't have to do anything. Megan's friend's got a heated pool, innit, so just bring your swimming costume or whatever?'

Innit, <u>really</u>?

'Hm. I reckon I'll be busy.'

This is mostly because I don't want anybody to see me in a bikini.

'I haven't even said when yet?'

'I already know I'll be busy, ta.'

Dad has moved from Brian's and has his own place – a one bed next to Brixton prison: 'But at least I'm not inside it, am I right, kids?' he jokes. 'Safest place in the world here – gotta be pretty stupid to commit a crime outside a prison now, dontchu?' He thumbs-up at his neighbours behind the barred windows; one thumbs-up back.

Violet thinks Dad's seeing someone: 'Cos, not being funny, unless Dad's wearing knickers these days, there are lacies in the laundry basket.' I feel sick. 'Sexy ones.'

'Violet!'

'Dad, man, what a rascal.' Violet shakes her head cheekily, teeth clattering on the lolly of her Strawberry Dip Dab.

Later, when we're tucked up on the pull-out sofa in Dad's bare sitting room, with nothing to do except sleep and David Attenborough is soothingly murmuring about whales in the background, I try to talk the situation through with my little sister (well, as much as you can with a thirteen-year-old who devotes their entire purpose on the planet to experimenting with how many different types of treat they can dip into a chocolate fountain with a skewer – that is her entire life). But I've got no other options. I can't talk to any of my friends about Lowe being off with me because then the love rumour mill will once again grind.

'Sounds to me like he's got himself a girlfriend,' Violet says, matter of fact.

'A _girlfriend_? How did I miss this?'

I am HORRIFIED.

'Take a hint, Ella. He invited you to his mum's funeral to be his friend, not to be his wife. Stop making it about yourself and move on.'

What she's asking of me is genuinely impossible. '_How?_'

'Just go and get a boyfriend of your own, _duh_?'

Violet's right. Why am I sitting around waiting for Lowe to fall in love with me? I need to get out there. I need to headhunt a side-lover project of my own.

*

One day, whilst eating untoasted Scotch pancakes by the fridge at Aoife's, I spot the logo for Lowe's school poking out of the recycling bin.

'What is that?' I say, pointing, my heart stopping.

'Oh, it's a prospectus, I think.'

WHAT?

'You're not moving schools, are you?' I accuse in an mix of jealousy, sadness and fear. It's hypocritical as I've been waiting to show Mum the prospectus for a Performing Arts School with a strand in stage and screen writing. But I know Mum will say no. And even then, it's unlikely I'll get in.

'No! It's for my brother Sean.'

'Phew. Bring it out then – share the wealth.'

We fish out the glossy magazine; it smells like holiday brochures. We flick the pages, admiring the building and its grandeur, its expansive grounds and not-from-the-Eighties computers.

'It looks far more epic than our old-fashioned cruddy school and *way* cooler,' I say.

'Well, there are boys for a start . . . '

Aoife leans over my shoulder, admiring the goods, chewing her raw pancake in my ear.

'*Loads* of *boys*.' I'm impressed.

Why, this thing is like a catalogue for boyfriends! How do I subscribe? No photos of Lowe unfortunately, but there are secret fit people we haven't yet been introduced to. Why is Lowe being so closeted about these potential suitors? There's a photo in a science lab, a double page spread: two boys are measuring some liquid from a conical flask into a test tube over a Bunsen burner. And I just get this feeling. I prod the photo, like choosing a kitchen appliance in a magazine.

'He's hot!' I point to the one on the left.

'He's wearing safety goggles. You can't even see his face, Elbow!'

Seeing as I fancy the helmets of Daft Punk, this view is generous.

'Yes, but look at his hands and his *way*. Trust me, Aoife – he's fit.'

As a last resort I *could* ask Mia but we've not spoken in a while so Aoife makes us hot Ribena and I get busy. Within an hour I've done my research. The Twins knew the guy from primary school; his name is Christopher. He works at the garden centre near Shreya's where their mum drags them. Good start – mature *and* reliable – meaning he might have enough money to buy me an H. Samuel heart locket one day. Shreya joins the three-way call to confirm that she doesn't know a Christopher but her cousin used to date someone who used to work at the same garden centre. This is a risk because people will know pretty quickly that I was *asking about* Christopher but it's a risk I'm willing to take right now. Twenty minutes later, we confirm that Christopher is indeed, 'safe, sane and single' and as tasty as a Gregg's Yum Yum.

Eek, this is IT!

That evening, I can't wait to speak to Lowe and ask him to set me up with this Christopher. This is the most exciting bit. Lowe is a bit taken aback.

'I dunno . . . ' His voice breaks down the receiver. 'Well, he *rollerblades* for one.'

'Lowe, you can't not set me up with a guy because you hate rollerblading.'

'I don't really know him that well.'

'Well, can't you *get* to know him?' I demand.

Lowe *does* do a good job of getting to know Christopher; they go for bike rides and play guitar together. But he also does a really good job of keeping us apart. It's like he wants this Christopher guy for himself!

Enough is enough! Us lot are forced to take it upon ourselves to go on a *little* day-trip down to the garden centre near Shreya's house to take a *look* (spy) at all the plants (boys). We all go, Aoife, The Twins, Shreya, Bianca and I (Ronks is at ballet), strolling into the outdoor, open air centre like it's absolutely nothing, like it's a no-big-deal normal day in our life to be shopping for bamboo screens, herb gardens, olive trees and trowels with about £1.50 between us. Trust Bianca to turn up *disguised* as a recent widow looking for a shovel to bury her late millionaire husband. Her eyes peer over huge sunglasses as she sashays past the bird baths and naked chubby cherub statues, hunting for Christopher.

'Flippity Hell – there he is!' Shreya screeches, SO LOUDLY, fingers digging into my shoulders.

'Who?' I ask, forgetting completely that I'm meant to be on a quest of fancying someone, secretly sad it's not Lowe, who's definitely off with oily Megan taking ecstasy.

'Duh! *Christopher*!'

Oh, I'll show you ecstasy alright, my friend.

'My God, he's so hot in real life,' Bianca gasps. 'He looks like Will Smith.'

Aoife sighs adoringly. 'Fressssshhhhhh Prinnncccee . . .'

He's wearing an oversized green sweater with the garden centre's logo, baggy jeans, quite cool trainers and a beanie hat. FUCK he's looking right at us. QUICK!

Shit. Shit. Shit. We all duck down behind some potted wheaty shrubs. Another guy, a little older but also FIT as HELL who looks ish-like Johnny Depp in the pony-tail days, in the same green top as Christopher but the polo shirt version, throws us a look and we hid – badly – again. They confer and then walk towards us.

'Hey.' Christopher smiles in that way you know means someone knows who you are, without saying it, like he was expecting this visit.

Shrey steps forward, does the small talk. 'This is Ella,' she says, shoving me forward, towards a cherry blossom and a stack of paving slabs.

'I'm Christopher . . . ' He sticks his hand out. Formal.

'She knows *exactly* who you areeeee! Don't you, Ella?'

Fuck off, Bianca.

'Err . . . how's your day?' I say, not knowing what else to really ask.

'Working?' he offers. Lifting all that soil. Pricing up them pots. Scattering . . . *woodchips?* . . . *How fit.*

'Awesome,' I say like a doughnut.

'Do you wrap up Christmas trees in those nets?' Bianca asks drunkenly, even though she's not drunk, like it's an innuendo, but she's not smart enough to think of one. This reminds me of the time she once tried to tell us that the plastic casing around a Peperami was a used condom.

'Errr . . . sometimes,' Christopher says suspiciously. 'In the month of *December?*'

'Maybe *Christ*mas will come early this year?' she giggles. OK, that was better.

'OK.' Christopher shrugs.

Bianca backs into a display of giant cacti, and Christopher warns, 'Be careful, those are spiky.'

'Would you like to get *spiked* Ella?' Bianca blurts and then laughs in our faces in that annoying way she does, nudging me with ZERO subtlety.

And Christopher gives it away, makes it very clear he knows I've had my eye on him, that the little birdies have been talking. The others go off to distract the manager, 'buying' packets of seeds. And within minutes Christopher and I are behind a shed, next to the Bleeding Hearts, kissing. He could have picked a nicer spot – the rose garden or those lemon trees but I appreciate him not taking me *inside* the shed where I might feel intimidated. His hands on my hips. His kiss attentive. The sound of a water feature bubbling behind us. The occasional waft of fresh manure.

And I think about Lowe. I imagine him – held hostage – Megan straddling him confidently, gyrating *aggressively*, with a mortar and pestle grind and I wish I could get her horrible fanny juice essence out of my mind. Even though I know he's probably loving it. Gag.

'So . . . ' Christopher says. 'Do you want to like . . . see how this goes?'

'Yeah,' I say. 'That would be cool.'

Cool.

K. Cool.

So it might not be Lowe but finally, it's happened to me: I have a boyfriend. And he isn't a weirdo. Or a pervert. Or a horse. Or imaginary. Or thirty-five.

And I wish I could just run away right then and tell everyone, but I have to hold it down because the girls are being ushered to the till-point by the manager, wheelbarrows loaded with hundreds of pounds worth of soil, plants and tools. When they see me – trusting the kiss has taken place – they say to the cashier, 'actually we're OK.' Dumping the barrows and running out.

Christopher waves. His friend, hands in pockets, gazes at us in that stoner way.

'Can't believe his friend didn't try it with me!' shouts Bianca fuming, and shouts, 'THANKS FOR NOTHING!'

EVERYONE is very happy and proud of me. It's like I've won some kind of trophy. Getting a boyfriend (pending) is like a thing for us *all*! It's like scoring a goal for your football team! Why everybody isn't throwing me up on their shoulders or giving me the birthday bumps, I don't know. I feel very grown-up, like I should be able to touch-type, ride the Underground, have an electric toothbrush. *Oh, you know what adult life is like? Bills, bills, bills.*

From then onwards I become so annoying. I like dropping Christopher's name into conversation: 'Let me check with Christopher', I gloat, even though there's absolutely nothing to check in with Christopher about. Having a boyfriend (pending) means I am on the radar with cool girls in school. They invite me to their coffee mornings at Starbucks. Isobel Chaser invites me to a Games Night at her house where all the boyfriends come and they get drunk and pretend they know how to play poker. I hear the last one got a bit *wild*, that they raided Isobel's dad's whiskey collection and refilled the empty bottles with cold tea. That they snuck into rooms and worked their way up the bases. It's a hard balance to strike: you have to hope you don't go too far and yet keep up with the pack. Ideally everyone in a friendship group gets fingered as the clock strikes the exact same hour but you can't always plan these things – it really is a game of trust and good faith.

'Oh, and bring Christopher,' she orders, turning away, like it's as simple as that.

Aoife looks at me as if I'm joining a suicide pact. 'You're not gonna go to *that*, are you?'

Course I'm not. I obviously don't want to *actually* drink coffee or hard alcohol or get fingered in real life!

'Maybe, but I'll check with Christopher,' I say.

How punchable am I?

Me getting a boyfriend (pending) is, I can only assume, the reason Lowe is off with me. He's abrasive. Moody. Can't he just be happy for me that I've pretty much settled down? He texts me one word answers, doesn't call me back. Sometimes he phones just to show me he's grumpy, in case I hadn't noticed. When I ask, 'Do you want to talk about your mum?' he says, 'No,' in the same tone I would use to tell my parents to 'piss off!' I say, 'I'm always here for you.'

And he says, 'K.'

You started it, Lowe! You were the one that started hanging out with a girl who wasn't me, do you think I WANT to be gathering emergency boyfriends like this?

Maybe I have to give him his space?

He says, suddenly, 'There's this girl, Saskia, in my art class who likes me apparently.'

I'm like, 'COOL.' WHATEVS.

'When she's eighteen, she's gonna get her clit pierced,' he says/ threatens.

Idiot. Don't act like you know where a clit is, Lowe. You can't even pin a tail on the bloody donkey. Fool.

'Great,' I reply. 'Good for Saskia.'

I haven't quite located my own clit yet but I assure you that once I do, there is no way in hell I am messing around with that precious pearl of nerves.

What can I pierce that will be cool and isn't going to hurt? A fingernail? Do people pierce their hair?

'What about druggy Megan?' I ask.

'What? *Who?*'

'I thought SHE was your girlfriend?'

'Ha. No.'

Don't HA me. I've gone out of my way to get a boyfriend here and he was single all along?

'I might invite Christopher over at the weekend,' I bait to make him jealous, to get him back for Saskia's clit-piercing plans, but then I reverse that hard work by adding, 'Come if you want?', really hoping he says yes. The way I'm always hoping he says yes. What I'd really like is for Lowe to say yes to coming to my house and Christopher to just not show up. That would be ideal.

'Christopher?' He cracks up, laughing *at* me, not with me.

'*What?* What's so funny?'

'He prefers *Chris.*'

It has become *that* pedantic. So, they're still hanging out, then. This is an uncomfortable cross of boundaries. We're two children fighting over the ragdoll of poor, sweet Christopher, Chris, using him as a pawn. A third party has got involved in our duel and we can't deal with it. Like, will Christopher pick a *side*? And what was Christopher saying about me to Lowe? Would he tell him if I was a good kisser?

'Well, *I* call him Christopher,' I defend defiantly.

'Whatever. You guys aren't serious anyway.'

I'm SORRY *what*?

This stings because it's true. Christopher and I haven't spoken on the phone *once*; we don't even really text. We haven't even kissed since that time at the garden centre and he was bored and possibly stoned. Now I think about it, I don't even know his surname.

Still, Christopher and Lowe plan to come to my house, together. I organize a house clean-up faster than any sixty-minute makeover you've seen on TV. I use a whole can of air freshener. Hurtle bleach around like salt to ward off bad spirits. My cleaning style: *rabid*. Nonsensical. Stuffing, scrambling, shoving stuff into cupboards, under beds, high up. Hoping they'll see 251 as shabby-chic, bohemian, *Takeshi's Castle* instead of a gothic death-trap. Rusty nails that stick out like werewolf claws: fun! Exposed live wires and pipes to trip on: thrilling! All snares, obstacles, for newcomers to confront, to earn respect, before Mum will even *consider* taking them seriously.

I'm more excited that Lowe is here. And we all know it. It's as obvious as the grass being green. Lowe, however, has come – it seems – purely to be a watchdog. Not that Christopher and I need watching.

'Woah, your house is so sick – it looks like the house in *Fight Club*!' People always gawp at our house like it's a museum, forgetting we have to *live* here. Christopher buys me a graffiti pen as a no-reason gift, *adorable*. Then the BOYS come to my room. The walls and furniture will be gossiping about *this* for weeks, losing their minds that the guy they've seen me dream about or lose sleep over is now here. I watch Lowe admiring my magazine cut-outs and posters, my photos of friends pinned to my noticeboard and silly ornaments on the shelves. *What does he think of me? Why isn't he SAYING anything?* We take turns to tag my wardrobe with the pen.

When Mum gets home she is excited by the arrival of 'strapping young lads!' And instantly, after taxing them for weed, sends them out to work on the garden with its upturned broken plastic chairs and metal barbed wire, broken glass and fox poo. Christopher is given the task of mowing the overgrown grass. I watch him, chugging away, working up a sweat, smiling, and for a second Lowe isn't the only person in the entire world I focus on. He sort of moves into the background a little bit and – for once – I'm able to *see* someone who isn't him. Perhaps it *is* possible that I could like boys who aren't Lowe. It's some sort of light at the end of a tunnel.

But my thoughts are broken as Christopher accidently catches a frog in the violent whirring jaw of the mower. 'OH SHIT! I am SO sorry!' he yelps. He shouldn't be the one apologizing.

I feel so bad for him, dark frog's blood spluttering down his light-blue jeans. The young boy in his face seems to jump out like a scare on a ghost train. It really isn't his fault; our garden is just such a mess we didn't even know we *had* frogs. 'That's not our frog,' I say, trying to make him feel better, but Mum acts like a disappointed zookeeper, like he now owes her compensation for the murdered amphibian. That will be a new unwanted core memory for poor Christopher. I look at Lowe like *oh, fuck off.*

The next day I text to check in, to see if the frog's blood came out of his jeans, and Christopher doesn't reply for ages. When he finally does, he says:

Soz ran out of credit. Blood came out. Thx. x

Even in the short lived hundredish hours of our small relationship, I know something is up. I pluck up the courage to call him.

His older brother answers and says, 'Chris' – oh, shit, it *is* Chris – 'it's some girl for you.'

I'm not *some* girl. I'm his *sweetheart.*

I ask, 'Is everything OK?'

He says, ' . . . Er.'

'Is it about the frog?'

'No, it's nothing to do with the frog.'

'So what's up?'

'I'm gonna step away if that's cool.'

Silence.

'OK,' I say.

Annoyingly, this is only making him fitter. Damn.

'I don't think it's working.'

Ouch. OK. I replay the day at my house in my head. All I see is Lowe. And the frog. I can't even picture Christopher; it's like he wasn't even there.

'No worries,' I say.

I can't work out if I just got dumped or not. I reckon I probably did. Which is annoying because now I just fancy him more.

Before I start work on my debut non-fiction on romantic relationships, *The Rejection is the Connection*, I should probably start sharing the news.

Lowe's dad answers. I don't even have to say it's me.

'LOWE!' he bellows and I wait, going over the minor details of my publicity spin as to why Christopher and I broke up. Do it like *Dawson's Creek*; they always know how to break up properly. Big words help. No words are better but I am not good at that.

'Hey.' He sounds breathless, like he ran for the phone. 'How are you?'

'Good . . . considering . . . ' I add, referring to my recent break-up, but he doesn't bite. 'You?'

'Cool,' he replies.

'So . . . ' I begin. 'Unfortunately, due to unforeseen circumstances – I mean you've probably heard; I'm sure the rumours are already spreading, given we were couple of the year – but Christopher and I have sadly decided to call it a day and go our separate ways. We really gave it everything we could but ultimately . . . we decided we're better off as friends.'

' . . . '

'Hello? Are you there?'

'Yeah, Chris said,' Lowe replies.

'What did he say?' *Did he mention that you and I are obviously in love, Lowe? That we'd make such a cute couple? <u>Did</u> he? And are you going to do something about that or no?*

'That you're just going to be friends.'

'Oh.'

'I mean, you guys were never really going out in the first place were you, so . . . '

'He bought me a marker pen.'

Stone. Cold. Silence.

That night I'm crying like I've broken up – not with Christopher at all – but with Lowe. I find myself beating my wardrobe up with a coat hanger so I'm clearly a girl on the brink. Violet walks in like . . . O . . . K.

'I know, I know I'm mad,' I howl. 'But I can't help it; this is what love does to you!' I push my finger at my temple like they do on TV and twist it like a screwdriver.

But there's only so much sliding down a wall into a crying heap to Britney's 'I'm Not a Girl, Not Yet a Woman' one can do. I've had enough of feeling so helpless.

I dig out the application form and apply for a place at the

performing arts school, stapling some of my writing to the entry form just like Mum did. One of my poems is about an old couple in love and their letters have been found by their great-grand-children. For authenticity, I've scrunched up the paper, stained it with teabags and burnt the sides with a lighter so it looks like it's from the olden days. Then, using one of the stamps I *had* saved for a letter to Lowe, I post it. Deciding I'll only tell Mum if I get an interview so she can't say no.

Once home, I say to myself, you know what will really help ease my chaotic mind? Redesigning my bedroom! New Bedroom means New Me. I put on Incubus and use my rage and sadness to shove the bed with my whole body weight. *CLANG*. I drag the furniture. BASH. The tips of my fingers white, red face melting in crying grunts until everything has been reconfigured. It looks utterly *sick*. Not that functional given that the bed is in the centre of the room and I can't quite open the door, but still, sick.

'MUUUUMMMM! COME LOOK AT MY NEW ROOM!'

I mean this is all far more healthy than chopping myself an anxious fringe.

And then it twigs. Wait, what's all this crying about?

So long as Saskia from art class is kept at bay, Lowe and I are single at the same time.

Beautiful, endless, rolling fields, open arms and flowing water, time stops and it's all ours . . .

Chapter 17

And it *is* all ours.

Lowe and I spend the summer back to back, side by side, sun on our skin, grazing away hours, sharing headphones and chatting shit. I'm certain I've failed my exams because I didn't know a single answer to any question. My only knowledge is pointless facts about Lowe Archer – unsurprisingly really, given that I've dedicated the past two years of my life to studying him, like a rare species I've discovered. But it's OK, because I smashed the interview at the Performing Arts School by talking 'passionately' about song lyrics being poetry, the beauty of radio, the wonder of everyday storytelling, conversation, making up plays with your siblings. How everything begins with a story . . .

Anyway, Mum's not mad. Mum's cool. Because Mum's met someone.

Mum towers over Ears, Nose and Throat doctor Adam, who wears fish-finger beige V-neck jumpers and has 14,000 degrees in every form of science you can imagine. He's the sort of person who does online IQ tests for LOLs. He can't get enough of the falling apart house and the wild garden. He doesn't have kids himself so his head is pretty much wrinkleless.

Once, when turning down a second bottle of beer, *just in case*, I hear him joke, 'No need for drugs and booze in this house! Every moment is a trip.'

I see my family as Adam probably does: psychedelic Austin Powers' extras, dancing in orange platforms, combusting into sunflowers. He watches on, gripped to the couch, tripping, in his mustard corduroy.

'Ha,' I reply. And we all know what 'Ha' means. It means *no offence but please stop talking.*

Adam takes Mum to lovely restaurants and wine bars. It's weird seeing Mum in a dress. They go to Paris for the weekend. When he buys me an iPod and the house a solar panel espresso machine and two Weimaraners, I realize neither he nor these great big hounds are going anywhere any time soon. I want to challenge Mum on this shift, given that it contradicts all of her morals but I instead use her good mood to my advantage and am allowed to attend the Performing Arts College – 'so long as it's free' warns Mum, which it is.

Both Lowe and I are moving schools for Sixth Form and on a night call our nerves are clearly showing.

I ask, 'Do you reckon everybody at college will have, like . . . *you know?*'

' . . . What?' We've never spoken about sex before. But it's ten o'clock on a Friday night and I'm a sixteen-year-old with everything to lose.

'You *know* . . . '

I laugh and he laughs and I laugh and *oh we're so funny.* 'Lost their *virginity?*' I whisper into the phone so my stupid family don't hear.

'Doubt it!' Lowe says reassuringly.

There is an awkward beat. My heart, pounding. I'm listening so hard I hear sparks of magic.

He asks, ' . . . Why, have . . . *you* . . . ?'

'Why? Have *you?*' I tell myself he hasn't.

'I asked first,' he says.

'OK, let's both say after the count of three . . . '

'Haha, OK . . . ' He laughs; I consider lying.

'Three, two, one . . . '

'No!'

We both cackle with laughter. I laugh because I'm relieved. That it isn't just me, yes, but also that he still is, so much so that I say with way too much gusto, 'LOL! We should make an agreement that if we haven't lost our virginities to anyone by the time we're eighteen, we should lose it to each other.' But I make sure I laugh loads so it means it could be a joke. 'AHAHAHA!'

'Ummm . . . OK.' Lowe breathes deeply into the mouthpiece. He isn't laughing.

Something *stirs*. And I wanted to reach my eighteenth birthday totally preserved, having not a finger on me. A handful of fresh snow.

We hold the line. *Why wait?*

I get hot and bothered and do a stress yawn. 'Aw, K, well, I should probably be getting to bed . . . ' even though I'm absolutely wired; my blood is on cocaine after that steamy exchange. We say goodnight and hang up.

When I turn around, Violet's Furby is staring at me with those awful crazy eyes Furbies have and Yes I Will Be Telling My Master All About Your Disgusting Conversation. I do the right thing and take out its batteries.

On the limbs of a bright shining silver star, I make a wish. I ask the star to *please* let Lowe love me back. Please let him feel the same way about me. Please don't put me through all of this for no reason. I stare into the star so hard I don't blink once; my eyes water. A tear streaks down my face – oh, this is *dramatic as fuck, perfect*. Then, because I've seen the film *The Craft* once, I utter, *light as a feather, stiff as a board,* and it feels right at this point to burn something to make it ceremoniously witchy. To *close* the spell. So I write Lowe's name on the back of a Domino's Pizza flyer using one of those tiny blue Argos pens and set it alight using the little box of matches I'm allowed for my incense. It burns up into a hypnotic technicolour flame, *shit, shit, shit,* it contorts, until I have to stomp it out. It crumbles into ash, and I have to kick and blow the grey shreds towards the fireplace. I'm not sure the star is going to even *receive* let alone *accept* that wish.

I dream of us living in the map house I drew, doing normal life stuff – making toast, lifting our feet so the other can hoover, reaching my hand out of the window, picking fresh fruit from the trees.

Chapter 18

Now

Aoife and I are on the way to a KTPLT party – one of the few times Jackson has said it's OK for us to come, a chance for me to network and meet commissioners who might need a writer. Jackson suggested inviting Aoife to keep me company in case the networking doesn't happen. He knows how uncomfortable it makes me but he has to *mingle* and doesn't want me to stand around on my own. There's no way I could invite Aoife without inviting Bianca too. I'd invite Ronke too if she wasn't getting ready to push a baby out. Jackson says, 'So long as Bianca behaves herself.' I mean, I can't make promises but I do know that Aoife and Bianca are both people you can trust to leave in a room with anyone and they will make friends. Plus, these parties can sometimes be quite fun. Canapes and fancy cocktails.

I'm *meant* to not be drinking. I've done eighteen days. My longest stretch as an adult. But now I'm worried about telling Aoife and Bianca. I don't want to dampen the night. I want them to drink freely, have a good time and enjoy the free drinks without worrying that I'm judging them – as if I would – or ask me why I'm not drinking. Maybe I can sip tonic water and *pretend* it's got gin in it?

I'm overthinking it. They're my friends – I'll just see how the night goes; if I fancy one, I'll drink, intuitively. I've proven to myself that I'm not reliant on alcohol and that I can quit anytime I want. It's about cutting *down*, not cutting out completely.

'When did East London get so *desirable*?' I ask. It's been a good while since I've ventured out of South London to go *out* out and to be honest, well, I'm shocked.

'Remember how nobody wanted to come to ours in Brixton because it was so apparently *dodgy*? And now those same people are buying there,' Aoife replies.

'I wouldn't even be able to afford a studio on Palace Road these days.'

'Peckham's next; everyone wants to live there.'

'I don't believe it.'

There's a small queue of people wearing expensive clothes outside a tall brick building – some exclusive members' club they keep hidden from the general public. A doorperson wearing black lipstick, a bullring nose piercing and dyed pink braids ticks off names on a clipboard.

Aoife looks down at her ASOS dress. 'Everyone's so cool around here. I'm so basic.'

'You're like a beautiful bag of ready salted crisps that when you open the bag, the flavour is actually something surprisingly twisted like Squirrel and Paprika,' I joke.

'Thanks.' Aoife nods like that's given her confidence.

We head inside. Polished concrete and rich-smelling candles. We take the lift to the fifth floor, checking our make-up in the mirrored panels.

It's open-plan: trendy media people chit-chatting, a DJ playing cool music I've never heard before. The nerves kick in. I feel the need to be switched on, in *work mode*. A waiter offers us cocktails in crystal-cut glasses. 'Picante?'

I haven't had a picante in ages. They're so good. And they look incredible. Really *well made*. I bet the tequila is posh. I'm sure expensive means a hangover is less likely. And they *are* free.

And just like that, willpower gone, I'm chinking glasses with Aoife.

She downs hers before slamming the glass back on the tray, none the wiser of my internal failure. We feel the gorgeous effects immediately as the tequila swims down to our knees.

'God, I needed that,' Aoife says, reaching for another.

'Bianca said she'd be here by eight.' I check my phone, pushing my hair behind my ear. I'm wearing cream silk pyjamas but with outdoor shoes instead of slippers. The pyjamas are covered in hand-drawn faces: *happy, apprehensive, anxious*. I thought it would look effortlessly cool and 'arty', but I just feel underdressed and frumpy. 'Kooky' and 'bubbly' – not in a good way.

I look about for Jackson. He's so tall I can usually spot him anywhere. He's standing by the bar, chatting to some stylish, sophisticated grown-up woman with a pixie cut. Jackson's glass isn't full of picante like ours. It looks like he's nursing a bloody Diet Coke. He waves when he sees us, signals that he'll be over in a minute. I can't help but feel a pang of jealousy.

'He's so good,' Aoife admires, 'working the room.'

Why did I have to go and drink? I already regret it.

Behind glass doors is an outdoor roof-top pool. Steam evaporates off the water. The pool lights reflect a ripple effect, painting dragonfly wings into the night. Behind, the view is startling: skyscrapers lit up in red, silver and gold, like a futuristic *Matrix* scene. It all feels very movie star-ish.

'So should we be *talking* to people?' Aoife asks, like, *please don't make me talk to people.*

'I suppose I *should* be networking,' I reply.

'Do you know anyone here?'

'A couple but' – I smile at the few faces I roughly recognize from the office – 'not gonna lie, I'd much rather chat to you all night.'

Aoife puts her arm around me and we head to the bar to get our next drink and pretend we're looking for someone to talk to. Jackson will be over soon, I'm sure; he'll introduce us to people.

'OIOI!' It's Bianca, hoofing across the room, looking for (and like) trouble, in a red mini boob-tube dress that looks as though it's been bought out the back of a lorry, Dalmatian-spot coat and shiny long snake-skin boots – none of these clothes I have ever seen before.

'God help us,' Aoife says.

'Is she smashed?' I ask, looking over at Jackson to see if he's seen her swoop in like a mad bat. This wasn't really the purpose of the night; a few drinks is fine but I don't think we're meant to get drunk. 'Please no.'

Bianca kisses us, brightly, cheek-to-cheek with an exaggerated *MWAH!* She stinks of cigarettes and vodka.

'Sorry I'm late. I went for some drinks with the *team*.' She rolls her eyes at 'team'. She loves having colleagues at the PR company she's just started at. It's good to see her happy. 'I've passed my probation; they're keeping me on! I've got a *real* job!'

'Bianca!' We hug her and scream; people look over at us and we apologize. 'Bianca, that's amazing!' Seeing her so genuinely excited just makes us even prouder.

'So,' she says, 'are we getting pissed then or what?'

'Yes, we need to celebrate!' Aoife claps her hands.

I know I'm at risk of getting in trouble with Jackson but Bianca's got good news.

'Don't look so anxious, Ella – KTPLT wouldn't have a party with free cocktails if they didn't want people to drink and have a nice time, would they?'

But why do we always have to take it too far?

The next thing we know, Bianca's requesting Black Eyed Peas' 'Pump It' from the irritated DJ who has told her 900 times that they don't take requests. '*Sorry, sorry, sorry,*' I say with Jackson glaring over at me. '*Sorry!*'

Bianca's sliding into people, boffing and barging, treading on toes, lighting up a cigarette *indoors* because she thought she saw someone else smoking (it was an E-cigarette). *OH GOD,* Bianca's spilling red wine, ordering shoestring fries that are actually tempura courgette – 'what are *these*?' – she sniffs, throwing the greasy strings across the room and wearing the metal basket they came in like a beret.

'Bianca, *NO!*'

People are staring, pointing, laughing, not impressed. Jackson is looking at me like *what is going on?*, and I mouth, 'Sorry,' and demonstrate that I'll try and keep her under control, sobering myself very quickly. Next, she gatecrashes a very serious-looking conversation and I have to steal her back like a teenage tearaway, arms looped in her elbows like that game where you pretend to be someone's real hands. 'No need to call security; we'll sober her up.' I apologize to staff. To everyone.

We drag open the sliding doors to get fresh air and feed Bianca lemonade through a straw. People are definitely watching. Oh God. The swimming pool, ring-fenced off, glimmers. Bianca smacks her lips at the water how a warthog might a muddy puddle on a hot day. Kicking her boots off, she jumps up onto a sun lounger and performs East 17's 'Stay Another Day' – the lyrics all wrong. *Shhhhh! Bianca!* Through the window I see Jackson, locked in conversation with the important-looking woman; *what's taking him so long?* He's using his hands to gesture, doubled over, holding his belly like he does when he finds a joke really funny. Like he used to with me. Pretending not to know us. He's not even said *hi* properly. He reaches for a cocktail from a tray. The same drink she's got. He wants to fit in, to impress her, to go with the flow, to make out he's FUN.

He sips the drink and then he *twiddles* his *ear*.

Fiddling with his lobe like he does when he's flirting.

'Who's *that*?' Aoife asks, coming up for air from babysitting

Bianca, hands on hips. But now Bianca's unattended so of course she takes a running leap – has the nerve to *pinch* her nose – and, knees in arms, *bombs* right in the pool. And Bianca is not a small person. The splashback is a tidal wave, splattering the glass window of the party.

'Bianca!' I cry. *Oh no*, this is bad. I put my hands over my mouth, frozen, and gasp.

Oh GOD, *getoutgetoutgetout, quick* . . . BI-*YANKA*! I growl, hoping that will make a difference but it doesn't. Bianca's silly face pops up from the water, lapping over the edge into the grates, *so* proud of herself, make-up trickling down her face.

'WOOHOO!' She fist pumps the air. The delusion. A few strangers applaud her. 'Why THANK YOU!' she says with glee, not getting the sarcasm.

'BIANCA!' Aoife and I try to discipline her but she won't be told. 'Get out!'

'NO! YOU GET IN! It's so warm!' She does a defiant breast-stroke.

People from the party are looking now. Pointing. Security are on their way, no doubt.

Jackson pounds outside in his fresh overpriced trainers. He doesn't want to admit he knows us but he knows not doing anything isn't a great look either.

'Ella, this isn't cool; this is my work.' He talks to me firmly, angrily, with his hand in a chopping action, like he's teaching me to chop an imaginary cucumber.

'I know, I'm sorry; she just jumped right in!'

'Get her out, Ella!'

'LOOK!' shouts Bianca. 'I'm a synchronized swimmer!' Dips down, feet up, back up for air. 'Do I look good?'

'I'll get her out!' I pad towards the pool. This is so bad I can't even look back at Jackson's fuming face.

'*Please*,' Jackson orders. 'I'll try and find a towel.'

I remind myself of a desperate dog owner, pleading with their disobedient spaniel to PLEASE get out of the pond! But she's enjoying winding me up with a 'you can't catch me!' Meaning I have to kick my shoes off to chase her round the perimeter of the pool in my frigging silk 'emotional' pyjamas, shaking a fist like the *wait 'til I get my hands on you* mother of a misbehaving toddler. People are just laughing at me. We're clowns, that's why. I'm pretty sure even security are laughing. The cool people – like Pixie Cut – aren't laughing though. The cool people are like *ew*.

'OK, I'll get out,' Bianca says, surrendering, paddling to the edge where she puts her hands out for me to help her. THANK GOD. I can already see her dress has sucked itself to her body; she's a goddess dripping from a fantasy lake, nipples pinging out like pegs to hang jackets. I don't want to embarrass Bianca or make her feel bad; she's celebrating. We hold hands and heave.

'Can't you use the ladder?' I ask.

Aoife grabs her other hand to help; we both anchor ourselves. 'Are you making yourself as heavy as possible, B?'

One, two, three, she's dragged us both in. FUCK!

We plunge under. A tornado of bubbles. Underneath I see Aoife's feet pedalling for dear life and I dread whatever will be waiting for me at the surface. All I know is it's very, very bad. I want to never come up for air again – can't I just live here? Underwater now, forever?

Returning with the towels, Jackson is not happy. 'Ella, what the fuck? I ask you to get Bianca out and now you're in too?'

By this point, Pixie Cut is enjoying staring me down; her spotless shoes are by my eyelashes, and I know I'm so badly in the wrong that I double down.

'Why aren't you ever fun?' I shout. 'I don't even like parties like this but *look*, I squeeze out the joy! I make the most of it!'

I'm not having fun at all; I'm freezing, annoyed and feel guilty and terrible.

'What are you on about?' Jackson asks.

'You're always so boring. You never want to have fun with me or have a drink.' STOP! My voice boomerangs the closed-in concrete and slate terrace.

'You wonder why?' he asks.

Bianca shouts, 'OH, JUST BANG YOUR GIRL FOR ONCE IN YOUR LIFE, MAN, WHAT'S WRONG WITH YOU? FEED THE SOUL! ELLA NEEDS TO GET PUMMELLED!'

I blink, astounded. *What the fuck did she just say?*

'TOO FAR!' Aoife scolds.

'Sorry but it needed to be said,' Bianca says. I mean, it did, but not like this, not by her and definitely not now.

'Thanks for that, Bianca.' I haul my body up the ladder, the cream silk sticking to me like clingfilm, revealing my bright-pink bra underneath and high-waisted knickers.

Jackson clenches his jaw but says nothing. Just holds out his arm and helps us out one by one, wrapping a massive thick towel around the three of us like we've been rescued from a flood and he's the rescuer, even though he did nothing except shame us. His – let's be real, *our* – KTPLT colleagues look on.

'I'm so sorry,' I say.

I wait for Jackson to say something like, *Me too.* But he doesn't say anything at all, which is worse.

In the taxi home, Jackson and I are silent. I'm shivering for dear life, even with the waffle dressing gown and flimsy slippers that the members' club gave us from the spa that KTPLT will be charged probably a hundred quid for, which I can't even appreciate because I'm in the doghouse. Underneath I'm completely naked. My silk pyjamas and underwear, sodden, are in a carrier bag from the members' club gift shop.

After brushing his teeth, Jackson goes straight to bed and turns off the light. I should wash the chlorine off me so it doesn't itch but I don't want to be any more of a nuisance. I'm not worthy of a shower. I just crawl in, next to him, where his back is turned, knowing I'll wake up with stupid waffle squares imprinted all over my skin like an actual waffle.

'Who was that woman you were chatting to all night?'

'Which woman?'

'The one you had a *picante* with?'

'What the fuck is a picanate?'

'Pixie Cut?'

'You are literally speaking fairy at this point.'

'Short hair.'

'Zahra?'

That's a cool name. 'Who?'

'KTPLT's president? From the New York office.'

Ooo, whoop de fucking New York dooo. That's mean.

'Who often employs *you*, Ella?'

'How am I meant to know that? I've never met her.' Her name does sound familiar from email chains but she never writes back.

'Are you joking me?' he says. 'You're obviously still pissed.'

I'm not and he knows it but it's an easy way of making me feel quite mad and shamed.

'I *wish* I was!'

'I've just secured a massive Christmas advert for us. She was saying, *Well done, thank you.*' He's diverting and distracting. 'You could try it sometime?'

I roll my eyes at his cliché line. 'All I do is support you!'

'Do you call tonight *support*?'

'I'm sorry – it wasn't me. Bianca had good news from work – we got carried away.'

'Yeah well.' Is his entire unfinished sentence.

I know what Jackson's flirting looks like. My chest starts to burn but I don't think it's jealousy; it's more injustice. Now is not the time to say it but here I am saying it:

'You were playing with your *ear*.'

'*Wow*. What are you on about? I don't play with my ear.' He's doing it now.

'You're doing it now!'

'Because I'm seeing if it's something I do. And it's not. I can't believe you and your dumb mates made it about yourselves. Such attention seekers.'

'Don't say dumb! It's offensive.'

'You're such a child, Ella. Grow up!'

SILENCE. The darkness envelopes us.

'I'm really sorry, Jackson.'

'Let's just pretend it didn't happen.'

'But if we do, it will just cause problems.'

'There already are problems, clearly,' he says.

'So, we should talk?' I say. SILENCE. 'Jackson?'

Knowing I won't be able to sleep if we leave it like this, he eventually says, 'Go to sleep – love you.'

'Love you too.'

And I hear this voice in the back of my head from nowhere say, *I wish he'd just cheat on me. Then I could leave.*

I understand there are lots of things in life that don't feel nice. Standing on a plug. Being heartbroken. Stubbing your toe. But waking up to press Day Zero on the sober app after a clean run of almost three weeks is really fucking shit and hurts even more when you're hungover. The whole screen goes black – just for a second – like I've died in a computer game – and then it offers me a motivational quote and the timer begins again. I click on the 'community' tab where I can see other Day Zero-er's; Self-loathing. Pity. Shame. Did I somehow think I didn't belong here?

But what hurts way more than hitting rock bottom, Day Zero, is letting somebody you love down.

I can't take it back. I can't parrot sorry at him all day. I can't 'treat' him with food or presents or affection; no, I just have to own this one. And I have to change. I have to grow the fuck up.

I'm up early. I wasn't properly sleeping anyway; my conscience wasn't having that. I haul my body to the shower. I wash my dirty hair and brush my teeth. Then I change into my leggings, an old sports bra and a t-shirt that I don't care about. I wrap my hair into a knot.

When he wakes up, understandably mad at me, I enter the bedroom with his coffee. 'Thanks,' he grumbles. He's frowning into his phone, rubbing his chin in that way he does when he's trying to solve a problem. The problem being me. He can't even look at me in the eyes.

'Are you going for a run today?'

'I run every day.'

'Can I come?'

He doesn't reply.

'Jackson?'

'What, to shake off your guilt?'

'No, so I can be with you, so that when we get home we're on the same page, so we can talk about last night – and all the other things – and see if we can make it better.'

He folds his arms. 'Ten K?'

'Ha! Five!' I blurt but read the room, love. 'No, yes, yes, ten K sounds absolutely brilliant.' OH GOD.

We run – my style more *shuffle* – down our street, which is OK because it's on a slant, almost downhill; if anything I'm scared I'm going to trip on my laces and smash my face in. Past the row of shops and down the backroads where everyone else is probably just being cosy and watching TV – jealous. My knee aches and my ankle feels dull – probably shouldn't put weight on it – arriving at the park gates. I was hoping that this would be The End because he knows this is the most I've run in a long time but *oh no*, it dawns on me that at the park there's kind of nowhere to go except follow the track around in a huge endless circle and if you wanted to, or were mad, you could just run that track around and around until the end of time. Very quickly my face goes bright red. My chest hurts as the cold air hits my lungs and burns. I am breathless and have had enough.

Come on, he says. I can tell he's hanging back for me. I cup my boobs to stop them bouncing. Gulp huge mouthfuls of air and exhale. There is snot. A lot. My nose won't stop running. Why do I suddenly have a cold? I want to cough. Then my shoulders start playing up – I'm hunching them: I remember to drop them and now it's my leggings, wrinkling up at the ankle. He says, *Keep going, you're doing great.* Are we not even going to play some music? Korn or Rihanna or The Strokes? Is he not irritable? Does this not make him annoyed? Jackson's so naturally light on his feet; he's like an athlete, swinging in these long power strides, human and cave-person-like. But then I see people walking with coffee cups and we pass them at speed, leave them behind in the dust. We see a dog chase a squirrel. Kids on bikes. Leaves bustling. Emerald, jade, chestnut, radish red leaves. Parakeets. Geese. Conkers. Pigeons. The sky above us, expansive and swallowing. And our breaths, *in out, in out.* We find a rhythm. Without forcing it, we find a pace. We're together. We don't talk; we just run. And then I start to feel it: the simple pleasure, of my feet on the ground, of my own body motoring me along, fuelled by my own steam. *I'm* doing this! The challenge, the reward, the sweat begins to come in little trickles but it's sweat all the same. I get all-over body vibrations, tingles, the stretch, the ache, the pain, endorphins and Vitamin D. My heart beating, flooding blood all around my body and at every point, when I promise myself I'll stop at *that bush, that lamppost, that tree*, I don't. I keep going.

When we reach the river, it's Jackson who stops first. He invites me to admire the view. But I'm bent over, huffing and puffing, hands on thighs. I look up to see he's breathless too. Hands on hips, face in an expression of I wouldn't say *enjoyment* but endurance. We are reasonably far from home. I look out at the water and then I just release. I begin to cry.

Jackson wraps his arms around me.

'I'm so sorry.' I sniff.

'It's OK,' he says. 'Life is . . . a lot. Neither of us can get it right all the time. We're just learning. Doing our best. It's OK.'

And we turn back and walk home.

Chapter 19

Then

My college doesn't feel like school. We do things like lie down, whilst a teacher plays political speeches at us which are meant to get us fired up but we're all too self-absorbed so just lie there, thinking about our own problems. We study Chekhov. Stanislavski. We turn Dr Seuss books into protest theatre. We bark cliché messages about anti-drugs. Anti-racism. Anti-bullying. Anti-sexism. Anti-homophobia. Anti-war. We stare at ourselves in the mirror to Massive Attack's 'Teardrop' and the aim is to cry. We make movement pieces. We are trees. We are ghosts. We have no tongues. We are mothers. We are cows. We then have to *become* a city, without talking, to twist and turn like the river, improvise. '*Trust*,' whispers the teacher as my hands link with a girl called Dominique – perfect eyeliner and an oversized washed-out tracksuit, which she somehow manages to make look like fashion – to mime a bridge.

'What the fuck?' I ventriloquist-whisper and this makes us both crack up.

Our school says: *you get out what you put in*. So we put in everything. Very quickly I realize I don't to be an actor but I do feel like I've met my kind, people who want to make stuff happen. Like Dominique. She's *made* her own coat; it's long and black with colourful felt shapes. It's incredible – just like her. Here, there aren't gangs and crews and groups; everybody meshes. Everybody can just be themselves. I am able to express myself outside of my notebook, in my clothes and body. I wear more bright colours, I accept my raggle-taggle look and scruffy hair. I am lifted, lighter, happier. A few months in, I find the confidence to share some of my poems with Dom.

'You should write us a play, Ella!' she encourages, wrapping her braids into a bun.

Really?' I ask.

'A hundred per cent!'

I shrug. 'OK, why not?'

Here, without even trying, I start to think – no, *believe* – that I am actually alright at writing, which I never did at the girls' school with its academic grades and unobtainable targets.

'I'm writing a play!' I rush in from school, slamming around my house. I need a notebook, a pen, a beret.

Violet rolls her eyes.

'If you must know' – she didn't ask – 'it's called *Bad Wolf* and it's a modern adaptation and feminist examination of—'

'*Little Red Riding Hood*?'

'Yes.' How did she know?

'Kind of obvious.'

'Rude. *ANYWAY*. It's from the POV of Little Red's gran – her lived experience of home intrusion as a senior female and how there aren't enough parts for women in theatre. Except it's set in Croydon and Little Red Riding Hood wears a red Nike hoody and gold hoop earrings and speaks in verse and we're going to perform it in the car park and school are going to let us use real cigarettes as props *if* we promise not to light them.'

Violet gags.

I squint at her, unsure how to take her feedback.

The rehearsals are full on. I still try to hang out with my old friends but I'm writing or sitting in on rehearsals or going to *new* house parties with my *new* friends. I find myself cancelling on Aoife, The Twins. Missing Bianca's calls. Not replying to Ronke's texts. I tell myself that long friendships are like stews that get better, over time – left undisturbed, flavour deepening and concentrating days after. I can no longer justify sitting on a common freezing my arse off whilst a spliff I don't even smoke is passed in front of my face. I see Lowe's name slip to the back of my *recents*, until the restricted memory on my phone is at full capacity. I delete around him, not having the heart to lose his messages.

It's Shreya's birthday at the Rainforest Café, a dusty central London tourist attraction in a windowless basement that's made to look like a rainforest and has a thunderstorm every half an hour. It's quite exhilarating when the robotic rubber gorilla beats his faux-fur chest, or the clunking trunk of the mechanic elephant sucks up stagnant water, its screw-loose eye wobbling around its skull. Shreya has been given her parents' chequebook to buy us all lunch and Coca-Colas. Bianca rebelliously orders a beer and Shreya holds up the menu and reminds, 'Coca-Colas.'

Bianca mumbles, 'Aren't we a bit old for the Rainforest Café?'

Aoife snorts into the garlic tear 'n' share bread.

'Sorry, Ella,' Bianca says, like there's no possible way she can go on with Shreya's birthday lunch unless she addresses the actual elephant in the room, 'have you changed your perfume?'

'Yeah' – I try to own it – 'it's DKNY *Women*.' I sniff my wrist. 'Justin Timberlake isn't the only cool one these days.' But that goes down like a shit baguette.

'We haven't seen you for ages.' Bianca pokes, 'Do you not love us any more?'

'*Seriously*? I am just at one of those schools where *you get out what you put in* and I want to do well.'

'We all want to do well!' Aoife bites into her cob salad.

'That's good to want to do well.' Ronks picks at her noodles.

A Twin asks, 'So will we see you in a production or anything soon?'

I just want this conversation to be over. The thought of The Twins dressed up in their silver spangly Oscar dresses, clutching opera binoculars, expecting West End ice-cream tubs, only to see me shouting about in a Sarah Kane play is too much.

'I've actually got a show soon.' After Violet's reaction, I can't bring myself to pitch *Bad Wolf* out loud.

'Yay!' a Twin claps.

Not *Yay*. I don't want to invite them; they won't get it (or the many layers). But I'll feel bad if I don't.

'I'll send you the details.'

The other Twin – the more outspoken of the two – let's call her Twin 1 – asks, 'And have you spoken to Lowe recently . . . ?' His name spikes me right though the chest. Just because she's going out with Sam now – as in Sam's house, where I first met Lowe – she thinks she's superior.

I haven't spoken to Lowe in a while; I've been so whipped up with college. We still keep our friendship cooking but things are . . . *scratchy*. We are less like a stew but a risotto that needs a sturdy hand and constant feeding of stock in the form of love and attention. We are no longer silky smooth and unctuous. We are starting to catch to the bottom of the pan. To *stick*. To get stodgy. And it wouldn't be long before we'd *burn*.

I say, 'No, not as much as before. It's not that I don't want to see him, but you know what it's like: he's at some music college now, which is in the total opposite direction. Don't you have to get like a *tram* there or something?'

'Hmmm,' Twin 2 adds like she knows otherwise. She's going out with Nas; they're double-dating friends like their life is a constant game of squash. 'Still, you should probably just call him.'

'What is *this*?' I feel myself sharpening.

'You don't have to get so defensive, Ella; it wasn't an attack. I just know he'd appreciate to hear from you, that's all,' Twin 1 says.

'OK. Thanks.' I sip my watered-down Coke. This is blatantly Pepsi. 'Why, did he say something?'

'Well . . . ' Twin 2 checks with Twin 1 if it's OK to speak and says, 'We bumped into him on the common and he said you hadn't really spoken to him since you started this new college.'

'He hasn't spoken to me either!' I snap back, shooting the messenger dead.

'He said he thought you might be too busy, that's all,' Twin 1 says.

'So now I'm the one that's too busy to see *him*? That's hilarious.' I'm thinking back to all the times he's been off on his BMX and never called.

'To be fair, you are quite busy,' Bianca adds, letting her fork clang on her plate. *Oh here we go . . .*

'I've written this production – the ONE I am going to invite you all to, obviously.' I am flustered. 'I'm rehearsing, reading—'

'—hanging out with Dominique . . . ' Aoife mimics my tone, letting her glasses slide down her nose like a challenging librarian – how did she get so cocky? I know Dom annoys them with her creativity and love for life. The others go quiet.

'Aoife? What the hell?' I laugh but not because it's funny. 'We go to the same college. What do you want, me to have no friends?'

Ronks sticks up for me again. 'It's good to meet new people.' *Thanks, Ronks.* 'You're blossoming, Ella, and it's glorious to see. Lowe will have to just suck it up.' But then she adds, 'You've always been too available for that guy anyway.'

'What does *that* mean?' I ask, my voice rising. 'Ronke?'

Shreya looks about for a waiter, desperate to flag down her *own* surprise birthday cake (that *we* were meant to bring out) to slice through the tension.

'It's like you're saying I'm some desperate people pleaser,' I add.

'No, we're saying you've *changed*.' Shreya drops the mic. 'There. Said it. You're *different*.'

The whole table is silent. *Ouch*. Changed is the worst. Changed means *Judas*.

'*Grown*.' Ronke finds a kinder word.

Bianca hides her face in the dessert menu; Aoife wipes a tear from behind her glasses. I've betrayed my friends by enjoying college. I'm having an affair on my whole entire past.

'This isn't even about Lowe, is it? It's about all of you.'

'God, I wish we'd never said anything now.' Twin 1 folds her arms.

'Me. The. Fuck. Too.'

Thunder and lightning strikes our table, the restaurant is thrown into darkness and drama, caught in an invisible rainstorm; a soundscape of hooting chimps, roaring lions and screeching birds; the gorilla beats his chest. A startled baby cries in a highchair on the table next to us.

'HAPPY BIRTHDAY TO YOU!' sing the waiters, winding through the tables with a cake on fire that, for some reason, Shreya's pretending she's never seen before, even though she ferried the bloody thing, along with the seventeen candles, in a fuck-off Tupperware, on the 159 bus.

And we're all looking very separate. The spaces between our chairs, huge.

That evening – as an olive branch – I reluctantly send a text inviting my friends to our show next week. They all RSVP yes.

I can't invite Lowe though. I'm not ready to share my new life with him. Or maybe share *him* with my new life. Why is that? Is it that I'm embarrassed of trying? I don't want him to see that I've been having a go of living outside of him.

Knowing my friends are coming to the play has instantly snuffed out my creative flair. I worry about how certain lines will land and begin to panic-edit the play at the last minute. Then I fret I've cheated myself by compromising my vision from fear of what others will think.

Cut to:

Aoife, Bianca, Ronks, Shreya, The Twins and their boyfriends, Mum, Adam, Dad, Violet and Sonny, all there to support me at 4.25 p.m. on a Tuesday afternoon, shivering in the school car park to see the production of:

BAD WOLF
By Ella Cole

And no one can hear a single line as the wind drags my precious words off into the distance. The forecast said 'sunny spells' – what the hell spell do you call *this*? I wince and cringe during the entire production. Begging for it to be over. Wishing that I, too, could get eaten by the bad wolf. At the climactic ending, I'm sure I hear Aoife snort with laughter but when I look around, she is nodding at the scene, feigning pensive and it's way better acting than ANY of these amateurs on stage.

At the end of the terrible production, one by one I hear the critics:

'Well, that was *interesting*,' says Violet.

'*Entertaining*,' says Dad.

'Very avant-garde,' says Stepdad Adam.

'What does *avant-garde* mean?' I ask.

'It means weird as fuck,' says Mum. 'Are you coming in the car home?'

I see Dom and the others in their outlandish outfits, walking in the direction of the pub where the bar staff turn a blind eye at our lack of IDs, half-waiting for me to join them. Then there's Aoife, Bianca, The Twins, Shrey and Ronks, standing around, talking about hot chocolates and jacket potatoes at the café near Bianca's. Even though I'm meant to be celebrating with the cast, I can't not go with my old friends; it would be unforgivable. Besides, in my eyes, there isn't a great deal to celebrate.

'I'll get the train with this lot,' I say to Mum. I see Dom and her wonderful long black coat with the colourful felt shapes turning away in disappointment, linking arms with the New Friends from college. To them, performing anything, good or bad, is what they love: playing, creating, experimenting. It's the process; what other people think is irrelevant and so, yes, there is much to celebrate – our wonderful weirdness, the refusal to cringe at our freedom of expression regardless of critique.

My Old Friends wrap their arms around me like they won the friendship battle, like they always knew they would.

'Now tell me *please*,' Bianca says, 'what the FUCK was that play about?'

And we all laugh.

As we are heading out of the school gates, this guy (from my class but we've not spoken yet; he's quiet – his name, maybe, Nile?) in a denim jacket who has the most charismatic face in the entire world, a big hooked nose and massive brown eyes, with the greatest Madonna gap in-between his teeth, walks past and without stopping says, 'Great play.'

I flush rose with embarrassment as our eyes hug and say, 'Thanks,' but he's already gone.

PING!

'Who was that *fitty*?' Aoife whispers in my ear.

'Some guy from school,' I say, a smile creeping across my face.

That weekend Dominique and I go to a *wild* house party with the New Friends. I'm wearing a pink spaghetti-strap dress covered in palm trees that Dom has convinced me I look 'astounding' in. A guy is going around cracking imaginary eggs on knee caps and letting the invisible 'yolk' trickle down because apparently it's like an orgasm. If that's true, I really don't get the hype over orgasms. We play a game called 'Nervous', where you have to let someone run their hands up your leg and see how high the person can climb your thighs until you shout 'NERVOUS!' There's a hot tub and the whole party clamber in with their clothes on, share bottles of sour alcohol and play spin the bottle – a *real* game of spin the bottle where everyone actually *plays*. I'm standing on the sidelines because I don't want to catch crabs.

He's in the garden, holding a bottle of cider. Nile. He looks like he's walked out of the Seventies.

I point him out to Dom. 'That's the guy who said he liked our play.'

'In that old brown suit?' she asks.

I nod, yeah.

He turns to face me, under the garden lights, and smiles. We stare at each other from either side of the bubbling tub, the bottle swinging back and forth in our direction, as kids from our year group kiss.

He appears beside me with a 'Hey.' He congratulates me on the play, for, and I quote, *having the bollocks to throw shit around*. I try not to take the word *shit* personally, even though the damage is already done.

'Oh, you've got an accent?' Like clotted cream and rolling hills.

'It comes out more when I've had a drink.' He laughs. 'I'm from Devon.'

He then tells me he is absolutely head over heels in love with London and I laugh. 'I'm not joking,' he says. 'I just cannot get over this place. The history, the clothes, the libraries, the literature, the shops. Do you have any idea how lucky you are to have grown up here? You have all this stuff on your doorstep! You can just *walk* to a gig! The theatre! And the food, my God. I don't sleep cos I'm so excited by it.' He laughs. 'I miss the sea though.' His face is calming. Like the sea. He says he's not been to Camden. Ever.

'What?' I say. 'You're going to die.'

The next day, Nile and I meet up at the station to go to Camden. He's wearing a Smiths t-shirt and a smile – toothpaste fresh. On the Tube, I wonder if people think he's my boyfriend. I take the lead like a tour guide. We stroll the markets: the overpriced band t-shirts, the latex platform boots, tattoo and piercing shops and sticks of incense, the troughs of luminous orange sweet and sour chicken. We sit by the canal, the sun breaking through the clouds, and eat pulled noodles. It's nice; it feels good. Simple. And easy.

Scarily, I find myself wanting to call Nile 'Lowe'. I've never called anyone else 'Lowe' before. The rare name, to me, holds such weight. Nile must be pressing on that familiar affectionate pad in my brain – I can't help but think of Lowe; what he's doing today, who he's with. How much it would break my heart to see him sitting by some sunny canal with a girl who isn't me. But I have to move on with my life. I'm almost seventeen now, so this time with Nile, I'm trying my very hardest not to friend-zone myself.

Pretty soon we're glued to one another. Some lunches, we skip the canteen and go to the deli. Nile speaks Italian to the staff because his mum is Italian and they can't believe it and feel sorry for him that he's studying so far from home – as if home is in actual Italy. 'You'll starve!' they say and gift him sheets of fatty ham, thin as glass, in waxed paper and posh plump olives with the pips still in, which Nile can expertly spit out from the corner of his mouth without having to nibble the flesh like a mini apple like I do. Once, for no reason at all, they give Nile a whole panettone that comes in a massive, decorated box with a ribbon, a box so flamboyant you'd expect to find Marie Antoinette's shoes inside. He quite sexily rips massive hunks off the sweet bread throughout the day, offering me handfuls.

Nile is the best actor in our year group. He's shy in real life and yet, on stage, he evolves into this charismatic, flamboyant wild angry man who is good at playing gangsters; shouting and pulling at his hair and punching his chest like the gorilla in the Rainforest Café, letting himself spit when he talks on stage, spritzing through the spotlights and we *sigh* in *awe*, like, *now THAT'S what I call acting!* Once he lets himself get slapped during a performance and the whole theatre gasps – even the orchestra stop playing their strings for a second – and real tears bulge in his eyes *and* in the eyes of the actor who slapped him (who never meant to hit him that hard), and Nile's left with a red diamond of a hand mark on his cheek. *Everyone* is starstruck.

It is all very fit.

Nile is the teacher's new prodigy.

He is also my new crush.

Chapter 20

Adam asks my mum to marry him. I was trying to suss out his game plan, but he has way more money than us, so it must *actually* be love.

My mum is NOT the romantic type, never felt the need to marry my dad, so I imagine it's taken a lot for her to say yes.

Aoife, Bianca, Ronks and Shreya are coming to the wedding. The Twins have gone skiing. I know *never say never* but I can already say with absolute confidence that skiing is something I'll never do. From lack of want, affordability and all the other awful reasons. Even though I've not spoken to Lowe in a while, Mum pushes me to invite him. 'I was going to anyway!' I tell her. I reckon it's just so she can give me the *you'll marry that boy one day* penetrative stare.

Lowe stands by my side in a crinkled light-blue shirt over his BMX t-shirt, still looking like everything I want. I watch Mum – the most unromantic stoic holding a bouquet made of homegrown wildflowers – say, 'I do' and she is the *happiest she's ever been*, and I think of Dad, all by himself, dissolving instant coffee into his BEST DAD IN THE WORLD mug.

Annoyingly, I am still too self-conscious to ever show my teeth in a photograph, even though my teeth are absolutely OK, but I'll get there, one day. As the photographer snaps photos of us and my hair that doesn't feel like my own, tousled into chipolata bridesmaid ringlets, people I haven't met before throw handfuls of dried petals in our faces and I look for Lowe in the crowd. But he hasn't left; he's right there. He takes my hand and holds it. His thumb criss-crossed over mine. And he doesn't let go. I think I've underestimated how much I need him.

We all take the absolute piss out of the free bar but Lowe takes it too far and throws up in a bush outside the venue. I hoist him up like a puppet and decide it's time to take him home.

He gargles, 'Leave me here. I'll wait for you – have a good time.' Crawling into the very same bush he's just thrown up in.

'Don't be silly.' I hoist him up. 'I've had enough anyway. If one more person tells me how much *I haven't changed a bit* . . . I'll . . . I'll . . . I'm too tired to think of the repercussions.'

Of course, I've changed; I'm a woman now . . . *aren't I?*

We get the bus back to mine. Me in my ridiculous velvety red-wine bridesmaid's dress that makes me look like I have hips in places that aren't even humanly possible and Lowe retching. He spits, throws up again, the doors of the bus swishing and swashing like oars, vomit sweeping back and forth like windscreen wipers until the tide touches my painted toes.

'I'm sorry,' he apologizes. 'Thank you for looking after me. I love you.'

He *loves* me.

And just when I'm about the say it back, he says, 'You're my best friend.'

Best FRIEND.

Let go, Ella.

A week later we're at WASP bar – a coffee shop by day, and by night a very illegal drum and bass club that doesn't seem to mind the fact that there are children's high chairs stacked in the corner and seventeen-year-olds raving and doing lines off their laminated breakfast menus. The only transition from day to night is that the chalk board listing all the coffee prices is swivelled to reveal:

NO HATS

NO HOODS

NO TRAINERS

Everybody inside is wearing one of the above if not all three. Still, it's always a relief to not have to memorize the star sign characteristics to match a fake ID with a birthday on it that isn't mine. When in reality no bouncer is going to ask me what traits make up an Aquarius anyway.

(*Honest. Curious. Creative.*)

I'm messaging Nile a bit from the party. He's at this late-night Film Club thing that he's started hosting. He invited me along, sweetly, but I said no because all my friends are here. Lowe's here, wearing a shirt again and it isn't even for a wedding. He asks me to go to the shop with him to buy cigarettes. He says he wants to talk.

For a second, I wonder if the star I wished on has actually come through, that my wish knew to activate just before things develop with Nile? We should just sack the party off and say how we feel, for real this time.

Once Lowe's bought his B&H from the off-licence, he mindlessly offers me one and I turn it down, annoyed that he would even think I'd want a cigarette. *Doesn't he know me?*

'You're so lucky to not have an addictive personality,' he tells me. *You don't know the half of it.*

'So . . . ' he begins. 'There's a girl from college here tonight.'

Oh. OUCH. ' . . . *And?*'

And, 'I like her,' he says. I think about how into her he must be to confess this; she must be driving him crazy. 'I need your advice, Ella. She says she likes older men so . . . '

'That's why you're wearing the shirt?' I ask (even though my mum's wedding is obviously what gave him the idea), smiling, finding out that *yes, it still hurts*, that I still hold feelings for him.

Trying not to cry, I reflex with humour. 'Cos you want to look like a bloody accountant?'

'Ha, yeah . . . does it look OK?'

He really wants to know, popping his collars up adorably; my opinion matters to him.

I could be a bitch but I can't.

'You look really lovely,' I say, because it's the truth.

'OK, thanks.' I'd never seen him so self-conscious. 'I just . . . really like her.'

Stab. K, bye. I'm dead now.

He squints, the cigarette smoke waters his eye. He rubs them with his fingers, childishly. 'You're the best.' he inhales. 'You're the best girl in the world.'

He exhales and puts his arm around me. And I'm where I should be, my favourite place of all – in his arms. But he's positioning me just right for the bullet to sink into my chest.

'I'll point her out when we get inside.'

Oh, will you now? Oh, FUCK OFF. Make sure you do.

'Great,' I say, even though I'd rather stick pins in my eyes.

And he does. The whole room is dancing to Cameo's 'Candy', leaving me out (I'm just jealous because I don't know my lefts from rights).

'That's Rachel . . . '

I see her in slow motion, sitting on a leather couch, sipping her drink. And that's when everything stops. Her head twists back, her long dark-brown hair swishing past, to look at me in the eyes, her face in full beam when she sees Lowe return. She likes him back, I can tell. She looks so much like me. But the Goddess version. Oh God.

I text Nile: **Are you still out? Would it be weird it I came to your film thing now? x**

He writes back: **it would be SO weird ☺ It would make me happy if you came. X**

Chapter 21

Well, Rachel may look like (a very much prettier version of) me, but it turns out she is nothing like me. The girl is seventeen and acts like a *woman*, clopping up and down Clapham High Street in a heel, getting blow-dries and takeout coffees in Chelsea like a divorcee. Rachel can drive. She and Lowe have actual sit-down meals at expensive restaurants like Café Rouge. I hear Rachel's tantrums are award winning. That she says , 'Oh, *fuck* you,' and then speeds off in her car. That her dramatic ultimatums are the stuff we only see in movies like *Ten Things I Hate About You*. That she has plans to move to California and work in fashion. The closest I've come to going to California is drinking a family bottle of Sunny-D by myself.

I know better than to compare myself but I can't help but think this is it for Lowe and me. It's over. For good. He's moved on. I can too.

And so, I kiss Nile.

We kiss at the bottom of the stairs at Sam's house. We kiss on The Twins' trampoline in the rain, raindrops on our faces. We kiss at Dean's party. On the common, under the willow tree. We don't need to make a handshake because we kiss. We kiss in the overgrown garden, our feet with the rotten apples and the weeds. He rides me home in the dark and kisses me goodnight.

I kiss Nile for every missed opportunity with Lowe.

Rapture.

'So . . . do you wanna be my girl then?'

I silently count down *five, four, three, two, one,* before managing a 'Yeah!'

I have secured myself my first proper boyfriend.

We do all that stuff I dreamt of doing with a boyfriend. Way cooler stuff than Lowe and Rachel do. Who needs a car like Rachel when we can miss the night bus and follow the route by foot so we don't get lost, many, many, many times? Who needs Café Rouge's unctuous onion soup and chive flecked cheesy crouton, when you can Eat As Much As You Like at Big Tums for £5.99 and get a twenty-four-hour bellyache because you ate yourself into a coma? We go on train journeys and fall asleep on each other's shoulders. We go to gigs. He makes me fruit salad and each piece of fruit is cut in such a perfect dice shape that if his acting dreams don't materialize he could get a job at a hotel breakfast buffet in a heartbeat. We take photos kissing in the train station photobooth. Although I find myself waiting at the mouth of the booth's printer, imagining that by some inexplicable twist of fate, it's actually Lowe's face developing in there on the four little photo squares . . . but it's Nile. We buy a whole loaf of tiger bread and scoop out the inside, tearing it off into little squidgy doughballs. But when we listen to music, every song reminds me of Lowe. I reckon I'll need that memory eraser like in *Men in Black* to ever forget him.

Nile lives with his Aunt Linda – for cheap rent, paid by Nile's parents. He has a cousin called Kirsty-Lee who hates us but apparently, 'it's not targeted.' Nile's bedroom is attached to the house like an after-thought, not too dissimilar to how he has been welcomed into Aunt Linda's home. Nile's two favourite charity-shop shirts hang on the back door. The carpet is the colour of sand. His single bedsheets are the colour of Blu-tack. The walls are covered in ticket stubs and band posters ripped from NME, stuck on with actual Blu-tack. And for the first time I am saying the words *I love you* out loud to a guy, and his name is not Lowe Archer and it's OK.

Even though it isn't *love* love. He doesn't hear the silent caveat: 'I love you as much as I possibly can love someone who isn't the person I actually love but they don't love me back in the same way I love them, so with all that in mind – I suppose I love you.'

And I feel happy that some kind of romantic feeling can exist outside of Lowe, at least in all the time and space that he isn't around. I can be OK. I can be content.

That's all fine until I hear Rachel takes the pill. That conversation we had before college still haunts me, the agreement we made. It wasn't a contract in blood and yet it seemed to have gone up in flames. I've not seen Lowe in months. What did I expect? Was he meant to ask permission? Check it was OK with little old me? Why am I going on like some cruel wicked virginity-stealing witch? He's not made a promise with a fairy-tale weasel. Maleficent. Rumpelstiltskin. Ursula rolling out the impossible-to-meet conditions with her tentacles: 'If you do not lose your virginity by the time you are eighteen it is MINE ALLLLLL MINE MUUUHHAHAHAHA!'

So, he's having sex. OK. Absolutely swell. I'm *chuffed* for him.

I realize that I'm going to miss out on so much love if I waste my time on someone who isn't even considering me. I like Nile, a lot. I have feelings for him and they're strong. We could have a nice life, me and him. We really could.

So one day after school, when Aunt Linda and Kirsty-Lee are downstairs eating a brick of Viennetta, watching *A Place in the Sun* with the volume so loud I'm sure they won't be able to hear the headboard gently shoving against the wall, I decide I'm ready.

Nile brushes my skin with the back of his hand; he takes my hair in his fingers and fondles every strand like it's angel hair. He holds the small of my back and kisses my neck. 'You're beautiful, Ella,' he says and I believe him. Nile is quite beautiful too. 'Should I get a . . . ?' He means a condom. I nod and I'm not sure if I'm meant to watch this bit – are we meant to do it together? Is rolling on a condom a two-person job – does he need my encouragement or is it in fact a very private moment and I should avert my eyes? I sort of do half and half. The boiler grumbles in the cupboard; the view of the dull grey suburban garden is there until it isn't as his bedroom window steams up, and I wonder if sliding my hand down like Kate Winslet does in the carriage sex scene in *Titanic* is a cool idea but I know I can't pull a move like that off.

He holds me so close afterwards, making sure that every single bit of our bodies is touching. He says I can stay the night or he can stay at mine, or he can even book us a B&B for the night! *Fancy*. But I'd rather be at home. I need to cuddle my teddies and be close to my younger siblings. Just to check that I can still access my childhood, that it isn't all gone now. But also, even though we used a condom, I'll HAVE to go to the Clinic ASAP. I'm definitely pregnant with triplets or have chlamydia.

'Course. Whatever you want.' He walks me to the bus stop without even asking. He buys me a can of 7-Up and a packet of plain Hula Hoops like I'm recovering from a tummy bug. *Sweet*. When the bus comes, he jumps on too and rides back with me all the way home, our fingers locked. That's at least an hour and a half round trip. That's love.

At home, I know I should feel like a Shania Twain song but I don't. My phone rings and of all the people, of all the times, in all the world, it has to be him – Lowe. Of course. Why now? It's like he knows I've just broken the pact and *now* he's calling me after months of silence. I couldn't write this, I swear. Don't tell me, he wants to meet up? I toy with not answering but I can't *not*; the idea of his voice sprouts a kernel of both excitement and terror in my stomach but it's probs just my phantom pregnancy.

'Ella, hey?'

'Hey, Lowe, how are you?'

'I'm good, been ages! How are you?'

'I'm . . . really so great.' After losing my virginity in Aunt Linda's box room.

He laughs. 'So . . . bit of a weird one . . . '

OH GOD. 'Yeah?' I pick at the wall.

'But . . . well . . . I'm in a band now . . . did you know or . . . ?'

'You are? Oh my GOD, OK, wow.' He's really doing it? I didn't know, no. How could I? This hurts. 'Congratulations . . . with *who*?'

'Some guys from college – don't think you know them.' Alright, *sorry about you.*

'What are you called?'

'True Love.'

True Love? The name takes me by surprise. I suppose it's more original than the other indie bands who just take any word in the dictionary, add 'The' at the front and make plural.

'That's a great band name.'

'Aw, do you like it?' Does he actually care what I think?

'Yeah, I really do.' It's beautiful.

'I'm glad.' He holds a beat. Maybe he does? Maybe he just knows how to work me. 'So, the reason I'm calling is that we actually have our first proper show.'

'Oh amazing! Your first show, like, what, *ever*?'

'No, not ever, we've done a few little things at college' – I bet Rachel went – 'a couple of house parties, but not anything proper. I wondered if you fancied coming down? I'll put your name on the list?' *List* sinks my heart.

It's not that I don't want to see Lowe play. I just have a resistance, an aversion to standing in a room sardine-canned at the front with every other name on the list looking and listening to *him*. Now everyone will see what I see. And I get this awful feeling that it is too late, that it's already out of my control: everybody can already see what I see. And everyone loves it too.

Chapter 22

I arrange to go to the gig with just Bianca and Aoife – keep it small, for damage control. Nile's going home to Devon this weekend anyway to see his parents, and I'm glad because I don't know how tonight is going to go. I've just begun to rebuild myself as a cool person and I'm not sure I'm ready for Nile to see otherwise. I'm nervous.

We get ready at mine. Vintage dresses, sparkly eyes and red lipstick. In our heads we look like Charlie's Angels, but probably we look more like the Sanderson Sisters in *Hocus Pocus*.

Before the gig even starts, near the train station, in the surrounding pubs and the whole area there is an energy. A buzz. Everyone is there, all the cool people who snow-leopard-creep out of hibernation for only the coolest stuff. The BMXers, kids from school. Christopher gives me an awkward wave; *hey*, it's like a bloody reunion! TRUE LOVE are low down on the line up but it's still quite surreal even seeing their name in a blocky font officially typed onto posters. Bianca is already drunk, chatting away to some guys with her handbag strap hoisted between her perfect boobs. Meanwhile my mouth tastes like paracetamol.

We buy beer in plastic cups and down the first two pints fast. The knots in my gut have loosened but one more beer and I could easily cry. And then I spot Rachel, with all the other cool girl-friends in their *whatever* girl-next-door jeans, like it's no big deal.

I'm as overdressed as a toffee apple. I get a text from Nile: **Hey, how's it going? Miss you! x**

I slide my phone back into my bag.

When the roar of a guitar strikes, the retching snatch of feedback squawks and an amp jars in that punk screech you hear on those documentaries my dad used to make me stay up to record on VHS for him about The Clash. People behind me *whoop*. And I feel scared. What was I about to see? I'm not ready to know how amazing he is, not ready to share.

The band walk on without ego, take their places; the lights come up. Everyone rams to the front and my stupid shoe is caught in a plastic pint cup. Fuck, it scrapes across the floor like an embarrassing boot. And *Eeesh*. Someone's cigarette burns my arm. *Oww*. The smell of my flesh barbecues in the darkness; this is not going well. Lowe wraps his hand around the mic – a beat of time – he holds us like this in the palm of his hand. And I realize that even though True Love are bottom of the bill, everyone in this room is here to see them. And it's the most bittersweet feeling ever.

Lowe sings like he has nothing to prove. He doesn't play the showman whatsoever, not turning it up for the crowd. He's wearing the clothes he always wears, nothing special, beaten up Reebok Classics and a scruffy t-shirt, like a shoplifter or one of those boys who works the waltzers. So unvain. So human. He's understated. Completely original and unique and yet it's like he's been doing this all his life. He's an *artist*. A *musician*. How the hell did this happen? He plays *into* the guitar, turns to his band, up close, pressing into the bassist; knuckles grind. He nods at the drummer. It's like we don't exist. He's playing at home, alone, to the mirror. And that makes us want to be noticed by him *even* more. I am desperate to be *seen*. He is *so* cool. His face screwed up, mouth lax, jaw clenches, then slack, wrists and fingers – controlled, yet relaxed, locked in, fixated and-then-comes-the-sweat, *oh boy*, I am not ready. He looks fucking phenomenal. I am fascinated by the apple in his throat. He swigs his bottle of beer, pours some in his hands and fingers it through his hair like gel. Gross. *Fit.* I see the needy painted fingernails of girls trying to nab the bottle. And I find myself anxiously making sure he'll have something else to drink nearby if they do. What if his throat dries? What if he loses his voice? Wait, where's his inhaler? The girls squabble over the set list taped to the floor, picking at the gaffer tape. *Who are these people?* These strangers lionizing my friend. And at the same time, I *so* understand their reaching fingers. Aoife, Bianca and I don't talk at all throughout the short set. We're too *stunned.* We just feel the raging tempest around us. Hearing the lyrics being bellowed by kids from Lowe's college, words *we* don't know. We get burnt by more cigarettes; we get warm beer thrown in our hair. I want to cry.

True Love are suddenly playing everywhere, all the time. 'Come and see my friends' band,' I invite the world. I'm stuffing flyers into hands like a jolly foot-solider, canvassing, spreading the good word to be supportive. I'm doing it again, aren't I? Protecting myself by doubling down; *if you can't beat 'em, join 'em,* as Mum would say. It's a cover-up, a veil. Just like I did when we were young, when I set Lowe up with Bianca but this time I'm setting him up with fans: Dominque, Nile, other friends from college. Always Aoife and Bianca. Each gig is ceremonious. A party. An event.

And Nile's obviously their overnight number one fan. He can't believe how good they are. 'They're ace,' he says. ACE. 'Thanks for introducing me to their music!' Like it's a cult. When I have no other choice: I *have* to invite Nile so that it's OK for me to go to these shows, for it not feel like I'm perving on Lowe. *I just LOVE the music.* As the price for tickets and venue capacities creep up, there are more shows in musty, cramped, squished up venues, deep dark dank basement clubs with sole-kissing floors. Rachel's always there, watching from the back with all the other

188

girlfriends, nodding along with her plastic glass of red wine. *Bleugh*. And I'm up front, pressed against the metal barriers like cattle, wishing my secret sorry love story didn't sound like the inspiration behind Avril Lavigne's 'Sk8er Boi', or thrust against the throbbing vibration of the amp with the groupies, because Nile just loves Lowe's band SO MUCH (FUCK MY LIFE!). He wants to stand at the front and sing every song, word-perfect, lyrics I can't stand because I feel them so badly, like they've been scratched on my skin with a razorblade. The ones I think are about me even though I know they aren't. And I mosh in the pit like a seal does tricks for a treat, balancing beach balls on my nose, with the other hardcore fans, getting knocked and shoved, feeling like a nobody.

Even though I am proud of Lowe – of course I am – it kills me, eats me up from the inside to attend. Lowe's evolved into this confident edible front man without me even realizing. He's got it all and he's still so normal.

The bigger the show, the harder it gets. The distance, amplified. It's like Lowe doesn't know me and I don't know him, not even when I take photos with my disposable camera because I should play the proud aunty. My thumb winding back on the plastic reel, wishing I could wind back to a time before this. Knowing I'll never get the reel developed because it will hurt too much. My eye behind the small square window, only there, with my face hidden. Can I let it be known how much I wish things could be different? How I long to be the cool girlfriend instead. But I'm caught in a trap. And snap, I steal the freeze-frame.

'HEY! Take a photo of me!' Nile shouts, posing in front of the band, big cheesy grin, thumbs up. I love seeing him happy, of course I do, but *PLEASE be cool, Nile, not a bloody tourist.* Professional journalists and their expensive cameras elbow me out of the way; my pathetic little disposable Kodak might as well get struck out of my hand and stomped on. Until I lose Nile to a crowd-surf and I'm glad the music is so loud so no one can hear a heart break like mine. But, oh, there goes Nile sailing past Lowe's eyeline like an inflatable dinghy!

'THIS IS AWESOME!'

He makes *that* rock sign with his hands.

Of course Nile wants to meet the whole entire band and stay for drinks after and *would he like to come backstage for a glass of whisky?*

'YES, PLEASE, ARE YOU FOR REAL?' he says, eyes pinging out of his skull like he's been invited to Santa's Grotto.

He can hardly believe his fortune. He's taken down the backstage corridors with the AAA pass strapped eagerly to his chest, looking back at me in disbelief, grinning, wanting more photos – it's so cute but it's also so . . . uncool. In the green room, which isn't green but dark and dingy where the sofas have seen the unthinkable, full of posters of the Sex Pistols and X-Ray Spex, Nile takes it in turns to talk one-on-one with Lowe's band members about how incredible they all are, which are his favourite parts. He wants to talk lyrics with Lowe: *what is he saying?* He wants to show off to everybody that I'm Lowe's oldest friend; he lovingly *brags* about it with pride and they all love him. They all adore Nile. He's so pure and uninhibited. They give him a True Love t-shirt. *Oh, for fu—* He'll be wearing that now non-stop now, won't he? Toodling around his bedroom with nothing on his bottom half probably like Donald Duck – *and* a poster, *is this necessary?* He rolls it up proudly, like a Star Wars fan with a toy lightsaber and I can't help but cringe when he asks the band to sign his jeans with a permanent marker. Really, does he *HAVE* to? On your *jeans*, Nile? Are you sure? Please don't. Ick. And I find myself thanking Lowe's band, how a mum might when the local fire brigade let her five-year-old son hold the hosepipe and sit up front in the driver's seat. *Aren't you a lucky boy?* They are all so happy that I'm going out with somebody who is so lovely, so difficult to dislike. It's what they'd want for me. I don't want Lowe to be happy for me, I want him to catch fire with jealousy. I feel patronized.

At the same time I'm envious of Nile's security and confidence, that he isn't threatened in the slightest of my friendship with Lowe, how some partners might be. He never asks if we had a thing in the past. He never hesitates to point out how cool Lowe is. He's only celebratory and generous with his kind words and energy, revving up their gigs for them. Nile really is lovely. He's free. I'm the lucky one.

I see Lowe step out, wrap his arms around Rachel from behind and kiss her swan neck. Her arms go up to hold him in; she smiles. They're the perfect couple. *I'm so happy for you, Lowe, I really am.*

If I'm so happy, why do I feel myself wilt like the *Beauty and the Beast* rose under the glass? We're both in love – just with other people. Maybe it *is* possible to be in love with more than one person at once? Maybe Lowe's really actually in love and I'm not and I'm just pretending and I'll never be set free from this curse and I'm not so happy at all. It's really fucking sad actually.

Night, we say, *night.*

That evening, Nile and I lie, heads touching in his bed. I ask, 'When college ends, what will you do?'

'I don't know yet,' he says, 'but one thing's for sure, I'm never going back to Devon. I want to stay here in London with you. Go to drama school, get a role in a great play, then a film, then win a BAFTA.' How beautifully delusional and great. 'Then maybe you'll marry me?'

I hear his smile.

I smile too, because it's so sweet how he says it.

And in the darkness I can just about see Lowe's face on the True Love poster already taped to Nile's wall, with all the other posters of the 'rockstars' we look up to who have no clue we even exist.

Chapter 23

Nile does well. He gets callbacks at most of the best drama schools and courses in the UK. He works hard. Too hard. He doesn't want to do anything else except rehearse his monologues. 'Test my lines again,' he orders, over and over. He gets impatient with me if he fluffs them. Like it's my fault. Whilst he rehearses, I write some monologues myself in my notebook, I enjoy it, stepping into a characters' shoes for a page. Only, the closer Nile gets to a place at drama school the more anxious he becomes. He punishes himself and it's horrible to see. He hangs around theatre box offices to get the cheapest seats and lurks around after to chat to directors. He pulls all-nighters – reading plays and watching films – and this makes him irritable. I say, 'You're making yourself ill, Nile; they shouldn't be making you feel like you need to put so much pressure on yourself. You'll be paying for this course, after all; it's *only* drama school.'

He talks about getting braces, closing the Madonna gap in between his front teeth.

'Are you for real?' I ask. 'Your lovely hippo teeth are one of my favourite things about you.'

'America don't like imperfect teeth,' he says.

'But, we're not in America. We're here. And if they don't like your lovely teeth then I don't like America.'

Every rejection letter is just another finger being lifted off the cliff from which he's been dangling, and Nile doesn't get into any drama schools. It's a disappointing shock for us all that leaves me furious at the broken system. But he doesn't want to hear about that. 'You can try again next year?' I offer, even though I can't bear to think of him going through all that again. Poor Nile. He scrunches up the letters. He can't get an agent without a play to showcase himself in and his parents don't have the money to bankroll him whilst he continues to audition off his own back in London, even if he was to live at Aunt Linda's. 'I'll just get a job!' he says brightly but his parents pull the plug on that. They have already set him up with a job back home – teaching Performing Arts at a summer school at the local arts centre. Besides, Aunt Linda has a new tenant moving into the box room and needs the rent. He sees this as insulting. His dreams, *crushed*. His bitterness manifests itself monstrously; it casts a physical effect over us. He very quickly cuts all ties with London. He say it's 'the worst place on earth'. He say it's 'overpriced', 'fake' and 'full of knobheads'. He asks, once, if I'd consider moving to Devon and when I say, 'I'll definitely visit you but not to live, I'm sorry,' he doesn't ask me again.

We don't break up, exactly. At the end of college, he says he's going back to Devon. For good. Too proud for the farewell drinks I suggest organizing.

'I love you,' I tell him. He doesn't say it back. I watch his train pull out of the station, more sad than I thought I'd be. I really loved him.

'My daughter,' Dad announces, smacking his worn Levi'd thigh, nudging his girlfriend, Lovely Naomi (who owns at least thirty pairs of glasses with the exact same frame just in different colours, has a twenty-three-year-old son who lives *off-grid* and is Lovely).

'Eighteen years old and the first in our family to go university, I can't believe it! You'll be buying me a house one day!'

Er. I don't think so, Dad. I smile, not wanting to disappoint him in front of Lovely Naomi. It isn't even a great university.

'Let's celebrate!'

Any excuse for a pint at the pub, a pint that *I* have to buy.

'Where's that nice Neil bloke gone?'

'Nile,' I correct. 'He's gone back to Devon.'

'Shame. Why can't he live here in London?'

I don't have the energy to go into details with my dad about why the world isn't exactly the same as it was when he was sixteen. 'Dad, NOBODY can live here. It's so expensive. I'm at university and I still have to live with Mum.'

'You could always live with me?' Dad asks.

'Thanks, Dad.'

Lovely Naomi sips her vodka tonic.

Twice a week I commute to my 'uni' to study Creative Writing in an old, empty, dead Lord's house. The course is taught by tutors who either don't show up, or, *if* they do, *very much* don't want to, and ignore us or slip off to have a breakdown. Or my favourite – just apologize, openly, for how embarrassingly bad the course is. I make *one* friend. (And yes, thanks to Myspace, they are a True Love fan. It's kind of hard to find someone my age who isn't.)

This is a hard landing after the joy I had at college, where I saw the world through rose-tinted glasses. Where life was bustling, it now feels stark. Meanwhile, Lowe's on tour with his band. I try to visualize an invisible silver chain, hoping he's still clenching to the links of us with our short and sweet exchanges:

Hey, Ella, we're in Scotland! How are you? x

I try to anchor the chain. **Cool! All good here, course is a bit dry but writing lots. Have the best time, miss you, hope the shows are going well. X**

And he doesn't reply and I can't help but feel I'm not an anchor but a ball and chain.

We talk less and less because the patter of small talk is just anxiety-inducing and exhausting, our lives so different. The days go on and on. I begin to avoid updates on him and the band like my bank statements.

To fill the precious time that I'm meant to be using to study, my dad's friend gives me a part-time job as a junior at his hair-dressers. I wash hair, sweep dead hair, check in clients, make coffee, people watch. I write poems at the front desk on scraps of paper and take the fluff out the tumble dryer. This way I can spend more money on food and alcohol but also theatre tickets and books and gigs. I write lots. I read lots. I watch lots. I eat, very lots, of sandwiches. And although university really isn't what I thought it would be, London is still the best city in the world. London has it all. I give myself an education.

That's what I tell myself anyway as I wave goodbye to Aoife and Bianca. They're headed for Gatwick airport, their towering backpacks loaded and strapped nearly as high as their expect-ations, for their gap year. They're going travelling, flying around the world. And with clever Ronke doing us proud at Cambridge, the only place I'm flying is off the handle. I'd watched Bianca hand-write out the names of hostels and night clubs and cram it into her camo bumbag; it's all so last minute. This is just *crazy*; No plan. No return ticket. No *jumpers*! Have they lost their minds?

'*Really?*' I ask again. 'Do you *really* not know *one* person out there in *Cambodia*? Are you really just going to leave it *all* behind? Are you *really* about to share rooms with *strangers*? Are you not . . . *scared?*'

'Of what?' They laugh like I'm cute.

'Errr . . . drugs, bugs, being mugged?' I didn't mean to make it all rhyme but they know what I mean. What about *rape? Being kidnapped? Crocodiles? Ayahuasca? Diarrhoea? Full moon parties?*

Their train pulls away and I wave them off, standing there

with their families like the left-behind little sister. We turn and walk away, making patent chit chat. Bianca's dad offers to buy me a hot chocolate from Caffè Nero as consolation, and obviously I say yes because he's loaded. A guy my age stands behind me in the queue wearing a True Love t-shirt. You've got to be fucking kidding me. *HOW?* I HATE THE INTERNET.

'Cream and sprinkles?'

'Yes please,' I choke, tears in my eyes. I feel like a sinking toad in the hole.

For someone who was already feeling particularly lonely, I am now just alone.

One night after work, I sit on an empty bus. I love sitting up front on the top deck so I can feel like I'm driving the whole damn thing. The night glitters. I can see the stars. I miss Lowe. I should text him. The space between us overgrown and abandoned, I could try and make a path towards him. *But what to say?* And what if he doesn't message me back? Should I tell him about splitting up with Nile? I'm definitely not going to tell him how much his band comes up in conversation, that people are now telling *me* about True Love like I've never heard of them. *You'd love them, Ella – they're so cool!*

Thanks for the tip.

I settle for: **Hey Lowe, how are you? x**

And he's calling me. Right now. Mini panic attack. Why is he *calling* me? *That's why I text you!* I hate it when people use a phone as a phone. Why did I have to be on the goddam bus and not in a limousine or out having the time of my life?

'You alright?'

His voice has a hint of *long time no speak* as though that's my fault, as though I've been difficult to get hold of.

'Yeah, I'm really good thanks.' Currently not great. 'You?'

'I'm actually in Brighton!' He laughs at himself, like it's a joke.

'On tour?'

'I'm actually . . . K, don't laugh but *studying* here.'

'In *Brighton?*'

BRIGHTON? Suddenly he seems so far away. It's a place you go for a day-trip, somewhere you need a full tank of petrol for. I want to get off the bus and walk this news off, but it's dark, so I let the feeling scramble about my body, trying to find a way to *place* this strange energy. I want to smash the 'break in case of emergency' glass, pull out the little red hammer and cave a window in just so I can breathe. I fiddle with my hair in the reflection of the window. It does not look like 'Karen O' like the hairdresser said it would; it looks like I'm wearing a wig. That's the last time I ever let a hairdresser 'have a play' with hair attached to my head.

'Yeah, I managed to get a place on the music course here last minute through clearing so, yeah, it all happened so fast. I'm a term late but Dad said I couldn't sign a record deal unless I at least *tried* to get a degree' – back-up plan, I guess – 'so I'm living in a dump with three guys! The high life!'

So, they haven't signed a record deal yet. The relief of normality rushes through me like a sea breeze.

'Wow, *Brighton* . . . ?' I say again. I conjure Lowe under the blue skies, the mint railings on the front, the pebble beach and the happy ice-cream faces. The town-houses with their sea-salt blistered edges.

'I'm not actually doing any of the coursework. I'm just using the student loan to pay for rehearsal space until they kick me out.' *Great plan, you salad.* 'It's nice by the sea. You and Nile should come down; we have some gigs coming up soon.'

'Well . . . actually, Nile and I have split up.'

'What?' Lowe sounds genuinely shocked. 'I'm sorry – I didn't know.'

'No, no, it hasn't been long and you weren't to know.'

'Aww, Ella, shit, man. He was a nice guy.'

So why does his voice sounds like he's smiling?

'It was the right thing,' I tell him.

'Come to Brighton? Stay with me?'

'In the dump?'

'Yeah, in *the dump*.' He laughs. He tilts his voice to make it sound appealing. 'It'll be amazing.'

Amazing? It *could* be. But that all depends on where Rachel is in all of this.

So my new haircut and I make the effort to go to Brighton for a visit. I write a silly detective short story – to let off steam – on the train. My heart is thrumming at the station where we've agreed to meet, me begging that he's not got Rachel in tow.

Here he comes. *Ugh, I adore him. Annoying.*

'Nice hair,' Lowe says. The wind traps in the station are not being too cruel to me and letting it sit still.

'You've shaved all yours off!'

He rubs his skinhead, as if embarrassed like I'm his grandma. 'Shall we go back to mine so we can drop off your stuff?' He eyes my giant bag. He probably just has his phone, card, key and tobacco all in his jacket pocket. 'Do you want me to carry it for you?'

'No thanks, I'm good. I'll panic I've forgotten it.' When really, I need the heavy bag to ground me; I'm so happy to see him my feet could lift off the ground like a helium balloon.

Lowe shares what is meant to be a four-bedroomed family house, which has become a many-bedroomed party house with definitely more than three guys. But it seems any guy who isn't him kind of blurs into one and multiplies. It's a sad forgotten place – too sad for a family – where there is never any toilet paper in the cold and musty bathroom. Where every cupboard handle is sticky. Dirty plates with congealed ketchup, ominous wet stains on the floor. The only glasses are dirty, stolen from pubs with beer brands on them, cigarettes floating inside, bloated out like strange new species of marine life. And stolen traffic cones because *hahaha, random*. The housemates can't get their heads around Lowe and me, our radical platonic relationship. It's blowing their schoolboy minds.

Ryan, who has actual man beard stubble and looks like a scarecrow, puts his fingers to his temples and dramatically says to Lowe as though I'm not there, 'Lemme get this straight: a girl that's *not* having sex with you is going to sleep in your bed? Alright, whatever, mate. I know when I smell a rat.'

Yeah. Me too.

'Sorry about him,' Lowe says, embarrassed, quickly shutting the scarecrow out. 'He's showing off because you're here. I don't know why he said that; girls aren't ever in any of our beds.'

Lowe's room is downstairs by the kitchen, brown and all very much on the floor. I look for signs of Rachel but find no left behind earrings or shoes, no love letters or photographs – just a bed, CDs and records stacked, guitars and laundry bags filled with clothes.

And to me, it is *heaven*.

I can see living away from home has already taken its toll, that Lowe looks not great, that his clothes are hanging off him. He's not eating or sleeping properly, smoking too much and not getting outside. His inhalers are empty and he's not bothered to chase up the prescription. The rings around his eyes are darker. I don't think the shaved head has helped matters. But sometimes, at certain angles, truly, the lack of hair just enhances his lovely face. A face so *stupendous* that if anything, hair only interrupted it. But the band are *thriving* in that underground unsigned way – there's momentous tension, pressure and buzz about their every move. Everyone wants to know.

'We're waiting for the right label and the right offer,' he shares. 'Until then, though, I've got about three pounds in my bank account.' He laughs in that way you probably can do when you're pretty certain you're going to be rich soon, picking a vintage Levi's denim jacket up off the floor, sliding it over a hoody and still managing to look like James Dean.

'So come on, let's go for a night out on the town.' He pops out his elbow theatrically like Dick Van Dyke and I link his arm in Poppins flamboyance, triumphant and jolly, ready to hit the town with our three pounds. And when the roads get narrower and we hit the lanes, he swaps the arm link for a hand-hold and I melt.

The weekend in Brighton is busier than when we met earlier and we can't even get from his place to the pub without being spotted a thousand times, without somebody wanting a photo or to stop and chat. Strangers want to be his mate, want him to be their boyfriend. They look me up and down like *oh so you're his girlfriend, you're the one he chose*. But I'm not. And Lowe, being Lowe, just keeps his hood up and muddles along, taking the time out to talk to every friend, every fan, every passer-by with a giant kind smile and interested eyes, smoking rollie after rollie, nodding along, not fazed. He signs an autograph with his left hand. His right hand is in mine.

We sit on the pier, the water licking the slats. We watch a tired caterpillar rollercoaster take screaming children through the bite of an apple, and mess about and talk, and those sad eyes of his truly go on forever, go to that *other* place I have only read about in books or seen in films or heard in lyrics that I've never understood. Trauma to me is watching *Moulin Rouge*, falling out with a friend, running out of milk. But he has witnessed the darkness of grief and returned, as if rescued, his eyes holding everything inside the tie-dye sprawl of their infinite wonder.

The colour of smudge. Where the sea meets the sky in a storm. Concentrated oil paint. Drenched in it all. Like a song.

I ask, when I am just about ready to hear the answer, because I feel obligated, 'How are things going with Rachel?'

'Alright.'

He tokes on his roll-up cigarette so hard I hear the nicotine travel to his lungs, his frown pinching at the top of his head.

'Rach's still in London and I'm here.' He shrugs and relights it with one of those cheap plastic lighters, blowing the end to keep it alight. 'She kind of annoys me, I dunno . . . '

Sometimes I feel like I'm a competition winner fangirl meeting him; other times I feel like a volunteer, giving him an hour to relieve his loneliness. I flit between the two sad states. It's for me. It's for him. Then, there are these times when I trick myself that we are a couple. That this is us. That it always has been, always will be. That might be the worst state of all.

'The band are my main focus anyway.' He nods, looking out to the water.

But I can see 'they' are on his mind. She doesn't call or text him the whole time I am there.

It's a few days later and I'm back in London, when I get a text from Lowe:

Rach has gone to California. We broke up. I'm OK. R u about? x

Chapter 24

Now

The blindfold is makeshift, made from one of those towelled tennis headbands. It's our anniversary. Five years.

'Almost there, Ells.' He shuffles me gently but pinching my elbow with a definite grip of excitement. The kind of touch a person only gives you if they want to let you know they would like to have sex with you tonight. But it isn't really foreplay; I have the spatial awareness of a clumsy, happy dog but we've been really trying for the last month, Jackson and I. Running. Talking. Taking the time to prioritize one another. We are getting our mojo back, and are better – than we've been in a long while – for it.

Through the autumnal Halloween park, I pretend I can't see a thing under the blindfold, but I can make out the grainy *Blair Witch* half-light of the brown-bread sky in the gaps between the blindfold and my chubby cheeks. The trees stand like an army of knives in a knife block.

'Just a little bit further . . . '

We pull onto a busy main street. Jackson, like a puppet-master, has to dodge the passing people; he's laughing now. I hear people mention the blindfold excitedly. This makes my heart beat.

I know there are doormen by the way the doors open simultaneously and sweep me in with crispy fallen leaves; the blast of a rich life hits us like interrupting an oven full of roast potatoes mid-bake. The clatter of service, clanging of trays and twanging cutlery, voices washing overhead, laughter and, somewhere, string music. Here, where the sunshine could switch on with the flick of a button like a lightbulb and shine red hot if you wanted, where candlewax drips thick as butter, pink lobster claws stare up at you, lemon slices come in handkerchiefs and you *know* the toilet paper is more quilted than your duvet at home. This place is posh.

I slip my burnt orange faux fur coat off my shoulders and onto a wooden hanger, with help from a staff member. I am special and loved and important and inadequate and inferior and self-conscious and guilty and consumerist and a brat and a fraud and a movie star, and all those things you're meant to feel when someone spoils you. And the blindfold comes off. The sign reads: LOGAN's. Posher than posh.

'You're a handsome Disney Prince,' I say and he is, valiant in his long navy mac and shirt. Radiant. Someone who will turn heads. I can see in his eyes that he's nervous by this experience too, that it isn't just me overwhelmed and flustered.

I take in the shining chessboard-tiled floor, like something from a gothic fairy tale, as we trip-trap towards our black leather studded booth. There is marble, wine glasses, salt and pepper pots so heavy you could kill a bear. Trolleys loaded with veiny cheeses and clouds of tiramisu. A gleaming wagon of an ice bucket, like a sledge on crushed ice, rammed with bottles of wine, ready to be yanked out. The twinned arched windows, the domed ceiling, the antique Tiffany lamps and fierce candles. One of those old-fashioned lifts with the ornate guards, and, above, a huge balcony that hangs overhead. I am reminded of Christmas for some reason, but nearly everything decadent makes me think of Christmas. A giant gold clock eyeballs us; the room seems to dance.

'Oh, you're sneaky . . . '

I go in to kiss him. He smells like expensive aftershave – the woody, smoky one he got in Liberty.

A tail of sizzling fish sails past on a speeding silver tray; heads turn; a woman tips her head back with a cackle.

'Happy anniversary, Ells . . . ' Jackson says, a bit calmer at the table. 'You look really beautiful tonight.'

'Oh, no, don't, you'll make me cry.' I catch his eye. *PING*!

Waiters fuss around us like we're superstars doing a costume change mid-performance – flapping huge menus and wine lists, reeling off specials; corn-fed chicken, steak tartare and dressed crab. Jackson and I take turns, politely murmuring, *Thanksthankyouthanks.*

We giggle like it's our first date as we overhear a table, in drunken broadcasting bellows, exchange conversation: pedigree dogs, country houses and recommendations for what I'm pretty sure is that procedure where you PAY to have your bum hole cleaned out with a plastic pipe. I pull a face at Jackson. Mutter, *These lot really aren't our species.* My appetite diminishing. I know Jackson wants to make an effort, as do I – I appreciate the gesture but I'm not sure this place is very *us*. I don't want Jackson spending all this money on *this*. We've just bought the flat. I'd happily have beans on toast.

I scrunch up my nose, to assess how he's feeling without sounding ungrateful, open my mouth to say, *Hey, shall we just leave? This place is a bit . . .*

And suddenly, no, he's reaching inside his jacket pocket, getting down on one knee now. *JACKSON.* You're fucking kidding me.

'Wait . . . ' I say. GET UP! GET UP! GET UP!

And then I see it. It. The navy velvet ring box and inside: a ring and all the things that come with it. I want to laugh but he's deadly serious. I can physically see the adrenaline in his eyes. I mean, this is wonderful, magical, special and so kind but—

'Jackson – what are you doing?' I find myself saying.

I clap my hands over my face and feel the eyes of the staff and diners at Logan's, an audience at this showdown. I see Jackson's shaking hands, *feel* his nerves, hear his dry mouth opening to say—

PLEASE, DON'T SAY IT.

'Will you marry me, Ella?'

His teary eyes are a jewelled promise of a good life. I know he'll be an amazing kind forever-partner. I know he would move the earth to make us happy. I know, with him, I would always be OK. Listened to, cared for, understood, valued. I would love him. He would love me. I know he'll get the big Dulwich house one day. The nice car. Holidays to the Maldives. I can see him as a dad, jeans rolled up past his ankles to paddle in the sea, two faceless children holding bamboo fishing nets. We'd never have to worry, solid for whatever life threw at us.

'El?'

I realize that Jackson and the restaurant are waiting for my reply. Even the chefs, flames turned down, are egging me on. The waiter's already peeling the gold foil from a thirty quid glass of champagne in anticipation. I'm not meant to be drinking but this is an exceptional circumstance, a once-in-a-lifetime treat. I've never told Jackson I was giving up for good and I suppose if I can break sobriety with my mates I can do it now, with Jackson, at something as momentous as this. As far as life events go, this is up there.

'Sorry!' I laugh and the restaurant laughs back like we're kids in a school play forgetting our lines. 'Yes?' And the room applauds. 'Of course, *yes*.'

YES. *YES?* YES! There, I said it. Relationships take work but, see, *this* is what happens when hard work pays off. You reinforce your commitment. You strengthen. You pour more love in and then more on top of that to lock in the love. Air-tight.

Jackson leaps up to embrace me and I fall into his chest. He kisses me on the lips, quite greatly. It's so romantic, tipping me back like this; *where did that come from?* People *whoop*, the champagne cork pops, shooting bubbles and glory into glasses – *ohmygodohmygod* – *this is a big deal!* Jackson slides the ring onto my finger. It twinkles under the lights, looking foolishly out of place with my chipped green nails and junkyard rings but I am walking on air.

And just like that life resumes; people order more drinks, starters, request the bill. The moment for them, already a memory, but for us, everything has changed.

We're getting married.

'I'll be back to take your order – enjoy and congratulations,' the waiter says.

'THANKS!' I gurgle, still not managing to find my voice, and both us and the waiter laugh at my giddiness.

'Jackson!' I tap his arm, sounding almost annoyed; it's the shock, the adrenaline, recovering from the scene that is so out of character for him. 'What on earth?'

'Honestly, when I heard you caught the bouquet at Mia's wedding, I was dying!' He laughs. 'How mad was that? I was texting Aoife like *how am I gonna keep this a secret?*' Bitch. 'All worked out though.' He squeezes my thigh, goes on to tell me how much I'd love the shop he bought it from, how special the jeweller said the ring is.

'Does it fit OK?'

'Yeah, perfectly.' It really is an amazing ring. I inspect it closer, wishing I had a magnifying glass to capture all its detail.

'It's antique, opal,' he says. 'You have to be careful getting chemicals on it, washing up and in the bath and stuff; they said it's called a water stone?'

So why is my finger scalding hot? Tight and burning. I feel extra pressure to take care of it. My ring and its demands.

'Well, cheers, to us,' he says.

'Cheers,' I say, toasting, as Jackson pretends to fancy things off this unappetizing menu. I take a mouthful of champagne. It doesn't taste good. I could have had a whole Nando's for this. I'm hot, light-headed, dizzy. My heart is racing rapid. I'm trapped under my own skin. I fan myself with the menu, inhaling deep. Is this a panic attack? Oh no. Not here. Not in front of all these people.

'You OK?' he asks.

Probably because I look as washed out as a poorly made cold cup of tea. 'I don't want to be rude – I'm sorry, this all very lovely, Jackson, but shall we get out of here?'

Jackson doesn't hesitate. 'You read my mind.'

He holds up some cash. 'My parents gave me this, to treat us.' He smiles. *Great, everyone knows. DOLLOP ON THE PRESSURE THEN WHY DON'T YOU?* Jackson tries to be cool by leaving cash on the table to pay for the glasses of champagne so we can make a swift exit.

'I don't think that's going to cover it . . . ' I say.

He places down two more and we make a dash for it, apologizing to the maître d' and front of house, who are baffled as to why we'd walk out, as they fumble nervously for our jackets like they've done something wrong.

We tumble out onto the street. I can breathe again. Alive with the possibility of a normal Friday night in Soho, I immediately feel better.

'Alright?' he asked.

'Yeah,' I say, my body in chills. 'Sorry. I think I'm just in shock? I'm *shivering.*'

'Aww, come here,' he soothes, stroking my back. Kissing my head, taxis honking past. One screams as it rushes by:

I don't want to marry you.

My head is playing tricks. I need to eat.

'Let's go to the pub,' he suggests, which he never does, so

obviously – now I've broken the seal – I'm at it like a rat up a drainpipe.

At The Ship, some sort of normality resumes: ordinary people in ordinary clothes, Pulp's 'Disco 2000' – oh, the safe, cuddly past – not a million staff shoving menus in our faces. Jackson brings over two pints and a packet of scampi fries in his mouth, drops them off like he's instigating a game of fetch. He's got an unmistakable spring in his step.

I pick up my pint and drain half of it.

'Woah, you alright there?' Jackson laughs.

'Sorry, so *thirsty* after . . . ' ALL THAT! I wipe my mouth.

Jackson, pint untouched, tears the packet of scampi fries open onto the dark wood round table.

'Yesssss, don't worry, I got you your little Frazzles.'

He jokes, knowing I DESPISE scampi fries. I grin at him, taking the crisps, my hands still trembling. I need one of those foil blankets they wear at the end of marathons and films like *Die Hard*.

Jackson rubs my hand, admiring his taste in engagement rings. 'Got a wedding to plan now!'

I slam the brakes on. 'We're broke! Should have bought the place AFTER the wedding like Mia did. That honeymoon money would have been useful!'

'Well, about that . . . ' He folds his arms and leans in close. 'Zahra's promoting me to MD. I get a bonus and it means I'll be an exec. So . . . '

'Aww, Jackson!' I wrap my arms around him. 'This is amazing! I'm so proud of you – you deserve it.' I hold the side of his face with my palms, in case he didn't hear me enough. 'I am so proud of you.' Which I am; he works harder than anybody I know, practically living at the office, on his phone.

'So, let's do it, Ella Wade!' he says, knighting me with his surname; I feel the need to dry-heave at this. 'Let's get married!'

'But let's not rush either,' I say and add, 'I want to enjoy this bit.' By enjoy, do I mean hatch an escape plan?

I cheers his glass with mine.

'Yeah, you're right. We've got all the time in the world.'

Me and Jackson together forever?

I don't want him to feel uneasy so I say, 'I'll have to talk to everyone like this now.' I accentuate all the actions with my hands unnecessarily. '*Oh hey there, hi.*'

He laughs. 'Are you going to tell your mum, then? Violet? Aoife?'

'Oh!' I say, like *thanks for reminding me.* 'I will, but later. Right now, can it just be us?'

After a couple more drinks, I've relaxed. We stumble home tipsily, in no real rush, taking our time; it's not too cold. We get piping hot sandwiches from the Italian bar that come in their foiled packets, fat, salty and perfect. Rickshaws whizz past, tangled in fairy lights, booming out 'Livin' La Vida Loca'. Buses breeze by.

Back to South London. Where the roads become clearer, the people fall away, the streets are darker, quieter. We pop into the corner shop and get a bottle of red wine to keep the celebration going. I take my time to choose the right bottle – I haven't chosen a bottle of wine in a while now – making sure it doesn't have a screw top, making sure it says the right description words – *smooth, full bodied, deep, rich in flavour . . . drinkable*? Who buys a drink that isn't drinkable?

At home I find two tumblers, rifle through the cabinets for a corkscrew and head into the living room where Jackson is putting on music. I already know which song he's going to choose. It's that kind of predictability of a long-term relationship. Even when the other one tries their hardest to be their least predictable, you are aware they are doing just that, so in a way the guess is even easier. Don't tell me – Nick Drake's 'Saturday Sun'. He takes his coat off and throws it on the armchair. He reaches his hand out to me and pulls me in, to sway in the living room. We kiss. It's nice, like in a watching *The Office* for the fourteenth time kind of way. I'm waiting for him to grab me, to squeeze me, to lift my dress up over my thighs or start unplugging my bra at the back with one hand. But it doesn't happen. Not even on a night like this, and before we know it, he's asking me if I want tea.

We sit together on the sofa, sipping our tea, the cork still in the neck of the bottle. Not able to even face resetting the Stay Sober app, I just delete it instead.

Chapter 25

Then

And finally.

At last.

We're both single.

Almost every weekend he waits for me at Brighton station. He's always early. Leaning in the same spot smoking a rollie. The way he jumps to attention at the influx of passengers boarding off the train tells me I'm an awaited gift. We completely clash: him in washed out, faded rinsed denim and wholesale sports socks, and me, a clown in sunshine yellow and bright red squeaky shoes that honk at every step like I'm tromping along to the circus, my heart a rubber duck. He's unwashed and greasy and yet so clean at the same time; his teeth shine, his eyes sparkle, his cheeks glow. And I'm here. One time, I have to get my photos taken to renew my passport for a family holiday and he waits outside as the booth flashes silver. I sit on the stool behind the little curtain, wondering what he's thinking. We wait for them together, and I pray I look decent.

'Can I have one?' he asks.

Really? 'Yeah, course' – ACT COOL – 'I only need two.'

And he carefully folds and rips off the bottom left quarter from the window of me. He puts it in his wallet, in the clear bit where grown-ups put the photos of their kids.

WHAT. IS. THIS?

He always keeps the entire weekend clear for me; I never feel compromised or a burden. He says we can do whatever we want – play the arcades, rummage the second-hand shops, go to the pier. Time glimmers here; it's perfect – a holiday away from home. We eat chips on the beach, buy matching tin turquoise thumb rings from a street market (like wedding rings?! *NO! Ella!*). We try on clothes, returning from the changing room curtain to parade. Some of the outfits make us crack up with laughter, but seeing him try on a simple jacket can bring me to my knees.

Lowe's housemates continue to be stumped by our innocent laughter filling the dusty corners of the living room, warming up the kitchen with our conversation as we make toast. They look at me with hungover, hungry, Lost-Boy-red eyes, like I'm Wendy here to darn their socks and fix their lives. We leave to wind the lanes, stopping on every corner for him to say *hi* to somebody, or take more photos with a stranger, and he always introduces me as his best friend.

'This is Ella,' he says proudly. Even though the fans definitely don't care to meet me.

And I love being with him and the torch I have for him is a phoenix rising, burning and ready to blow. The volume of my life is louder, my surroundings brighter and brighter – shooting day for a postcard bright. I feel I have enough heat in my heart that I could evaporate the sea to sand. We hardly go back to his little brown room, just stay out all day, charging our phones in coffee shops or under pub tables, or just allowing the battery to completely drain and die and we're off-grid, invisible and free, together. Letting the day do what it wants with us. At night, we go dancing, to clubs and venues, where one time I regrettably sing Linkin Park at indie-karaoke with possibly too much *zest*. All the while, *many many*, so many girls try and hug him, kiss him, tell him that they love him.

Lowe is a heartthrob; girls fall at his feet, but he always makes me feel like the only girl in the room.

I stand behind the decks as he DJs an after-party. He's put a pair of headphones around my neck to make me look legit but I haven't got a clue what I'm doing. I watch girls with love-heart-shaped eyes trying to hypnotize him with their drunken glares. I feel the need to shake them and say, *He's just a guy, get on with your life, wake up!* Forgetting I've been in a Lowe-Love-coma for years. *None of these girls love you like I do. Not one.* He plays my favourite songs.

Some nights Dom from college and her girlfriend Ruby, who lives out here and smokes rollies and has incredible hair right down to her bum, come along too and I meet all their friends. And all the bands' friends. And Lowe's housemates. And their friends. And everyone knows everyone and everyone knows the others we've scooped up between us, over the years, along the way. Nobody questions our friendship because we're both 'adults' and single and nothing is happening. WHY *ISN'T* ANYTHING HAPPENING? 'Wow, they really *are* just friends – well, isn't that remarkable?'

Our friendship restores faith in humanity, yet at the same time I feel shit about it. It's a total scam on my part: my love for Lowe, if anything, is only getting stronger. Cementing. Crystalizing. I am a barnacle. A wart. Stubbornly refusing to wash away. A tick. I wish I could be de-rooted, tweezered out, before I get eternally trapped under his skin forever. Like Carrie Bradshaw, *I couldn't help but wonder* what he'd be up to if I wasn't here with him. How many of those girls he would stop and talk to.

On a night out, a girl who looks like a model from the Sixties wants to talk to Lowe *outside*. Outside means away from me. She drags him by the zip of his hoodie, eyelashes fluttering. I can see him, faintly, through a stained-glass window – candle-lit diamonds in blues, greens and reds over his face – but not clear enough to read his expression, to see if he's looking for me. *What are they talking about?*

Now I feel like some estranged cousin who his parents force him to hang out with whilst they're in town. To occupy, to keep busy, to tag along.

Ryan, Lowe's scarecrow housemate, finds me on the leather couch. He invites himself to take a seat, his flat pint splashing froth on my yellow velvet flower print dress. 'Whooops, sorry!' He makes himself laugh and I laugh back even though I'm annoyed. He eases in. 'So . . . you and Lowe, then?'

'What about us?'

'You guys . . . ?' He criss-crosses his hands, his fingers inter-locked. 'A thing? Or just . . . ?'

'No!' I shriek. 'We're just friends.'

He wiggles his finger at me sloppily. He's pissed; he has a stain down his front; he's harmless, possibly trying to flirt. 'No, no, no, don't play games. You sleep in his bed every week – you're together all the time. You're single; he's single – what's the deal?'

'There is no deal.' I laugh it off weakly, to be polite – not that I owe the scarecrow anything. But there is a problem – Lowe's outside with a girl. Ryan swigs his drink, offering me some. I shake my head, looking for Lowe over his shoulder.

'You really don't fancy him then?' he asks me, plainly, rubbing his stubble. *Oh no, he's gearing up for something – I can feel it.* 'You don't *like* him?'

'I do' – but I don't want it to get back to Lowe that suddenly I'm in love with him because I don't want whatever this intimacy is to stop – 'but not like that.' I put my hands on my lap. Clasped. My prison of a secret, safe.

Ryan, somewhat convinced, nods, his tongue clicking. *Don't do it – oh God, he's doing it.* 'What about a drink with *me* one day, then?'

I laugh it off. 'Ryan, you're not serious; you're drunk. You've seen me looking a state, eating cereal out of your pint glasses for weeks—'

'I like it! It's nice having a woman's touch around the place!' he defends innocently, not realizing how offensive that is.

'I'm not Snow White!' I can only imagine how Ryan sees me, singing whilst letting the deer from outside lick the plates clean like in the cartoon – which by the way is not the way to clean a plate. 'Anyway, I'm not really looking to date.'

'Aw, *please*?' he begs. 'I won't look like *this*.' He drapes his hand down his body and it makes me laugh. I look up at the stained-glass window. Lowe and the Sixties model are gone. I swallow. Fear sets in. The bass of the music bolts through me: where is he? Don't tell me he's gone off with that girl. He wouldn't do that to me, would he? How *can* I even be so sure?

Ryan is still there, coldly blinking, eagerly waiting my response. 'I'm a nice bloke, I promise.'

'I know you are, Ryan,' I say. 'But I really don't want to be your Mrs Scarecrow.'

'One drink?'

'Fine. Yes. OK. One day we can have One Drink.'

Ryan has more chance of having a beer with David Bowie.

'Yessssss!' He fist pumps. 'Get in!'

'Please don't do that again,' I say, but then we actually find ourselves laughing.

'See? This is why I need you around.'

Lowe makes his way over to me. Where the hell has he been? Where's the girl?

'Nightmare,' he says. 'One of our friends' ex-girlfriend. Keeps trying to chat to us about their break-up.'

Really?

His loyalty surprises me every time. No matter what happens on any night out, who we speak to, dance with, who steals us for a-too-long-cigarette or corners us, robs us of each other, we always walk home, hand in hand through the navy night along the seafront. Walking away from everyone like the last two people on earth. I wonder if it's the same for him – is he so happy he could die too? Because I'd go like this, in this state of felicity. The elements battle, rain so hard it's needles. My shoes are puddles but he's the one for me; with the lantern of him in my heart, I can do anything.

We hurry inside for tea, the key wet, slippery in his hand, his housemates sleeping or still out for the night. We play 'house' in the dark. I towel dry my hair and feel the black flecks of running mascara smudge on my fingers. I wish I could look sexy soaking wet, like one of those beachy-hair girls who let their hard nipples point through soaked vest tops but I know I look like the Penguin from *Batman Returns*. He kicks his jeans off with a smile. I put them on the radiator because I know he wouldn't do it, and the smell of wet pub floors begins to brew. We brush our teeth at the same time, staring in the mirror, polishing our smiles. Then we slink back into the bedroom to listen to soft music for a bit, and I admire the room he's built for himself. I soak in his human-beingness. How if he's hungry – he eats. If he's tired – he sleeps. If he's cold – he puts clothes on. If something's broken – he fixes it. Nothing needs to be new; it's used or worn until it falls apart, and if it isn't used he gives it away.

His silhouette, like a protective guardian, hangs over me. I catch sight of his skin, his ribs, his freckles, his soft belly and his arms. His armpit hair. *Oh God.* And he politely waits outside whilst I change into my silly actual matching teal pyjamas. I never attempt to look hot. 'I'm gonna melt your heart,' I joke as I reveal my scrubby twinset. He slams his hand over his heart. 'Oh, I'm melting!' and he watches me crawl towards him in his little lived-in brown bed that to me is like a four-poster super king with Egyptian cotton 800-thread-count sheets at the poshest hotel in the world, and my room service is strong tea in some mug that doubles up as an ashtray. He keeps a photo of his mum taped to his side of the bed, by his pillow, her face watching him whilst he sleeps. He looks so much like her. *Beautiful.*

Nothing happens, not once. We just hold each other the whole night. His tender arms – smooth, naturally sculpted, just right, how a human's arm should be, rather than pumped from weight-lifting – wrap around my gigantic bursting heart.

Once, when we're waiting to fall asleep, I ask, 'Have you ever fallen over on stage?'

'Of course, loads. I fell over on tour; I had a pint in my hand and tripped on the top step. I was covered in beer; I had to just get on with it.'

We both giggle in the darkness.

'Did people see?'

'Everyone saw, Ella. I, like, *properly* dropped on my hands and knees! Like a . . . cow position.'

We belly laugh; tears spring out of our eyes.

'Did you laugh?'

'Yeah, how could you not? It was so funny . . . '

'What did you do?'

'I was just like *oh*. And had to carry on.'

'Aahahaha! Sorry,' I cry. 'It's just the image of you, thinking you're so cool and then down you go . . . '

'Down I went.'

Our stomachs ache. We manage to collect ourselves for a moment of peace. And then one of us splutters into laughter, and we're off again.

Another time he says, 'I like your eyes.'

And I say, 'I like yours.'

And that's it. Then we roll over. We sleep the night, soundly, back-to-back, spine to spine, like the Kappa logo.

He says, 'These are the favourite nights of my life. When you're here. I'm at my happiest when I'm with you.'

He says, 'Goodnight, Ella Cole.'

I worry that in the morning light he'll be regretful, itching to get on with his day without me, like he can't wait to pack me back on the train to London with a takeaway cup of black coffee and sober frostiness, fumbling the ice-cold kiss of fresh mint toothpaste and reset: 'See Ya.'

But no: it's the opposite. I will never forget his face in the mornings, seeing me there on his pillow; he seems to hold me even tighter. Are we friends? Or something more? I don't know. But I do know how comfortable I am in his sheets, in my skin, in the bungalow of him.

This goes on for a few weekends in a row. Constant consistency, speaking in shorthand, day after day, late nights, proper fry-up breakfasts, tea in bed, me reading books and him listening to music on his headphones. We share cups, socks, jumpers, money, food, ideas. I know what he likes. White chocolate. Cheeseburgers. Satsumas that he splits with me. We are bound. *Waiting*. For Lowe to get his shit together, to muster the courage to switch us into a new gear. For what we'll become.

Stepdad Adam takes us on a family holiday. An all-inclusive, three-star hotel in Egypt with seven curly waterslides and watered-down Coke on tap. Every evening, after a day of falling in and out of sleep and reading and writing poems by the pool, I come back to my room and sit, whilst Violet and Sonny watch stupid comedies and eat almond Magnums. Hair dripping, on the edge of my bed, I speak to Lowe when I can from the hotel room phone (I get *badly* in trouble with my mum and Stepdad Adam about the bill). I've never been so far from him. I have perspective; I feel like I'm recharging somehow. Preparing to return, *glowing*, and for everything to fall into place.

On my return, True Love have a big gig happening. Their biggest yet. The major record label that has been chasing them for months and has offered a deal is coming down. So of course, I'm going to Brighton to watch them play. I'm staying with Dom and Ruby because Lowe's been in rehearsals. I've not seen him for almost a month.

I wear cut-off red tights, a blue denim mini skirt. A second-hand shirt speckled in bunches of purple grapes. I spend a good twenty minutes doing the buttons up and down, not sure if I should show a glimpse of my pink bra or not, but then decide against it.

I meet Dominique and Ruby, Lowe's housemates – yes, Scarecrow Ryan – and the rest of the new Brighton lot at the pub beforehand. We bump into loads of people we know. Friends, super-fans, groupies. Everybody is saying *how well* I look after my holiday and I know it isn't the holiday at all that's fired up *this* glow. It's Lowe, the effect he has on me. We drink pints and feel the electricity that comes before a gig, especially *their* gigs, like a birthday party. We sing along to every word. Especially in front of record labels – then we really exaggerate our singing. We have a role to play tonight and we are ready.

Ryan swings open the heavy door to the venue, his palm pressed over my head, making an arm-arch for me to walk under. Our wrists stamped, out tickets torn, he says, 'Have you met Lowe's new girlfriend yet?'

And it just hits me.

Like that.

I burst into water like *Amélie* does in the café scene.

Landslide.

Like somebody has reached inside my bloody chest, ripped open my ribcage like a set of jaws and yanked my bulging heart out – all the important tubes still attached – and is now crushing it, before me. Behold the butchery of me, my carcass upside down, drained and hollowed out, swinging on a hook in the foyer of a club. People push past my ghost with their tickets, to buy t-shirts, to worship my murderer.

Well, that's taken the wind *right* out of my sails.

The only feeling worse than being heartbroken is having to pretend you aren't.

'No,' I say. 'I haven't.'

'You still up for grabbing that drink soon?'

But Ryan's bumped into someone he knows. I hear him introduce me but I'm already walking away from his small talk that shouts so big. I feel so fucking sorry for my own self, swishing about like we're something when this very housemate and all the others know he has a new girlfriend. I feel like a mug.

Why hasn't Lowe told me? Why hasn't he *said*? I didn't even know he'd met anyone. And *why the fuck would he do this*? What in the world would let this happen? I look at Dominique, wincing and cringing, and I can tell she knows, and probably, definitely, maybe just didn't know how to tackle this with me because *I've* never tackled Lowe with me. As I said, everyone knows everyone. What did I think? That I could just dip in and out of Brighton and London, squeeze in a holiday and assume the whole place would freeze in time until my return? Did I think things didn't *happen*? That people didn't talk. Didn't move. Didn't touch. Maybe this has been going on longer than I thought? Maybe I was just his little weekend girlfriend?

I tug on Dom's sleeve to get close. 'What's she like?' Because I have to know; she has to be pretty special, otherwise there is no single excuse on this whole earth's crust why he would love somebody who isn't me. Or maybe she made a wish on a star that actually paid attention? FUCK! I want to storm into Lowe's dressing room and say, *You've made a fucking fool out of me. You've broken my absolute heart. What the hell was all that? What are we? Who even ARE you?* and then smash up the whole room.

And Dominque replies like she'd been asked the question a hundred times before, or more likely she's rehearsed it. 'She's . . . *striking*.'

STRIKING.

I wish Dom was a liar.

I might as well pull the elastic of a sling shot back as far as it'll go and launch a rock at my own face. 'What's her name?'

'Heather, I think. Yeah, Heather,' Dominique says. *Heather.* 'She's from New Zealand, studying here.'

I've always wanted to go to New Zealand. It seems so fresh, green spritzy and peaceful, doesn't it? I don't why know what tells me that this Heather is here to stay.

And I'm right.

Of course, after that bomb, I try to dance at the gig. I try to sing along and be *that* friend. I try to stop my eyes from peering through the bobbing heads to identify this mystery 'striking' girl, but the room is a blur. Someone takes a photo and I'm beaming with delight, grinning like a Cheshire cat. You'd never know; you'd never have any idea that inside my guts are decaying in fast-motion like those flowers in ET. Like the documentary we watched in primary school of the mouse decomposing sped up. That's me: mould in my tummy, in my lungs. In my mouth and chest and throat. Mould in my eyes. Mould in my heart.

This sharp shock blading through me. I'm still so soft, I'm still that overripe peach; I cut so easily.

No, I don't hang around after the show, even though Lowe's calling and texting, asking where I am, where the after-party is; he's got me a *gold* wrist band, WHOOP-DE-FUCKING-DOOP! *Oh, thanks, how about FUCK YOU? What, so I can make you look great in front of your new A&R? I don't think so.* I keep myself to myself. No, I don't want to meet *her.* I don't want to cradle her at her first show for him. Play babysitter whilst Lowe chats to his record label all night. Buy each other rounds. Welcome her to the family. *Where we're all just fans, Heather.* Hopeless fans! I am nineteen. FIVE years. *Just MOVE on, girl. GET YOUR LIFE TOGETHER! Two years was too much.*

Three years insulting. Five years: you're the mug. Loving him is not compulsory, Ella. It is not all you know. There are options. Other ways to be loved.

I really thought all of *that* was *it*.

What a waste of make-up.

It's too late to take the train so I sleep at Dom's. But I barely sleep. I lay my rag of a body down on the sofa. Dom holds me but says nothing. I've come to know this feeling well: of intuitive friends knowing what I can't say out loud. I drink a mint tea. 'With a sugar?' *Yes please.* I say I have a stomach ache. But the pain is in my chest. If a doctor were to give me an X-ray they would see that my heart is broken. They would see Lowe swimming in my blood. *You've been infected,* they'd say. *How long has this been going on? How long have you been living in pain? How long have you been doing this to yourself?* They would diagnose me with foolishness, naivety, gullibility, desperation, lovesickness, embarrassment.

The next morning my phone is actually ringing inside my pocket as I step onto the train. It's Lowe. I let it ring. For the first time, Lowe Archer is calling me and I ignore it. I find a seat. I look out of the window, catch my reflection; my hair is growing out of the bowl cut and into the helmet of an astronaut; the process of change, like anything, is always quite ugly but I know, just like the poisonous sky, it won't last forever. I put my headphones in and wait. Until at last, the train pulls away.

Chapter 26

The following Saturday is tropical hot and I'm sweating at the salon. It's like a greenhouse and we're hot-boxed in with the power roar of hairdryers *and* it's fully booked. The whole planet is on fire because of us, roaring our hairdryers and rinsing all the hot water. I'm dashing up and down, checking in clients, making coffee and taking payments. Basically running that goddam joint now. I don't even have time to wee – forget drinking water or having lunch. And then I see it, appearing, like I have to double-take. It's him, his name on my phone.

Lowe.

I feel equally elated and queasy. It's been a week since that Brighton show and we've still not spoken.

When I finally get to my phone, his text reads: **hi ella, i'm in london, are you around? be nice to see you. x**

Be nice. Like fuck it will. Maybe he wants to talk? Maybe things didn't work out with Heather? Maybe he's changed his mind?

Or wait . . . maybe he means *with* Heather?

Oh hell.

We've all tried stalking her on Facebook and MySpace, but nothing comes up, which makes her even more annoying. How dare she be so private and mature? I throw my phone into my open bag.

I fold warm towels. I brush the cakey mouldy damp off the walls. I drag clags of hair like rat tails from the drain. I use my mum's technique of cleaning mirrors with vinegar and balls of newspaper and it works a dream. I wipe down fashion magazines and *National Geographic*. I light a scented candle. I get told off for not scooping leftover colour into the bin before the sink. *It's bad for the environment; do you want fish to eat bleach? No, of course I don't want fish to eat bleach.* I wash hair, LOADS of hair, with rosemary and peppermint, chamomile and orange, eucalyptus and patchouli, and with it the humdrum of the day comes off – the Tube, the rain, the cereal bars. And it swirls down the sink in bubbles.

It's astonishing how vulnerable the baptism of hair washing can make a person; their brain in your hands, their eyes in yours. It's intimate: you listen; you wash it all away. I shampoo a woman's hair and she starts to cry; her tears roll into the sink.

'Are you OK?'

'My husband of forty years has been diagnosed with dementia.'

'I'm so sorry.'

'Life's too short,' she tells me. 'You're young; make it count.'

And I want to give her the best hair wash of her life. Respectful, thorough, treating her head as if it's a delicate crown of gold leaves. She closes her eyes, trusting me, snatching a minute of peace.

I text Lowe back.

I tell him I'm at work. And he – *please not with her* – can meet me when I finish at six. He might have an explanation? If not, it'll be closure, our final goodbye.

It's BOILING hot outside but, with no space in the beer garden, Lowe is sitting *in* the shady pub with a beer. I guess his tail is too in-between his legs for him to have the courage to change our meeting spot and begin calling the shots. When he sees me, his

224

face sunshines like it always does and it's hard not to smile back even though I'm aching like a freshly yanked tooth. He buys me a pint and we down them fast, agreeing it's too nice to be inside. Just before we head out, in the hope of leaving this conversation behind here forever, I say, trying to not sound *too* heartbroken but also refusing to avoid, 'I didn't know you'd met someone . . . '

Lowe looks down at his empty glass. 'It's only been a couple of weeks but yeah . . . '

Down. I. Come.

'Heather . . . I want you to meet her.'

Well, I used to want to run away with you somewhere far away like . . . I dunno . . . Jersey and live forever and have your baby, but it wasn't going to happen, was it?

Does he think I'll be there next week welcoming his new girlfriend into my mum's house and asking if she takes sugar in her tea? Hellllll, no! I get it now. It's clear. I can see it for what it is and this empowers me to sit comfortable in my new stance.

'We're really different' he reassures me. 'Like she knows no music or anything – she's not really into what *we* like or . . . she doesn't drink . . . she's studying, so . . . she's quite hardworking.'

Oh, great, she's all the things I'm not. How I wish I was a child again and couldn't acknowledge and recognize this horrible heat, these tight muscles, this strained migrained twinge in my forehead, this bubbly unpleasant feeling as jealousy. How I wish I could just behave like a child, unfiltered, hurt that it's not gone my way and could indulge in a straight-up tantrum, kicking a wall. But I have to hold it inside. And it eats me like worms in my core, acid in my organs.

Wishing it would turn my way is like wishing the weather to change on a holiday, praying the dark clouds will lift, that the sun will break through and we can run to the beach and be happy. Or wishing that the end of a book could be different and they all live happily ever after.

'I'm just gonna see how it goes,' he adds.

'Cool.' I nod. No, not cool, not cool at all.

'It's good for me to have someone to make me feel *anchored*.'

I was the greatest anchor you've ever seen.

Outside I am grateful for the oxygen and everybody looks like Greek gods, splayed out, half naked, seduced – eating and drinking. We buy more beers from the newsagents. I feel like the people sitting around with their bottles of cider recognize him; somewhere a prosecco cork pops. The smoke of outdoor barbecues billows roasting meat and cobs of corn. The music from outdoor sound systems bumps, the vibration pulsing through the grass. The shouts from the basketball players and skateboarders with their tops off and their sun-kissed shoulder blades. The weather is on my side and love is still young.

Immediately, we forget about Heather or whatever her name is (it's definitely Heather). Anyyyywayyyy, we're too long in the tooth to let the thoughts of her distract us. We kick our shoes off because we want to feel the cold soil under our feet. Lowe smokes rollie after rollie and I'm hypnotized by the ritual – the way he licks his thumb and cocoons the paper, crumbles the tobacco shreds in his fingers, the way he wipes his hand on his jeans and then – the lick – steady and quick. And I come to love that tobacco smell so bad; it's like a rush. And I'm glad because after everything, Lowe is still *Lowe*. It's so hard not to pay him a compliment, but I don't.

'So . . . we signed our record deal.'

'Oh, my word, wow, that's fantastic! Congratulations!'

We chink our beers and hug.

'I'm so happy that you're happy,' I say. 'Then what will you do?'

'I wanna look for somewhere to rent on the seafront.'

'Oh, you're not coming back to London?'

'Not right now; we'll be away on tour anyway so Brighton will just be a nice place to come back to and . . .'

Don't tell me, it's closer to Heather, but he tails off.

' . . . I just like it there right now so that's what I'm doing.'

He shuts down like I was about to try and change his mind.

'Sure.' I nod. This really is the end, isn't it?

Why does crying always feel worse when it's sunny?

Dream career. Girlfriend. New house on the seafront. About to perform his art around the world.

I live at my mum's. Am single. Work part-time at a hairdressers and the only view I see is someone's roots getting done. Plus dandruff – heaps of the stuff. But my writing – at least I've got that.

'I'll still come back to London though,' he says.

I know this is for me. A little dangling carrot. A patronizing pat-a-cake baked just for me. He *does* know what he's doing. That he's hurting me. But if anything, this allows me to loosen my grip.

We finish the beers and get closer. Lowe lies down sideways beside me, propped up on his elbow. I let my eyes take him in for the last time as he rolls his t-shirt sleeves over his shoulder. The sun drools. The cap on his head to one side – necklace catches the light; sweat beads chase. He pulls at the grass blades and racks them up into neat rows near my leg, like one of those cognitive tests to show me the inside of his brain. I think about the pattern I would make if it was me laying them out, but I don't want to hurt the grass. I want to tread as gently as possible and not hurt a fly. Not like Lowe, going around breaking hearts and hurting grass.

He takes out his inhaler, presses it against his mouth and chokes, spluttering out a mouthful of filters that have been rolling loosely in his pocket and got trapped in the mouthpiece.

'What the heck?' He spits the filter out. 'Why are you laughing?'

'Your face!' Tears begin to run.

'Could you imagine how ironic that would have been, if I'd

died choking on *cigarette* filters that were pelleted at the back of my throat by my inhaler?'

As the sun goes down, insects muscle in to feast on everyone's sweet blood (except mine). Lowe goes to buy another pouch of tobacco and a bottle of vodka. *God, he must be about to become seriously rich.* The light shifts, slanting through the trees in spaceship cone beams. The streetlamps ping on. We take turns fidgeting at the unrecognizable rip-off non-brand label, tearing it off into little rice-shaped shreds, the sky now sweet amaretto. Before we know it, we are two kids under a tent of pitch-black darkness and the open sky is ours and the moon is blushing for us. Even the ducks are quacking, *JUST FUCKING KISS HER, MAN!*

But we drunkenly practise our stupid handshake instead, for old times' sake. *Clap, clasp, twist, link, thumb to thumb, spiral, spud, punch, hug.* Any excuse to touch.

'I have a free house . . . if you want to come back?' I ask. Because this will obviously be the final time we ever hang out ever, ever, *ever* again.

The night bus rolls us home, back to mine, and we have a headphone each. Every lyric remotely mentioning love clings to me, and, maybe it's the alcohol, but I find myself latching on like Velcro once again, believing everything is a *sign*, about us, urging me to take a leap of faith and that – TING! – maybe, instead of saying goodbye, MAYBE I can finally tell him how I feel? Maybe if I wait for him it will never happen? So sick am I of being passive, my bold brain begins to chant, *tellhimtellhimtellhim* and the vodka spins the lights of London into hazy drunken stars, and sparks crackle and we slide into each other. How can I say goodbye to Lowe when we're like those jelly alien toys that come in a plastic egg of slime, the ones that were meant to have babies if you pressed their backs together for long enough? When every touch with Lowe is like a vow of some kind. Different from any hand I've ever felt.

I *have* to tell him I love him. Now. It's got to be now. Before it gets too serious with Heather and then there's no going back. I might never have a chance like this again. Before it's too late. I've got to. *Be brave, Ella – you can do it.*

But how the fuck do I begin a sentence like that?

And the bus goes too quick; time just disappears and I don't want to ruin the moment or our friendship, which I feel like I've only just won back. I don't want him to get off this bus. To change his mind.

Usually this walk down the South London backstreets frightens me but not now. Not when I'm with him. Not when I'm love-struck. Walking on air. Bouncing on the trampoline of the moon.

I rush in the house first, my key jangling in the front door, vibrating with nerves about actioning my confession. Lowe hangs back to finish smoking on the doorstep. And I am manic. There have been a few renovations on the house – new heating system and a few licks of paint – but I still feel that shadow of embarrassment.

They say people only take actions from a place of love or fear. Well, right now, when it comes to Lowe, I am suffering, severely, with both. We have both drunk more of the horrible vodka by this point – truth serum – and we are doing that thing where you pretend to be drunker than you are. Like a game that if you yourself aren't playing would definitely be annoying. It's a balancing act; I want to let my guard down, but I don't want let myself *go* completely, be head down in the toilet, crying. And yet I need to have enough alcohol in me for *insurance*, so I could afford to *blame* the alcohol if I had to, as an excuse. *What did we do last night?* And of course, I want to remember every single detail of whatever happens between us so I can *dwell* the hell out of it for the rest of my days but that's just it – *nothing* ever happens, does it?

Adrenaline fights the alcohol anyway, burns like a blue flame over a damp brandy-soaked Christmas pudding. But right now, I cast a magic spell, a placebo to let us do the things we wouldn't normally do when we are sober.

I find more vodka in the top kitchen cupboard and we fill our glasses, but I'm so giddy I'm not even sure I'm metabolizing it properly. We head up to my messy bedroom. Sit on my bed. I put on music, too giddy to worry if he'll judge me for it, 'Heatbeats' by The Knife, which I'm sure will make me look pretty fucking cool actually.

'So,' he says, like he's been building up to something,

'So . . . ?' I grin back.

And to my surprise, he says, 'What's all this about you and Ryan then?'

What? 'Ryan? Your housemate?' What's that scarecrow got to do with anything? What a way to kill a mood.

'He said something about you two . . . going on a date or some shit?'

'A date? With Ryan? I said we'd have a drink.'

'A date is what he said.' Lowe acts like he doesn't care, his sixteen-year-old self shrugging me off. 'He said he asked you out and you said *yeah*.'

Wait, are his feelings hurt?

'Yeah, but like not like a date! Lowe! *Really*?'

'*I* didn't say it!' Lowe puts his hands up, spraying nervous laughter. He ponders. 'He said some other stuff too . . . '

'Like what?'

Lowe is quiet for a moment, runs his finger around the glass. 'Doesn't matter.'

'Gosh, Ryan's been busy, hasn't he? Tell me then, what did he say?' I hold my nerve.

Lowe watches me, not saying a word until he's absolutely sure, trying to work me out before he lays down his cards. 'That you two get on really well?'

I've never seen him so unsure of himself; he wants me to fill in gaps for something that didn't happen.

'Right?'

'He's just obsessed with you basically.' He lies down on my bed, hides his face under his cap.

I'm confused. Is he now trying to bundle me off with his mate?

'And . . . ' he begins, his voice muffled under the cap.

'And?' I ask.

'. . . He said what great friends we are.' Lowe peeps his head out from under the cap to look at me. He rolls his lips together like he's stopping words from falling out.

'Well . . . ' I say proudly, 'we are great friends . . . aren't we?'

'Yeah, course.' He looks at me, properly; he seems disappointed somewhat. 'Best friends,' he adds but like he's being sarcastic.

'Wait, Lowe . . . ' Was Ryan asking me how I felt about Lowe . . . *for* Lowe? Did Lowe ask Ryan to ask me how I felt about him to see if I felt the same? And I confirmed we were just friends and *then* Ryan asked me out. And *then* Lowe went and got a girlfriend? But obviously I say none of that.

'Like I said' – Lowe rubs his face; he, like me, is tired of our complicated situation and game-playing – 'what does it matter now?' He drains his drink, coughing at the strength of it.

But it really does matter.

Why the fuck didn't he just ask me himself?

I'm stunned. I just sit there, like, *what now?*

And then I think, if there's any chance for something to happen, it's now.

It's time.

Be cool, be cool, be cool.

But my word, is it hard to act cool when you're *fizzing?*

I find myself saying, 'Hey . . . erm . . . so . . . *we've* . . . my mum . . . we've got this new steam room fitted; it's kind of *weird.*'

'Weird' is safe. A neutral word to use when you don't want

to say if something is *good* or *bad*. It invites an opinion without giving anything away; it means *I'm interested, I'm curious* but also allows wiggle room if the other person gets freaked out. It would definitely not be unusual to describe somebody you extremely fancy as 'extremely weird'.

I add, 'Do you wanna try it?' *Wanna? Jesus Christ, calm down, girl.*

'K. Definitely . . . ' he says.

Well, then, don't give him a reason not to, Ella; get going, love.

The steam function takes a while to heat up. So, I get it on immediately. I prop up a bottle of Herbal Essence; it's empty but it's for display purposes only. I hope Lowe will know the brand for girls on TV with their bouncy floral hair. These little signposts are important. I flush my brother's straw-coloured wee he left in the toilet, remove any traces of coiled pubes and hide my stepdad's psoriasis shampoo. Nothing that would put Lowe off.

He heads outside for another cigarette and now I have about three minutes to transform. I run to my room. Oh FUCK! I haven't planned this. I didn't even know I'd be seeing him today! I was gearing up to say goodbye, not strip down to a bikini and confess my undying love! I bought the bikini especially for Egypt – and thanks to Egypt's climate, I am the shade of an all-butter crois-sant – but I can't find it now. I'm hurling my clothes around; I can't think straight. I find the top part of my bikini, but not the bottoms – oh FUCK it. I am just going to wear my underwear – that'll have to do, and then just as I'm about to give up, I see my bikini bottoms, hanging out of my still unpacked suitcase. *There is a God. And she is a woman.*

I look at myself in the mirror. The bikini is orange and dotty and I got it in a size bigger so it didn't dig into my curves, didn't press in around the fanny area to make a chubby fanny pouch – which I practise accepting and celebrating daily – didn't spread and stretch my fanny hairs taut or bulge the fillets of back fat so they suddenly go from a bit of harmless cute chub to something you'd happily pick up in a supermarket and fry up with butter and garlic to feed a family of four. 'You are BEAUTIFUL,' I say, trying so hard to mean it. I'm not there yet but I'm hoping that one day I will be. I'm a late bloomer. I'm only just getting the hang of this 'love yourself' stuff, you see. They don't teach it at school.

But better late than never.

This is my first bikini. He is my first love.

Here goes nothing . . .

Chapter 27

We stand half naked in the shower.

We are *meant* to wait for it to fill up with steam before stepping inside but I don't want it to be over before it's already begun. Don't want him to change his mind, to acknowledge that this is extremely . . . possibly . . . definitely . . . a bad idea.

One that will, as Mum would say, 'end in tears'.

The tears being mine. Obviously.

It's a new function, the plumber worked on Mum, *a shower and a steam room in one; everyone's getting them these days.*

And it's all leading to THIS moment.

This is close to the edge for us. I've never seen Lowe this *naked*. Sweat glitters, soft focus, moisture, the bathroom light. I want to touch him but I can't because my hands might shake. He is wearing boxer shorts that are jersey soft fabric in a muted grey. Probably from some multipack. I'm not sure what I was expecting but I'm glad, *good, nothing too intimidating*. Nothing that screams he's some experienced person at spontaneous shower-steams with girls. Or expecting anything.

But at the same time, I also want him to have made an effort: *I'm seeing Ella tonight; I should wear some nice boxers.*

I think of Heather, a pang of guilt, but my nipples, this close to Lowe, go stiff.

OK, body. Thanks for totally giving the game away.

I don't want to look in *his* direction; I don't want to know what the roomy boxers are doing. If he's *interested*, I will get nervous and feel sick; if he's not, I'll take it personally. I don't know if I'm ready to look at him like that. But what if he doesn't look at me at all? I want him to respect me and be the most courteous anybody's ever been in their life. But I also want him to *want* me – to push me up against the tiled wall and kiss me like people kiss when they've spent months resisting and they have no choice but to inhale and exhale, both, through their dragon flaring nostrils.

Ella, calm the fuck down.

We're just two best friends who happen to be a boy and girl who get half naked and have steams together. We're just letting off steam.

WHERE THE FUCK *IS* THE STEAM?

'It's not broken, is it?' He looks into the steam-making contraption as if he might try and fix it himself.

'No, it's new. It can't be.'

My confidence in the technology dwindling, panic sets in, as if the steam function is a new machine gun that has let me down mid zombie attack. *PLEASE, DON'T LET ME DOWN. NOT NOW.*

YOU ARE SO FUCKING HOT, LOWE. YOU ARE A BEAUTIFUL RARE CREATURE IN MY GRASP. An exotic bird that has flown into my open window by mistake. And I'm worried you'll wake from this dream and you'll be butting your head against the glass, wanting to leave . . .

Come on, Ella, deep down, you know he isn't better than you. I'm nineteen years old and I am on form, boy. I am magnetic. Electric. Kinetic. Scalextric? Whatever. I'm not the chubby one who friend-zones herself with knotty hair, who wears oversized baggy jeans and Limp Bizkit t-shirts and bitten-down nails any more. I'm on the cusp of womanhood. I'm almost at peace with my stretch marks and bumpy skin. The spots on my bum and in-grown hairs. My sharp, characterful nose. And wonky boobs.

And touching thighs. I know the word vulva is not a brand of car; I have looked at my vulva face on in the mirror more than once and I am *trying* to be OK with the view. Even though she looks like a snarling human-eating plant and nothing like Georgia O'Keeffe's *Orchid*.

In the shower there is a little fold-down seat like the jump seats on planes.

Lowe sits.

And suddenly I have one thigh between his knees. Did I put myself there or did he bring me closer? I test it, pull away a little to see if he'll draw me back in, and he does, but with a touch so light it could also not have happened.

What is this?

I try to catch glimpses of him. Secret photographs with my eyes. His shoulders. *Snap*. His wrists that I've watched so closely I could draw them by heart. *Snap*. His knuckles, that I've watched wrap around the handlebars of a bike, the neck of a guitar. Lovely fingernails, hands, near my jelly-scared legs. The fabric of his grey boxers dampens with condensation. *I'm too scared of what happens next.* I'd only been with Nile before and it was love, yes, it was sweet, honest, *wholesome*, I got lucky – sure, but it wasn't this. It wasn't *Lowe*.

Nobody ever is. That's the problem.

And eventually, the steam creeps in.

You took your time.

Before I know it, we're hot boxed in.

OH SHIT!

A flaming flamingo-pink hot high voltage, drumming through me like a marching band, firing off alarm bells. I'm a lolloping piñata mid-smash. Not butterflies but albatrosses fly here. The dull thump in my knickers when I'd make my Barbies kiss. *Is this what it feels like to fly?*

No, this is love.

It's not normal for a heart to stop and start as much as this without it being considered a medical emergency, surely?

Say it. Don't say it. Go on. No, don't fucking say it. Ella, this is your chance. Think about it – you're drunk. Ella, you're not drunk but you can pretend you are if it goes wrong. Don't do it. You've only just got close again. But if you don't, it will be too late and you'll regret it like before. You've grown up – look at you! You wear bikinis – you're cool now. We're cool.

Do it.

Somewhere, a lioness is about to lunge at an antelope. Someone is about to cuff a Wanted Man, take the final penalty, pull the table cloth at a magic show. About to take *that* leap. And so am I . . .

'Lowe?'

He doesn't look up; his fingers gently brush my legs, sweeping past my thighs so gently.

Don't ruin the moment, Ella; you don't have to talk. See how he's speaking with his hands; can't you do that? But the words are detoxing from my pores with the steam; the confession is bacteria.

'Lowe, I know you've just met somebody; I know you're really into her but I just have to tell you that . . . '

A long moment passes.

. . .

'I love you.'

. . .

There.

I said it.

I'm numb and stinging at the same time, I've been feasted on by leeches, rolled around in nettles. It's like I've unpacked a box and everything just won't go back in its place, the lid won't close. The physical withdrawal kicks in, like a thorn has been removed from my side. But could the procedure be fatal? The feeling boils down to a hot burning gnarl. My bright-red heart is clanging, beating *outside* of my chest like a cartoon.

Did the words even leave my mouth or did I dream it?

Did he hear me?

Should I say it again?

Have I got this all wrong?

Am I dead?

I feel the words retreat now, afraid; they're hiding in the trenches of my throat.

He looks up now so I can't take it back. He suddenly doesn't seem one bit drunk but immediately lucid, present and stone-cold sober. His big eyes clap on mine. He licks his full lips. I can't see his reaction through the continuous clouds of steam pumping out like a dry ice machine at a teenage disco, *pssstttttt*. This isn't sexy any more; there isn't sexual tension or chemistry. I just need an answer. *DO YOU LOVE ME BACK OR . . . ?* I mean, he must know.

'What?' he asks, with a smile that's about to break into laughter, like it's a prank.

'I love you,' I say, firmly this time. 'I've always loved you.'

And then he laughs. *Why are you laughing? Please don't laugh at me; I'll cry if you laugh.* He shakes his head like I'm winding him up. Like this can't be real. He needs further convincing. I go in harder.

'Since we were kids,' I try. 'How did you not know?'

Like it's *his* fault for not helping me out with this freight in my heart.

'Did you really not know?'

'No.' More seriousness now. He's in shock. Total disbelief.

I see it hit him for the first time.

'I didn't know,' he says. 'I thought you wanted to be just friends. I honestly had no idea.'

'Well . . . ' I gulp. 'You do now.' *OH GOD*. 'And I know you've just got into this new thing with this girl Heather and obviously like I'm SO happy for you.'

I stand with my back against the cool dripping tiles, hands

behind me like I've been cuffed. Like I'm in trouble. I speak almost defensively, apologetically.

' . . . And I would never normally get in the way of any-body's relationship, especially yours – I want you to be happy, Lowe – but I feel that if I don't say this now, I might never and the idea of . . . I don't know . . . let's say *dying* without saying it . . . will be ironic . . . actually . . . because that could . . . very well be the very thing that in fact kills me.'

THAT'S ENOUGH, ELLA!

'In the autopsy, my cause of death will be keeping in the secret that I love you as much as I do.'

He is too shocked to laugh at my terrible humour.

'Look, I don't want to cause any harm. You've not been with her long, so before it gets too serious with her' – *it's rude to say her* – 'With Heather —'

He interrupts. Is he angry? Hurt? This is the least calm I've seen him. 'You told Ryan you didn't feel like that about me. The next thing I know Ryan's going around telling the world and his mates that you're going on some date with him and then you go on holiday!'

Ryan? That JESTER? What kind of Shakespearian tragedy is this?

'Ella, I honestly thought you just wanted to be friends.'

'And then you met Heather?'

He says nothing. He hunches over with his elbows on his knees, face in his hands. Then he puts his hands over his mouth and stares out into space.

'I'm not looking to have an affair.'

Affair – please, girl, you're nineteen.

'But – I just had to finally tell you that I love you.'

YOU'VE ONLY SAID THAT TWENTY-FIVE TIMES.

'And so . . . if there's any chance – then . . . then please tell me . . . '

Chapter 28

We sleep in Mum's big brass bed.

Well, he sleeps. I toss and turn.

I see the sky turn from midnight black to some other denseness through Mum's self-made skylight – *don't* ask – that makes me feel horribly alone even though Lowe's right there.

I should feel relieved, but I don't. I wish I could take it back. There is a Before and an After now, and this is After.

In my head there is a storm. Regret thunderbolts crackle. Shame rains. The scene replaying in lightning silver shocks, so cringe they are blinding. Guilt, a fog I can't seem to clear. WHY DID I SAY IT? WHY DID I SAY IT LIKE *THAT*? WHY IS HE STILL HERE? How does he have the capacity to just say nothing back? How does he have such a tolerance for silence. How can he just sleep as though it's nothing?

Maybe he's thinking on it?

Sleeping on it.

Dreaming on it?

Tomorrow is Sunday. I don't start at the hairdressers until midday. Maybe in the morning it will be better? Maybe Lowe will have clarity and we can go for breakfast before I start work. Maybe we'll get lucky and the café with the individual toasters on each table will have space for us for once and we can talk about our lovely future. I'll order a Cappuccino, and he'll be impressed. And I'll go off to work and Lowe will call this mystery Heather whilst I'm earning £45 for us towards our life together (maybe more if I get tips) and say . . .

I really like you, 'Hev', you're very <u>striking</u> (well, let's see what comes out in the moment) *but you see, there's been a huge misunderstanding – well, many, there's been many misunderstandings but this I know to be true: Ella and I are in love. We've been in love since we were kids. In fact. I think it's fair to say this is TRUE LOVE. The kind of love people wait for. And I'm sure that as a human being yourself, you can understand that anybody in their right mind wouldn't let a thing like that go.*

And she'll be upset but she'll say . . .

. . . Of course, I understand, Lowe; I am new on the scene and I always knew there was something magical between you and Ella. I'm disappointed, but I understand; who would turn the love of a lifetime down? Go get 'em, tiger.

And then it happens.

Out of nowhere, in the darkness, I feel his hands on my body, wrapping around me, not sneaky but definite, deliberate. He presses his body into mine, I suppose like a spoon, if a spoon had hands – maybe a pasta spoon? I'm not sure if he's holding me to say sorry. Or that he feels bad. Or guilty. Or that he doesn't want to lose me because of everything we've been through together. I let him hold me. It's not unlike us to hug in bed, but never like *this*. Then, as a lover would, he breathes me in and I realize he's trying to *begin something*. I say his name, 'Lowe?' to see if he's asleep. He doesn't reply, just spasms out of sleep – *OK, he's drunk.* But then here he is again, closer this time, so tender and gentle, yet clumsy. I hear him deep breathing . . . *Is he asleep?*

I want something to happen but not like *this*, not when he still hasn't told me how he feels. I don't want him to cheat with me behind Heather's back. Or allow something to happen only to wish it never did, go back to Heather and never talk to me again?

All I know is, he knows that *this* isn't *me* or something I would do.

Maybe he's flattering me, smoothing it over? Maybe he's that fucking arrogant, thinks I'm *that* desperate that I'll take a pity fuck? Maybe he's just horny and I'm the only girl within arm's reach? Maybe he's just like that now, got a bit famous, plucks girls like grapes and spits out the pips? Maybe he's willing to trade our friendship off for one awkward night? Maybe he really isn't who I thought he was? Maybe I don't know him at all? Maybe he quite simply doesn't care about me or Heather or anyone? Maybe he thinks *I'm* Heather?

And so no, in the sternest barbed voice, I say, firmly, 'No, Lowe, *don't*.'

And his wandering hands snatch away like they've been stung.

In the morning we don't talk about it; we communicate through murmured mumblings, no eye contact and pure friction. 251 is colder than ever. I can't look at my favourite face. We make Mum's bed together, hoisting the sheets up and over, either side of the gulf between us that is the lavender throw. The air rotten and stiff. Lowe is clearly hungover – his sunken eyes sorrowful, his mouth dry. I can see his cracked lips but he doesn't ask for water; he asks for nothing.

We're both too confused. We can't come back from this. We're too young to know how to make it right. The damage is done.

There's no mention of the café with the toasters. Fluorescent with regret, in the flurry of it, I see him shiver, teeth chattering with nerves and fear. I silently offer him Dad's turquoise hoody. This will annoy me for years because Dad doesn't live with us any more and I wear it when I want to feel small and cosy and safe in his 'Dad' arms but it's the first warm, clean and big enough thing I see and I want this to be over.

And now Lowe has it.

And will probably lend it to Heather to wear when she's cold.

Chapter 29

Aoife reads the line-up for FEVER FEST down the phone on the three-way call.

'*Weekend Plans, 200, Wet Paint, Sleepover, HERO, TriggerTrigger . . .* '

So long as True Love aren't playing I really don't care. I haven't spoken to Lowe in almost a year. Not since their album release. Not since they've blown up. Not since I can't go anywhere without them being everywhere.

But I'm still looking for an excuse to stay at home and say, 'Not my *dream* line-up . . . '

'No, Ella, don't back out. You're doing it,' Bianca orders.

Aoife and Bianca are both sick with wanderlust and, this time, they're determined not to leave me behind. Aoife is willing to blow her entire student loan in one summer and Bianca's already quit her temping job. I'm definitely still playing the little sister. Unable to step into my big boots and catch up with them, I lag behind, unable to imagine the big world they've seen. The changes come out in little reminders, like when they can identify street food at Camden Market. Or when they wear their matching Havaianas and I'm in my plimsolls. Or the way they salute the sun and I sit, spine like a bent coat hanger, watching TV. And, of course, the eternal reminder is Bianca's shit tattoo, which we all know doesn't say 'serendipity'.

'Is it going to be . . . *OK*?'

Obviously, I'm PETRIFIED. But Aoife and Bianca aren't; they're like expert travellers now, explorers of the world.

'For God's sake, Ella, *yes*,' Bianca says.

'Elbow, listen,' adds Aoife. 'You are TWENTY years old! It will be exactly like going to a festival in the UK, just better because it will be hot and everyone will be in a good mood and fit.'

'And nothing you do out there can come back to bite you on the arse cos you can leave it behind in Spain!' Bianca screeches.

I know they think I'm boring. As far as they're concerned, my life has stood still. Frozen in time like forgotten fishfingers. They've stepped out of their comfort zones; I'm just ticking along. I still live with Mum and Stepdad Adam, arguing over who ate the last onion bagel with Sonny and Violet. Still studying very un-Creative Writing at the same university. No boyfriend. Same job. Journeying only by writing love poems about 'love' when all I really know about love is Lowe. My pen is my battered passport. Whereas Aoife and Bianca have all these new experiences under their belt, names and numbers in their phones, big plans. They certainly aren't fussed by the barriers of money: 'It always works out,' they reassure me, 'what more do you need? Sun, sea, music! People will always help us if we get stuck.' That sounds like *begging* to me. Freeloading. What kind of hippy chat is this? 'Besides, this is what money is for!' Aoife says. *Yeah, no shit, because I'm the only one with a job right now.* They think I'm uptight. But I've worked so hard at the hairdressers to save up for this damn festival – long enough to see a client's spontaneous break-up head-shave grow out into Rapunzel's luscious locks – so seeing the money go out of my account for festival tickets *and* a flight feels outrageous, luxurious, unnecessary, mostly because I can't see myself actually doing any of this. Will I *really* see any of this through? But even the stylists at the salon are ushering me along now. I suppose it will give me will give me some new material to talk about at the basins when I get back.

The festival website is stressing me out: half of it's in Spanish; there are all these different campsites – some are better than others apparently; there are tips in the reviews . . . warnings about overpriced bus tickets and dangerous, long, off-road walks that aren't lit, about the extreme heat, drug dealers and touts. I try not to bore Aoife and Bianca with the mundane logistical stuff that's keeping me awake at night like *how* will we get from the airport to the festival? Will our phones work out there? Can we drink the tap water? And where will we sleep? We don't have a tent!

But Bianca has it all worked out. 'We can take my cousin's tent! It literally *flings* up in seconds. It's like a palace.'

I'm yet to meet a tent that's a palace but we say bye and hang up.

'Why are *you* so stressed?' Violet asks, judgmental and disgusted. Just because she's studying Food Tech now she thinks she's the only one who has the right to be stressed. She's been trying to make us use different coloured boards to chop vegetables and protein but we don't pay attention.

'Have *you* ever been *travelling*?' I ask dramatically.

'*Travelling*? Ha! For *eight* days?' Violet says. '*Please*.' And walks off scoffing.

I change up my money. Write down some key phrases. It's hard to pack summer clothes that are suitable for boiling weather and also demonstrate my sense of *fashion*. Sun cream, insect repellent. Sunglasses. Two days before we fly, I remind Bianca to borrow the tent from her cousins; we need to air it out before we go. 'Will do,' she says before asking her dad to pass her the remote. She's not listening. I text again to remind her, not wanting to sound anxious, but I definitely am.

The day before we fly, Bianca organizes another three-way call.

'So . . . about the tent.'

'What?'

'It's currently in the New Forest,' Bianca says, without apologizing. Typical.

'*What?* So where are we gonna sleep?'

'Under the stars! It's just a tent. Loosen up.'

'Errr no,' Aoife snaps.

'You've got to be joking, Bianca; we'll get bitten to death. Or RAPED.'

'Ella's right. I fucking hate rapists. Why can't men just leave us alone? Let us sleep, man.'

I don't *really* understand how the added millimetre shield made of polyester, nylon and a zip is going to act as a rape preventative, but I've got enough to worry about already before catastrophizing. Why didn't she sort the tent before now?

'Well, I know *we* don't have one,' I say. One of the only things my parents do still have in common is that they both hate camping.

'Ugh, I think we have one,' Aoife offers. 'But it's a hundred years old and weighs a ton; it really is a last resort.'

Bianca calls us back. 'Rob's got one.'

Rob is Bianca's toxic stoner 'friend' who is eight years older and the type of person our parents don't like us using the internet because of. He scares the living day lights out of us because, well, let's face it, he's an actual *man* man.

Aoife hesitates.

'What? You don't want to sleep in Rob's tent?'

'It's not that but . . . ' Aoife tries but I take over.

'I really don't want to sleep in Rob's tent; it will feel like sleeping in Rob's *bed*. With his armpit hair, coffee breath and adult pubes.'

'Look, we haven't got a better option – I wanna get some weed to bring with us so I have to see him anyway.'

'Bianca, you can't bring *weed* to Spain!' Aoife shouts.

'You lemon, course you can! It's Spain, it's like going to . . . I dunno . . . *Eastbourne*. Chill. As. Fuck. Trust me.'

'Get the tent but please don't bring the weed and don't forget to set your alarm – we've got our flight in the morning,' I tell her.

'Good idea . . . ' Bianca says. 'How do you set an alarm on your phone? Rob will show me. I'll bring my passport to Rob's in case I end up sleeping over – I can just leave from his in the morning.'

'PLEASE DON'T DO THAT!' I bark.

'Are you sure you should sleep over? What about all your stuff? Is that a good idea?' Aoife blurts.

'Yes, don't be ridiculous; it'll be FINE.'

And lo and behold, at 4 a.m. my phone goes off. It's Bianca.

What now?

She's crying. 'I had my passport on my chest when I was sleeping so I didn't forget it – and . . . '

'OK, and?'

'It rolled off and . . . ' She starts really crying. 'It fell into a pint of orange squash.'

'Shit, is it salvageable?'

'It's been in there all night – it's *soaking*.' She sobs.

I can tell she's still drunk or stoned or both. I'm not interested in making her feel any worse.

'I'm so sorry,' she cries.

Her dad was meant to be collecting us from the bloody airport on the way home. Bet he would have taken us to the Burger King Drive-Thru too. Livid.

'Dad's found a tent!' Aoife says down the phone. 'But it's a bit *crusty* . . . '

'We'll buy a new tent,' I tell Aoife.

'With what money? I'm spending my money on beer not

248

tents! And the shops are all out – it's festival season. We're out of options.'

Mum reluctantly drives me to Aoife's house where her dad has dug the oldest, ugliest bright-orange tent from the Seventies out of the shed where it nearly sliced off our toes like a guillotine. It's as heavy as a desk. It has bazillions of chunky metal poles and thick ropes and massive wooden pegs – and no instructions. It's like something from the original Girl Guides' handbook or Clipart.

'OK, let's buy a tent when we get there? This thing will weigh a ton on the flight.'

'And risk not having a tent at all?'

'But, Ella, how am I going to bring a guy back to that?' Aoife whispers to me. And I don't have the answer to that question.

When we get to the festival, we follow an ant-trail of very cool people, heaving our bags to the tropical campsite, the best on the map. We track through the dust to find the perfect spot, overhearing some know-it-all saying, 'Close to the bathrooms but not too close, sun spots but mostly shade, good ground . . . ' Aoife takes the piss, stomping her Havaianas on the floor like she knows what she's doing, when in reality we're copying their every move. That is until their tents pop up and they run off to the bar. Meanwhile *we* have to resurrect the skeleton of what may as well be a diplodocus. This can't be real. We're sweating; every pole is like lifting a log and it doesn't even have a zip, but—

'Oh, hell no, not *toggles*.'

Toggles aren't going to stop us getting attacked – *oh no actually they might*. We start laughing crazily; people stop and stare at us and that makes us laugh more.

Done and dusted – no literally, it is like we've deliberately rolled in dust, and we're so sweaty everything seems to stick to us – we take a cool shower in the communal block and then, finally, arm in arm, we plod down the dry crumbling brown sugar dirt hill to buy a pack of cold beers and a massive bag of delicious holiday crisps.

With the festival not beginning until tomorrow, we want to save our energy. We lie on the ground, outside our tent, close to the stars. I feel like I'm in that book *Where The Wild Things Are*, and feel a sense of bravery and pride. But also, the distance gives me a chance to reflect. For a year, since Lowe, I've been motoring along, trusting that my brain is processing the heartbreak, the rejection; I hoped it was filing the thoughts and taking care of itself without me actively caring for it. But maybe the wave is hitting me now?

'You OK, Elbs?' Aoife asks.

'Yeah, why?'

'Quiet, that's all.'

So much happened when Aoife was away. Only now am I made aware of how much my friends don't know; could not sharing such a big part of my life with them be holding our friendship back? Could it be costing us our bond? We've been friends our whole lives. What a relief it would be to get it off my chest. To tell Aoife everything about Lowe and me from the start. My heart clutches but even in the night air the prick of shame engulfs me and I'm unable.

'Sorry, yeah, I'm fine.'

The new morning at the campsite reveals new horrors; there's an ambulance treating kids with sunstroke or who've been found fitting in the showers. Hydrating with cheap spirit. Eating too many pills and not enough food. The sun's damage rips skin red raw, peels boobs, blisters noses and makes nostrils bleed. Aoife and I whack on as much sun cream as we can find and wander down to the local village where we sit at a paper-cloth table with toothpicks and grains of rice in the salt pot and order bread and tuna salad, which we drown in oil, vinegar and dusty grey pepper. The Diet Cokes here taste sensational – ice cold with lemon in slim cylinder glasses. We float the little shops, admire the ornaments and wave to the locals who are utterly perplexed as to why all these parentless kids are trudging round their hometown like they own it. The festival starts at night when the air cools, when the floor isn't melted lava and the pebbles aren't hot coals, when the molten sun slips away behind the hills and leaves a tang over the landscape. Soon the music will come to life.

When we get to the site there is such a buzz. We can all feel it. It's so incredible to be at a festival without anoraks and wellie boots. Here we come with nothing but beer money crunched up in our pockets and bras. We stand by the ginormous blue fans that spritz a mist of water and cold air at the same time and we all spread out like starfishes and coo like babies. The bar's already packed with beautiful people: braids, flowers, ribbons, feathers, glitter, face paint, open shirts and bikini tops. I hardly know where to look. I fancy everyone except for the fucked-up kids with the rolling back eyes heaped in corners, who have peaked too soon. Here, next to the warm rub of bare flesh and cups of beer, I feel excited; all those times I'd hunted for boys as a teenager and asked myself where the *hell* they were hiding – well, turns out they were here, at this festival.

We all gather to hear the opening act, the kick-drum, the feedback scoring a line through the sky, and thousands of hands rattle, stirring a tidal wave as the lead singer says coyly, 'Hello' and the song opens up. We howl like animals. Strangers share cigarettes and beer. My heart skips a beat. Friends jump on shoulders, bare thighs around necks, a sea of hands, surfing into nowhere, and we all scream as paper cups are thrown and plastic bottles land on our bare feet; the hands and elbows of others are comforting and close. When we sing, it's like a whale song, a frequency. We move like a swarm of bees, in ripples. I feel beautiful and happy and young and carefree.

Until a rumour starts that the headline act, Weekend Plans,

have pulled out. Gutted. We're having such a nice time it shouldn't be a big deal but of course it is.

'I'm demanding a refund,' Aoife states. She loves Weekend Plans.

'Hold on, let's see who the replacement is first?' I ask. I'm actually enjoying myself now.

We think about asking someone but we don't want to look anxious or annoying or desperate. Like we *care*. And we're not about to go and ask the INFORMATION desk like losers.

'I'll get my brother to look online.' Aoife texts her brother, Sean. That text will cost about a fiver to send.

We share a bag of sugary churros in the shade and wait for Aoife's brother to reply. We watch a really horrible electronic band on a small stage, a boy on pills dancing to a song no one else can hear.

Eventually Sean texts back.

'SHUT UP!' Aoife screams and reads the message out:

Forums are guessing true love?

Stop.

'SICK! How great is that?'

True Love? Impossible. No way. What does that mean? That Lowe is coming *here*? As in TODAY? As in he could be here *now*? Well, that's my holiday over then. *Buh-bye*. That's my free spirit chained.

'You're right!' I change my tune. 'Who organized this shitshow of a festival? We should demand a refund and go home.'

'Ahaha!' Aoife thinks I'm joking, head still down in her phone. 'Has Lowe said anything to you about it, Elbie?'

Once upon a time, I'd be the point of contact.

Instead, I'm over here, privately bleeding, his name a dagger in my chest. A dagger that turns when our names are said in the same breath like wedding vows. God, Aoife really has no idea, does she? Is this what it's like having an affair, hiding a whole other side of your life?

'Why would he say anything to *me*?' I add, scratching the question off me uncomfortably, 'I haven't spoken to him for ages.' I thought he might ask me to come to a show at some point but he never did. Then again, I never messaged him about his album release. I acted like it didn't exist even when the posters were everywhere. Those milestones just seemed to come and go.

'Shall we just text him?' Aoife asks, openly searching for his name in her phone, like it's as easy as that, even though I'm sure she must sense I'm acting weird. 'I've not seen him in *so long*; has he still got the same number?' She asks so casually, like we're asking about Shreya or The Twins. Wait, does she think we just TEXT each other still? Does she really think we're *normal*?

I try to deter her. 'We don't know if he's playing for sure though, do we?'

'Ella! It's worth a try! He might be able to get us *backstage*!' Her eyes bulge. 'We might be able to sleep in their air-conditioned hotel and have a buffet breakfast with posh ham? We can get out of the shithole campsite! We're in Spain at the *same time*; what are the chances? He's still our friend; we should let him know we're here! Be fun!'

'OK' – she's not going to give up – 'but let's do it after the show; we don't want to put him off.' I manage to delay her.

'Cool,' she says. 'Do you reckon he's a trillionaire by now?'

I don't give a fuck. All I'm thinking is about all the ways *I* could get out of tonight? I could say I have stomach cramps, food poisoning, water poisoning, period pains, my drink's been spiked? But the idea of being alone in the dark campsite whilst everyone is screaming along to Lowe's band makes me quite sad. I'll say I have bad news . . . I need to fly back to South London. Immediately. Or at the festival I'll just get *conveniently* lost, go have a Nutella crepe and find a nice radio stage where undiscovered alternative acts play, instead? How cultural.

But, of course, we're heading for the main stage like everyone else, in a daisy-chain of wrist-banded hands we've only just met. 'We should just plant ourselves here!' some girl shouts over the music. 'We've got such a good spot and we don't want to lose it.' Everyone else agrees, everyone except me but I say nothing, just sweat it out like translucent onions in a pan.

'NO WAY!' Aoife yells. 'Is that *Mia?*'

'Mia *Bennett*? Where?' I look through the crowd ahead to see the most free, luminescent girl with white-bleached hair, wearing cut-off shorts and a crochet bikini top on someone's shoulders. It *IS* her!

'MIA!' we scream. 'MIA!'

And she turns, face full of glitter, so happy to see us. 'ELLA! AOIFE! OH MY GOD!' Blowing us huge kisses with both hands, she appears so cool and breezy; her energy is quite amazing. 'YOU ON FACEBOOK?' she bellows, balancing her paper cup on her stomach and the head of the shoulders she's sitting on.

'*I* AM!' Aoife cries. 'ELBOW'S TOO COOL FOR FACEBOOK!'

'I am not.' I dig her in the ribs.

'MESSAGE ME! LET'S MEET UP!' Mia signs off with a thumbs up, turning her back on us and spreading her arms out to the stage.

We pass water bottles filled with alcohol down the line, filling our cups, just spirits so we don't keep having to use the toilets. The crowd around us shoulder to shoulder, in gridlock. The rumours have clearly gone round, everybody is shouting, 'WE WANT TRUE LOVE!!' and *I* want to crouch down into a ball with my hands over my ears. It is killing me to know that Lowe's quiet little nobody band is now famous enough to pacify all of these paying people! That it's got *this* big. I was so in denial. I'm so insignificant. He doesn't even know I'm here. I'm not even a second thought. The crowd starts singing their songs and I pretend I'm loving it because Aoife (and everyone that Aoife has told) keeps looking at me like I must be SO proud that all these thousands of people are singing our friend's song. They must think I'm absolutely loving it when really I'm drowning – drowning in the song of him. Death by his music. How did he smoke me out? How did he *find* me here? It's like he KNOWS. *You win, Lowe. You win. I surrender.*

'WE WANT TRUE LOVE!'

As the silver floodlights smack on, the audience unleash a Hitchcock scream, and I need a sachet of Dioralyte. The empty stage is a *gift*. SURPRISE! Everyone's eyes lift as the artwork appears on the backdrop, a giant bleeding heart, *oh God, it's them* and the crowd go absolutely NUTS. I look down at my sandals and see my stumpy little emerald painted toes and give them a wriggle just to check I'm still alive. I try to escape but I'm locked in. Breathe in, breathe out . . . *You can do this, Ella – you've done it before.*

Aoife grips my hand and looks at me wide-eyed. 'Here we go!' Like we're about to sky-dive together. I wish I could be her right now, just able to enjoy the show. I wish I *was* skydiving. That would be easier; I'm not in love with the sky.

True Love explodes. My friend is a star.

I don't know these songs. I have gone out of my way to *not* know these songs. I look for the supportive eyes of Mia but she's disappeared. Lowe gives the crowd want they want: everything. Why is he acting like he doesn't have asthma? I feel the need to waggle my finger in his face like a teacher: *Fame, money and success don't stop you from having asthma now do they? You're not too cool for health you know!* He's a frontman, a showman, and it's his job to perform. The old recognizable real parts of him are background noise, fading fainter and fainter until they are completely covered over, trampled on with this cartoon celebrity alter-ego. *Fucking actor.*

There are these tiny moments though, in the cracks of quietness, where I see him, humbled, having fun. Or a bit scared. It must be quite scary, all these dehydrated drunk people roaring at you.

Loving you. Wanting you. All that pressure. These are the times I remember him, in his little downstairs bedroom in Brighton, watching me crawl towards him in my matching pyjamas. *I'm gonna melt your heart.*

Torture.

The show finishes and somehow I've survived. I'm still standing.

'Wasn't that INCREDIBLE?' Aoife squeals, her skin steaming,

'It really was,' I reply, which is true, in the out-of-body experience bits, where I was able to dissociate and forget I know him.

'Do you want to call him?' Aoife nudges.

I appreciate her handing that role over to me but I can't. 'Phone's out of battery.' I tut. 'Soz.' But there's a massive charging station right next to us.

'Don't worry,' Aoife says. 'I'll text him now.'

PANIC. 'What are you saying?' I ask. 'Don't beg it.'

'I'm just going to tell him that we're here and see if he wants a drink?' Aoife stops, readjusts her contact lens with an itch. 'What's up?' she finally observes through her drunkenness. 'Are you like worried that now he's famous he'll be a bit of a dickhead?'

'No, I just don't want us to look desperate.'

'How can you be desperate with your friends? He'll be happy to see us, *you* especially,' she says, which kills me. 'I'm sure it will mean a lot to him. There, *sent*.'

I watch everyone else at the festival, free from this burden, move on to the dance tents, the bar. And I wish I could go home.

Aoife's phone rings within minutes; he must have just that second stepped off stage. She shows me the screen. She's got his name spelt wrong in her phone: LO. I like it that he has the same number, that not *everything* has changed. 'See, told you . . .' she gloats and answers, rushed and delighted, making a plan and gushing. Firing off confused directions of our whereabouts. Aoife is never like this; it's jarring to see her starstruck.

'Yeah, I'm with Ella,' she says, looking at me with what can only be described as *glee*. I wonder if my name pierces his heart? She ends the call with a 'see you in a min'.

'He's sending a GOLF BUGGY!' Like a golf buggy is a helicopter. 'Bet they've got free beers in their dressing room. Air-conditioning!' She sniffs her armpits. 'Deodorant, please lord.'

My whole body is in a state of threat as the crowd disperses, leaving us in a field of paper cups. The sky is pitch dark, the temperature dropped ever so slightly but not enough to warrant these shivers.

'There it is!' Aoife points at a white golf buggy, trucking along towards us. 'OH MY GOD! It's him, El – he's *driving* it!' She claps her hands together joyfully like he's the bloody night bus.

There he is: his face, his smile, that post-adrenaline-buzz glowing about his person. I see his eyes on me and gulp. Something still stirs, shakes me up.

'Isn't he worried about paps and psycho fans?' Aoife's says as he gets closer. 'I suppose it's dark; people might not notice him.' She's just talking to herself at this point. 'Nice of him to pick us up though, don't you think?'

'Yeah,' I say, 'it is.' Very humbling. Very fit, I suppose. Damnit.

As Lowe approaches, I involuntarily break into my happiest of faces. That's what he does to me. And he smiles back with his happiest of faces, and I know *all* of his faces; that's what *I* do to him.

To be funny, he speeds up, skidding the buggy when he pulls up, jumps out with the vehicle still moving like a stuntperson. He runs straight towards me and then he stops. I replay our last moment together, the frosty, clunky awkwardness but he seems to have shaken it off—

'*Ella.*'

I love it when he says my name. Bypassing Aoife, he puts his arms out for a hug, making sure I want him to, which obviously I do.

He breathes me in. 'I can't believe you're here. I've missed you so much. I can't believe you're here,' he says again. 'I'm so happy to see you.'

We're magnets.

We jump in the buggy with Aoife doing an ecstatic wiggle dance in her seat and ride back through the festival, flying over the thousands of footsteps we've walked today. Lowe waves us through the backstage area with little, if any, interrogation from security with a 'they're with me'. People stare but he doesn't seem to care. He knows he's famous but he doesn't act like it. He only cares about talking to us, making us feel special and important and wanted. Aoife links fingers with me and squeezes my hand. In the dressing room we see the rest of the band. It's been a while. They stand to hug us; the fact we're all away from home seems to break the ice, level us out a bit. Lowe hands out cold beers from the fridge and tells us to help ourselves to whatever we want. 'Is this all for you?!' Aoife says about all the snacks and alcohol, and the band laugh. We open our beers and take a seat on the couch like we're teenagers in a fit older brother's bedroom. Knees touching.

Aoife gets talking to the drummer and Lowe says, 'Do you want to come outside and chat whilst I . . . ?' He holds up a cigarette.

'Sure,' I say. What does he think about the last time we saw each other? What on earth is running through his mind? Does he remember it like I do?

There's a dividing fence between the backstage and crowd, and I'm on the inside with him.

'This is mad. I wasn't expecting to see you at all.' He holds his cigarette like a cowboy; his fingers make the OK gesture. He takes a drag, eyes on the sky like he wished on that same star I did all those years ago and it obliged, *thanks*.

'You're the one that joined the line-up!' I say cheekily. 'If I'd known you'd be here I wouldn't have come!' I joke but FACT.

'*What?* Don't say that! Why?'

'We haven't spoken in a while, have we?'

'No. I've been shit. Sorry about that.' He exhales smoke with the words; silver spools sail past my face. He offers me a toke. 'Oh, you don't smoke, do you?'

I shake my head.

'I shouldn't really.' He admits, 'My manager would kill me, but . . . it could be worse – I could be addicted to heroin.' He cracks up. 'What are you up to these days? How's your writing going?'

'I'm actually working on a collection of poems.' I regret using the word 'collection' out loud; it's off-putting. It makes me sound like a clothes designer who works only in the colour *shell*.

'That's great.'

'Working at the hairdressers mostly.'

'You're still there? You cutting hair now?' He sounds genuinely interested.

It actually takes years to train to be a stylist; it's not that simple but anyway. 'No, the desk, *that's* where I'm working on the collection of poems,' I joke. But again, true.

'Hahaha, nice.' He sucks on the cigarette. 'It's so cool you're here.' He looks at me then down at his busted trainers which you'd think by now he'd have sorted. He lets a thought drift over him. He rests his head on the fence. 'I miss being around you, Ella – I really do. Can we meet up properly in London?'

My mind immediately springs to: *In what way? A date?*

'Yeah, that would be nice.'

'This whole thing's been so . . . emotional.' And then he says, so loosely like he doesn't mean to say it, 'I don't think I can do it without you.'

'What? Life?' I joke, hoping that's, in fact, precisely what he meant.

'No, this whole band/fame thing.'

Oh. I feel my face snarl in a disgust. What does he mean by that? Why does it feel so gross when he uses the word 'fame' about himself?

'You wanted it,' I clip. *All I wanted was you.*

'I thought I did but turns out fame is more like . . . a mental illness.' He laughs.

'In what way?'

'I dunno . . . ' His voice goes quiet. 'I get paranoid . . . You think everybody just wants to be your friend because of who you are, the band. You find it hard to trust anyone. There's pressure. Anxiety. Expectation. To be good. To be *fun*. You don't sleep and you eat shit cos you're always on the road in different time zones. I get homesick.'

He looks at me like I have the power somehow. He clicks his tongue like he's thinking. 'I really want to be friends again.'

Oh, no, no, no, here we go.

I want to say, *How the fuck could we ever be friends again? It would never be the same. How could we ever be equal when you have fans, Lowe? People that think you're God's Gift. How long will it be until you start believing that what they think of you is true? And how, in all that mania, will you ever find me or my miniature day interesting? Your feet don't even touch the ground. You're a famous rock star. I'm a friggin' receptionist wannabe writer at a hairdressers. Your record went to number one in the charts; meanwhile I'm excited because my boss has just cut me my very own key to lock up the salon with.*

But I say, 'Yeah me too.' Knowing deep down that we won't be meeting up when we get back because I can't do it again.

Especially not when I see a *striking* girl with dark curly hair, heading towards us, Lowe looks down at his feet (annoyed? Embarrassed?), stubs out his cigarette. 'I can't remember if you ever met Heather?'

Heather looks me up and down like she's heard *all* about me. 'I've heard so much about you.' She proves my point. *What have you heard?* Sticking her hand out towards me like an accommodating kind *vet*.

Lowe clears his throat. 'Heather, this is Ella, my best friend.' Bullets to the head.

You know when you smile so hard it's an act of violence?

'So hot, isn't it?' she says.

'So hot, yeah.' *Try sleeping in a tent with toggles on a mountain. Bet you're both in a five star in Barcelona.*

'Well, I better find Aoife,' I say. *Hold it together, Ella, even though the scar tissue isn't healed and you're a sack of feelings ready to split and bleed everywhere.* Lowe tries to talk but I'm walking away already. Luckily it's dark so nobody can see my sad face. Luckily it's dark so I have my shadow as a friend.

I wonder if I owe myself an apology? For being so hard and harsh on myself? For all those years of grinding myself down and self-deprecation. Self-care isn't a new pair of shoes; it's finding the compassion to say sorry to yourself: *I was a bitch to you back then and I'm so sorry. You didn't deserve that; you're a bloody lovely person. You did nothing wrong except love.* There have been times in our story where I actually thought I wasn't good enough for him. The self-sabotage brings me to tears. It's time I put some scaffolding around myself. Time to shed a skin. And this time, it's not because I'm hoping to whittle down the wood to reveal a perfect – smaller – statuette hidden inside. This time I'm polishing down something that is already there, so I can shine. Thank you so much Lowe, thank you for waking me the fuck up. Now I can go into my twenties, the rest of my life, choosing to put myself first.

I stick my head around the dressing room door where Aoife is deliberately letting her bra strap hang down and flirting with the drummer.

'Aoife, we're going.'

She is stunned by my assertiveness. 'But we only just got

here . . . ' she says, with a look like *ARE YOU FUCKING HIGH?* The drummer looks at me like I'm a boring mum.

'I need to talk to you.'

'Can't it wait?'

'Not really,' I reply. I've only waited six years already.

'Sorry . . . I'll be back.' She excuses herself and glares at me. She's pissed off. (She won't be back.)

'Grab some of the beers from the fridge,' I add.

'Are you serious?' she asks like I'm really taking the piss now but does as I tell her, awkwardly bending past the band to cheekily steal their alcohol with a *thanks, bye*. They've had MORE than enough support from us over the years; it's the least they can do.

'I was about to get with The *Drummer*! Have you seen biceps like that in your entire life?' Then she sees my face. 'Ella? Are you OK? What the fuck is going on?'

And I say, 'I don't even know where to start . . . ' But somehow I find a way.

On the journey back home, I decide I'm going to pull all those poems I've been writing together. Maybe I could turn them into a pamphlet, a book of some kind. Not because I'm looking to get published, just for closure, a way of signing Lowe and me off in one place rather than him and me forever floating around my head. So I can glance over at that collection and think to myself, *That was a story, once . . .*

Chapter 30

Now

I've been wearing the engagement ring of somebody I probably shouldn't be marrying for twelve hours. Although there are *hints* of comfort and security, a tiny buzz, the overriding sensation in the pit of my gut is *what the F are you doing, Ella Cole?*

I'm already looking for ways to get this restraining security *tag* cut off me with industrial shears. But that comes with its own heaviness: guilt, betrayal for both Jackson and myself. It's not right. But then why would I *not* marry him? What are we going to do, tread water forever? Why am I forgetting I can swim?

What's wrong with me; why aren't I *buzzing*? Oh, why did he have to go and do this? Things were going so well. Now this stupid opal, so pretty you can't believe it's natural, has gone and shoved a sword in my back, forcing me to leap off the plank into choppy waters. Girl overboard. If I end the engagement, our whole relationship will be thrown up into the air for debate. Jackson will ask me the big questions I've been avoiding, like: 'What *do* you want from this?' *I love you but I want more space and time to work at what we have. I'm just not ready for forever. I'm not sure. Something is holding me back.*

But that's unfair. Jackson's nearly thirty-six. He's going to want to start a family. We have a mortgage. It's got the word Mort in it. Mort in French means DEAD. Until death. He might end it.

Say I'm wasting his time. People will ask questions. Think I'm a bitch runaway bride and I haven't even got to the altar yet. His parents will HATE me.

I have to talk to him. He'll know what to say. But how can I ask Jackson for advice on whether to marry him or not? I can't imagine his advice will be impartial. I'm making tea, looking like I'm normal, my mind a helter-skelter quietly whirring at a million miles an hour, when it all changes.

'Oh no!'

It's the kind of *oh no* he makes when he's spilt a cup of tea but I'm making the tea.

'You OK?' I call back.

'*Shit.*'

'What?'

He's silent.

'Jackson, *what?*'

I enter the living room.

'True Love have split up.'

I look at him like *who?* But it's to buy myself time before I have to decide how to react.

'The band.'

He's looking at the laptop screen, trying to read more about it. It doesn't sink in. I reach my hand out to grab the first stick of furniture I see to steady myself. A very unreliable standing lamp.

'True Love?'

Even saying their name feels like summoning some kind of spirit. Lowe has been fossilized for ten years in my heart and now he's here – unearthed, dumped on my table – and needs dealing with.

'Yeah. It says here—' He points at the screen.

'Well, what does it say?'

Not to make it about myself but *why* am I finding this out

from Jackson? I mean, I didn't expect to hear from Lowe but it feels back to front.

'It just says they've split up, that . . . '

'Read it.'

'OK, here, *after fourteen years together, Indie* . . . hate it when they write Indie . . . '

'Me too, carry on . . . '

' . . . sensation True Love have decided to part ways.'

'Oh, FUCK.'

'Lead singer Lowe Archer says – *it was a mutual decision and we still* . . . '

'OK, that's enough,' I snap.

'Don't you want to hear?' he asks, reading over the words to himself.

'Stupid journalism; it's not going to be the truth.'

'So, you should give Lowe a call? Check in on him.'

'I'm sure he has lots of people to support him. We've barely spoken in years.' We have the *occasional* text, once a year if that. 'I can't just call him up out of the blue.'

'Still, though, Ella, I'm sure it would still mean a lot to hear from you. You guys were close right?'

Jackson doesn't know the half of it.

'Send him a message?'

'Maybe.'

'Aw, I'm heartbroken,' he mutters as he leaves the room, tutting, to go for his run. 'They were one of the greats.'

Jackson doesn't really even listen to True Love but I know it makes him look cool at work to say I know them. No doubt he'll be listening to them now as he runs around the park.

I head into the kitchen. I should take out the teabags; the tea will be getting filmy stains on top. I stare at my phone. Nothing. Why am I expecting to hear from him? It's nothing to do with me. He doesn't have to inform me. I don't have True Love on Google

Alerts. What can I do anyway? It's not little old Ella, dropping him off at Fame's doorstep all those years ago and here to meet him on the other side. Helping him acclimatize into the ordinary world with the ordinary people. 'We go to TESCO; this is where you get your BASKET; this is how you use the self-service machine; this is called a TRAIN.'

I shouldn't really – it's like picking at a massive dangerous scab – but I start scrolling. This is bad for me. I can only flick radio stations for so long. Talk really loudly when friends have True Love's music on at parties, pretend to be OK when my drink tastes extra bitter. Or when they play True Love's song for the 'cool down' of an exercise class and suddenly he's soundtracking the stretch of my tight glutes. Why do I care that a video of them has gone viral? That their fourth album is number one in the charts. NUMBER ONE IN THE CHARTS? *HOW?* That the billboard near my house replaced a BOND movie poster with their new album artwork. That Lowe is a name so rare it sometimes doesn't even need a surname in the press. Meanwhile the sound of a BMX tyre on the pavement still tiptoes along the tightrope of my spine. It probably would have been easier for me to just fold in and become a fan. The more I scroll, the guiltier I feel; he's meant to be my friend. It feels like exploitation. Like stalking. Finding invented answers to questions I could just pick up the phone and ask myself.

The news is trending, photo after photo. I'm winded, sick. LOWE. LOWE. LOWE. My thumb blasts over articles and their horrible puns: *TRUE LOVE NEVER DID RUN SMOOTH.* Or *not all love lasts.* Photographs of heart-broken fans . . . photographs of the band over the years, of Lowe when he was younger. How *I* remember him – his hair, his hoodie, that face. I'm terrified to see a photo of him with a girl. There are some rumours – one an actress from a TV series, but it turns out she just did a sex scene to one of his songs and afterwards said how much she loved his band. He's a private person. The more I burrow, the harder it is to turn back. I've not allowed myself to do it for so long but DAMN he looks so FIT now. He's grown out his hair, he's . . . I need to do something cleansing . . . like . . . eat plain yoghurt.

There are tributes from bands we love. If little Lowe that wanted to be in a band could read them he'd die. Articles mention new songs and latest records, all of them unrecognizable to me, words that go over my head, that I've blocked out, albums that whenever people ask if I've heard I just ignore or avoid. Track titles that, honestly, I wouldn't get right in a pub quiz if I was about to win £500. I hide away, to keep myself safe. I wonder if Lowe ever sees girls who look like me in the supermarket? On a dancefloor? Serving him coffee? Sitting next to him in the cinema? Taking his blood pressure? Selling him a t-shirt?

I go to find his name in my contacts, a couple of numbers saved for him, unlike me, same-number-Ella. My thumb hovers over the one I'm sure is the most recent. *I could* . . . Jackson *told* me to. It would be a short exchange if anything, if he even replies.

The last message exchange is just a long ladder of 'happy birthdays'. Once each every year; we take turns in this drawn-out heart-crumpling dance.

No. I can't do it. Everyone will be calling him right now saying the exact same thing. Or wanting to hear the gossip about the break-up. I want to make sure he's OK but I don't want to be another sock lost in the wash of Lowe, but then why am I here trying to get my wording right a million times? It's *weirder* to say nothing. Cold, even. I write: **Hi Lowe, just seen the announcement, I really hope you're OK. You should be so proud of yourself! x** *Don't force him to reply; that way you won't take it personally if he doesn't respond.*

Big kiss. No, little kiss. No, big kiss. Little is good. **x**

And away it goes.

I sling my phone across the bed. Immediately I hate the thing. The power it has and the trouble it causes. But one second later I'm reaching for it again so I can insecurely add: **it's Ella by the way.**

I immediately regret sending it. I stuff my phone under my pillow. I feel bad. Like I've cheated. And then embarrassed. I get an adrenaline *rash*. It comes up now, here, alone in the darkness, fierce and in flames, angrily rumbling up my neck and face, wrapping around my throat like a boa constrictor, like I've been held captive in an Iron Maiden and somebody has rescued me *just* in time before the spikes drive through my skin.

I should never have messaged.

He won't reply.

Why did I text?

And now there's no going back . . .

Chapter 31

He hasn't replied.

It's 8.52 a.m. on a weekend. *Ella, calm THE HELL down.* I stress-eat granola straight from the box. Maybe it's my phone; maybe it's broken? I switch it off and on. Flick airplane mode on *just* in case. *Nope. OK.* He's blanked me. *Wow.* Whatever. I don't care anyway. I throw my phone down again like an old banana skin, and within seconds I'm drawn back, rereading my stupid message.

Hi Lowe, just seen the announcement, I really hope you're OK. You should be so proud of yourself! x

What did I mean he *should be so proud of himself*? He doesn't need my permission to be proud. I don't even know the guy any more. He could still be with *whatsherface?* (Heather) and her big curly hair and ideal curves. He could be in bloody New Zealand with her now. I bet she never got jealous, bet she only felt flattered. I can just see her glancing at my name popping up on his phone.

Poor Ella, she fancied you so much, didn't she? Bless her.

Or does he keep me a secret? Bottle me up like I do with him?

Could be the time difference, or just *all* the differences.

I've probably, *obviously*, pissed him off. Why did I do this to myself?

I need fresh air. Jackson's back from his run and offers to come but I say I need to call my sister (as IF! Vi would rip me to shreds over these dilemmas!).

'All OK?' Jackson checks.

'Yes! Just a lot to talk about!'

And he relaxes, as though Violet and I are going to be hunched over Pinterest getting bridesmaid ideas. Outside, I hover around like a hologram being pathetic. Glitching. I. CAN. NOT. STOP. CHECKING. MY PHONE. I'm checking my phone so much that I worry I might break it. That the robots – you know the ones that report to the algorithm department to only ever offer me adverts for memory foam mattresses – might be panicking, thinking my phone has been robbed? I'm out of control. Why did I listen to Jackson? He has no context! I wish I could throw my phone into the River Thames but what if Lowe calls and my phone's slinking to the bottom of the riverbed with the bent beer cans and murder weapons, crying out his name?

I should do something nice like go squish Ronke's baby daughter, Avanna, but I don't want to infect her with my rampant anxiety.

I return to the flat. The granny fireplace chuckles at me. The old boiler cackles, *you fool, you never should have texted.*

By now a few friends have reached out about the split. Some writer friends send me links to more news sites; some of the stylists from the hairdressers share gossip about 'the real reason' True Love broke up. Annoying. Mia texts me the news like I haven't already heard and even The Twins come out of the woodwork: **Bianca gave us your number – hope that's OK. Just heard about Lowe's band 😔 made us think of you. We're in Suffolk now but when next in London we should defo meet. Be good to see you X**

Dom calls to chat about it. She's in shock. *Why now,* she asks, *when they were at the top of their game? Have you spoken to him at all?*

Their whole USP was the fact that as a band they were all friends, that they promoted friendship, a brotherhood that ignored competition and bravado, that they truly *loved* each other. And here are horrible articles stirring the pot. That must be so hard. Growing up publicly, the whole world looking on. I hate to think of him in the eyeball of a media cyclone.

My phone—

Ella! so good to hear from you, how are you? fancy meeting up for a coffee soon? Lowe x

Shit. Ella. He wants to *meet.* I write back instinctively: **hey, I'd love that, I work from home so when is good for you? x**

Chapter 32

Now

It's a few days later and the weather is frigid in Waterloo, the sky wet, cold and hard. Me and my fourteen-year-old expectations stand by the stairs leading up to the South Bank, with puppet string legs. It's so early. Early is good. Coffee, and then I'll pretend I've got somewhere to be. I'm wearing a bright-pink flowery dress with a matching coat, and sandals. *What was I thinking?* I was so flustered getting dressed. I hold onto the silver rail of the staircase to steady myself, to take it all in. *Ella, you have a fiancé. Go home and make pasta bake.* I swallow. My adrenaline is making me shiver. *Wait, are my knees knocking?* My teeth, *chattering.* It's not *that* cold. I use the little mirrored apple-logo on the back of my phone to make sure my mascara isn't leaking. I hate *so bad* the idea of being just another girl in a pretty dress in Lowe's jumble-sale pile of broken hearts. The foolish way I was always so sure that I was different from the rest.

I read the note back that I emailed myself on the train.

Ella, everything has changed; you won't still feel the same after all this time. It would be very weird to love someone you barely know any more, strange to love someone based on the past. Grow up and get your fucking shit together. You're getting married to Jackson now. Lovely Jackson.

I look at my engagement ring. The opal, a spy. *I've got my eye on you.*

I need a song. Headphones in so I can keep my stride cool and steady, feel like I'm on a catwalk. I have to remember this moment. But it can't be a song I'd catch Jackson whistling whilst he takes a piss.

J.Lo's 'Waiting For Tonight'.

I'm nervous. Exam nervous. Doctor's appointment nervous. Submission nervous. I should turn back. This feels *wrong.* I'm making it all up in my head. But I'm still walking.

The riverbank is almost empty. I linger. Don't rush. I take my time to see the boats and birds. I let the new morning take me. The South Bank buffers the wind with its boxy concrete and blank blocks. And just across the river, a skyline waits like a tray of chocolates. The emptiness and opportunity of the new day gives me the freedom to be in my favourite place: the music video of my life. My Co-Star: Lowe.

This will be the first time in more than ten years we've been alone.

I imagine us spending the entire day together, falling through a trap door in the universe where nobody can find us. *Do you want to run away together?*

And then I feel stupid about that thought, insecure, like a fan lurking outside the gates of an actor's hotel.

This Titan from my past stands before me, a figure in the distance, unzipping through the clearing like it's nothing. A pair of scissors gliding through wrapping paper. The coolest guy you've ever seen in your whole life – Lowe Archer shark-finning his way up the riverbank where, for him, everything gives way. His stride, swinging, with intention but not arrogant. He grins – *you can't fake a smile like that* – and I turn to goo on command. I do a stubby excitable wave, ridged, an Action Man greeting, like somebody wearing a too-small jacket afraid to tear the seams.

I smile. He smiles. I fight the urge to run to get to him faster.

Lowe looks older. A whole-the-distance-we've-been-apart *older*. I wasn't expecting that. I thought he'd stay young forever. His thick hair is *longer*, long enough to fold behind his ears but I know that – I've seen the press photos. His moss eyes. His face thinner and sculpted, clean shaven, jaw squarer, nose, wider. Lowe is a *man. Of course, he's a man*. But he's still all there. Preserved, like he never lost a *drop*. He wears black skinny jeans and pointy boots, an expensive-looking mac with the collar starched up. He's so refined. I still wear the same cheap perfume I did when we were nineteen. The one that triggers people our age because it reminds them of their first finger. Only now I've got grey hairs sprouting out my scalp like resurrecting skeletons from the dead.

Should I instigate the handshake? *No, he won't remember that surely? Don't make it weird.*

We hug. And time seems to halt. It's been ten minutes and a hundred years at the same time. We're just like riding a bike – muscle memory; we can't forget. We pedal along, finding our balance.

I want to fall into him. To buckle my legs and collapse, to let him carry me, like the last ten years of hunting and wishing have taken their toll and, finally, I'm home. Mission complete.

I've got to stop telling myself these stories, that he's too cool for me now, that he'd rather be out with someone else, got every one of our idols' phone number on speed dial these days, seen the lively, jerky boobs of a thousand girls. Trashed the best hotel rooms. Got original cowboy boots from Texas. Eaten black cod in Japan. Climbed a mountain. Killed all his brain cells with cocaine. Been to wild parties that I've only seen in films where they drink from Red Cups. I probably can't talk to him about music any more because all music now belongs to him. That's just his thing now, his industry; he'll have opinions on it all. That whilst we're out he'll get spotted by fans.

And how he's probably told himself stories about me too. That it never happened for me. *Sad little bubbly Ella.*

We walk side by side. He's quiet, sometimes laughing, sometimes responding, clearing his throat. Side by side is good because it gives me a second to catch my breath because I'm motor-mouthing my way along the river, panting. Can you pass out from walking and talking at the same time? Lowe has always been comfortable with silence. I am not. I'm rattling around like a pinball machine, lighting up and firing off memories and stories and total rubbish.

I talk my way past the spray-painted colourful Mexican food truck. Past the second-hand bookstalls under the bridge, trestle tables already smelling of damp and spiders' eggs and others' hands. We talk about TV. Books next. Hop-scotching along. It feels like everything I mention he's not into or has never heard of. It's miss after miss. 'Have you really not seen that?' and '*How* did you miss *that*? Gosh, you really do live under a rock, don't you?' Of course, ironically, I'm the one who lives under a rock of fiction and Lowe's been touring the world, witnessing his magnificent dreams come true.

We see an early-riser kid skateboarding, echoing on concrete. He's probably seventeen but I feel the same age as him. And, in the distance, I see her: the sitting, waiting, wanting girl on the sidelines. A cheerleader, watching the boy as though he's as impressive as the Northern Lights.

We find a plump, squashy purple velvet sofa in the corner of a cinema café that is empty except for one waiter unloading the dishwasher. The high ceilings shrink us and every move we make feels spot-lit and gargantuan. The sofa eats us up.

'We're like *The Borrowers*,' Lowe jokes.

I laugh and he does too.

Our knees knock; our legs touch. *CHING.* I obliterate.

We look at the menu.

Lowe reaches inside his jacket pocket and puts on a pair of glasses. GLASSES? I can't even bring myself to look at him in them. *Just keep looking at the menu.* But my eyes aren't looking, not really; I'm simply trying to steady my heart, stop my mouth from being so dry, trying not to gulp – lots. He's all tentacled up with his bag and I long to be the strap of that bag, twisted up with him, close to his chest.

I spot his jewellery: his chain, his rings. And I find myself sitting on my hand, squashing my week-old engagement ring in-between the sofa and my bum cheeks, like how I might hide a blade if I was trying to escape a hostage situation. I won't keep it there for-like-you-know-*ever*. Just until I calm down. Then I'll relax and tell him my great news.

Well . . . NEWS . . . I'm engaged.

Hey, so, Lowe . . . My boyfriend, Jackson and I are engaged.

So, guess who's getting married . . . ?

Once I say it. That's it. It's done. It's all over.

I thought if maybe I *don't* say Jackson's name it might not come up. Don't worry, I know that's not good. I know that's *bad*. It's a bit like a challenge, a game, to see if I can tell every story I've experienced in the past few years and casually leave my partner's name out, but I must get the pronouns right, remember to say *I* instead of *we*. I know I can't keep it up forever. I know that Lowe will know the truth eventually; I just want to keep the hope alive, somehow, just for this one sweet coffee – just today – to live out the dream, make it a possibility, that I'm free and then go back to my life. I know nothing is going to happen, I just don't want to give it up. Not yet. Not when I'm sitting here imagining what our baby would look like.

And what about him? What about Heather? Or someone else? He could be married; he could have a kid?!

'Where are you living?'

'Peckham.'

Aoife was right! What's so bloody good about Peckham?

'Just renting, temporarily.'

WITH *WHO*?

'Still South then?'

'Course.'

Don't course me when you were the one off recording albums in LA – but I'm careful what I say because then he'll know I've been searching his socials and I don't want to slip up.

We have to order at the counter so up we go. The bar is lined with jewels of coloured bottles like the windows of a church, a sobering reminder that we're meeting before 10 a.m. *That this is definitely not a date.* It's hard coffee in the morning. I order and the waiter smiles at us like, *you guys make a cute couple,* or maybe I just made that up. Or maybe it's because even the waiter knows how in love I am with Lowe; he can *smell* it, it's *that* obvious. My vulnerability, my weak spot – Lowe is what would get me killed in the wild – and the waiter pities me. Where's my personal *growth*? My *development*? My *progress*? What do I have to show for myself? Maybe he just recognizes Lowe and can't wait until he's made the coffee so he can run off and text his mates: **GUESS WHO I JUST MADE A FLAT WHITE FOR?**

We find the sofa again. Flashes of cinema surround us – images of other lives of lovers and families. How I wish we could just press pause on today like a film, rewind back to the beginning, to when we first met, and this time not fuck it up. This time I would play it out to the end. I imagine Jackson walking in right now, how quickly I would spring up, and that's how I know that I still have feelings. Oh. This is awful. I should probably make an excuse and leave. *JUST BE HIS FRIEND.*

Our coffees arrive on a silver tray; mine is basically frothy milk and tiger lines of chocolate. I reach for the sugar pot, stuffed with coloured paper sachets. And that's when I see him spot my ring. BULLSEYE. Glinting like a bullet. A gold filling at the back of the devil's mouth. I quickly hide it underneath my bum again. But I know he's seen it. I should have left it in the little soap dish by the side of the sink and pretended I'd forgotten to put it back on but *that* would have been deliberately deceptive. That, I couldn't live with.

I change the subject. 'I'm sorry to hear about the band splitting up.' Has his mood changed since he's seen it? I can't tell.

'Thanks, yeah, it's shit but it was time.' Cucumber cool.

'Think back to when we were young, when you first picked up the guitar. If someone told you that making music would be your *job*! That you'd go on to achieve all you have? Can you imagine? I mean – it's incredible, Lowe.'

He goes shy.

'Your mum would be so proud of you.' I want to put my hand on his leg when I say that bit, but I don't.

'Thank you, Ella.' He takes a breath, brushes crumbs off him that aren't there. 'I just don't know what I'm gonna do with my life now; we've been playing since we were kids – I don't even have a CV,' he jokes. 'Got any jobs going?' he says to the empty room and I laugh. 'We're still so young anyway. We've got time.'

'How did you feel about turning thirty?'

'Fine,' he says. 'Another trip around the sun?'

I guess thirty is perfectly pleasant if you've achieved all your life dreams already. He must be pretty happy then.

'Did you have a party?' (Like the one I conjured up in my head with all the cool people and me not being invited.)

'Well, I don't drink, do I, so . . . ?'

'You don't drink?' This surprises me; I thought he'd be living some hedonistic lifestyle. '*Why*? Sorry, I didn't mean that – I mean *how*? I've tried so many times to quit and just can't seem to do it.'

'Yeah, it's hard – it's everywhere, all the time, especially on tour and it was just getting in my way. Not helping. So I stopped.'

'That's incredible. Well done.'

'Once you start seeing drinking for what it is, it's easy – but you're right – that first bit is tough.'

He changes the subject to me.

'So what have you been up to?'

What a question; we laugh awkwardly because it's been so long.

'*Where to start* . . . ?' I joke. 'Well, other than letting my hair grow wildly long, spontaneously lobbing it off into a bob, regretting it and repeating the cycle endlessly for the rest of my days, not a lot.'

He smiles at me how he used to. 'Are you still writing?'

Ouch. There goes my favourite question.

'*Still*, you know?! That's the sort of question a great-uncle asks at Christmas.'

'Sorry!' he corrects. 'I really didn't mean it like that.'

I pretend to be a great-uncle. 'Do you *still* do gymnastics and listen to NSYNC?'

'I still ride my bike!' he defends.

'That's your *hobby*! Yes, Lowe, I *still* write.'

'Music's my hobby too, though.'

I didn't want to talk about my writing with Lowe. He's achieved – a million times over – the dream of making a hobby a job – which I know is more of *my* problem than *his* – but still, it doesn't make it any less hard to accept that he's reached the top of the mountain enjoying the view, whilst my career hasn't even rolled out of bed and brushed its teeth yet. But the main reason I don't want to talk about my work with Lowe is because of my first book of poems; that was all about him. I don't know if he read it; I'm not sure if he even knows it exists.

'I've just finished my first novel, actually.' It sounds aloof and pretentious. To compensate, I put myself down. 'It's just . . . a bit of *fun*.' CRINGE. (And perhaps there lies the answer as to why it comes across as a hobby.)

Lowe nods. He wouldn't call his band *fun*.

'That's great. I remember your letters. They were always so, what's the word? . . . *Alive*.'

Alive. We hold eye contact. I go back there through the portal of his eyes. Whhoooossshhhh. *ZAP!*

'I do other writing bits and pieces, to pay the bills.' LIKE MY MORTGAGE. WITH MY FIANCÉ.

He nods, like bills are something he doesn't have to understand.

I bring it back to him. 'So what about you? Are you *still* making music?' I take the piss.

'Yeah, that does hurt actually. Sorry,' he says, rubbing his hand over his heart. 'We still have the studio, so I'll be in there *pretending* to write music, although I'm not sure how much the world is begging for my depressing solo album to be honest. *But* I'm sure at some point I'll find the misfired confidence to inflict a release of some kind upon the world.'

'That'll be good,' I say. Awkward silence. Have we run out of things to say?

Our arms kiss.

Time for a round-up. 'So, Ronke has had a baby – Shreya has settled down with four kids but we haven't spoken in years. The Twins are in Suffolk apparently. Aoife's got some high-flying corporate job in the City where she gets paid to eat sushi,' I tell him. 'We're still close.' He likes that, *loyalty*. 'Bianca is *Bianca*. She's just got a new job actually; she's doing great.'

I think of her beaming face in the swimming pool at the KTPLT party and I'm finally able to see the funny side.

'—and Mia – just got married actually,' I say. 'I caught the bouquet at the wedding.'

WHY DID I SAY THAT?

'What does that mean? That you'll be getting married next then?'

He saw the ring. I'm sure he saw the ring.

'I'm not superstitious.' I blush. 'Also me, not stepping over three drains on the way here.'

'I still do that too. And I have to get to the bottom of the stairs before the toilet stops flushing or something bad will happen.'

'Like what?'

He looks like he wants to say something but doesn't. We've spent so much of our relationship not saying things, it just seems normal to us now.

Lowe gives himself into the chair. I catch the elasticated waistband of his Calvin Klein boxers and nod to myself like I've seen too much. I realize I've been gazing.

'I like your chain.' CRINGE.

'Thanks,' he says. 'It was my mum's.'

I nod. 'It's really beautiful.'

~~So are you.~~

And the coffee is done.

'I'm just gonna wee and then . . . ' I excuse myself.

I wonder if he's watching me walk away? What do I even look like walking away? Then I remember that what I look like from behind is none of my business. Is that *it*? Ten years of waiting for *that*, throwing out stagnant small talk, tepid touch. Was that the very best we could do? I don't know what I was hoping for, *expecting*, but it's sad that he'll go back to his life and I'll go back to mine.

Good, I think. *Good*. That's where I belong. With Jackson.

So why do I want to cry? The toilet mirrors are unflattering in this horrible bright-red light and they ping everywhere like a house of mirrors. And when I sit down I notice that I've sat on my hand for the entire time. My engagement ring has crushed a red crimped line into my small finger and it's actually quite painful. It serves me right. Poor Jackson. How would I like it if he avoided talking about me? I love him – why would I do this to him? To us.

Just go home, love.

By the basin I check my eyes to make sure there's no reveal of regret. Or pain. Or longing. Or clear as daylight desperation. I head back upstairs where Lowe is leaning against the bar how only pro models lean. I suppose he has done a lot of those photo shoots. He's waiting for *me*. I almost can't believe that for this one sweet second, Lowe Archer is waiting for *me*. How right that feels. He's chatting to the waiter, nothing too much but it already feels like an in-joke. He gets on with everyone. He always has a cheeky face like he's up to something. But he never is; he's too honest.

'What?'

'*What?*' Lowe says back, smiling.

'What?'

His face spills into a massive laugh. He tunes into the music faintly pattering away in the background, his head bouncing from side to side mockingly. I bashfully reach for my card to pay, shyly, as the waiter hands Lowe his receipt, smoothly, like he's in on some gag. Lowe slides it into the back pocket of his jeans. The younger me would have scrapbooked the hell out of that receipt.

'I wanted to get it,' I offer.

'You can get the next one.'

The *next* one. And there it is, the chink in his armour: he wants to make sure I want to see him again. He bites his bottom lip. It's a plump lip. Succulent. And I'm slung back. Years of loving somebody isn't just going to evaporate because of one frothy coffee.

We walk towards the station, the voltage between us sparking. Walking by his side feels normal. Like being next to him is always a touchstone, a place to start. I begin making a case in my head now, gathering the evidence up nice and neat into a big stack of why we would never work, even though absolutely nobody asked. He walks so close he almost bumps into me. *See? It will never work.* If our walking is like this just imagine the clunky sex we'd have. We should go back to being *old friends and me secretly but not secretly at all just being in love with him.* It's so much easier this way. Or going forward, we can be like brothers? Two brothers who go on fishing trips and wear plaid shirts and sit in silence.

At the tall steps of the station, we hug. He squeezes me so wholly he's saying it all. He smells like washing powder, the air outside, the coffee he's just been drinking. I smell weed somewhere and this only compounds the memories. Until he brings out his vape, which is as big and as heavy as how I imagine a gun to be, and chemical sour-sweet exhalation is blasted over us.

'Oh no, no, no.' I blow the smoke away.

'Sorry,' he apologizes, fanning the air. 'I've quit so – I'm addicted to this thing now.'

'That's good you quit, but *this?*'

Our eyes lock in. WE STARE. Does he have a girlfriend at home? What's his life? How is he so *mysterious?* Somehow I've revealed *all* my cards and his cards are held so close.

'See you again soon?' Lowe asks.

'Definitely.'

I nod, even though I'm scared he just wants me as his normal friend from his normal life, proof that he was *liked* before he got famous, and I'll have to make friends with his wife and go to Winter Wonderland with them and watch him have babies and become their *crazy fun* Fairy Odd Mother. KILL ME NOW.

But also don't kill me; let me live here, eternally next to him. Where I can talk to his tongue. Open his jaws. Clamber into his mouth.

And then he says, 'Oh, hey, by the way, Ella, I read your book, your poems and . . . ' He lets the words hang . . . AND? . . . 'You should be proud of yourself too.'

The word lands like a match, strikes my heart. I do a face as if to say *hardly.*

'You read books?'

'Only yours.'

I download the sober app once again and hit Day Zero. The clock starts ticking and would you believe that from that moment on, for the next month, I am feeling so fucking good. It's like I've been rebooted. I'm *inspired.* I don't wear my rings when I write – I need to write hard and fast – so I can almost forget the opal ring and its diva requirements, its power and conditions. It sits in its soap dish with the others. Days turn into nights, the back and forths pick up with Lowe, like nothing ever changed, like no time or distance has passed between us. We never talk about meeting up, which is good – just song recommendations, screen grabs of my sober milestones, stupid memes. Innocent, light and friendly – maybe we can just be pen pals? I find myself laughing out loud at his messages. My heart soars every time I see his name appear on my phone. Jackson is at work more than he is home. Taking calls from Zahra and the team at weekends, past 10 p.m., before 9 a.m. – where I'd usually nag, I don't.

Once, Zahra is on loudspeaker and I hear her call Jackson 'Jackie'. He goes quiet when he's stressed, insular. Burning off the racing thoughts and congestion at football, tennis, cricket and all those 10ks. When he's distracted with work, he's distant with me; he pulls away. Usually, I'm the one to pull us back, carve out the space to bring us together: a new TV series, dinner, a night away. But this time, I don't. He notices the changes. *You're on Cloud Nine,* he says. He thinks it's the engagement that's making my mood lift, not that I'm high off the dopamine of getting a text back from my favourite human.

And I'm working. Doing it, editing and fixing. I help Jackson finalize the story for his big KTPLT Christmas advert, a simple one about *giving the gift of love*, with hidden messaging about sustainability (got to hide those greens of goodness in the creamy mashed potato). The main character is an adorable animated carboard box with a bow of string for hair. It's very cute. I enjoy working creatively together with Jackson in this way, our brains tessellating.

But if anybody asks, I'm writing my book. And I don't care how ambitious or ridiculous or audacious it sounds because once again my world has been set on fire.

By November, I, finally, hover my finger over the button and press send to my agent, cross my fingers and hope for the best.

My agent replies, so fast it's like an Out Of Office auto-response: **Is this a prank?**

Chapter 33

Already smashed down by the terror of sending out my work, I feel vulnerable and tremulous, forgetting that absolutely nobody can read a giant novel and give you feedback in an hour. I meet Aoife in London Bridge to silence the voice of my inner critic and self-medicate with food. I am DETERMINED not to drink but meeting up with my best mate in a fancy place is a test. She's clearly feeling herself: high-waisted leather pants and her clip-clop boots, swinging her TK Maxx handbag. Aoife's recommended this pasta bar where they cook the pasta in front of you. *They don't take reservations,* she says, *but you can drink in the queue.* Queue? For *pasta?* The queue is at least fifty people long and next to an alley that smells of vomit, piss and fish blood, but apparently *it's so worth it.* I'm sorry but have you ever watched anyone make pasta pesto in front of you?

I manage to dodge the queue-drink by offering to go to the shop whilst Aoife holds our place. I return with the two bottles of Peroni she requested and tell her, 'I'm just SO thirsty,' whilst cracking open my sparkling water.

Aoife's tipsy by the time we're seated at what she calls 'front row' at the bar looking over the kitchen. She claps her hands excitedly, leaning over, naming ingredients very loudly to impress the chefs. Ah, that's why she likes it here. 'They're tattooed, bearded and Italian' – a chef wipes their forehead with a rag like a Diet Coke advert – 'and *stressed.*' Her eyes flicker at the untame, orange flames, snake-charmed.

She glances at the wine list, ripping at the (very good) bubbly bread, whilst perving over other people's burrata. 'Order whatever you want – I'll expense it. Red? Or white? To start?'

'I might eat something first.' I buy myself time.

'A carafe of the *Rosso Toscana*, please?' she tries to pronounce in her South London accent to the waiter, who returns with two glasses. I let them fill my glass with delicious-looking red wine but don't drink.

'So, I'm having doubts,' I begin, but it isn't easy to talk; it's crowded and loud. We're sat in the middle of a chain of strangers and the plates come small, quick, and in no order, interrupted with top-ups of water and small talk with others, the staff. Aoife's acting like we're on holiday, here to make friends, twirling pappardelle, catching eyes.

'About?'

'Jackson.' I wince.

'It's definitely the engagement; it's freaked you out.' She's so sure she barely looks up. Wipes her bread around a ramekin of grass-green oil, sprinkles on crystals of salt.

I nod; already this is bringing me great comfort. I prefer this diagnosis to having to leave him, which is much more effort.

'You two were happy before this. We always thought you saw things long term with Jackson. *We* told him it was a good idea,' she confesses.

'It's not *your* fault.'

'And the way you ran for that bouquet at Mia's, *I mean*—' She chuckles to herself in that way that makes you sometimes want to punch your mates.

'I can't pin my future on catching some flowers.'

'So, turn the engagement down a notch? Buy yourself some time to figure out if it's Jackson or the commitment? He's always working anyway – as if that guy will find the time for a wedding! It might never happen. Just talk to him.'

'I can't. He's on a high with work, got a deadline, we've just got the flat—'

Aoife sits back to analyse me, holding her wine close to her chest. 'What? Why are you looking me like that?'

'Could it be that things are just a bit *too good*?'

'I don't want to sound ungrateful but I'm not sure it's what I want.' Silence. I chew the inside of my cheek and add like it's another part of the story. 'I met up with Lowe last month?'

She's not surprised; then again not much surprises Aoife. 'And are these two things related or . . . ?'

'No!' I blurt. 'Well, no, not like *that*, but it has given me *perspective*. Reminded me of who I was before and how it's *meant* to feel to, you know, *feel*.'

She doesn't like this. 'We're not kids any more, El,' she says like I didn't know. 'It's normal to be *intoxicated* and *entranced* by these *celebrities*.' The word 'celebrities' is said with almost no sound at all in case journalists are everywhere.

I laugh at her hysteria. 'He's still Lowe!'

Aoife looks at me like I'm naive, like she could say a million things about Lowe but will – just this once – spare me her opinions, filling her mouth with a forkful of rocket salad. I watch her tackle it and then she leans in closer.

'Elbow, don't be *mad*. Jackson is FIT!' she jokes, then softens. 'He's successful and kind – he's as good as partners come, and, most importantly, he loves you, Ella, and you *love* him.' I see now she's pissed, enjoying playing the role of independent-female best friend in a movie but here, with the wine and the surroundings, it's kind of working. 'It's because we're used to chaos; we run away from love, from accomplishment and nice things, but look—' She holds her hands out to present the chefs as an example of *nice things*.

She continues, 'It's cos our mums were raised by women who

didn't get a say, who didn't have ambition, who they just saw cooking, cleaning and having babies, so they became such feminists. Now, they've hammered that trauma into us – *we shouldn't settle, be conventional blah blah* – but it's just turning us into desolate islands!' She orders a second carafe of wine, transferring the wine from my glass into hers. 'Should have just got a bottle.' She considers me. 'You're not preggers, are you?'

I shake my head.

'I've had enough of drinking right now, it isn't doing me any favours. I don't like how I am when I drink.'

'You don't even drink a lot though, El.'

'I know, but it's enough to be horrible to myself the next day.'

This somehow permits me to order a lemonade.

She can see I'm still being eaten up and admits, 'That kind of romantic lovey-dovey thing you think exists out there does *not*. Dating apps suck; *trust* me. Don't break up with Jackson, not in *winter*. It'll be lonely as hell. It's *not* a good time to make big decisions.'

When we can feel the restaurant wants our seats back, Aoife unapologetically zips her leather pants back up with force, debating whether or not she can be bothered to go to the house of the new guy she's seeing. I should have asked Bianca for advice instead; she would have just screamed, 'LEAVE HIM!' Though at least Aoife's advice means I don't have to act right now. I can just keep doing what I'm doing: waiting.

When I wake up, Jackson's already at the gym and I have a message from Aoife: **I was fucked last night 😵 chatted crap, sorry if I said the wrong stuff. Should have just been a good friend and listened. Always here if you wanna chat, I'll keep my big mouth shut, I promise! Love you. Dreaming of that 🍻💜 Need not to drink so much! X**

I text back: **you are a good friend x**

And an email from my agent: **Ella! Couldn't sleep, read your book. It's fucking nuts but I really love it. Lots of questions but I think we can do this. I might put the feelers out? Let me know your thoughts. And well done. It was worth the wait.**

And I put my hands over my chest, pull the duvet up over my head and squeal. The first and only person I want to text about this is Lowe. To share the news, but very quickly the news feels news-less and needy. Nothing concrete to get excited about. We never share intimacies like this. The back and forths are irregular, about nothing much, few and far between. And I think it's probably safer that way.

Chapter 34

It isn't until a month later, when Lowe suggests meeting again:
hey, fancy a ◗ x

Christmas is coming on this early afternoon. In town there's an etherealness that only comes with the heaviness of December: the shops strung with lights and decorations; on street corners, candied nuts (that smell better than they taste) are scooped into paper bags that stain with oil immediately; happy people loaded with big square shopping bags and day-time prosecco. A shiny brass band play 'All I Want for Christmas Is You' under the chest of a silver angel, wire wings spread out towards the clouds, and it makes me giddy.

Does it have to be SO romantic? JEEEEZZZ.

My brain's mumbling to itself: *Hey Lowe, so I've been meaning to ask you . . . it probably sounds ridiculous now but just wondering, did you ever love me back then?*

If you were to see me walking down the road at this moment you would see me physically shake the thought out of my head: *Ella! Stop it! He is your FRIEND!*

We arrange to meet in a strange little café in Soho. It looks more like a gift shop than a coffee shop: black and white sofas; marble tables covered in art books and fashion magazines; the coffee served in ridiculous deep shiny black cups with giant saucers. The owner is a rude woman my mum's age.

The reason I suggested here is because the owner has ten dogs. They all hang around, posing and showing off in glamorous dog beds that look more expensive than my own with collars that would make you gasp if they came in your Christmas stocking. Dogs make a great ice-breaker. One of them is particularly adorable, a brown and white floppy King Charles Spaniel with one working eye and the other sewn shut, who sits by you, looking like she could read your fortune. *PLEASE, READ MY FORTUNE, TELL ME WHAT TO DO, DOG!*

I arrive first, carrying bags of my own Christmas shopping (to look busy and to make it clear Lowe wasn't the *only* reason I faced the Underground). I take off my oversized, fuzzy, royal-blue hooded coat, order a coffee and wait, bags now by my feet. I obviously immediately regret the coffee; that's not going to help with these *jolts*. I flick through a comic book that I found on the table to make myself look artistic, occupied. On the page, inside one of the little rectangles, a cartoon woman cries giant globular tears into a telephone. On the next she has a cape and is flying.

Annoyingly, the entrance to the café is a side street/alley, so I can't prepare myself for his arrival. Still, I gaze anxiously out the window. Watch the people and daydream.

And the door swings open.

We turn our heads.

All ten dogs stare. And me.

Lowe looks knickerbocker glory delicious today. The structure of his face. His hands. He wears a pendant around his neck, something old but new for him, with stones – a ruby maybe? Turquoise? He wears a shirt, red-wine red. Black jeans and boots. He orders a coffee and I watch him give the best smile of his life to the woman who owns the coffee shop – she doesn't deserve it – and I see *even* a woman of her impenetrable stature falter. I watch him pet the dogs, all sniffing his legs and licking his fingertips. I long to be their fur, their chins, their paws. *Lucky bitches.*

I cross my legs, lean my head on my elbow. I notice that Lowe mirrors my position. If I sit up straight, so does he. If I arch my back, so does he. If I cock my head to one side, he does too. If I sip my coffee, he sips his. I mean this is basic armchair psychology, isn't it? If somebody is mirroring you it means they like you, right? Well, the guy is a bloody mime!

Smile versus smile. Eyes versus eyes. Hands versus hands.

'So how've you been?' he asks.

'Good.' *Sound strong, Ella.* 'My book's about to go out on submission.' Realizing that's probably just how most men in my industry talk about their work.

'Wicked. Let me know how it goes.'

We still talk about our lives as 'I's and 'me's in total singular without ever mentioning partners.

'What are your plans for Christmas?' he asks. 'You going away or . . . ?'

'I'm just going to Mum's. You?'

'I'll go to the coast with my dad.'

'You still do that?' Since Lowe's mum died, Lowe and his dad created their own Christmas tradition of driving down to the coast to cold-water swim, and eat a picnic of sandwiches and coffee from a flask in the car. 'Will you *swim*?'

'Course we'll *swim*!'

'You're crazy! I bet that's an amazing feeling.'

'I mean, it's a *cold* feeling' – he laughs – 'but it's addictive.'

'What about New Year?'

'There's a few parties but I reckon I'll just have a chilled one.'

We're getting good at this.

'I've had my fun anyway.' He jokes like he's old.

He doesn't mention True Love. Only looks in my eyes and

smiles and laughs at everything I say. *How dare somebody so beautiful as you just tread the universe?*

'I've been writing actually.' He looks shy to tell me this. 'See, told you I'd get there!' I like that he refers back to our last conversation. 'I've just been playing around with some ideas, seeing what comes and—'

'What?'

'Sorry, it just feels weird and bit embarrassing talking to a proper writer about writing.'

'Lowe! I'm not a proper *anything*!'

'Yeah you are.' The way he says this makes me think he isn't talking about writing any more. The conversation is so close up and intense I forget to breathe.

I can't take it. I'm going to burst; my feelings are breaking the seams of my clothes, tearing out like the incredible hulk – in velvet.

'Ella, Ella . . . ' Lowe points down and I clock the one-eyed fortune-telling spaniel pissing on my coat. OH, FOR FU—

The owner stalks over. If my dog pissed on a customer's coat, trust me, I would not be *stalking*. 'Oh, she does that – she's old,' she says, without apologizing. The fortune-telling dog looks at me like, *how's that for a prophecy, bitch?*

I can tell Lowe's annoyed on my behalf.

'Here, let me give you some money towards dry-cleaning . . . ' she half offers, not even really opening up her purse properly.

'Give it to charity,' I say.

And she scurries the money back and into her purse without even offering us a free cup of coffee.

Lowe says in his loudest voice, 'Wasn't that your most treasured irreplaceable coat that you inherited from your beloved deceased great-aunt, Ella?'

I catch on the joke and say, 'Yes, it was.' I sniffle like I'm crying. 'It's all I have left of her.'

And Lowe puts his arm around me, tutting and walks me out of the dog café.

'It is a nice coat though, even with the dog piss.'

Once again we walk side by side. Side by side is good, remember? People take walks like this when they have difficult conversations, or they take long drives or sit by a fire so they don't have to look each other in the eye. *Did you ever feel the same about me?* But side by side means I see the stares of passing people. 'Oh my God is that . . . ?' Somebody stops to ask for a photo. And again. And again. He's so lovely to everyone. 'Sorry.' I can tell he wishes they'd leave us alone.

'Don't apologize,' I say.

'I'm going to put this on.' He pulls out a cap clipped to the back of his jeans, just like the one he used to wear when we were younger and it just sends me back and twists me up. 'Is that OK? I feel like it's rude.'

'No, it's OK.'

We pass the Christmas displays in shop windows, squares of theatre, an electric toy train full of shambolic model-mice passengers wearing sunglasses and party hats, looping complicated tracks of consequence like that Mouse Trap game, tipping over glasses of wine, shooting through a turkey and splatting in trifle. Lowe and I crack up like we're kids. Everything just makes us so happy. The last window is of a winter snow scene. Escape. Desolation. A magic effect of mist and mirror makes a forest of tiny plastic evergreen trees infinite. It's like Raymond Briggs's *The Snowman*. Lowe's grin is huge, his hands behind his back, taking it all in.

'It's so amazing!' I say. 'How did they do that? It's so clever.'

Lowe is quiet, enchanted.

And then, at the very end, the selling point: a jewellery display. The centrepiece an engagement ring.

I should be going home.

'I'm walking this way if you want to?' I say.

'Sure.' Lowe follows; like one of those people who has nowhere to really be, he slides along next to me, aimlessly. 'I haven't been around here for ages.' *He's* lost this time. He doesn't seem to see the odd person who recognizes him, the way strangers nudge each other and whisper when he walks past. And if he does, he pretends not to or he's used to it. We walk like we're sharing a sleeve, laces tied together for a three-legged race, deliberately, clumsily.

At Seven Dials I ask, 'What are your plans for the rest of the afternoon?' Then kick myself because this is what I usually ask when I've had enough of someone's company and I'm looking to wind things down, whereas I ask here because I genuinely care.

'Well, we're buying a house so—'

We're.

I hear a gameshow buzzer siren go off with the word 'we'. By the way his face falls, I know this means he isn't single. This means he's buying a house with someone else.

A bloody mansion, I bet.

I don't know who *we* is.

I imagine Heather's face in his wallet. I only met her that one time at the festival but did I mention she's also the face of my nighttime sleep paralysis.

Aoife found her on LinkedIn once. She's nothing like us. She's a grown-up. A proper one. One of those organized women who wears suits with trainers to work and then changes into her smart clippy-cloppys when she arrives. Brings in her own salads with a separate bottle for dressing so it doesn't go limp. It's too easy to see her French-manicured nails wrapped around a Biro, filling in mortgage applications. Straightening out the paperwork how a newsreader does before they pretend to notice the camera. Get real – he doesn't need a mortgage.

'Oh, Lowe, I'm so happy for you,' I say.

Because that's how my parents raised me, to say kind things at times like this, to be happy for others' happiness, even if it hurts. So I play easy-breezy, good old resilient Ella. Although this seems to sadden us both further.

It begins to feel cold and dark. Bleak.

This is no longer an indulgent fantasy but an ugly nightmare. He sticks his body close to mine; he's trying to make it alright but that's a fucking joke. Each step stings. Like warm hands on cold-water fish scales. I can physically feel the Christmas presents I've only just bought crunching in their bags, four crystal cut gin and tonic glasses I bought my mum, cracking to pieces.

We say goodbye under the dripping railway bridge.

'We've got a Farewell Tour next year; you should come down to a show . . . I'd love for you to be there.'

'Definitely,' I say. 'Wouldn't miss it for the world.'

When I'm already thinking of all the ways I can be sure to absolutely miss it for the world.

'OK . . . well . . . '

He lingers; he doesn't want this to be it. He knows something's shifted. And we can't win it back. We hug. Warm and tight. For ages. And I'm about to cry so I pull away first. His eyes are wet, but I think that's the wind. Maybe if he was single, I'd definitely know it was time to jump ship, not to be *with* him but to spend time with him, freely. I'm not just going to sit there on Heather's sofa now, am I, sobbing and eating Ben & Jerry's? I want to cry more for working my major life decisions around him. Then I want to cry even more because I have to be brave and there's nobody to hold my hand.

'Merry Christmas, Ella.'

'Merry Christmas, Lowe.'

Crushing.

I hear the awkward 'Excuse me?' from some guy with eyes as big as gobstoppers – I can already guess what he's about to say:

'But you're not . . . sorry . . . are you *Lowe Archer* . . . from True Love?'

I take this moment to get away, waving goodbye, Lowe calling out, 'Ella, wait?' and I pretend to find my train home with the cracked gin and tonic glasses and dog piss-stained coat and wasted day. We forgot to even talk about my solid streak of not drinking. When I'm out of sight I go back on myself. Jackson's at the KTPLT Christmas lunch (freelancers not invited – no surprise there) and invited me to come down for a drink after. I hadn't planned to; I don't want to beg it – the last KTPLT party didn't exactly end well – but I feel the need, now more than ever, to throw myself into my life with Jackson, to be sure one final time.

Lowe texts, just simply: **X**

I don't reply.

Chapter 35

They have moved on to Pub. A proper one that's packed and noisy, decorated with red and gold tinsel. The kind of pub I would have loved to drink beer in all night long. I can barely get through the suited pint-holding penguins with my bashed bags (I'm just carrying broken glass at this point), to Jackson, at the bar.

'Hey,' I say. My face is stung from the outside air.

'You made it.' He wraps me in for a hug. I need it. He's pissed. He smells savoury, yeasty like beer. I say *hi* to those I know and Jackson begins to introduce me to those I don't, giving up halfway as he gets distracted. They're all drunk. The whole building is drunk. I'm left out of a big drunk joke. I try and squeeze through the elbows at the bar to order a drink but don't seem to get noticed.

Now that he's an exec, Jackson has to talk to everyone. I watch him pull out the same old stories of his childhood from his back pocket – to make him look human, relatable, like his co-workers are being let in on a revealing side of him. Those animated hands, those excitable eyes, like when I first met him. Pats on the back keep coming – 'well done, mate,' they say, 'you deserve it' – about the success of his Christmas advert, his promotion. Drinks line up on the bar behind him, like offerings. He's drinking like he's good at it, which is news to me.

'Do you do non-alcoholic beer?' I shout to the bar staff over the room. They don't. 'Do you do anything non-alcoholic?'

They shout back the word, 'Coke.'

I take my Coke and stand under the shadow of Jackson. Zahra, teeth stained with red wine, says to me, 'You must be so happy?' I assume she's referring to our engagement but it's about 'Jackie's' promotion.

I reply, 'Of course I am – he's the best.' He really is. 'I'm so happy seeing him happy.'

She adds, 'Oh, and the Christmas advert is great by the way – good job.'

Jackson says, 'Sorry, I'd have said not to come down if I'd have known it would be so busy.' My head cranes upwards, trying to hear what he's saying. 'Why don't you go on home and I'll see you there? I reckon it's going to be a lot of . . . ' He castanets his hand to imply networking.

'No, I want to stay with you.'

'I'm still kind of working . . . '

I can tell I'm cramping his style, he just wants to hang out with his friends.

I take the hint. 'OK, if you're sure?' We kiss. 'I'm very proud of you, Jackson.'

You'll find there are rooms in your life, special rooms in special times when you're a Very Important Person – it's your birthday, your best friend's birthday, or you're just simply on fire that night – and the room needs your heat. But most of the time you can walk away from a room and the room will be OK. It will stand just fine without you. In fact, it might not know you've gone. Or that you were even there at all.

Wandering back through the lit city at night, I begin to catastrophize: what if I am alone forever? The trope hag at the top of the hill, with the garden gates all locked and overgrown with my pubes? Will all my future Christmas dinners be leftovers underneath some sweaty clingfilm from a golden-hearted next-door neighbour? What if I never love again?

I call Vi. I call Aoife. I call Bianca. Ronks and Dom too. I say the same thing in all its variations – 'I have to leave Jackson,' I say. 'I can't marry him. I love him but I don't. It's not fair any more; he deserves better' – until it becomes a narrative, until that narrative reinforces itself and becomes a plan. And this time not one of them tries to stop me. Not because Jackson's not great. Because maybe I'm not as great as I could be.

It's me. I'm not great.

Mum rings. Violet's obviously told her. Even though I specifically asked her not to yet until I could get my thoughts straight.

'Alright?' she asks like she's just calling for a *chinwag*.

'Not really.'

'Adam's out; I was just about to decorate the Christmas tree if you want to help?'

The same mammoth tree that normally lives potted in the garden, Mum's already hoisted inside, naked and plump. She shouldn't have carried it herself but she won't be told. Opening a box of family Christmas decorations can be more emotional than looking at photographs of the past. Each one precious, sentimental or humorous, wrapped individually in newspaper over the years, in faded faces, old stories. The cardboard snowman Violet made from the toilet paper holder and pipe-cleaner arms. Sonny's painted star with the red ribbon from nursery. The glittery green garden trowel I got Mum as a present. Then there are younger additions to the collection. Colourful pound-shop baubles Vi and I got to bulk the tree out one year to replace all the smashed glass ones. The expensive gold Cherub that Mum treated herself to. The haggard angel, with wooden peg legs, to clip on top of the tree with the cotton wool hair and the painted face. And the tangle of broken fairy lights, which look like my scrambled brain.

But it's peaceful. The smell of pine, the fragrant mixed spice pouches that Mum's made to hang on the tree: clove, cinnamon, orange, star anise. Mum makes a log fire and it meditatively crackles with comfort, throwing off hissing hot rocks into the charcoaled guard, heating us from the inside out, the living room a sauna. Spy snores happily in front of it. Mum and I quietly work in harmony as we wrap lights and hang ornaments. Mum hums. It's soothing to do a focused activity that takes my mind off things. Calmly navigating, changing positions – arms up and down, bums squeezing past each other to get around the waist of the tree. Pausing to ask *what do you think?* Or to share a memory, to catch each other's eyes.

She says without looking at me, 'You know, I used to suffer with the worst anxiety as a teenager *and* in my twenties. Nobody spoke about it back then like they do now. I used to think I was having heart attacks and all sorts of crazy shit. But it all calmed down once I understood that those flare-ups, those "attacks" were my body's way of warning me, keeping me safe – guiding me. They calmed down once I practised not being upset by them but *listening* to what they have to say. They weren't always right, but I listened all the same. Now, I'm grateful for those warnings; they're like my body's alarm system.

'You have a good instinct, Ella – you get that from me.' Of course I do. 'My advice to you, if you *even* care what I think, is trust your gut. You were never one of those kids who threw themselves into dangerous situations, not because you were boring – because you were smart. If something doesn't feel right, Elliebellie, it usually isn't.'

Once the tree is up, glistening (and wonky) as it should be, Mum and I sit down on the sofa to admire our work. The tree gleams. 'Well, we've made Christmas,' Mum says. 'Mulled wine?' Before I can *impatiently* remind her that I'm trying not to drink, she says, 'It's non-alcoholic; it might taste like shit but I got it for you.' And that warms my heart more than any fire or Christmas tree could.

Lowe texts to say: **Did you get back OK? x.** He's obviously testing the water; it's hours after I would have arrived home and he knew today was scratchy. I can only imagine it took him quite a lot to send; he's reserved like that. I write back: **yep, thanks, call you soon x**, but I'll never make that call.

I hear Jackson tumble in drunk around 3 a.m. – maybe even 4? They went back to Zahra's; I got a text. I've slept in patches. A lucid dream where I felt broken glass shards in the bed. I wake to see actual scratches on my calves, although I think they're from my big toenail and anxious itching. My jaw clenched so hard I've made a tiny hole in the gumshield. Jackson falls into the bed and begins to snore within seconds. I hold his back tightly and cry into his t-shirt. *I wish I was in love with you.*

The next morning, I'm sitting on his side of the bed, trying to be assertive but I know I'm more Annie Wilkes in *Misery*. He stirs awake with a 'What the—' and I say, really calmly, 'Jackson, I love you so much.'

He's bewildered. 'OK? I love you too.'

And I begin to cry.

'Ella?' He sits up. Looking frowzy, smelling like a wolf den.

I cry more and he wraps his arms around me and I say, so quiet it's a whisper, ' . . . I can't marry you, I'm so sorry.'

He tuts, like *silly*, how a parent might comfort a child for believing there's a monster under the bed. He puts his warm hand on mine and says, 'My hours have been crazy but it won't be like this forever.'

And I shake my head. 'I could quite easily live like this with you forever – and that's what frightens me.'

'Is it me?'

'No, you're amazing. I love everything about you.' I stroke his hair but my hand is shaking so I stop. 'I don't even mind that you just sit there and pick your nose in front of me, even when I watch you twiddling your bogies and I know they're going to fall to the floor and stick to my socks. I find your cauliflower fart *comforting*. I honestly *hate* every other cup of tea I drink that isn't made by you – I even didn't mind that time you blow-dried your balls—'

'—that was one time!' He manages a laugh.

'—but I didn't mind, did I? I liked that you felt comfortable and secure with me. Staying here with you is for me and my comfort, not for you. You've always said I need to grow up and you're right.'

'No, you don't, Ella. I didn't mean that. I love the way you are.'

'Jackson, I think I have to break up with you.'

'OK, well, please don't do that?' He laughs again but his brows are pinched. 'Is it the engagement? It's just a ring! I don't even really like weddings! I thought you were the one that wanted to get married. Let's just call it off?'

He brings me round and holds me tight. I feel his heart pounding through his t-shirt into my chest. I cry down his shoulder. My whole face steams up.

'I'm so sorry, Jackson.'

I take off my ring and tuck it into his hand. He shakes his head, and puts the ring on the bedside table, hoping, I guess, that it will be back on my finger in an hour. Then he pulls me back and we lie together in silence.

Maybe that's the kind of maturity that only comes when you reach mid-thirties?

Is that it? Have I done it? Have we broken up?

Of course, it doesn't end that simply. We tripwire ourselves into an argument. He's pissed off. Annoyed. Hurt. He talks about the mortgage; he's rattled at me and my 'impeccable timing'. He blames Aoife and Bianca for 'making my decisions' for me; he says, 'They're jealous, they just want you to be single with them!' I say, 'Aoife wanted me to stay with you!' The fact that we've discussed him hurts him more. I shouldn't have said it. I call his colleagues workaholic money-obsessed privileged *snobs*. I go off about Zahra. *You answer the phone to her at 11 p.m.* I say we've got nothing in common. This makes him mad and sad. He tries to kiss me; I don't kiss back. I say, 'I love you.' He tells me to 'fuck off'. He sits on his phone whilst I lie in bed with the covers pulled over my head. He comes to talk to me and I flop the covers off, only to see him clip a hangnail on the cabinet and shout like I've never seen him do before. I shush him. 'The neighbours!' He goes for a walk, slamming the door. I make tea. He returns crying. He begs. We cry. We hug. We're exhausted, red-faced and hungry. We eat beans on toast, in silence, heads in our hands.

It's as though Lowe has exposed my capacity to love. Unlocked some kind of forgotten door. It was never Lowe's or Jackson's responsibility to feed and water my self-esteem. Finding Lowe again after all these years was not a waste; it's given me the courage to kick that door open wide and here it is, swinging off the hinges and I am walking through it, alone, whether I wanted to or not. Into the complete unknown.

I imagine myself ducking out of my life like the woman in the Scottish Widows advert, but I just take the 137 bus back to Streatham, scraping a wholesale multipack crisp box full of books down the road towards 251, muttering promises to myself that I'm going to love myself better than anybody else can.

I get a buzz on my phone – my agent: **We've got a nice offer in, Ella! Your novel is going to be published! Merry Christmas! x**

If only she knew.

18 MONTHS LATER

Chapter 36

I've watched the spring thaw on the windscreen of Mum's car until it becomes a trap for golden tree pollen. The forget-me-nots and acorns. I've watched the same tree get dressed and strip. I've been back at 251 for almost eighteen months and, yes, I am the cliché of arrested development: thirty-two, single, always wearing leggings and that same Foo Fighters t-shirt, and, now that our flat has sold, 'saving for a deposit'. My brother and sister have both moved out. Sonny's moved in with his friends; Violet lives above her café. So it's just me. People who don't know my mum might list the pros of living at home – the money I must save, the washing she must do for me, the nutritious home-cooked meals I must eat. Well, as said, these people obviously don't know my mum.

And yet, my raw newborn skin is soothed by the harsh, itchy blanket of my mother. I feel at home. It's what we both needed: I needed to be taken care of; she needed a new project. We've bonded over cooking Thai curry, books we're reading, and she's even writing now too – yes, it's her memoir. When I moved back home, I helped Mum and Stepdad Adam with the garden. Mum gave me a patch of my own to grow vegetables and I laughed like, *yeah right*. But I surprised myself and have grown beans, peas, and beetroot and knobbly cucumbers as big as my arm. Having soil behind my fingers has even stopped me biting my nails. The patch is now a great pleasure of mine. Turns out I'm way more like her than I thought.

It's not all been easy, learning how to sleep on my own again, nobody to check if I've eaten (not that I forget) and I've been tempted to dig out that old rape alarm for the backstreets after 9 p.m. It's mostly a lot of writing and watching TV alone on my laptop, but I no longer need to wear a gumshield at night. My aching teenage self haunted me from the corners of my bedroom until I invited her to lie in the bed with me, where I held her tight, kissed her head and lullabied her to sleep. My vegetables are growing nicely and my book, just like me, is almost ready to face the world.

I've done an interview about it for the newspaper (only the *South London Express* but still): a profile piece on returning to writing and coming of age.

'They could have used a new photo,' Mum says. 'You look like a thirteen-year-old.'

I get a few messages about it. Dad, his wife. My friends. An email from my girls' school, inviting me back to give a talk to the students. *Ha! Knew you suckers would be back.*

And then Lowe. *STING.* His last message was way over a year ago when I turned down an invite to a New Year's Eve party. I wasn't in the mood for parties or seeing him kiss Heather as the clock struck twelve. It's difficult not to search for True Love updates online but I don't. Anyway, he's probably enjoying the stability of not touring, the peace of not being under the microscope, just living.

He says: **Ella! My dad just showed me you in the paper! You've got a new book coming out? That will be the second book I've ever read! 😄 meet soon? Lowe x**

It's surreal that he's the one reading articles about me for once.

I write back: **aww say hi to your dad! Yes, come to the launch if you fancy it? But no pressure, defo up for meeting x** And I send over the invitation to my book launch, thinking he'll never come.

There's a heatwave in London when Lowe and I meet again, on the South Bank like before. I carry a hand fan now, like one of those nans you see on postcards in Greece sitting in cobbled lanes on little straw chairs outside tavernas. I spread my legs when I sit down like them too. I've embraced my age and, you know, I'm looking forward to getting older. My wireless bras. My hairy legs. My high-waisted everything and flat summer shoes all-year round.

There's an energy in the air, like carnival, like a night only just getting started. There's no real cause for celebration. For new lovers on a first date to kiss, for drunk girls in bikinis to be grinding next to a speaker. For the busker to sing another song. For plastic cups of beer and dewy ice buckets of rosé. For kids to run in the fountains. But tomorrow doesn't matter; that's what this kind of weather does to humans.

I'm wearing a jade dress; it shines like mermaid skin in the sun.

As always, Lowe is magnificent. He rearranges his posture, pulls at his dark clothes, boyishly, to look smart. He's never been good at dressing for hot weather. Hey. *Hey.*

'What would you like to drink?' he asks. Just being near him is a tonic. He's having lemonade.

'Sounds good. Me too.' I smile and he smiles back. 'I'm just going to find the toilet.'

I have to wee upon arrival anywhere, ever, always.

In the toilets I am sweaty. My moustache is very much *thriving*, and my lipstick has made its very own puddle in the well of my upper lip. In my reflection I see a woman. Oh, shit, it's me.

Lowe's managed to find a table by the river and I sit opposite him, surrounded by talking people.

'I got you this *mock*tail . . . .' He pushes it forward nervously like he prepared it himself.

'Oh, fancy!' I say.

'Because it has strawberry in it and you always used to drink strawberry Ribena.'

I'm touched he remembered. 'It's very pretty.'

He looks at me, my hands (for a ring?), and then looks away.

I keep it moving. 'So you're gonna come to the launch then?'

'If you want me there.'

I kind of want you everywhere.

'Course I do.' And being the martyr I am, I say, 'How's things with you? The house?'

Lowe stretches back on his chair; sweat starts to form on his head. He rubs his jawbone.

'I wasn't going to tell you . . . I don't know why I'm even . . . ' He admits, 'I've been living at my dad's for the past year.'

WHAT?

'On Orchard Road?' I whip out my nan fan and start whisking myself crazily but it's not doing anything. If anything it's pure cardio.

He nods.

'Are you OK?' I ask. 'Why?'

'Oh, sorry, that wasn't me being presumptuous,' he says. 'I just thought you . . . OK, sorry, do you remember Heather?'

How could I forget? Does that make it harder to digest or not? That they were together for more than a decade? It's a really long time. I feel sad for Heather too now. I nod.

'She had all these problems with the house, *then* she started talking about moving home to New Zealand.'

HUH?

'So she went there to look at houses and I guess I just freaked out? And' – he looks at me like I'd judge him for the next bit – 'and, yeah, hid at my dad's.' Squints his eye from the sun and my opinion.

I like it that he has obviously has money to rent anywhere he'd like but chooses to live with his dad.

I sink my mocktail, hard and fast, even though it's basically just juice.

He watches me with curiosity and says, 'Can we walk?'

We walk along the river and it's like the skies of our fate want us to keep moving in a certain direction, breadcrumbing a clue to a secret destination. We get caught up in a colourful balloon parade, where people squeeze us so tight we're forced to lock fingers so we don't lose each other in the crowd. Cornered into the machine brown of the Tate, we stumble upon a guy singing an unknown song that is probably the most romantic thing I've ever heard. Lowe and I take a step away from each other because it feels too well-timed to be true. We turn back the way we came, not wanting to get too far from the station so we can go our separate ways after; we just want a pint, that's all. We end up cutting through by Gabriel's Wharf where we pass a carpenter who handmakes beautifully rough and natural children's wooden rocking see-saws in the shapes of ducks and horses.

'I used to come here as a kid,' I say.

'No way,' says Lowe. 'So did I.'

I can't help but think about all the times our paths could have crossed.

'My mum and dad would drink in the pub there and we'd play on these. Really sweet of the carpenter to let us.'

'They're probably even better once they've been played with, helps wear the wood down.' Lowe rocks one with his hands, as if testing it out. 'If I had kids, I would buy them these for the garden.'

I wonder if he's thinking about his mum.

'Yeah,' I agree. 'Me too.'

'Imagine how many times we probably crossed paths when we were little . . . ' he says. 'It's almost like we were meant to meet.'

'I was LITERALLY just thinking that!' I HAVE to STOP saying LITERALLY!

The path widens and we head back onto the river where it's

slightly quieter. Primary-colour bunting hangs like fruit from the trees overhead. The smell of popcorn. A child catches droplets of trickling ice cream from its cone like a tap.

We find a quiet bar, upcycled from a converted airstream, lightbulbs like tomatoes on a vine, two young bar staff chilling on their phones.

'Beer?' I ask.

'Why not?' He seems to listen out for the *something elseness* that's hovering around us.

We play sword fight with our cards. 'MY round!' I say, pinning his card to the bar.

We sit opposite each other, sipping our beers, smiling our faces off. And here it comes . . . I have such a strong urge to ask him.

Go on, Ella.

Ella! Stop! You've been there, done that and bought every damn season at the whole damn shop for an embarrassingly long time now. Let it go.

I try to ignore it as the question circles around my head once again. Pecking at the squashy bits of my brain. *Ask him. Now is your chance.* I sip my beer to stop the words that are filling my mouth, rising up, pressing the back of my teeth: *ask him.* But first, 'What's going on with you and Heather now then?'

He sighs deeply and scratches the back of his neck. 'She's living in New Zealand.' He puts his hands out like *what more can I say?* When there's obviously a lot more to say.

I can't even look him in the eyes right now; it's too intense. My heart is *howling*.

'Deep down I knew it wasn't right for a while but I was away on tour so much – life moved so fast; it's either all a blur or you slip into habits. I know it might sound strange to someone who doesn't live like that but you don't get the chance to address the problems and ignoring them just makes them bigger and bigger until they implode.'

314

I don't speak so he continues.

'I don't think living away from home, her family being on the other side of the world, helped. It was isolating for her and a lot of pressure for me. I guess I felt like I had to make it perfect for her all the time to make up for them not being around. And well . . . New Zealand's *far*.' He sips his beer. 'But selling a house in different time zones is NOT easy.'

'I'm really sorry, Lowe. You guys were together a long time.'

I put my hand out across the table to comfort him how a friend might.

He takes my hand, nicely, not cornily, and with a cheeky flirt, says, 'So where's your ring then?'

I nearly spit out my drink.

'Oh, *that old thing*,' I wheeze; he's caught me off-guard but there's nowhere to hide now. 'It didn't work out.'

'That's good,' he lets slip. His eyes widen. 'No, not like that, like *good* you're OK about it. I mean, *are* you OK about it?'

'Jackson was a really lovely person; we took good care of each other but it wasn't right.' He nods at this. 'Maybe you need your twenties to find out what *is*?' I fan myself. 'So, you're not the only one living back at home like you're fourteen again!'

We laugh. Hold. On. Does this mean we're both single at the same time? As adults? There really isn't anything stopping us now. The prospect makes my belly do science – fizzing and foaming and frothing like Mentos in Coke. The sun slinks into the river.

Lowe plays with his bottle, tapping mine. 'Do you want another one?'

'Do *you*?' I ask cheekily, taking the hint.

'I'll have another one,' he says. 'I can drink these like I'm getting drunk!'

'Well, let *me* get these.'

One of the bartenders is sitting up with their bare feet out, eating crisps and playing a game on their phone.

'Two more?'

'Yes, please.'

The other whispers, 'So how's it going?' Like it's a first date. I look up, startled.

'We're not . . . on a *date* or anything . . . '

'Oh my bad. I could feel that first date *vibe* between you guys.'

'No, no . . . ' I laugh it off. 'We kind of always have that.'

I look back to make sure Lowe hasn't heard, but he's just vaping and looking out to the river. The bartender winks.

I inhale, deeply, I'm nervous as I walk back, hoping that the spell is still alive since my departure. *I'm going to ask him. I have to.* I am sober. Clear-headed, full of clarity; natural confidence, healthy nerves and some wisdom of adulthood. There's joy too – an abundance of pure joy running through my system. I know what I'm doing. I'm free and able to make choices.

'I'm just going to ask you' – I clear my throat, not quite as cool as I'd hoped – 'did you ever *feel* anything for me back then?'

Lowe's smile is completely wiped from his face. He sits up, seriously, like he's been waiting for this question his whole life. I hadn't expected this reaction from him. He goes to speak but then he can't. 'I . . . errr . . . ' His teeth flash, nervously, and then he leans back in his chair. Trying to settle himself, his response, he straightens out again.

'Yes, of course I did.' He shakes his head, in disbelief. 'Of *course* I did, Ella.'

'You did?'

I am surprised – just like that – how simply he said it. All that build-up, volcanic intensity only to come down to simple words.

'I think that's my fault,' he carries on. 'I really kind of messed that up.'

He can see me beginning to get emotional but he doesn't say anything; he wants to put a hand out but he doesn't know if he should touch me or not.

'That night, at yours, after the shower *thing*, I was trying to show you that I felt the same, that I loved you back . . . and then I felt you thought I'd overstepped the mark.'

'Why didn't you say anything?'

'I was just . . . so *badly* embarrassed. And ashamed. Like I'd let you down, or like you thought I was . . . trying to *hurt* you . . . ? Or that you were drunk and didn't mean what you'd said or that I'd wrecked our friendship . . . I just . . . really messed that up.'

I'm crying now.

'This isn't because I'm sad,' I defend when it's definitely because I'm sad. 'These are tears of relief actually . . . because I thought I made it all up in my head.'

'No, no, you didn't, Ella. I hate that,' he says with such sincerity. 'You didn't make it up. Any of it. And I'm sorry if I ever made you feel like you did. It was all my fault. I'm the one who lost out.'

'Why didn't you . . . *do* anything – why didn't you try to get to me?'

'You were wearing a ring! I thought you were getting *married*!'

'Before that?'

'I gave it all to the band; my head was all over the place, I was a mess – not dealing with losing my mum, self-medicating – my confidence was so bad – I dunno, I was pretending to be someone I wasn't. You've always seemed to really *like* yourself, Ella. I felt I didn't deserve you.' His voice cracks. 'Then I met Heather and she seemed so *together*. I knew that – with you – it would be forever and that would be a problem because I wasn't in that headspace.' *Forever*. 'I wasn't ready for forever.'

What about now?

Chapter 37

It feels wrong being out late with Lowe, like we're *lost* in another country. Like someone might *tell* on us. Moments like this make me all the more grateful for my sobriety. I know tomorrow I will just feel tired – not shit.

He says, 'Do you want to come and see the studio?'

We stroll, arm in arm, past the booming nightclubs of Vauxhall roundabout, past the speeding cars and traffic lights. There are loads of people on the streets, drinking and chatting in clusters. I love watching people gather outside pubs on warm nights. He asks me about my new book. It's been over ten years since I last published anything.

'And where do you want to be in the next ten years?' he asks.

'Awright job interview!' We laugh. 'To be happy? To be a good *mum*?'

'I think you'd make an amazing mum.' He squeezes my hand. Stitch by stitch I feel myself undo.

His studio is beside a derelict car park, cornered off by a barrier. There's only one car in there: a banged-up silver dad-car.

'That's my car. Don't laugh.'

I like that's it's not showy-off or flashy.

Shrubs of grass, crates and flattened boxes, graffitied walls and overflowing bins. There is a church next door, signs that GOD WANTS TO TALK. Pyramids of broken mirror. The studio door is protected by a silver metal cage with a chunky padlock; bit by bit the door becomes looser and looser.

The lights aren't working down here so he switches on his phone torch. I see cold white cement walls, the grey shiny slap of marked lino. We begin climbing stairs. It's cold, but the air is so warm outside still, it's OK, like entering a damp cave in a hot climate. There are no windows in the stairwell. I feel myself bumping into boxes, passing a bike. He holds my hand firmly as we go up. 'OK, here we are.' I have to step over a ledge. 'Just one sec,' he says. 'I have to turn on the power.'

And it's like being inside a spaceship. The whole room sparks into power. The studio is open, all on one floor but split into sections divided by plants, sofas and artwork creating little pockets: vocal booths, pianos, writing areas – guitars – everywhere. An old-school carpet overlapped with patterned rugs. It's natural and worn and lived in but clean. Full of makeshift improvised seating areas made from old cinema chairs and upturned boxes. Handmade unpainted shelves filled with instruments. I recognize the old doll's house from Lowe's childhood home. I don't want to touch anything in case my fingerprints remain eternal, in case I break anything, in case I have to protect myself by pretending I was never here, in case we don't see each other for another ten years, and that makes me want to touch it all in case I never get the chance to come back. I'm not gonna lie – it would make the most impressive apartment. The windows are HUGE. Spread out and up high, on a slant, with a view of London. To me, this is a holy place. A wonder of the world.

'Wow.'

We play music. Nostalgic music we used to listen to before it all got serious. We sing as loud as we want, knowing every word and equally resenting and praising our brains for remembering it all. Lowe scrunches up his face and sings along with the same dedication he'd sing any of his own songs. We crack up at how much effort he puts in.

'D'you want a cup of tea?'

We sit on an old trunk, leg to leg, sipping our teas from chipped True Love mugs. How I would have waited ten more years to feel this feeling. Of me and him. All grown up. Together in this special room.

Sitting, I'm able to see the stacked boxes.

'Just some stuff I'm storing from the house.'

The reality that there are still ties to another life – thin ties but ties all the same. There's no real reason why we can't roll around on the floor but it doesn't feel right. Not tonight. I finish my tea and stand to leave.

'This was really nice,' I say. 'It was really nice to see you.'

'Yeah. It really was.'

Chapter 38

For the first time in my whole life I don't sleep at all for an entire night. Not one wink. I watch the trains rush and rattle past until they don't and then when they do again in the morning. I can't eat. I can't even hold down tea. I open one of the warm mini bottles of tonic water Mum keeps down by the tumble dryer and sip it because I'm pretty sure doctors prescribed it like medicine in the Victorian days, when lovesickness was an actual real disorder. It's six in the morning. I should wait it out, until at least eight, but it's clear, warm and light. I can't stop the clubbing palpitations in my chest, this heart-dropping feeling. My thoughts are taking my body hostage; I'm completely in debt to my emotions.

I shove on the first pair of shoes I can find, throw on a hoodie over my pyjamas, and walk. I just open the door and begin to walk, then I speed up to a bit of a run . . . I'm following my heart. I can't stop now; I don't know what I'm doing; I'm fucking crazy. I've completely lost my mind. *HERE I AM*. I run down the high street, and I can see us, that night he cycled me home when we were kids, *my arms wrapped around his chest, my palms over his beating heart*; that was all that mattered then. Past the train station where we'd bunk tickets in the rain. Through the common where we'd chat shit on the swings until we were just silhouettes and our faces were outlines, where time was a half-pipe dream, an exhale, a cloud of smoke, a polaroid picture. Where we'd share drinks, lips wet with fizzy sugar. We were in love. I can taste it now. I'm reversing the spell. At the traffic lights I stop for a second. *What am I doing?* This is insane. *Red. Amber. Green.* And off I am again, running into the present, to the sweet little street and the early risers and the flower market. And I'm there. At his dad's house on Orchard Road.

Quiet. The blinds down. I'm here. Just one mad woman on the street.

I ring his phone.

'Hello . . . ?'

'Hello . . . ' I pant, breathlessly. 'I'm outside.'

'You're joking.'

'No, I'm not.'

Lowe opens the door. His eyes are gemstones and wet; he's wearing everything he was wearing from the night before, as if he fell face-first into bed. Still the same old Lowe then. His dad is out. He's home alone.

Our fingers moving closer and closer. I feel the tips of our noses meet; our lips nearly touch, his mouth near mine, hands go underneath my hoodie where it bunches and I'm just wearing a vest. His fingers tuck under the fabric and onto the skin of my belly, which shrinks under his reach and I can tell. I know he knows it's time to use words.

'I want *this* . . . '

I smash like a chandelier crashing towards a ballroom floor and finally all these years later the guy's learning to clarify so he adds, ' . . . to be *with* you. But I want to get it right this time. I do. I want it to be for real. I still have to sell that bloody house; Heather is still involved and I don't want you to get caught up in the mess of that.' What is he worried about? That he's going to get *papped*? 'I'm sorry but I don't want us to run away with the idea that . . . '

'Run away with *what*?' I am fucking fuming. 'Lowe, I just *ran* to your house. RAN! No, no, no!' I'm pacing, zipping my hoodie up to the neck. 'No!' I find myself pointing.

He tries to explain but I don't let him speak. He tries to bring me close again but I push him away.

'Maybe I'm overthinking it' – *YOU ARE OVERTHINKING IT* – 'but I want us to have the best possible chance to make this as great as it can be.'

I feel so fucking angry and betrayed. I can't believe I'm here again, saying my feelings, being all vulnerable – for what?

I walk towards the front door. *Stupid, stupid girl.*

He rubs his head in distress; his eyes are starting to plead. 'I really believe that if you trust me, if you wait . . . '

'*Wait?* Are you really that selfish? Have you slept through the last . . . ' I count on my hands, which isn't easy under pressure ' . . . EIGHTEEN YEARS?' Eighteen. Christ almighty. It's BAD. Only over half of my goddam life. THAT'S how long I've been in love.

'I just want to be ready for you.'

'What do you mean *ready*? You're not a bloody virgin bride, Lowe! I'm *here*.' I bang my chest, standing by the front door, waiting for him to say something, anything, and as always, silence. 'And you're not here at all. All you do is break my heart over and over again. I can't take it. I wish I'd never met you.'

I open the front door and walk away as fast as my body will take me. I don't look back. Not once.

I pound down the road like I'm on fire. And no one will put me out. So instead, I singe everything in my path. Trees crumble; cars rust and wreck; people blister.

I run into a café. Tremoring. Not drinking makes you feel a LOT. I order coffee. *No, tea. No, coffee. No, tea. Please. Sorry. I'm just— Thank you. In a takeaway cup. Yes, please.* A little girl eating an iced cinnamon bun stares at me, eyes locked in that intense way kids have, frosting on her mouth. I must look like a friggin' banshee. She holds the bun out to me. And it just makes me cry – not ugly crying but enough to know I'm just a little girl in a scared woman's body in a café crying in the face of a child.

Back out onto the street, which is too overcrowded and thin for drama like this, and he's there, searching for me as the city stirs, as people try to get in and out of the coffee shop, step around him. The yellow yolk of the morning breaking, spilling out everywhere.

'Ella.' He's breathless; he doesn't want to do this in front of strangers, to cause a scene. 'Ella, please, can we find somewhere to talk?' He steps towards me. I step back into the seating area of the coffee shop, on the pavement with the fold-away tables and chairs that rattle. 'Ella, please, I'm really sorry. I'm just trying to do things right. Please can you just let me talk to you?'

'After nearly twenty-*fucking*-years of silence?' It's way too early in the day for outdoors swearing but I'm hurt and embarrassed, annoyed at myself.

I see real fear on his face. The type I've never seen when he's on stage or riding his bike. He's endangered here on the normal street, without the backup of his band or the gang of mates that used to fly behind him on bikes like a V of geese. But I'm comfortable here; this is my territory.

He puts his arms out how he might approach someone thrashing about a sharp knife. People stop and stare; a florist throws a bucket of water down the drain, eyes on us; a bin-collector whistles to state they are minding their own business. Lowe puts his hands back in his pockets.

Prams push; kids scoot; dogs bark; joggers run. Lowe steps into the road, to make space on the pavement. I see him catch his ashen reflection in the coffee shop window; the urge to fix his messy hair must be enormous. He hangs like a soaking anorak in a lost property office. His eyes hit the tarmac, his feet. Is he going to cry? Because tears are rolling down my face, burdened with yesterday's mascara. His expression, a mix of he-knows-he-deserves-this acceptance, pleading and utter powerlessness. More passers-by stare, and I hear a faint *'Isn't that the singer from . . . ?'* The little girl with the bun steps out of the café, holding her parents' hands. She turns her neck to look us, at raw adulthood and the way it bleeds. I manage to produce a smile for her and she turns her head like *we're not mates*.

'I used to think you were the love of my life, you know?' I can tell the words are hard for him to hear. 'But you're not even my friend. You're an *enemy*.' I want to scream *plus, my fucking book comes out next week, you selfish prick!* but I don't want to look like a privileged artist raging in the street or make it seem like I'm doing some inventive performative promotional stunt. Instead I say, 'This is NOT how friends treat each other.' My voice breaks. 'I've realized you're actually lucky to even *know* me.'

He nods, and says, more desperately now, 'I know I am, Ella – you're incredible.' He tries to laugh, but it doesn't work. I just scowl. 'Please give me a chance – please forget what I said about waiting. You're right, let's try, right now – please let me take you out?'

Of course, everybody on the whole street is looking now, waiting for my answer.

And I say, 'Sorry, Lowe. No.'

And nobody likes that.

I turn and walk away from him, standing there, thinking *What the fuck was that?*

See, it hurts, doesn't it?

He chases after me. I do like it that for once he's the one chasing me, but, turns out, being chased makes me feel extremely anxious, so I turn and snap, 'Just leave me alone!'

And that makes him retreat. He stands there, for I don't know how long; I don't care to look back and see. Just bolt up and off the main road, down some side street where the houses are in perfect rows, promising lovely freshly squeezed orange juice lives. Lowe is ringing my phone. I screen the calls.

I ring Aoife instead. 'Whaaaat?' She's half asleep; I'm crying. She clears her throat. 'What's the matter?'

I say, 'I'm a dick. I've done it again.'

She just says, 'Oh gawd.' Like she knows exactly what I'm talking about. 'Come now.'

We hang up and I try and get my shit together to make my way over to hers, walking in *a* direction, I'm just not sure which one. Lowe is calling and texting: **please answer, I'm sorry, tell me where to come and I'll be there.**

Later, I will learn that Lowe drove his dad-car round the streets for hours to find me, his head hanging out the window. He drove to 251 Palace Road and back again – where every person looks just like me but nobody is.

At Aoife's I say big and bold things like how *I've got to pull my shit together. I've got a book to release. I'm sorry, this guy is not GATECRASHING the next decade of my life!* And Aoife feeds me toast and tea, and says things like, 'Absolutely!' and 'Totally' and 'A hundred per cent' and 'You're right.' I feel insecure and self-conscious. I want to live a quiet and simple life, to shut myself inside, to not get out there and live. I announce that 'I have doubts about my book; nobody needs a pointless, stupid shit book like this!'

Aoife says, 'Fuck off! *I* do! I love pointless, stupid shit. It's the best. That'd be like saying nobody needed *Bridesmaids*!' She holds my hand. 'We need that shit.'

Later, Ronke comes over with Avanna, who plays hide-and-seek with Aoife's bra that's hanging off the clothes horse before spreading a bowl of pasta everywhere and being put to sleep in Aoife's bed. Ronks shows us photos of her incredible new house. We're so happy for her; she works so hard. Then Bianca arrives and I decide it's finally time to exorcise this unceasing love story for Bianca and Ronks, whilst Aoife – who has heard it many times now – orders takeaway.

'We always always knew you loved him,' they say, 'but we always knew he loved you too.'

Chapter 39

I always pictured the launch of my first novel in one of those quaint little bookshops in Portobello, next to the bricked houses the same colour as the Love Heart sweets, an upgrade from the pub function room where we had the launch for my poetry book. One with a ladder on a runner and brown paper bags and an old cat sleeping by the window. Proper champagne, red wine, pistachio macarons and a hunk of cheese, which everyone nibbles at.

But, of course, it's *my* book launch, so I have to beg Colin and Tamika at the local bookshop up the road to let me read out loud in a corner in front of my publishers and friends, have a few margherita pizzas and bottles of room-temperature cheap white wine in plastic cups. I'm being harsh. It's actually very beautiful. And I hate the sound of stinky shared cheese anyway.

I'm wearing a down-to-the-floor green dress covered in golden embroideries of the sun, moon and stars. It has big billowy shoulders and tight crimped sleeves. I look like Princess Fiona from *Shrek* when she's an ogre – the exact look I was going for. And the best bit about it? The dress belonged to my mum when she was younger (hence why it's so long).

My whole family is here. Violet's made a chocolate cake, decorated with the cover of my book – not *quite* big enough to spell out the *entire* title but I appreciate the gesture. Mum and Adam are here, Sonny and his new girlfriend, Dad and Lovely Naomi. Aoife,

Bianca, Mia. There's Ronks and gorgeous Avanna. Shreya – who I haven't seen in years – who I never expected to say yes but has the night off from the kids so she's up for a party. Dom and her new fiancée, Soph, The Twins. Even Nile, who has his own theatre in Devon now. He followed me on Instagram and I extended the invitation, never thinking he'd show up but here he is, standing at the back with his girlfriend, looking proud. 'I've always loved your weird work,' he says. 'Write a play for us one day? But not *Bad Wolf*.' There are stylists from the hairdressers, my one friend from uni, from college and some writer friends. The room is full of my loved ones, sharing seats and stools, sitting on the counter, leaning on the walls, more full than I could have ever imagined.

My phone pings; it's Jackson: **Smash it. Proud of you, Ella x**

I will cherish that.

And I write back: **thank you ♥ proud of you too x**

After my editor says a few words, I climb up onto a wonky wooden stool to read. I open up my book, feeling the weight of it in my hands and my mouth is so dry, but I take a breath and say:

'Maybe you've never been in love with someone who you're sure is the one for you? So sure that birdsong sounds like their name in the street. Like *déjà vu*. Like recognizing a face from the past. The way you know your parent is your parent. The way you know you're about to be ill. Or that milk is off. It's that voice that says *you can rest*, that says *you're here, I've got you*. It's in that rising tide of happiness that happens for no reason when you're listening to a song that you can't put into words but up go the hairs on your arms.

'That person is hidden in those spaces, between being awake and dreaming. They're there. Always. And time can stretch on for miles, years, without contact – life drifts on, does its thing and you're almost able to forget that you love that person and the fact that they belong by your side because you're doing OK without them. You're doing quite well actually.'

The room laughs at this. I feel able to look up and take a breath.

I see my family shedding tears, my friends filming on their phones – CRINGE. I compose myself and try some more:

'And then *something* happens. And you're sprung back to it all, like an elastic band that tricked you into thinking you had already broken from its grasp ages ago but no, you've snapped right back to where you started, to that very moment and all the beautiful, terrible, wonderful, terrifying feelings that come with loving somebody, with being in love with them still, and wondering if they ever loved you back. This book is for everyone who's ever felt like that.'

The room applauds, probably happy that they can go back to drinking and chatting now the formal bit is over but still I'm rushing from the fear, surprise and overwhelm, relief. I sign books (only by the very last do I feel like I've mastered any sort of professional autograph) and take photos with my friends. I look around the room, thinking that *of course* Lowe will push through the door and appear any moment, that *of course* he wouldn't miss my *book* launch – it's my fucking book launch! I'm eyeing the twee bell above the door, waiting for it to *tinkle* open with his arrival but it doesn't. It's just Bookshop-owner-Colin taking out the clanging recycling bins, full of empty wine bottles. I hear him mutter, 'They're worse than a hen party, this lot!' Dropping major hints for us to leave. Bookshop-owner-Tamika's complaining that someone's spilt red wine on the carpet and *it won't clean itself.* The carpet is red; it's very hard to see where the stain is. Aoife lays down kitchen roll. *That'll do it.*

When we've successfully sold out of books and my party have drunk our booze supply dry and overstayed our welcome, Mum shouts, 'Everybody back at ours for the *afters*!' Sonny and Violet groan weakly at Mum's attempt to be cool. Bianca pulls the one copy of my first poetry book from the shelf and – away from the owners' stare – slides it in the window display. I wink at her like, *thanks mate, appreciate it.*

We link arms, out into the warm evening. We bundle drunkenly onto the bus. Even Dad and Naomi and my publishers come, folding into taxis, any way to get back home to Mum's. This is where the celebrating will really happen, in a house I'm no longer embarrassed of.

We're loud, singing and talking over each other. Drinking and dancing. Until the music is snuffed and Mum chinks a glass with a fork, like she's about to go and give a speech. *Oh, she's about to go and give a speech.*

'Oh no, please,' says Sonny,

'Does she *have* to?' Vi mutters, covering her face with her hands.

'YES ANTONIA!' Ronke screams (Avanna been collected by her dad so now Ronks is ON it!). Stepdad Adam looks at Mum in awe like *that's my girl*. Dad excuses himself to 'find more beer'.

'Since you were a child I knew you lived inside your head.' Mum directs her words only to me, as though she's forgotten seventy-five of our loved ones are also here. 'I used to ask myself, *what on earth is that child thinking about?* And well, now I know.' She holds up the book and laughs. 'I mean, what an overthinking, highly sensitive anxiety-riddled little shit you are—'

The room applauds and laughs. Aoife hangs around my neck crying with laughter.

Violet whispers, 'Do you want me to make her stop?'

I say, 'No. She's good.'

'But you are also fearless and brave and full of so much love. My word, am I *proud* of you?' Her tears make me cry, and everyone *awwwws* at our mother/daughter bond, which now I think about it, is probably the real greatest love of my life. 'And if anyone wants to know where she gets it from . . . ?' *Oh, here we go* – she looks like she's about to point at herself, loving the attention. ' . . . I have no fucking idea. I *wish* I could say it was me.'

And my dad re-enters to hear this bit, and blows me a kiss.

I, through tears, hug Mum as the room claps. There's so much commotion – laughter, talking, crying, music – that I don't hear the knock on the door. It's Violet who leaves the room to answer it.

'ME NEXT!' Bianca screams and everyone protests as she takes a half-full bottle of prosecco off the table, holding it like a microphone. 'I was actually Ella's first *commission*. Sorry about me, she used to write my love letters for me back in the day to help me catch boyfriends . . . '

Violet taps me on the shoulder, whispers in my ear; she says, 'Ella, that was Lowe.'

I say, 'What was?' I think she's referring to a song that was being played (when it was definitely Elvis Costello) but I can see by the look on her face she doesn't mean that.

'At the *door*.'

'Now?'

She nods.

FUCK! I squeeze past Mum's annoying friends loitering in the hallway sharing a spliff – the friends she HAD to go and invite to the 'afters' even though I told her not to – with Mum's dress hitched up to my knees in a bundle, so I don't trip; the thing is like a bloody wedding dress with a train of its own. Out of the wide-open front door, the gate on the latch and onto the street. I'm buzzy and warm from the feeling of the night, the love and now *this*. I look up and down the empty road, the streetlamps breathing their honey-and-lemon-lozenge luminescence, see Lowe climbing into his same old dad-car. Oh. My. Days. *There he is.*

'Ella.' His voice seems to echo. 'I didn't know you were having a party. Sorry, I knew your book came out today. I just wanted to say congratulations and give you this' – he holds up a carton of strawberry Ribena – 'but I appreciate that looks *not that* great a present now . . . ' The straw in its plastic casing limply falls off onto the road. He picks it up, awkwardly, scrunching it in his hand.

'It's good to see you.' Really good but maybe a bit sad. I feel bad he wasn't at the launch, that he didn't feel he could come.

'No, no, thanks, it's your night. I *do* have something else for you though, and it's not flowers because I know that's . . . whatever.'

He looks even sweeter when he's shy. He pulls out a pizza-boy bag and goes to open it but Bianca storms outside – *uh-oh, here goes.*

She demands, 'What the fuck is going on? What are YOU doing here?'

And then Violet. Aoife. Ronke. All of my parade, piling out onto the street.

'Lowe! Come in, have a drink!' Mum drags him towards the front door and he looks back at me over his shoulder like *Is that alright?*

Even though I know it's virtually impossible to say *no* to Mum I say, 'Can hardly say no now, can I?' whilst secretly screaming *YES YES YES!* But I'm not giving him that.

My friends follow Mum inside, dutifully. She is the boss, of course.

We pile back into the kitchen. The guy is OUT. OF. HIS. DEPTH. All eyes on him as he skulks through our house.

He's so nervous his hands are shaking. Mum pours him a drink, and he tries to find the furthest place in the back of the kitchen, so he can wallflower himself and become invisible which, if your name is Lowe Archer, is pretty impossible.

'Poor thing,' says Dom, 'he's been thrown in at the deep end, hasn't he?' And she goes over to keep him company.

But before she can get to him, it's Mum who shoots Lowe right between the eyes. 'Perfect timing, Lowe. We were just giving speeches. Is there anything you'd like to say to Ella?'

Heads *swoop* round to face him.

The silence is deafening. Lowe flushes luminous with horror.

'*Mum!*' I say, defending him. 'He just got here!' I look at Lowe. 'You don't have to say anything.'

He's already making his excuses anyway: 'No, no, thank you, I honestly just wanted to say congratulations to Ella. I won't stay—'

But he's met with my colosseum, the loyal pillars of my family and friends staring back at him, unimpressed. Lowe, the speechless showman in the room, famous for wowing crowds (and stomping all over my heart), is now flustered, in the spotlight at his toughest gig yet. He clears his throat, sweetly with his fist, and goes to speak—

But Bianca gets in there first, pointing: 'Excuse me, you can't just come in here, *Lowe*, and take over Ella's night. I know you think you're some hot-shot celeb these days but this isn't about you, mate. Ella – tell him?'

Lowe looks at me apologetically.

I fold my arms and grin. 'It depends what he's going to say, doesn't it?'

Lowe's face falls as the jury of my loved ones await his words.

'Ummm. OK. Let me just think . . . ' Lowe puts his left hand on his chest and rubs it over his hammering heart. The room quietens. Then he says, faintly, 'If you know Ella, you know she's a storyteller, always exaggerating, embellishing and making everything around her a poem or fairy tale. What she doesn't realize is that *she* is a poem. *She* is the fairy tale and we are just characters in the story of *her.*'

GULP.

'GORGEOUS!' heckles Mum. And the room claps.

Lowe then puts his arm up, to stop the clapping; he's not finished. 'I'm sorry, sorry . . . I . . . err, maybe I have to say what I actually came here to say tonight . . . I just didn't expect to do it in front of so many people.' He doesn't take his eyes off me.

'Ella, I thought that you'd be home after your launch, *alone*, so I could tell you that . . . ' He takes a deep breath like it might be his last and says:

' . . . I love you, Ella.' He speaks, loud and clear, firm, like his life hangs on these very words. 'I've always loved you—'

Mum gasps. (CRINGE.)

I grip onto the fireplace to hold myself up, not even caring that my fingers are definitely touching some old jar filled with something rancid.

He reaches for his bag.

'He's pulling out a bag – oh no, what *is* that bag?' Ronks whispers.

And inside is everything I'd ever want to see. Proof. Evidence. Like the photo of 'Jase' I found in the unwanted roadside drawers as a kid but for real this time. He holds the items up one by one. All the letters I ever sent him. The mixtapes too. A scrap of leather from my shoe. And a lace. A bottle top. A travel card with my lipstick marks on it. My hat. Even my dad's hoodie that I assumed he'd lost. His old wallet, in front of the worn travel cards, a passport photograph of me aged nineteen.

'I've been holding this stuff at my studio for years,' he says. 'You were sitting on top of it!'

The trunk!

'Oh God.' Aoife bursts into tears.

'That's done it. I'm absolutely finished,' says Bianca, pulling a stained tea towel off the oven to stop her make-up from running.

Lowe clenches his jaw, straight into my eyes like it's the most real anyone's ever looked at me and says, 'Ella, I think about you every time I play guitar, every song I hear – I think about you when I'm awake, and when I'm asleep I dream of you. Every time an aeroplane flies over my head it's you I think about. When I eat. When I'm with my friends, I'm thinking about you. I think about you when I'm driving. Even when I was on stage – I was thinking about what you were up to. When I had to go to the dentist and had an injection in my gum, I thought about you. I think about you when I ride my bike. And when I'm not thinking about you, although I'll admit these moments seem to be less and less these days, I'm wondering why I'm not thinking about you and go back to thinking about you again . . . I love you, Ella. Everything about you. I just . . . love you. I'm completely ready if you are.'

And . . . he moves in for a kiss; I move in for a kiss; he moves in, I move in, heads tilted, eyes closed. . . . Is this EVER going to EVER happen? WILL YOU JUST KISS ME FOR GOODNESS SAKE and . . . he does. He kisses me.

'Fly Away' plays and the volume of the world drowns out. And the universe has done something right for once. And that star will grin. And the kid versions of us are caught in the rain, hugging. And holding. And laughing. And jumping up and down on some trampoline somewhere in the past, celebrating like they've pulled off the greatest of stunts: *We did it! We did it! Look what we made happen*!

I like you. I like you too.

But the kiss is kind of in front of everyone – including both my parents – so it's weird and awkward. I laugh and say out loud, 'Why does this feel like a wedding?'

Chapter 40

The next morning, I feel like I've woken from a fever dream. Aoife and Bianca lie head to toe, passed out on the couch, Dom and wife-to-be Soph on the floor as they missed their train back to Brighton. It's like bloody Glastonbury in here. Then, I turn over to see Lowe, fast asleep.

All these years of searching for him in the corner of every room, in the cavity of every party, every gig, every festival, every window of every passing train, every alcove of every pub, subconsciously waiting for him to sit down next to me on every bench in every park, half an eye on every door, only to find him here, on the pull-out sofabed at 251.

He opens his eyes and says, 'Oh, it's you.'

I say, 'Yeah.'

And then we both laugh. He leans up and puts his arms around me, kisses me on the lips. On my cheeks. On my eyes and face. He says, 'Well, this is a pretty good day.'

And it's not even begun.

After cleaning up cups and glasses from last night's party, we open the windows and doors to let the honey sunshine pool through. It's too nice a day to waste. I pack a bag. We bundle into his dad-car. We play the songs we love and sing out loud, summer kids on summer mornings, his hands on the wheel, his knees next to mine, tearing out of the city. The roads widen and spread, the houses more distant. Greener and greener, bluer and bluer.

We stop on the way to get petrol. I watch him from inside the car, interacting with strangers, smiling at everyone. After he pays, he cracks up as he walks back towards me, waving a toothbrush that he's bought at the garage. He rings hotels on the way and everywhere is booked. But someone's had a last-minute cancellation – a little house on the hill. We park and hike up a narrow mud path, through thorny brambles, over crumbly peaks and craters to get there. It's a small wooden place, perfect, with a kitchen area, a little blue sofa, bed and TV – almost like a kid's playhouse. The sun melts into the sea like butter in a hot pan. Far in the distance children collect crabs in buckets. A woman in a swimming costume helps her senior mother across the pebbles to reach the sea, bodies alike, holding hands. They swim out further and further until they're dots. A soft dog that we don't know comes to chill by our feet. We drink ice-cold beers on the front porch and stroke the dog's head and admire the still air, the feather clouds, the way things fall into place. We talk about it all, the misfires and miscommunications, although none of that matters any more. Call it foreplay. Hearing him tell me his version of events tames the galloping horses of my heart. I've been living with background noise for so long I had forgotten the sound of peace.

In the darkness, off the beaten track, we scramble down the werewolf-tree hill, through bushes and bracken, our city shoes not prepared for the treacherous slopes, to a pub. Instant warmth and life, the smell of beer and roast potatoes, fresh lobster and clams. The ceiling covered in rotten copper pots and pans, compasses and pirate ship wheels, tankards and rope. We find ourselves on a worn sofa in a cramped cosy corner, where the locals don't know or care about us or our love story. And it's nice to introduce ourselves to the world as a couple without question. We just are.

We watch a fiddle band and sip our drinks. Lowe taps along to the music, his hand on my thigh. I feel thirty-two. Any earlier would have been too soon.

Later, on the blue sofa, I say in a voice so quiet it's almost a whisper, 'Don't be scared.' And Lowe kisses me for nine hours straight. Kisses me for so long my lips flare up. We inspect and explore every freckle and print on our skin, as if there's anything new we could possibly see. New scars, old burns and everything we've imagined.

We know that when we get home, there will be things to sort. Things to do and face. But there will be a day in the future, when we find calm inside that house, not quite the picture I drew when I was young but close, very close, with one of those wooden rocking horses in the garden, and he'll play the guitar and I'll write stories.

'What are you writing today?' he'll whisper as I finish the last line, not wanting to wake the sleeping baby lying in between us, as I soar towards the ending, his cherub curls stuck to his face, chest rising and falling. He looks like us both.

I will say, 'True love.'

I've always wondered how I'll tell our little boy about us. I suppose now I can just show him this.

Acknowledgements

Thank you to my wonderful agent, Ariella Feiner.

Thank you to my incredibly talented editor, Clare Gordon.

Big thank you to Emily Kitchin.

And an enormous thank you to Judy Parkinson.

Gigantic thank you to Amy Mitchell. Amber Garvey. Molly Jamieson. Thank you to Stephanie Heathcote. Angie Dobbs. Halema Begum. Tom Han. Rebecca Fortuin. Brogan Furey. Georgina Green. Fliss Porter. Angela Thomson. Sara Eusebi. Hannah Lismore. Lauren Trabucchi. Kom Patel. Sarah Lundy. Emma Pickard (the flumps! The playlist! The Ribena!). Shan Sawjani. Lauren Gardiner. El Slater. Dan Usztan. Phoebe O'Donnell. Jodie Hodges. Lily Down. Alex Stephens. Georgina Le Grice. Jane Willis and United Agents. Myar Craig-Brown.

Thank you to my family; you are my world. Jet and Luna (yes, see? I told you I'd put your names in a book!). My incredible friends, you know who you are because I call you a hundred times a week. And Siobhan, for it all. Thank you to the bookshops and booksellers, libraries and librarians, schools and teachers. NLT,

BookTrust and those organisations that support my work. Thank you tea, pink lipstick, my slippers, electric blanket, Sunflower the cat and Jennifer Lopez.

Thank you to the *Guardian* for commissioning me to write the very article that inspired this novel. Thank you to Hugo, the real life inspiration behind that very article. I love you, I love you, I love you. After years of keeping it a secret, now everyone knows, don't they? So that's embarrassing but URGH the relief to get it all out! I wrote a book about us, gross.

And lastly, to little me, young Laura. Sorry I gave you such a hard time as a teenager. You were actually pretty great. Sing your grungy little heart out and eat all the Kit Kat Chunkies you like, girl. This one is for you.

ONE PLACE. MANY STORIES

Bold, innovative and
empowering publishing.

FOLLOW US ON:

@HQStories